All rights reserved, no part of this publication may be either reproduced or transmitted by any means whatsoever without the prior permission of the publisher.

VENEFICIA PUBLICATIONS UK
veneficiapublications.com
Typesetting © Veneficia Publications
UK October 2020
Additional editing Fi Woods.

Cover artwork created by Sem Vine
with the kind permission of Kizzi Syme.
Original photograph by Avon Hardy.
avonhardy.com

"Written under the duress of a pandemic lock down, in memory of all those persecuted for differing views and beliefs. Long may their names live on in us."

Defoe Smith

Wytches are the Evolution of a Sacred Breed persecuted in pure ignorance by the un-evolved."
Taloch Jameson
facebook.com/Clan-Dolmen

"Bringing to life the suffering of those Witches and innocent people over the centuries, reminds the current generation of Witches how much freedom we now have, how far we have come and how grateful they should be to those who went before."
Merlyn (CoA)
facebook.com/groups/childrenofartemis

"The Witch walks a tangled path of dissident sorcery. Those accused of witchcraft (whether rightly or unjustly) bear witness to a recurring crime against humanity; when those with power, single out certain people and dehumanize them Their stories should be told."
Jonathan Argento
facebook.com/LyceumWitchcraft

"I weep for the witches who have been and continue to be beaten, shamed, raped, murdered, wronged by societies through misunderstanding and fear. As a witch today, I strive to act in ways that validate witchcraft as a positive, vibrant and life-affirming path."
Moira Hodgkinson
moirahodgkinson.com

"The witch trials' legacy includes literature, art, film, and the Wiccan foundation myth "The Burning Times." It is poignant and powerful to read this contemporary Pagan exploration of the enduring fascination of the figure, fantasy and magic of the village witch."
Dr Melissa Harrington
Paganseminary.org

"Shadows and midnight, have always been favoured haunts for Magicians who seek to understand the Mysteries. We have rarely found solace in mundanity. Meanwhile, society tries to tame the wild soul of those who don't fit in. The Witch trials show where that fear can lead."
Damh the Bard
paganmusic.co.uk

"The witch hunts were an emblematic era, in which all the inner demons of Europe were expressed, against women, against magic, against the suddenly targeted innocent. There is no richer source material for creative exploration, as we see in this wonderful new book."
Christina Oakley Harrington
Treadwells.com

"The path of today's witches is drenched in the blood of those who went before us; their sorrow,

their joy, and their power can be felt in our veins. Within our songs, our dances, our stories, and our moments of silence their magic is ever present."

Diane Narraway
facebook.com/Clan-Dolmen

"The central themes of this book are prejudice and violence. Whether modern neopagan witches identify with people accused of malefic magic, in the past or today, is perhaps less relevant than our shared humanity and our desire to see an end to persecution and intolerance."

Julian Vayne
theblogofbaphomet.com

"Our conduct, words and actions today reflect who we are as Witches. The way we carry ourselves should be to honour those who went before us in the name of the Craft."

Rachel Patterson
Rachelpatterson.co.uk

"May the drums revere those whom the fire consumed but failed to silence. My feet dance to the legacy that they came to transmit: the voice of the Bird Woman that no one dares to look at. Terrible mother, we are your daughters today the same as those of yesterday ... our voice shines in

the darkest times to dissipate the ignorance of this world."
Verónica Rivas
facebook.com/melogyeshe

"This collection is a fine testimony to the continuing power of the witch figure to move hearts and inspire minds and pens. In their two-thousand-year progress, spanning three continents, its stories embody the nobility and the tragedy, the horror and the pathos, the beauty and the poetry, the redemption offered by nature and the evil inflicted by humans, that are all bound up in the image of the witch. No other human type has the ability to produce such a variety of reactions and associations, and all are represented here."
Professor Ronald Hutton
Author/Professor Bristol University

"Thou shalt not suffer a witch to live."
King James I
KJV Exodus 22:18

INQUISITION
Diane Narraway

'Twas ecumenical poison
That started this war,
And arrogant bigotry
Brought it to my door.

With accusations of witchcraft,
My torture is justified
As you drink the blood
Of one crucified.

Demons and devils
I allegedly conjure,
Yet I healed the sick
While you peddled torture.

Macabre afflictions
Grace those you defile,
Staining Christ's name
With accusations so vile.

And as Lucifer's consort,
I should truly repent
As your rapacious appetite
Defies your sacrament.

To confess all my sins,
Of my clothing I'm stripped,
And in the name of the Lord
Raped beaten and whipped.

And the Holy Testaments,
Absolve you from this lie.
But Cain's mark all can see
As I'm sentenced to die.

You cry, "Secular whore!"
Oh! Puritanical fake
With bell book and candle
I'll burn at your stake.

And just one of many
Whose blood you have shed
In the name of the Church
So many lie dead.

So, inquisitive inquisitor,
What did you hope to find?
Did this sordid violation
Bring you true peace of mind?

CONTENTS

THE INQUISITON – Diane Narraway — viii

INTRODUCTION – Diane Narraway — xv

OF FLOWERS AND THORNS — xviii
– Earl Livings

THEORIS OF LEMNOS — 1
A Greek Tragedy – Diane Narraway — 3

PETRONILLA DE MEATH — 13
'A Matter of the Faith' - Geraldine Lambert — 15

PETRONILLA DE MEATH — 40
The Whipping Girl – Sem Vine — 42

GILLES GARNIER — 52
The Hermit of St Bonnot – Fi Woods — 54

AGNES PORTER — 73
The Wight Witch – Marisha Kiddle — 75

AGNES WATERHOUSE — 90
Satan's Widow – Scott Irvine — 92

AGNES COLLINS — 101
Redress – Donna Hayward — 103

URSULA KEMP	116
They Say – Marisha Kiddle	118
DR JOHN FAIN	120
Devil in the Detail – Scott Irvine	122
ANNA MUGGEN	142
The Cobblers Curse – Diane Narraway	144
RICHARD WILKYNS	152
A Life Undone – Rachael Moss	154
JOAN, MARGARET & PHILLIPA FLOWER	183
The Flowers of Bottesford – Esme Knight	185
GOWANE ANDERSOUN	229
'The Fates of Men Are Their Fates Alone' – Tarn Nemorensis	231
ELIZABETH CLARKE	263
An Unremarkable Life – Issy Ballard	265
ISOBEL GOWDIE	304
The Second Coming of the Hare – Lou Hotchkiss Knives	307
LISBETH NYPAN	327
The Last Witch of Trondelag – L. N. Cooper	329

MADDALENA LAZZARI	340
Those Eyes – Diane Narraway	342
TEMPERANCE LLOYD	353
The Bronze Plaque – Defoe Smith	355
TITUBA	370
Obeah Magick – Diane Narraway	372
GILES COREY	402
More Weight – Diane Narraway	404
JANET HORNE	427
The Divil of Insch – Diane Narraway	429
BRIDGET CLEARY	441
If of The Devil You are, Burn – Sem Vine	443
AMA HEMMAH	448
Burn Bitch Burn 'Fly Free Upon the Winds' – Diane Narraway	450
THE WYTCH – Sam R Geraghty	453

ILLUSTRATIONS

Theoris and Her Visions – Various Public Domain

Collecting Herbs by Moonlight – Geraldine Lambert

The Whipping Girl – Sem Vine

The Hermit of St Bonnot – Leroy Skalstad

Tonight, You Burn – Marisha Kiddle

Satan's Widow – Various Public Domain

Redress – Public Domain

So, They Say – Various Public Domain

Devil in the Detail – Art Tower

The First Drops of Rain – Various Public Domain

The Noose Tree – Grotesco Joe

The Flowers of Bottesford – GDJ & Schueler Design

Witches and Devils on the Wind – Tarn Nemorensis

Drunk on Power – Public Domain

The Second Coming of the Hare – Various Public Domain

Lisbeth Nypan – Donaldmac.photography

The Judas Cradle – Bekki Milner

The Bronze Plaque – Public Domain

Obeah Magick – Various Public Domain modified by Diane Narraway

Giles Corey's Punishment and Awful Death – Public Domain

Maternal Kiss – Mary Cassatt

If of The Devil You Are, Burn – Sem Vine

Let My Spirit Slip Away – Various Public Domain

All images, regardless of source, are solely intended as an artistic representation of the stories.

INTRODUCTION
Diane Narraway

Witches carry an ancient and sacred bloodline; their DNA encompasses the memories of ancient practices: the ability to commune with the spiritual realms and first-hand knowledge of personal sacrifice. For this they have been persecuted, tortured, and sentenced to death for several millennia, and in many countries nothing has changed; thousands have died since the beginning of this century in India and Africa alone. Many witches in the USA, especially within the Bible Belt, remain firmly in their broom closets for fear of verbal and physical attacks.

In the earliest of the ancient laws, present in Ancient Egypt and Babylonia, malevolent sorcery and magic were punishable offences: the punishment often resulting in death. Likewise, the Ancient Roman Empire had laws in place which forbade the use of Black Magic, making it a capital offence. This included anything from blighting crops or spreading disease amongst livestock, to causing death by the use of enchantments.

It is estimated that between 2000 and 3000 individuals were put to death in Ancient Rome. Ironically, and somewhat amusingly, this stopped with the arrival of Christianity: Christian laws were similar concerning witchcraft, but their punishments were far less severe. At least they were in the first millennia. They appeared, however, to have a change of heart a few hundred years later, and by the 14th century 'Witch Fever' was rife in Europe and rapidly making its way to the new world. This was just the beginning of what would come to be known as the 'burning times.' The purge of heretics had increased to include Witches and Cunning-folk; all of whom were deemed to be in some way working with the Devil.

Whatever the cause, the end result was the same: the persecution of around 50,000 men and women; and these are only the ones we know about. These days, those of us in the UK enjoy a certain amount of freedom and are able to practice our spiritual beliefs relatively unhindered. There will always be bigots and those who condemn us through ignorance, but on the whole, since the repeal of the Witchcraft Act in 1951, we are doing ok.

As we look back throughout history, we realise that the persecution of witches was, and still remains, a global phenomenon: it spans centuries, affecting men, women, and children, making no allowances for age, physical illness, or mental health. Whether through ignorance, fear, or religious propaganda, countless human beings have been brutally tortured and slaughtered for their beliefs and practices.

The aim of this book is to bring to life those who are all too often little more than a name and date on a plaque. For some, not even their date of birth or death is known. Through the stories in this book, fact and fiction are cleverly blended to breathe life into lost memories and pay tribute to all those who lost their lives and those who continue to suffer. It is both heart breaking and sickening to consider what they went through and how frightening their world must have been. As you read their stories, you may shed a tear; several even. Perhaps you may smile at their defiance and resolution; who knows? Whether you empathise or sympathise with the witches in this book, I can't say, but I am sure you will never forget them. At least a few of those souls, lost to time, will come to mean more than just their dates.

In our hearts and through our actions, long may their memories live on.

*A Halo Made by the
Breeze and Moonlight.*

OF FLOWERS AND THORNS
Earl Livings

She comes to me with ripped clothes, a pale face swelling and purpling with bruises, her legs caked with dried blood. I hold her for a long time before the sobbing stops.

'What happened?' I say.

'I was fetching water. He grabbed me. Pulled me into the bushes. I couldn't scream. Couldn't get away.'

She shudders uncontrollably. I fetch a blanket and wrap it around her. Not the first time I have done this.

For generations, girls from the village have always found their way to this hut. They have listened well to the ancient songs in the old words only their mothers can teach them and come here even though it is well hidden behind thickets of brambles and thorn. They come whenever they need help. Powders for making a man look their way. Potions for unwanted babies. Pellets for turning a man grey before his time. Ever since tin was found within the northern escarpment and a miner's camp was set up at its base, they come more often nowadays.

'Who did this?'

'That short dumpy miner with the crooked teeth and lopsided ears. When he finished, he hit me again and told me I was his. Told me to come back tonight or else he'll burn down my family's hut, with all of us inside.'

Ah, yes, I know him. Have seen him swagger-chesting his way through the throng on market day as if he were a hero back from slaying a dragon. One evening, a year ago, I caught him pushing a girl barely out of her Blood-Blessing against the back wall of a hut. She fled while I beat him with my yew walking stick and chased him off. Left him with some vicious welts. I'm stronger than I look. In many ways. Though my time to join the ancestors in the whispering deep is coming.

Still, that man will never stop. Just like some of the others. Time for a lesson.

I give her a spoonful of powdered willow bark and honey to calm her and reduce the pain. Chew up a wad of yarrow and bandage her face with it. Make her eat some of my evening soup, even though she struggles to swallow because of the swelling. Sit with her, hold her, soothe her when great wracking sobs return. Leave her sleeping in my bed. Go out with my walking stick and my cunning bag, the same one my mother used, my grandmother, and others before them.

The full moon lights my way through the forest. Somewhere to my right, a fox barks a greeting. I cough one in return. To my left, something snuffles through the undergrowth, a badger likely. An owl swoops along the thin path before me then disappears into the dark of a gnarled oak I climbed when a young girl myself, so I could touch a star. That night, the moon goddess called me to my task and my mother started training me in earnest. It has always been that way, but the work is much harder now, with priests fanning abuse, and worse, at those who still follow the old ways. As my mother found out when she was returning from a laying out. Men beat her for being a witch. The next day, we held hands and sang the spell of bright travel as she passed over.

As soon as I can smell the putrid aroma of sweat and piss, liquor and burnt meat, which tells me the miner's camp is nearby, I step off the path and make my way through gorse and hazel to a small clearing within a grove of rowan trees. A slab of rock with glints of quartz beckons. I sit on it, open my senses to the night. Scent of wild garlic on the warm breeze. The criss-cross of buzzing insects. High wispy clouds stretching themselves westward, disappearing.

When the moon is nearly overhead, I open my bag, take out dried meadowsweet, oak and broom flowers, and arrange them on the grass in the shape of a woman lying down to feel the earth. I have done this only three times before in my life, twice with my mother, all after the miners arrived. Before that, my mother and grandmother did it only once each, because the old ways were more respected then. Satisfied, I bow to the moon nine times, bow once to each of the directions while giving thanks, return to the east and lift up my arms. I breathe deeply and call out in the old tongue:

*'Oh, goddesses of sea, land and sky,
come to my aid this night.*

*Oh, spirits of tree, stream, and stone,
come to my aid this night.
Oh, spirits of fur, fin, and flesh,
come to my aid this night.
Come to me for the making and taking of
 life.
Come to me for the blessing and the curse.
Come to me for the life I will gift you.'*

The breeze drops. The grove wraps itself with silence. Moonlight and starlight sparkle each trunk, branch and leaf. Blades of grass ripple and sway, each to their own rhythm. Tiny wings of light hover above the shape on the ground. They are waiting.

*'My thanks to you all. May all our
generations continue to serve you, bless
you, and be blessed.'*

The wings form a spiral of light that swirls moonwise around the laid-out flowers.

*'My thanks to you all. May you carry the seed
of our desire this night, so that we are all
protected.'*

The spiral thins at its bottom and descends.

*'My thanks to you all. May you be the mirror
for those who lust after us, who care nothing
for us, who care only for what they can tear
from the earth and from us.'*

The tip of the spiral touches the belly of the flower woman. Spreads out. Blossoms into curve of body and breast. Stretches into limbs and long-fingered hands, into the flowing shapes of hair and robes. Carves gentle eyes, pert nose, quivering lips in a heart-shaped face.

She stands before me, reaches out her right hand, and strokes my cheek.

The more she shimmers, the more my wrinkles deepen, my body shrivels, my eyes dim. I have barely enough breath to speak. This may be the last time I summon her because the magic takes more from me than it did my ancestors, who did not have to struggle with a new faith and a ruined land. But we must go on. Do what we can for our kind and for the future.

I bow to her. 'We are grateful you have come again. He is waiting.'

She smiles. Nods. Turns and glides out of the grove towards the camp and the man's dilapidated hut. She knows what to do.

She will appear before him at midnight. He will think she is the girl he aches for.

She will open her arms. He will try to grab her.

She will smile and step away without a sound.

He will curse her. He will try to punch her, shake her, choke her. She will dance out of reach.

He will howl his anger. She will smile again and race outside.

He will chase after her. He will blunder

through bracken, ferns, and thorn. He will ignore the scratches and the bruises as he stumbles over fallen branches. When his foot catches in a rabbit hole, he will swallow the pain and hobble after her. He will scream for her to stop. He will clamber over logs, claw at heather-covered slopes, pull himself through sliding scree and over jagged rocks. Many times, he will bend over panting, then burst into a run when he hears her distant laughter.

He will stop, lungs aching, muscles quivering, fists shaking.

She is standing before him. Arms open.

Beckoning smile. Her hair a halo made by the breeze and moonlight.

He will forget everything but his need to hold her again, plunge himself into her again.

She will not move as he wraps his arms around her.

She will let him kiss her. She will then take one step backwards.

In the morning, the workers find him broken on a pile of rocks at the bottom of the escarpment, not far from the mine itself, his face a rictus of fear, his hands clutching fresh flowers of meadowsweet, oak and broom. Some shake their heads and mumble while they cart him away for burial. Those who still know of the old ways tremble as they burn the flowers.

That evening, because I have no daughter and my breathing has not eased since the rite, my bones aching, my heartbeat unsteady, the whispering deep calling me, I begin to show the girl the ways of birthing, healing, and laying out and how to use the cunning bag.

We will have need of it again soon enough.

Voices from the Ashes
Resurrecting the Wytch

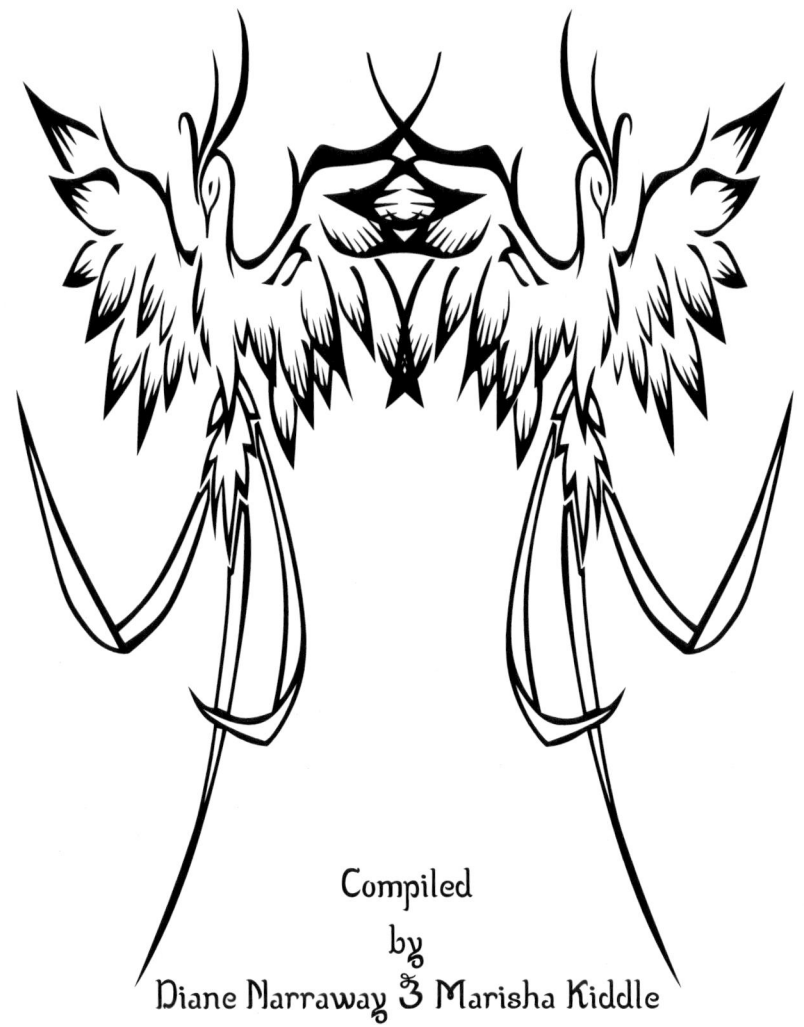

Compiled by
Diane Narraway & Marisha Kiddle

THEORIS OF LEMNOS
(Died prior to 323 BCE)

Theoris of Lemnos was an ancient Greek woman who lived in Athens in the fourth century BCE and was known as a witch or folk-healer. She was tried and executed for crimes including witchcraft along with her children. Although the exact date of either her birth or death are unknown, and details of her offence are unclear, there are three ancient accounts which survive describing her prosecution. They provide us with the most detailed account of a witch trial taking place in Classical Greece.

The earliest source is from a speech given by Demosthenes against Eunomos' brother Aristogeiton.

The second account is from the Hellenistic period and is credited to later sources, the atthidographer[1] Philochorus. The final account comes from the biography of Demosthenes, written by Plutarch and is dated to the 2nd century AD

---

[1] Atthidographer – In ancient Greece atthidograhers were historians from Attica (a region of Athens) who wrote the histories of Athens.

Theoris and Her Visions

A GREEK TRAGEDY
Diane Narraway

"She will be the ruin of you. She will break your heart ... chew you up and spit you out like gristle and bone ... I tell you brother. She will destroy you! Surely you've heard the rumours?" The constant argument between the two brothers was in danger of defining them. If Aristogeiton's concern for his twin brother was in any way fuelled by anything other than his own financial concerns, Eunomus was failing to see it.

"Enough. Really enough I grow weary of this, your constant drunken babblings ..."

"I am neither drunk nor babbling ..." snapped Aristogeiton taking yet another large swig of wine "You are both!" And with that, Eunomus left, heading for the home of the exceptionally beautiful Theoris. There was no disputing either her beauty or her wealth were anything other than mesmerising, plus the latter was currently helping Eunomus to pay off his brothers latest fine.

Aristogeiton, the younger of the twins had a penchant for wine, which was inevitably followed by political or moral crusades. All of which, to date had resulted in Eunomus paying in some way or another. The current fine was for his latest political ramblings against the more accepted orations of Demosthenes.

— *Rumours ha! They can't be true. Theoris is far too beautiful. And as for that brother of mine, well, he is determined to be as our father; imprisoned, alone, and broke ... such a waste of a life and I wouldn't mind if it cost him, but it doesn't ... Besides, she asked me to call round.*

As angry as he was, the sight of Theoris cooled his temper and warmed his heart. He was putty in her hands and he knew it. She was a rare beauty and not just in his eyes. There wasn't a man in Athens who didn't lust after her. Some more secretly than others, and all more secretly than Eunomus.

He had met the beautiful Theoris back in Lemnos some ten years earlier, and for him it had been love at first sight, but at the time she was married. There was no love between her, and her then husband. It had been a convenience for her; he was a wealthy landowner with several vineyards. Not only did she need children, she desperately wanted them, but it was the one thing her husband seemed unable to provide.

She had become known as a folk healer and had tried every potion, incantation, and petition known to her. She wore amulets of bone and gem and had lay still for hours after she and her husband made love reciting incantations and ritual petitions to Hera. She had trained and become a devoted priestess to Hera, but all to no avail. Like all women, her focus had initially been on a male heir but after 2 years of trying she would be as grateful for a daughter. As for her husband, she had no real love for him. She had no real love for any man; her preferences lay elsewhere. She and her maid Phaedra had been lovers as long as she had been married, and at times she wondered if her infertility was punishment for loving another more than her husband, especially a woman. Lemnos was under Athenian law and such practices were taboo.

Eunomus had come to Lemnos on business although it was never clear what business. Whatever it was it had brought him to the home of Theoris. He got little joy from her husband but was captivated from the moment he met her, and although she viewed him as a poor specimen of humanity, she could see that his infatuation for her and his need for money may work to her advantage. She waited until her husband was away before inviting Eunomus to her house.

"Eunomus I see how you look at me ..." she schmoozed, taking another sip of her wine, and looking seductively up at him. One flash of her deep brown eyes made his heart melt. "I feel much desire for you also, but alas I am married, and we could never be more than ... well, lovers. But surely, a man such as yourself would not be happy or content being a secret love. Oh, Eunomus I am torn!"

Eunomus could feel his hands become clammy as he struggled for the words to respond. There was no playing it cool or casual. He was lost for words, drinking in her beauty, the fullness of her breasts and flowing black curls. Her olive skin, deep brown eyes, and perfect lips. To him, she was a goddess, and she knew it. Sidling up to him she planted a soft kiss on his lips. From that moment he was helpless and hopeless.

"I can never truly be with you, but if you give me children I will fund your business" she whispered in his ear. "Does that sound a worthy proposition ..." she continued, nibbling gently on his earlobe. He nodded, he was powerless and the most response he could manage was a breathless "Yes."

Their affair in Lemnos lasted 3 years during which time they had two children, both boys. Shortly after the birth of her younger son her husband fell ill. Eunomus had returned to Athens to bail out his drunken brother yet again but remained ever hopeful that Theoris' husband would not survive, and that she and her children, his children would move closer. Eventually his prayers were answered. She sold her husband's vineyards and moved to Athens; having left a respectable amount of time of course.

Eunomus never questioned her husband's death nor her desire to continue with their arrangement. Nor did he question how close she and her maid seemed at times. There were rumours, plenty of them, and she was openly affectionate to Phaedra in his presence, but there is none so blind as those that refuse to see! And Eunomus refused to see alright. 'An oblivious fool' was what his brother called him, but then he was a drunk, so what did he know?

She had long ceased any intimacy with Eunomus, that had stopped the moment she got pregnant with their youngest child, but she kept his brother out of jail and him plied with enough pharmakon to remain literally 'under her spell.'

Tonight, though things would change. She had asked him round.

— *Perhaps she is to end this secrecy. Perhaps she wishes to marry me. Perhaps this is just wishful thinking on my part. We shall see. Just be still my beating heart, you confound my thoughts and I suspect I need a clear head. There she is my beautiful Theoris. Gods, how I love her.*

"Eunomus my love. Come quickly"

"What is it? Why the urgency?"

"I have had a vision."

— *Oh yes, Theoris and her visions.*

"A vision of what my love?" Eunomus rolled his eyes internally, he daren't actually roll them, having no desire to offend.

"Something dreadful is going to happen, I tried to heal the Priestess of Hera and she died. It is dreadfully sad; I fear they will blame my pharmakon"

— *What is she saying? Why should they blame her?*

"Surely they will not. You are a good person. You have healed many."

At no point did it ever occur to him that perhaps she had intentionally poisoned either the priestess or her late husband. Totally ignoring the fact that she lavished affection on her maid, including the time, he had caught her sucking her maids nipple and fondling her crotch. Or any of her other public behaviour which openly fuelled the rumours concerning her sexuality. Oblivious to the fact that she had been the Priestess of Hera back in Lemnos. She was a seer and a pharmakis, and her use of either was nearly always subjective.

"Eunomus my love please listen to me. I need you to do something for me."

"Anything ... Just name it" Poor fool that he was would have walked to the ends of the Earth for her; on broken glass if she requested it.

"Take these, my potions and other paraphernalia. This one ..." she said pointing to a large bottle on which, unlike the others had the ingredients clearly written on it "... will cure the sacred sickness. Please take them all and dispose of them ... and only use the large bottle. Bury the rest, burn them, whichever you deem best but never, I implore you speak of it again."

Eunomus, being Eunomus dutifully obeyed. Theoris kissed Eunomus goodbye for what she knew would be the last time. She fiddled with the small vial of hemlock she had tightly clasped in her hand behind her back.

— *Now to deal with that treacherous maid Phaedra. I know she has betrayed me. What have I ever done to her, other than love her, that she would do this? I have no idea, but I trust my visions they have never failed me.*

Theoris' thoughts were interrupted by the arrival of two men from the court to arrest her. There was little formality; she was accused of practicing witchcraft to cause harm and witches got no special considerations. In the following confusion, and with a crowd gathering many things were said, only fragments of which she heard, "... Witch ... Pharmakis ... Murderer ... Slut."

They dragged her out of the house more roughly than necessary and in the process she managed to drop the vial into the street. The words cut through her heart like a knife, as one of the men shouted, "Bring the children!"

This had been hidden from her vision. Her children. Her beautiful, beloved children.

—*What could they possibly want with my boys? They are scarcely more than babies. Monsters! How could Phaedra my love; my one true love do this to me?*

Tears rolled down Theoris face as she approached the court. Many had followed shouting insults and abuse as she was dragged through the streets to the Hill of Ares, with the sound of her children screaming behind her. Her heart was broken and her spirit with it. The once proud and beautiful woman that Eunomus and Phaedra had both fallen in love was now dying inside. It was a broken woman that stood before the court, a

9

mere shadow of who she once was. As Phaedra gave her damning evidence, telling those present how her Mistress had used potions and enchantments to bewitch her husband, Eunomus and Theoris both hung their heads. There was a time when she would have stood tall, stared Phaedra in the eye and used every womanly wile and cunning magic at her disposal, but that time had passed with the arrest of her children.

She wasn't on trial for using magic as such; she was on trial for using magic and magical knowledge to commit murder. Her knowledge of herbs and her magical practices had provided her the knowledge to commit murder without trace.
Without Phaedra's evidence there would be no charges, but of course Phaedra had been handsomely rewarded. Theoris wasn't sure why her activities should be of enough interest to warrant a reward, but at this point it didn't matter.

Eunomus had gone to the court as soon as he had heard. His drunken brother had taken great delight in telling him of her arrest; too much delight Eunomus thought. Through watery eyes he heard the love of his life sentenced to death. And not just her, her children too. His children too. This was Draconian law where murder or even attempted murder carried a death sentence, and in the event of witchcraft the court deemed it best to apply the same sentence to the defendants offspring, in order to remove the malevolent and cursed bloodline.

There were no last words or requests, nor was she held until an executioner was available, instead Theoris and her two children were led unceremoniously to the precipice. The Varathron[1] lay silently waiting below. The tears fell from Eunomus onto the dusty ground; he turned and walked away unable to bear the pain of either watching Theoris hurled to her death or endure the sobs of his children as they followed their mother.

In the burning heat of a hot summers day Theoris was not even pushed, but kicked to her death, while her children just six and seven years old had their heads held to prevent them looking away. Still sobbing, and with the sound of their mothers body hitting the bottom of the Varathron ringing in their ears her children were hurled over the edge to their deaths. Their soft little bodies lay disjointed, broken, and bleeding at the bottom of the deep trench. The only mercy was that they had all died on impact.

Phaedra was handsomely rewarded, not by the courts but by Aristogeiton whose motives had been to save his besotted twin brother any further humiliation. The bitter irony was that he had used the money to pay for his outstanding debts which had been given to him by Eunomus, and ultimately had come from Theoris. She had effectively paid for her, and her children's death.

A few short months later, Aristogeiton was arrested for not paying his debts and jailed despite Eunomus' testimony the public orator

Demosthenes gave a damning speech against both brothers. Demosthenes, who had himself been the subject of one of Aristogeiton's public speeches as he called them; drunken abusive rants would be a more accurate description was no fan of either brother.

Eunomus' involvement with Theoris, was brought up by Demosthenes and due to his involvement with the witch Theoris, he was denounced as a credible witness. Aristogeiton's attempts to save his brother from further humiliation had backfired. Not only that, but Eunomus' testimony being discredited meant Aristogeiton was imprisoned.

So, Aristogeiton lost his freedom and with it came delirium tremors and seizures, which Eunomus could have cured had his brother not been incarcerated. Theoris lost her life and faced eternal damnation. Eunomus, lost the love of his life, his children and with it his lust for life. And Phaedra? Well, who do you think taught Theoris in the first place?

---

1 Varathron – Execution was carried out by throwing a criminal off a precipice (usually a high, steep cliff) into a deep trench. In Athens this was known as Varathron.

PETRONILLA DE MEATH
(1300–1324)

Petronilla was the maid of Dame Alice Kyteler, a 14th century Norman Irish noblewoman.
 Following the death of her second and third husband, and the debilitating illness of her fourth husband, Dame Alice Kyteler's in-laws sought legal charges against her. Their primary concern was her practice of sorcery and these matters caught the attention of the appointed Bishop of Ossary, Richard Ledrede. The Bishop petitioned to use his experience in inquisitional methods, previously learnt at Avignon, France, to accuse Dame Alice and her group of practicing witchcraft. Petronilla was charged with heresy, as one of her accomplices; she was imprisoned and confessed that both she and her Mistress were guilty of witchcraft. Petronilla was flogged and burnt at the stake in the year 1324, in Kilkenny; she was the first recorded case of death by fire for the crime of heresy in Ireland.

Collecting Herbs by Moonlight

A MATTER OF THE FAITH'
Geraldine Lambert

THE VISION IN THE CHURCH

I will always remember that night at the church; treading upon the worn steps leading to its entrance: they were ground down by the enduring times of the land and its people. I had never imagined I would take up and learn the powers and follow my mistress in her uncanny ways. As we entered the porch, the nave smelled of old leather and stone-damp. The soles of my feet felt cold upon the aged tiles and my arms jumped with the chill in the air, but how my heart beat fast as we all called the conjuration. As soon as I had sparked the candles, our mistress first called the words and then we followed. We were gathered there, united in our sorcery, calling to the old ones of time and mystery. There were ten of us in all: Mistress Alice, Annora Lange, Alice Carpenter, Elena Galrussyn and Syssok, Eva de Brounestaun, Johannes, and William Payn de Bolu, myself and my daughter Sara Basilia. Sometimes William Outlawe, the son of my mistress, would attend our gatherings or otherwise be associated with us. He was high-born, like my mistress, and I worked at his house as his mother's chief maidservant. I was also her chief mediator in our magical workings, and this gave me an air of importance and pride.

At first it was still and dark inside the empty building, although the wind hammered outside at the tower. How the younger ones jumped at the knocks and raps of branches hitting the roof, as the shutters drummed loose by the strength of the fierce breeze. I remember it took us a while to get used to the disturbances within the old chapel; its ghostly magnetic and hollow atmosphere beckoning us to stir. Waiting in that still darkness, the mist gradually came like ribbons of grey silk encircling our cold breath. It was so strange and tense, and so exciting too. As we waited in that sublime moment, Dame Alice took the mixtures of powders and herbs and combined them in the dish of fresh albumin. Reciting her words of conjuration, she added the runny compound into the skull cap, which was already prepared with dead insects, worms, and flakes of dried blood. I then stirred the concoction with a thorn stick, before adding the contents with cooled cloth water, from the clothing of an unbaptized village infant. The mixture spun slowly in the bone cup with its heavy density of new life and death. We watched the candlelight glow upon the strains of threads as they tangled with the worm parts, weaving the destiny of our purpose and desire to be sewn into each fate. With trepidation, we handed the bone cup around, each of us supping the bitter, disgusting mixture. This wasn't our first time in conjuring the spirits, but it was eerily different, and we weren't sure if we were doing it right. I tried to catch mistress's eye, but she laughed at my expression and made me feel foolish in front of the others. Then some of us giggled, our nerves were so sharply heightened.

After leaving the remainder of the mixture on the floor before us, we then duly followed our usual routine and spoke the chant to attract the spirits:

> "The mare will fly, riding with tooth and hoof,
> The gander will fly, riding with wing and ring,
> All our Lords and Ladies, come, come, come."

We whispered the words again and again, until the echoes of our voices spun into an amalgamated hum and our mistress called us to cease. We continued to denounce our faith in Christ and the church by the calling out of all the parts of our body, from the top of our heads to the soles of our feet, each in turn, one by one. This was to entice every part of us to pay homage to our 'old ones' and to allow every bit of our body to witness and belong to the ceremony. When we were finished, Mistress Alice called me to my duty; in doing so, the others stared at me intensely, biting their lips while their minds waited for the interpretation.

Foreheads and contoured shadows flickered in the bobbing candlelight; stone faces from the statues of olden kings and aged saints seemed to dance upon the walls. I now had to carry out my concentrated performance, which arrived with spectral images after a brief meditation.

At first, I saw a shaggy black creature standing still in the centre; it was staring out with flickering mirrored eyes and crawling within their reflective surface was the shape of black rags with torn shreds and tight knots hanging, flowing, flickering, and twirling. I saw movement and whoops of dusted shapes, thick ash lumps of a charred burnt out hump. Then, on the central alter steps, an old dread lady appeared, wrapped in black sack cloth, with piercing dark eyes framed within the crevices of her skeletal fleshless face. Her features were strong, yet slight, with a fair grey hue and dark ashen lines where the movement of her skin had etched with time. As my seeing eye continued, I felt my soul and spirit move within her presence. In the silence, as I concentrated, her hooked hand slowly slid out of her sleeve and beckoned me with her fore finger.

Standing by the north side, I stared at the sooty outline of her thick ridged fingernail, whilst holding my composure. I turned quietly to the group, stood, and spoke alone.

"A mighty spirit has come to us: a Lady of the dark of time, a grand mare mother. She comes with the gift of sight, and great power to give ..." The monotone words came freely without, the thought of mind as I continued, "She cannot guard the embodiment, but has come to protect the heart of our being, the vital force within; she is always with us though she might not appear again ... so, she will, as is the way."

This spirit of such age, with the appearance of all fearfulness, then slipped behind the font, but I caught her with my eye again. I was anxious, but strengthened, and her appearance gave me a feeling of significance because, on this occasion, the others couldn't see her. She just sat rocking back and forth on the long stone step, then she slowly raised herself and darted to peer into our eyes or flicker to the side of our faces. We all felt the cold, silent, and dreaded emotions that struck within us, and oh, such a sense of majesty and power coming from the spirit realms.

When the vision rolled away, Mistress Alice asked me to describe exactly what I had seen; I told them all, with a voice flat with caution, whilst a sensitive echo rang between the pillar stones.

"The old mother of power, knowledge, and dread ... she says more with her eyes than with her thought ... tread well and carefully where whispers hold ... she places her finger against her lip. We have the blessing of secret courage; she grants us knowledge but warns to be silent ..."

Dame Alice and the group asked questions for me to interpret. The answers appeared as images, glyphs, and sometimes, whispered words in riddles. The face and body of a man in dark cloth, standing behind an arch of yellow flames, shifted, and dissipated so suddenly that I wondered if it were a message or just my imagination.

However, it left an imprint on my mind. After the visions and messages were gone, we then continuously called curses to those who had wronged us. We also cursed those who had scorned Mistress Alice because of her wealth from two of her four husbands. We focused upon the relatives of Adam le Blund: her second husband, who had suspected Alice of murder, especially when his death-will was read, leaving all his proceeds to his son. Alice had been forced to sue the relatives of her third husband, Sir Richard de Valle, so that she could get her widow's share. His relatives had suspected her of murder, and had even claimed that her present husband, Lord John le Poer, had become emaciated through the use of her potions and poisons. So, it seemed only fair to make calls for ill luck to catch a hold on Dame Alice's in-laws, and to make charms to stop and punish those relatives who had publicly instituted litigation before the clergy. One of these was the particularly fastidious and annoying Bishop Ledrede, who was always deciphering details and facts concerning the affairs of the villagers. On different occasions we called for some of the townsfolk to appear ugly, with the horns of goats and rams arising from their heads when their beloved menfolk looked upon them. We began to giggle as we pictured them under the coverlets, talking before lovemaking, and suddenly changing into horned beasts. We laughed so much it was a great release, and we wet ourselves with the jest as it took a hold of us. We were angry too, as we howled our curses upon those righteous, devout, and fervid uncomely people we mistrusted or thought themselves above us.

On finishing our ceremony, we thanked the spirits as we blew out the candles. We all knocked or clapped three times, as was our custom, and made sure that no trace was left behind us, except for our moments of ritual memory. William and Syssok waited until we had left the porch before locking the heavy church doors, then we walked our own way in silence back to our chambers and the warmth of the hearth. There were plenty of other times too. I loved the power of sorcery – its changing upon us in our ordinary mundane lives. How the air would appear still for a moment, then change into a torrent force of energy and power. How our spirits would flow in unison with our surroundings as we began with humility, then rose with mischief and command whilst calling to remedy those who had wronged us.

FRUIT, ROOT, AND BONE.

Once our group had become established, and we became more familiar with one another and our individual ways, we settled into our workings. We learnt that the sacrifices we made at the crossroads would set the space for the flow of the magical forces to travel in all directions: north, east, south, west, above, below, and everywhere in-between.

Sometimes William used his tame animals and birds as sacrifices. Often the women took turns to prepare the cock birds; their torn feathers and scattered innards paid for the success of our enchantments and helped us to read the future with their symbolic patterns. The fodder of the cocks, spiders, and worms, the luxurious flags of the peacock feathers and wildflowers, the flax cloth and the brains of the unbaptized child were all beautiful and fascinating things. The scent of blood and flesh, grass and grime, filled us with an earthy prowess. We prepared our sorceries with full intent and, as our group developed, we became more proficient in creating, harnessing, and liberating the forces.

Dame Alice knew when I first sought employment with her that I had the gift of sight: she said it was in the dark colour of my eyes. She taught me how to read the tides, select the right parts of plants, and split the skin to extract and boil the properties of fruit, root, and bone. She also showed me how to mediate between summoned spirits, channel and direct what to do and when to ask for prophetic answers. Last year we summoned together an incubus who became a mysterious friend and guide to us. His name was Robert Artisson, and he appeared in broad daylight in the bed chamber at Williams's house. We had prepared a mixture of crushed night berries with petals from henbane and monkshood flowers, together with herbs and rubbed it into the veins of our inner forearms. After following with words of power and much meditation, we noticed an outline in the tapestry that seemed to move and overlap in a corner of the room. Shapes appeared and flickered as we clinched our eyes, then a great dark shade emerged which roiled into three tall, black, shadow men holding iron rods. The figures cautiously rose out from the wall and stood before us, as Mistress Alice and I gasped. They were so tall; their teeth, large and white, gently shone out against their darkened skin. Eventually, the three figures combined into one: the two taller forms becoming wings on either side of the central figure; we now call him our good friend. We could scarcely believe that the demon would actually *appear* in broad daylight, let alone take the hands of Mistress Alice and seduce her; although it didn't take much to persuade her. After much caressing and touching, he undressed Mistress Alice and moved her onto the bed under him. His muscles gleamed with sweat;

Mistress was in full ecstasy, and I had to shut and guard the doors in case anyone heard the rhythmic bangs of the bedposts whilst he struck into her. When it was finished, and Mistress was greatly pleased, he grabbed the hemp sheets and vigorously rubbed himself dry after their physical enjoyment. We then cut and saved those dried sections from the bedsheets, which held his salty life force, and later added the stiffened cloth to our collection of sorcerous mixtures.

It seems a time ago now, but I still remember the majesty of that moment in the chamber, and how it changed my thoughts concerning the intensity of our secret world. So pure and dark, so frightening and calm, and so ominous was the moment when he first appeared and spoke to us. He told us that he was from the lower middling realm of hell. His resonant calm voice spoke to me, a maidservant, as though I were a Queen. The atmosphere in the air was so still and tight, I could cut it with a knife.

PESTIFEROUS WOMEN - SPRING 1324

So much has happened since those magical days. An air of unease built up around the town because an English bishop named Ledrede, has caused much affray amongst the nobles due to his particular interest in those involved in witchcraft and sorcerous acts. He has been investigating allegations made against Dame Alice and our group.

The more the Bishop enquired, the more his clergymen spoke of whispers concerning instances of maleficium: causing injury by magical means and sorcery, undertaken using occult powers for one's private advantage. When we first heard of the bishop and his enthusiasm for hunting out heretics and those adverse to the usual ways of the church, we didn't fear much. We thought that if we were unlucky enough to be caught, we might be placed with the same people who were classed as common criminals. We also knew that Dame Alice's son William, and other powerful family members who had influence over authority and the law, would not want to cause any hindrance upon us. We had also believed that torture was forbidden under King Edward's English Law, so we duly expected an easy sentence: perhaps a fine, or charitable services for the poor for a certain time. We didn't fear because we knew that Dame Alice, as a lady of influence, would provide the costs,

25

having been a money lender from the time of her first husband and son, William. With her ample allowance, she, William, and noble family friends would protect us all and get us out of trouble; that's what we thought.

Regretfully, what we did not know was that Bishop Ledrede, in all his sacred finery, intended to show a new type of clerical power to our people. He was a man of the church, who was prepared to cause much fear and anguish to achieve his goals. We later learned that he had previously been influenced by the legislation preference of inquisitorial prosecution upon divination andsorcery. The bishop paid distinct interest to the factions of heresy, and it was said that he had paid precise attention at the start of the inquisition in Avignon. In 1258, before I had been born, Pope Alexander IV was in favour of finding and punishing heretics. He passed a bill which stated that whenever there was the 'scent' of heresy, in the form of a group or sect of worshippers different from the Papal doctrine, they should be sought out and punished. Likewise, Bishop Ledrede saw women like us as 'matters against the church': devil worshippers and witches with dark energies, who drew power from the devil to use against those 'good Christian people' within the larger communities.

He called us 'pestiferous women' and roused the powers of ecclesiastical law against heretics to round up Dame Alice and our group for punishment. Lord Arnold le Poer was the seneschal of Kilkenny, as well as a long-standing in-law and friend of Alice and William. At first, both Arnold and William openly fought to evade the chaos that Bishop Ledrede had brought upon us all. When Lord Arnold heard that his friends William and Alice had been implicated, he succeeded in arresting the bishop for not following due legal process in his enthusiastic pursuit of heretics; the Bishop was imprisoned for seventeen days, which was highly unusual. However, some of the townsfolk felt such pity for a 'man of the church' to be locked up that hundreds of them paid him visits, bringing so many gifts of food and wares that his cell resembled a guest house. Following the bishop's release, Lord Arnold and the bishop agreed to settle their differences; however, this was after many proceedings and letters, discussing who had the power of authority to judge and condemn regarding matters of the faith and the law.

I remember the long process of time when the nobles and clerics were trying to settle these matters. Many families were torn between the power of church law and that of the land; this resulted in the severing of allegiances between the loyalties of the family, and that of their official roles, together with clerical license. In some circumstances, individuals were obeying the bishop and his clerics on one day, and then, by the evening, observing the laws of the secular court. It was likened to a whirlwind of pure chaos and confusion, between the importance of the church and the clerics with their spiritual laws, and the definitive noble authorities and their secular laws of the land. Some clerics of high authority even had differences of opinion between themselves! All this perplexity had been initiated by Bishop Ledrede, with his scrupulous and meticulous thorough investigations into those who committed heresy and those who aided and abetted them.

Dame Alice and I sometimes thought that the bishop was terrified the church would lose its vast wealth and power to any disparate soul who sought to find a better life by using a different way of devotion. We had heard he disliked the beguines in Europe and wondered how he could command such a didactic approach to something as private as spirituality. We sometimes even laughed when we imagined a whore beckoning him into her bedchamber, and his reaction whilst reading the scriptures in his autocratic and fastidious nature. But sometimes we had been very wary of the bishop; I remember the days when we became fearful of being charged and were ducking and hiding from the bishop's orders. The company of our group gave a lift to our spirits during those times of pressure and unease.

THE DREADFUL BISHOP

The balance of the law dramatically changed between our Irish secular law and that of the ecclesiastical. The dreadful Bishop Ledrede came into our lives and upset the balance within the law of our land, our Ireland. He came as an English man, a foreigner, to intrude in our laws and ways of being. He did not bring peace between the feuds of the clans but sought out the darkness of difference, with his scrutiny of church laws and his meddling. It is because of this so called "holy man of God" that a whole nest of vipers was born, with his questioning amongst our people concerning folk paganism and the likes of magical practices gleaned from our mistress' texts.

In time, it followed that Bishop Ledrede found the sacks of powders, oils, nails, and hair that we had kept hidden in the chest at Mistress Alice's home. He made a big public display of burning our magical collection within Kilkenny Square; the town's folk watched with pinched cheeks, and hands to their mouths in astonishment, although of course, I don't recall them looking so astonished when we gave them the herbs for their healing. All that time we had spent making those powders; how we spent those long hours selecting, bruising, drying, grinding, and enticing magical life-force into those mixtures. They were then destroyed like a puff of dried ash, as though they had no importance at all. To us, they represented the keys to our magical needs, and now they were gone, like piss in a puddle.

The bishop continued to challenge and investigate our characters, even appearing in front of the court at Dublin, until he finally succeeded in obtaining testaments and warrants for us. We were so shocked, although much was true, to be charged on numerous accounts of heresy. The charges included: denying the faith of Christ and the church, being in possession of a familiar, and using sorcery and potions to control Christians. Later, at the hearing, the Bishop held an inquisition on the first group of six, which included Dame Alice and other members from our group. We were at first defamed in front of a great crowd of priests, clerics, and other high nobles from the surrounding districts; then one by one, we were publicly accused and openly dishonoured. I felt intimidated standing with the others, in our humble shifts and patched up clothing; I felt so exposed with our secrets coming out before the judging crowd of important men. I had always believed that our magical ways were so the ordinary people could fight for justice within this world of inequality. I recall the times when I had served some of those nobles and clerics: I had always given extra helpings, more meat, bread, and ale when they were staying at Lord William's Manor. I made sure the others would serve them well, make their chamber fires and ensure they were comfortable, with fresh rushes on the floor. Those men of importance knew all this, and yet they would not oppose the bishop's proceedings. It was as though they were all defeated and conquered by the bishop's continuously dominant conniving persona. The nobles were ground down by the bishop, like a sorcerer grinding down a victim, like charcoal crushed into dirt.

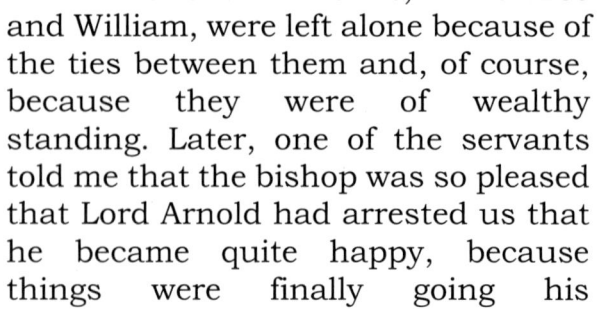

The hours passed by and I recall the rain lashing down against the heavy courtroom door. The officials droned on and on, as we watched like frightened horses until the bishop set about to arrest us on the charge of heresy. Eventually we were all committed to prison, including Mistress Alice and Lord William. Lord Arnold had previously called support for us and had even described the bishop as 'that low born tramp from England.' However, the change in law had turned Arnold's tune when the bishop called for the inclusion of those who had previously aided and abetted heretics. Lord Arnold, realizing the shift in power regarding his previous support, turned to preparing our imprisonment. It then transpired that Lord Arnold made sure his friends, Dame Alice and William, were left alone because of the ties between them and, of course, because they were of wealthy standing. Later, one of the servants told me that the bishop was so pleased that Lord Arnold had arrested us that he became quite happy, because things were finally going his way. However, the rest of us being of poor standing, were then incarcerated in different prisons. This was the last time I would see my daughter, Sara Basilia, and Mistress Alice. Unknown to me then, it would also be the last time I would live my life as I had known it, even though I felt sure we would be freed within a few days.

THE HOLDING - KILKENNY CASTLE

I was taken to a damp raw cell at Kilkenny Castle, in one of the basic holdings. I remember it was very foreboding and cold, with a tiny wood-framed window that let in little light. Marks of old, brown blood splatters had made patterns on the dirt- engraved stone wall. During the days of my incarceration, I could only eat what the servants of William Outlawe were able to secretly poke through the shutter. On some days no one came, everyone was very afraid of being connected to me. The silence and isolation of that holding room left me distracted and confused; my imagination began to trick my thoughts and I sometimes lost hours and days in strange reverie. Adrift from the others, I was anxious, restless, and very unsure of what would follow.

One grey day the bishop came to question me in my cell; accompanying him were two clerics and a burly masked and hooded man, who looked uncomfortable in his gait. The masked man placed the hand ropes and screws before me, and the splatters of old blood and trapped hair wrapped around the weave and iron alerted me to the other people they had been used on before me.

The bishop proceeded to tell me about previous prisoners in France, and how he witnessed their suffering at the unbearable pain caused by the torturous art. The attendants nodded in unison with his words; their gleeful eyes catching a fragment of candlelight as they sensed my vulnerability as a torture novice.

I tried to remain serene, although my legs refused to move when they ordered me to sit upon the bench. The bishop and his men began to terrorize me with the knot rope, binding and then crushing my fingers backwards as they twisted and lifted against my joints. My shouts of pain did not stop their questions; they repeated them again and again, before I gave the answers they wanted. In-between the confessions, the bishop would give me a short break before continuing whilst his man prepared another device to cause me further agony. I was numb from the fear of what would come next. After the terror, desperate and worn down, I confessed to several accusations. Some were true: causing injury to the bodies of the faithful with potions and concoctions and arousing feelings of love and hate amongst people within the village. However, much of the answers I gave were exaggerations and made-up tales when the torture wouldn't stop.

I think I also confessed to many more detailed sorceries and practices, but only one that had involved Mistress Alice. I told great secrets of our craft, including how we had consulted with demons and received answers from the beasts of Hell, and a pact whereby I would be the medium between Dame Alice and our friend Robert Artisson.

Throughout my wheeze for breath, I even admitted to aiding Mistress Alice with the murder of her husbands, even though I hadn't yet been in her service. It went on and on ... the ripping of reason and the breaking of my true self, as I admitted to more and more things I didn't know or do. The deadly silence afterwards was broken by the clerics scribbling, their quills scratching upon the parchment.

It was during the time of my confinement that I heard Dame Alice had managed to elude prison. She was the centre of all our magical sorceries, but despite this, she slipped through the net and was able to make her escape quite openly with my daughter Basilia. She probably used Basilia as an identity disguise.

Dame Alice had been mistress and mother to us all. With all our hearts and bodies, we willed our deeds to protect one another, as any secret society would do. However, I felt betrayed; the hope I had expected would no longer come; it was lost with the news of her escape. Those of us who were imprisoned had become the scapegoats bound to take the blame for all.

I was later told by the same informant that William had been given a hefty monetary fine for aiding and abetting us heretics. However, I doubt he will carry out his penance; he always had his own rules on how to spend his money and often tried to elude mass, never mind attend three times a day for a year.

William had not been as lucky as Mistress Alice in escaping punishment, but he was, however, given a lesser sentence compared to the rest of us.

RETRIBUTION- 1324 – 1325

The day Lord William was placed in shackles and given a new penance set by the magnates, I was sentenced to be whipped throughout the parish and taken to the stake to die by fire. This had happened before in Ireland; I recall how embittered and disillusioned I felt that these horrors had been instigated by a foreign bishop in our own land, our Ireland. Wretched and torn, my swollen hands shook uncontrollably as they dragged me to walk along the parish road, while the strap tore the flesh on my back. I remember flinching every time the leather struck, but although numb from shock, inside I felt as hard as a rock. Some of the parishioners stared as we passed them and a couple shook their heads, but their expressions and stances did not appear to gloat. They knew of my low status and any one of them could have been me: a servant to those of wealth. My courageous self-regard was buried deep within, although my stride and appearance were week. Several times I stumbled and was hoisted up by the demeaning leather rein and rope.

William had not suffered in this way; I heard that he had been instructed to travel to the holy land and to hear three masses every day for a year. He was present with us on so many occasions, it has become very clear how unequal the law is. The common folk always pay more than those of status, more than the nobles and the clergy, with their false responsibility and humbleness. We, the poor, pay in sweat, servitude, misery, and blood.

Trying to keep my balance on the muddy stone roads, I walked on, step by step; by this point, my mind was spinning with the raging injustice of it all. I cursed the bishop and his piteous clergy, as well as all those in the town who were of high-standing, including Mistress Alice. As I fell again, face downwards into the mud, my cursing became louder with the annoyance. The hooded man pulled me up and my nose began to bleed; it dripped onto my lip and I sucked it in because I was dry. How my body ached for a woman of twenty-five years. Although blooded, dirty, ripped, and torn, my thoughts continued. I thought of pleasant things for a while, to appease the pain: the taste of rose hips and honey, the colours of summer fields, moon light striking the woodland, the scent of lavender ... But I return soon enough to muttering curses; the promise of revenge made me feel stronger.

When the humiliating walk and cruel whipping was over, I was taken back to Kilkenny Castle Square. Here, I was straddled over the shoulder of the big, burly man from the prison and quickly taken, without ceremony, to the platform of the stake. It was surrounded by a heap of dried wooden faggots, all tightly stacked and crossed like a rook's nest. The ropes tying my hands at the front were re-tied behind my back and I realized they were preparing to hide the torture wounds on my hands from the audience's glare. My arm muscles pulled as the wooden stake jutted into my torn back. I clenched my teeth together and stared out at the people watching me; it was the moment to state my final sentence. My voice yelled with driven determination, as I spoke to all the clergy and town people present. "Under the influence of Dame Alice, I totally reject the faith in Christ and the church." I noticed some in the crowd raised an eyebrow or nodded, and some placed a hand to their mouths in a gesture of surprise. But the bishop stood still and upright, without expression.

I stood there on the lonely platform, my mind thinking forward and back in time. Seeing the lighted bushel, I wondered how long it would take to die, and whether I would scream or go into shock as I felt the flames bite my pale skin. I then wondered what would happen: would the fire choke me to death, squeeze the air out of my mouth as I gasp. Would it take two or five minutes to die, or up to an hour, as I had heard?

As I felt the heat rise upon my skin, I knew that my death was soon. Moment by moment the fire increased, with the yellow flames dancing higher to greet my face. The spectators held still as I yelled so hard that I couldn't rest for breath. Like a banshee, I screeched bitter curses and foul crimes upon Bishop Ledrede. I peered through a gap in the choking smoke and my mind suddenly recalled the vision during that night at the church. It was the dark frame of the bishop surrounded by an arch of flames. I then caught his direct glance in the crowd. Our eyes locked for a few seconds, as glimmers of his future began to come into my mind. The ethereal images blurred in and out of focus because my eyes watered in the smoke. I willed them all to be true: Fire, Storm, Destruction, Collapse, Attack, Rebellion, Wrath.

★

I then found myself lifting into the air above a thin, charred, blackened body. It was a slight female figure, humped over with hands tied behind. She had a streak of auburn hair, just like mine, and her clothing, once terracotta, was now dissolved into fraying embers. I sensed a sublime familiarity when I peered at the blackened skull face; it was turned sideways and tipped with a smoking halo of flowing mist. The remains of the inferno with its combustible heat had left an illuminous glow, which resembled the peering eyes of the 'forgotten' surrounded in pitch.

I was then guided to the Castle, where to 'need' and to 'want' is defunct, and nothing is forbidden to the people of our kin.

OR PERHAPS ...

PETRONILLA de MEATH
(1300 – 1324)

In more recent times, Dame Alice Kyteler would be considered a serial killer, one who had become titled, wealthy, and well connected through the calculated murder of several husbands. Indeed, despite the religious paranoia prevalent in her day, when her disinherited step-children accused her not of murder but more subversively of heresy and witchcraft, she was able to action a brief imprisonment of the bishop, allowing her time to abscond.

However, this history is not written for she who escaped the flames but for she who fed them. Petronilla de Meath, regarded as Ireland's first witch burned at the stake, served in Kyteler's household, and was arrested as an accomplice. The charges included flying, summoning demons, and brewing foul concoctions in the skull of a decapitated thief, all of which, under torture, she confessed to. William Outlaw, Kyteler's son, was also accused of heresy, but on confession his sentence was commuted, through the influence of powerful friends, to visiting the Holy Lands and arranging funds for St Canice's roof. In the heart of Kilkenny, Alice Kyteler's house still stands. Local opinion differs as to whether the spirit that presides there is of Dame Alice finally returned from hiding, or of Petronilla, the servant left behind.

Wind from Water, Earth to Flame
God sold my Soul, which I Reclaim

THE WHIPPING GIRL
Sem Vine

WATER

The glimmering haze gathered itself into a face, eyes ice-grey, flesh framed black, and lips parting as if to speak, but a sudden stab of pain shattered its form, and the vision fled. Petronilla fought to follow it, but she could only mouth the smothered cry of dreams. In a moment she came to, the pain reduced to a thrumming ache where her head had struck the flagstone floor.

'Petronilla! Petronilla!'

An urgent call from the kitchen.

Petronilla rose up, staggering like a marionette. Taking a breath, she touched her thin fingers to her forehead to steady herself.

'Petronilla, come here girl, I need you to help me!'

Her mistress's voice, even after these long years in her service, still sounded so foreign. Mistress Alice would tell her of the long voyages she had travelled, over distances that Petronilla found hard to imagine. 'Everything is change,' she would say. 'We think the world is an old one, but it can wrack itself new in the beat of a bird's wing. It constantly spins oil into its waters and kindles fires in its heart. People must take the chances life gives them or perish in the maelstrom.'

Petronilla knew this was true. She thought of the long years of the Rains. She remembered the piercing cold of the streets, thin bodies falling into the mud, a perpetual autumn of flesh, more of bone than skin; she remembered seeing her lifeless mother face down in the water. But still, despite the cruelty of those years, she could not imagine travelling the seas to escape them. She had heard stories of vast oceans, their wildness and depth, where swam monsters that were broad as a house and as tall as a tower. Even the river that ran through the town could kill the strongest of men, they said, without him so much as wetting a finger with it, such was the power of its stench.

'Go fetch me water from the well.'

Petronilla had found Mistress Alice stabbing vigorously at the blackened logs in the kitchen fire, fresh wood at the ready to feed its flames. The table was replete with finely chopped vegetables, delicate portions of rabbit, and a bowl of oats. Mistress Alice liked to cook, especially now that Sir John seemed so unwell. He must have pottage daily, prepared so as to exactly balance the humours; and, of course, only Mistress Alice knew the perfect proportions of ingredients for her husband.

Autumn was coming. Stepping out into the courtyard, Petronilla saw itsapproach in the warmth of the light. She felt it in the breeze and smelled it in the air, even above the pungent stink of rotting bones and effluent that hung like mist throughout the streets and alleys of this prosperous town. Each season brought its own test of spirit, but of all the year's wheel she dreaded the days of the cold and dark the most. She hauled the brimming bucket to the top of the well and rested it on the wall while the ache from the effort subsided. Petronilla gazed into the water at the pale reflection of the sky; a shadow bled into it.

'Here, let me.'

It was Will. He took the handle from her, poured the water into the kitchen pail, and made for the house, spilling dark patterns onto the path. Petronilla followed him into the kitchen.

'Mother.'

'Son.'

Dame Alice narrowed her eyes almost to smile, and watched her son place the pail near the fire and sink heavily onto a chair.

'It's not good.' There was a hoarse gloom in his voice.

Petronilla quietly fetched him a mug of ale. He took a long draught and wiped his mouth on the back of his hand. Petronilla caught him glance at her with his ice-grey eyes.

'He's been to see Bishop Ledrede.' Alice turned to Petronilla.

'Petronilla, will you check on Sir John; see that he's comfortable.'

Alice allowed enough time for Petronilla to reach the top of the stairs, then sat to face her son.

'Do you mean Richard?'

'Yes.'

Alice muttered something in her native tongue; Will had never learned it.

'Arnold says the Bishop can't arrest us. He says that Ledrede's only recourse is to apply to the King's Chancellor.'

Mother and son instantly shared a sublime moment of knowing.

'Ah, dear Uncle Roger; how useful he is. That may give us a little time. So, what are the charges?'

'Usual deviltry, which will, of course, be modified and moulded according to the latest papal paranoia.'

'Never underestimate the power of paranoia.'

Alice held up her hands, dampening Will's flippancy with her prescience. 'In a few short days, we will be at the crossroads, feeding demons flesh dripping with blood and enjoying endless pup-noddy with them night after night. Sorcery is not what it was.'

'Mistress Alice,' came a timorous whisper from the doorway.

'It's Sir John. He's asking for you.'

'Very well.'

Alice rose and took some coins from the small leather pouch that hung from her belt. 'Go fetch bread, milk, and more ale.'

When Petronilla had left, Alice made for the narrow stairs. Will caught his mother's arm.

'Did she hear us?'

'No, I always hear her first.'

AIR

It was not until her head touched her pillow in the quiet of the night that Petronilla could reflect on her fall that afternoon. So far, she had been able to keep these shadowy faints a secret for fear of being sent back to the streets, or worse. Now, away from the endless work of the day, her head began to ache furiously. She closed her eyes and beckoned for sleep, but all she could see was the black hole of the well; her futile dreams drowning in the whirl of its waters, stealing hope away with her mother. Water took life as well as gave it.

— *Eyes open. The moon is so bright.*

Petronilla moved to close the shutters.

— *How close the moon seems, its patterns like moss on a stone. I see it trespass the day sometimes, when the sky is blue, and the stars are sleeping.*

With the shutters closed, the ice-grey moonlight could only pierce through in slivers.

— *Ice-grey; the colour of his eyes.*

— *What had Mistress Alice meant by feeding demons bleeding flesh?* In the Great Rains there was talk of people eating the dead, even though everyone was so thin, all skin and bone. Only the rats seemed fat and many. And then what were the things Alice would say came to her in the night? In the night, Petronilla wrapped her blanket so tightly around her, it felt as if she were being held. Dreams would come and the embrace was real and kind, and Petronilla would feel the burden of living leave her; its troubles exiled by the weight and warmth of a passionate being, by a lover's heat.

— *Surely such solace could only be sacred?*
— *Surely such warmth is compassion, and all that which is deemed Divine.*

She lay cocooned and expectant. Thoughts, like the pain, gnawed at her weary mind, while a wind began playing strange music on the slivers of moonlight, a chill bitterness in its breath.

— *Change. Life leads, while death beholds me.*

EARTH

— Death is watching, and I cannot follow life, for I am in chains.
— Mistress Alice. Mistress Alice!
'Mistress Alice, Mistress Alice. Where is Mistress Alice?'

Spittle from the interrogator's hot, foetid mouth slabbers her face. She wishes she knew. One morning, she cannot think how long ago it was, she awoke, and her mistress was gone, no sound in the house but Sir John's groans and a violent hammering on the door. Since then, these men had stolen the night and the day, dictating the terms of nature. Rush lights, carried by her tormentors, made for a cruel sun, lighting her stone cell and illuminating their callous work. Whenever they left, taking the light and leaving her in agony, they ushered in a canvas of nightmares.

'Where is Alice Kyteler?'
'Please, I do not know.'

A sudden blow sends her thin, bruised body to the floor, and darkness descends like the embrace of her winding sheets, comforting as the clemency of love.

Behind the door, the Bishop of Ossory peers through the eyehole. His fingertips sweep oily crumbs from the corners of his mouth, which he wipes down the front of his already grease-stained alb. There is a shadow beside him.

'The only word is that she is in the company of a man,' murmurs the shadow into the holy ear.

'Making for Dublin?'

'We have men heading there now.'

'And what of William Kyteler, the son?'

'He has confessed, your Excellency.'

His Excellency's lips thinned.

— *That murdering bitch will be on the seas by now. Her 'companion', her 'saviour', will soon find he is more victim than lover. As for contriving my arrest, the imprisoning of my ordained person ...*

The Bishop strikes the door with his righteous fist.

— *She will see the tides turn, for the Pope's Word is the Word of God, and He is omnipotent!*

'The girl must not sleep!'

Petronilla opens her eyes to see she is lying in a flood of noxious water, and knows it is her blood that threads through its surface in scarlet curls...

— *oh, my mother*

A hand clutches her hair and violently tugs it high, forcing her upright.

There is no peace for the wicked.

— *Pain exiles all but itself.*

— *Death waits.*

FIRE

— *This girl begins it. So, shall it be if it be Thy will.*

His Excellency avows in quiet prayer, while his brow betrays his temper.

Petronilla lies still in the moonless dark.

— *They say that Will says it is true, all true.*

— *A demon, it was, in the dark of the night, not the bliss of my dreams nor of a man.*

— *And the Son of Art it was, he who was fed with blood and bleeding meat.*

— *And Mistress Alice stirred her cauldron, adding all kinds of monstrous things, while poor Sir John, the next of her husbands, paled and vomited the stinking green of his insides.*

— *And now she has vanished to unnamed places and none will find her.*

Silent men, careful to neither touch nor look at her, release the chain that binds Petronilla to the floor. By it, she is led like a dog and taken from the windowless confines of the cell into a world that is changed, the last of all tenderness swallowed by a cold-hearted November mist.

— *I have been corrupted. am corrupt, and for this I have earned hell on earth.*

Faces appear carved from the grey air, suspended above ragged bodies, wretched effigies of the damned. Petronilla falters as she passes the gathered townspeople, and though the weals from the whip bite at her ruthlessly, she can sense the waves of their fearful dread.

— This was the place I once lived.

Ahead stands a figure in a blaze of colour and white, shining with a brightness which burns through the ashen brume like sunlight. With him is the Host, the talisman, the body of Christ, and all that has forsaken her. The potent secrecy of his chant affirms her banishment as she, breathless now, is secured to the funeral pyre. With a cool air of licensed authority, Bishop Ledrede motions for the kindling to be lit, and as the flames take and the girl who is to feed them begins to retch on the acrid smoke, the fires of rage, which have been devouring the Bishop beneath his cold finery, are not appeased.

— For I have failed.

— Here, now, in the presence of all, is the sum of my mediocrity.

—This will not, and cannot, end.

Through the curling fog of heat and tears, Petronilla spies a face she knows among the fire-lit masses behind the Shining Man. Eyes ice-grey, flesh framed black, lips tight shut.

— Will?

— W ...

A sudden lightning of pain surges to consume the final sensations of a brief life. The vision is engulfed by its savagery, and the crowd sees Petronilla mouth a cry that is silenced by Death's indifferent mercy.

GILLES GARNIER
(died circa 1573)

Gilles Garnier was a native of France-Comte, a very small country between France and Switzerland. He was a hermit and alleged cannibalistic serial-murderer, who was convicted of lycanthropy and witchcraft. Garnier, his wife, and their two children were burned at the stake in 1573. Garnier was to become known as "The Hermit of St. Bonnot" and "The Werewolf of Dole."

The Hermit of St Bonnot

THE HERMIT OF ST. BONNOT
Fi Woods

Although those of the nearest village considered it to be nothing more than a "hovel," Gilles and his wife, Apolline, were content. They had walls to protect them from the winds and a turfed roof to shelter them from the rain. They had no concern for its shabby appearance; it mattered not. They managed well enough together, but it wasn't exactly what you'd call a happy marriage. They were very poor and were sustained only by the animals that Gilles could kill in the surrounding forest. At least he had plenty of scope for his hunting: their home was isolated within the forest to the point of almost being inaccessible. Nonetheless, the acquisition of sufficient food was a constant worry, for although the forest was home to wild boar, small deer, moles, hares, shrews, and dormice, these were difficult animals to trap or grab.

Gilles and Apolline had been married for five years, since Apolline was 15 and Gilles was 25. Apolline's relatively well-off parents had finally grown tired of coping with her periods of staring into empty space, pulling her hair, clapping her hands over her ears, pacing, and her frequent "conversations" with nobody but herself.

'**Ahh, my sweet Apolline.**'
'You're not real. Go away.'

'*I am indeed real; do you not feel me inside you as well as hear me?*'

'I don't want you; you make people think I'm mad and my dad puts me in the cellar. I hate going in there; it's dark and cold, and I can hear rustling, scratching noises. It's so horrible that I fight against it, then my dad gets the groundsmen to help him force me in there.'

Claude and Jeane, her parents, were embarrassed by their only child's behaviour, and felt that it lowered their standing in the town. They believed that Apolline was viewed with no small amount of suspicion by the town's folk and they'd often heard the case of Gilles de Rais being discussed; something they talked about back at home. They didn't understand it; Apolline had been an ordinary baby, beautiful in their eyes, but when she was five she changed. It seemed at first to be just a normal case of a child having an invisible friend, but it quickly became apparent from the "conversations" that her "friend" was malign. They wanted rid of her, but how?

Gilles' odd behaviour had been noted by villagers on those rare occasions when they saw him. They had also been able to hear him having what sounded like shouted conversations, even though they knew him to be alone. These "conversations" seemed to be at their worst during a full moon.

'Go away, just leave me alone.'

'*But I don't want to leave you alone; I like having someone to talk to.*'

'I don't want to talk to you.'

'*But I've been lonely for so long and you're lonely too.*'

'I am not lonely, and I have no need of any other.'

The villagers kept their distance from him, and they frequently discussed the case of Gilles de Rais: did they have a similar monster in their midst? Garnier watched them retreat and heard all they said but took no notice; his concern was simply survival and being left alone.

Village tittle-tattle reached the nearby town and thence the ears of Apolline's parents. A man who apparently shared the same behaviours as their daughter? They saw their chance and took it: they approached Gilles with a cow and some hens, along with basket of bread, meat, and several jugs of ale. It was his, they explained, as long as he married their daughter and she never darkened their door ever again. Gilles really didn't want a woman in his life: he'd already discovered that women were nothing but trouble. The bribe though, for of course that was exactly what it was, was powerful enough for him to accept the deal. And although her parents said they never wanted to see her again, he reasoned that, given time, they would miss their only child. Then, he thought, they would both be welcomed into a wealthy family. Apolline struggled as she was thrust towards the scary-looking man, 'Mama, Papa ... what's happening? What are you doing?' Disbelievingly, she watched as her parents turned their backs and walked swiftly away.

'Come back Mama. I'll be good; I promise. Where are you going?' They were gone from sight, without another word or look, leaving her with the man.

The villagers were suspicious and fearful of Gilles: his appearance was more than enough to scare them, without taking his behaviour into account. He was a tall, ugly man, with a pronounced stoop. His hair was long and matted, as was his long, grey beard. His rough, bushy eyebrows stretched the entire width of his lower forehead, from the outer corner of one eye to the outer corner of the other: in a single, unbroken line. He was sombre, with a pale face that contributed to an overall impression of ill-health. Gilles spoke as little as possible, and when he did, it was in the broadest patois.

Whilst Apolline had been quite a pretty girl when they first married, slender with a heart-shaped face and long hair as black as midnight and stunning blue eyes, the years of marriage and hard living had taken their toll. She had been brought up well, had a good education, and was used to comfort and plentiful food. Now though, she could easily have passed for a woman of 40 instead of 20. Gilles, likewise, had aged and looked like a middle-aged man.

As if one hadn't been enough, the villagers now had two people to fear; double the strange behaviour, twice the concern, and the end of doors being left unlocked. Folk now securely locked their doors behind them and were very wary before opening them. They never used to live like this: they'd always popped in and out of each other's houses without a second thought. They were all on edge and they weren't happy.

During the course of their marriage, Apolline had borne two children: both boys. Pierre was born during their first year of marriage and Nicolas the following year. Apolline had never come to like Gilles' touch, not even merest brush of his skin against her. The thought of having sex with him was untenable, but he was bigger and stronger than she; his will prevailed. She cried through the burning pain inside her, but his thoughts were only of himself. After that first time, she'd learnt not to fight, to just be passive and get it over with. Although as parents they tried to love the children, it was a very difficult time: how could Gilles or Apolline hear a baby cry over the voice that shouted into their ears? The children were undoubtedly a source of pressure and stress, as children are and caused a great deal of discord between Gilles and Apolline. Neither of them had particularly wanted children, but seeing as Gilles had a woman there, he felt that he might as well make use of her, and children were the inevitable result. Prior to marriage, Gilles had only himself to feed and look after; then came the responsibility of a wife and now there were another two mouths to feed. Their cow had supplied milk and the hens gave them eggs, but they had both been long slaughtered for their flesh. Their life together near Dole, in Franche-Comte, became very strained and their "conversations" with invisible people grew ever more frequent. The times of the full moon was the worst, for both of them. The voice they heard was louder and more insistent: it was impossible to shut it out, however hard they clapped their hands over their ears.

'There might come a day when you're glad to have me around.'

'No. No. No. I *don't* want you. Go away and give me some peace; that's all I want.'

'You can have peace, but haven't you realised yet that I am always here, whether I'm talking or not?'

Gilles one minute and Apolline the next.

'Ahh, sweet Apolline.'

'You're not here. I've left you behind.'

'You can't leave me behind; don't you know that?'

'I don't want you; I never did. Look what's happened: because of you, I'm stuck here, and my parents have completely disowned me. I've lost everything: I had beautiful clothes, a wonderful bedroom, a maid, three meals a day ... look at me now. I am dressed in little more than rags, I have children I don't want by a man who makes me shudder, and I'm always hungry. You did this. This is all your fault. Now go away. There are two men in my life, and I don't know which I hate the most. Just go.'

Every time the villagers heard the shouting, they wondered about Gilles and Apolline and talked again about Gilles de Rais. The two men even shared the same name, and if such a high-born, titled man could commit such heinous crimes, what might this pair be capable of?

Although the murders, sodomy, and heresy of de Rais took place way back in 1440 and 400 miles away in Nantes, the acts that he was found guilty of were such that he would never be forgotten.

The winter of 1572 was particularly harsh, and prey was hard to find; however long Gilles spent in the forest, he rarely returned home with any meat. One night, as he hunted, the voice came upon him again:

'Well, well. Hello, who'd have thought I'd see you here?'

'I've told you before to go away and leave me alone.'

'Food's got a little tight at home, hasn't it?'

'I'll find something. Go away.'

'As you wish; perhaps I'll go and have a chat with Apolline.'

'You've started to feel hunger now, haven't you my sweet Apolline?'

'Gilles will bring something back.'

'I've never known a winter like this, so cold. There may come a time when Gilles is simply unable to find any prey, however hard he tries.'

'My husband will provide for us; he will always find something. He will not let us starve.'

'Let us hope you are right.'

'Now begone. I am tired of you and Gilles will be back soon.'

'I am Gilles.'

'No, you're not. Whoever and whatever you are, leave me.'

'I am Gilles de Rais; I'm sure you have heard of me.'

'I do not believe you. Now go.'

Eventually her husband arrived home, with a couple of shrews, a dormouse, and a small hare. It was barely enough to sate their hunger; the milk from the cow which filled their children had long gone, and Pierre and Nicolas now needed real food. Gilles was worn out and dispirited. It had been so much easier when he'd only had to feed himself. As they ate, they talked, for the first time, of the voice that each of them heard. Apolline told Gilles about the voice telling her that he was Gilles de Rais and how often her parents had talked about him. Garnier stood, in shock.

'I'd never thought of anything like this, even though I always heard the villagers talking about de Rais when I was around.'

'He's here again,' said Apolline.

'You were right about one thing, my dearest. It is because of I that you are here. Who do you think whispered 'de Rais' into your parents' sleep night after night?'

'I don't want to be here. I want to be back at home, and I want you to go away so my parents will love me.'

'It is what it is and what's done is done. I have long been in both of you, and now I have you together. What could be more perfect?'

'I don't like you and I don't like him.'

'That is of no concern to me. You both belong to me and that is all that matters.'

A couple of nights later, as Gilles hunted through the forest, he heard de Rais:

'You've not much food left now have you?'

'We've enough.'

'For now. Hunting's getting hard, isn't it?'

'I can manage.'

'But it takes such a lot of effort to feed you all, doesn't it? There are far easier sources of sustenance to be had.'

'Such as?'

'Children. Easy to snatch and kill. Plenty of meat on a child.'

'Are you mad? I'd never do that; I'd rather starve.'

'I'll leave you to your fruitless task then, while I go and chat to your wife.'

63

'**What about you, sweet Apolline? What say you to an unlimited source of food?**'

'I don't want to hear you; I'm not listening.' She clapped her hands over her ears and began to sing, louder and louder, in an attempt to smother the voice in her head.

The next night, Gilles was startled when a spectre appeared before him in the forest.

'**You've been out here for three hours and caught nothing. Do you remember I said that there might come a day when you'd be glad to see me?**'

The spectre, recognisably de Rais, threw his head back and laughed at the moon. The laughter seemed to go on for ever, until Gilles thought his head would split plain in half. He screamed and yelled at de Rais, telling him to stop, that he was scaring away whatever prey there was. Eventually the laughter subsided to chuckles and Gilles saw that de Rais was holding a pot out to him.

'**It's an ointment, made of jimsonweed, henbane, and other plants. It'll turn you into a wolf and it'll be far easier for you to catch the prey necessary to feed your family.**'

Garnier saw no harm in taking it: he didn't believe what de Rais said, but at least it would get rid of him.

'**Happy hunting.**' said de Rais and went silent.

Garnier rubbed some into his arm and wrinkled his nose at the smell; as he did so, he realised that his sense of smell had sharpened. He could smell flesh and followed his nose, which led him to sight a young girl. He dragged her into the nearest vineyard, strangled and stripped her. He was drooling at the thought of sinking his teeth into her. As he tore flesh from her thighs and arms, a tiny spark in his head tried to question what he was doing, but it was easily and quickly extinguished. He revelled in the meat, in the blood running down his chin and covering his hands, the strong coppery odour. When he'd eaten his fill, he licked his lips and tore some more flesh from the body and took it home.

'Apolline, children, I have brought meat.'

'That doesn't look like any meat I've seen before. You've done what de Rais said, haven't you?'

'He came to me in the forest; he made me half wolf so that I could get enough food for us all.'

'Well, seeing as you've done it, there's no point in wasting it I suppose, not when we're so hungry.'

Hungry or not, Apolline had to force herself to pick up a piece of meat and put it in her mouth. She looked at her two boys and thought about what the parents of the child they were eating must be feeling. The very idea of someone eating her children made her sick to her stomach and she struggled to keep the mouthful down. She knew that if she couldn't keep it in her stomach, the boys wouldn't eat it and they so badly needed nourishment. She worked hard to maintain an impression of normality for their sake:

'Eat up boys; there's a good meal in front of us, let's enjoy it.'

Pierre, and Nicolas ate with gusto; they were so hungry, and it'd been so long since they'd had so much food that it was easy to ignore where it had come from.

'It tastes like pork.' said Apolline, as she took another handful.

The minute she'd said it, she was brutally reminded of where she'd come from, where she was, and what she was doing. She remembered the banquets, organised by her parents, and attended by other suitably endowed townsfolk: the smell of roast pork from the whole hog on the spit. She could eat no more, so, claiming that she was full, she passed extra to her sons.

A couple of weeks later, Garnier attacked another girl, biting and clawing her. He had to flee though when her screams attracted the attention of passers-by. Her screams followed him all the way home, through the forest and it wasn't until the next month that he again pounced. He spotted a boy and dragged him into a field, where he killed him. He had nothing short of a feast on the boy's thighs and belly, ripping the flesh apart and sinking his face deep into the blood and meat, before tearing off a leg to take home.

'Dinner.' he called as he arrived home.

Apolline and the boys had been waiting for him; the males enthusiastically partook of the meat, eating until they could eat no more. Apolline nibbled at little bits.

The next day Gilles arrived home empty-handed. 'I was strangling a boy but had to run when I was interrupted.'

He made up for the loss with his next kill though: he sank his teeth deeply into a boy's stomach and ripped him in two, with several shakes of his head, much as a cat might do to a bird or a mouse. Then he ate the boy's belly and all his innards with much enjoyment and satisfaction.

'It's the start of a new year, wife. I'm going to bring back something to celebrate.'

He arrived back at home with a girl's leg, having strangled her and eaten her meat. The four of them had a feast fit for a king.

The dead and missing children were, of course, noticed and the deeds were blamed on a werewolf; no human could possibly have committed such appalling desecrations of the flesh. The province authorities issued a decree proactively encouraging and allowing the villagers to capture and kill the werewolf. One evening, a group of men from a nearby town saw, in the dim light, what some thought was a wolf and others thought was the hermit. Whichever it was, it had what they believed to be the body of a dead child.

Despite the fact that Garnier hadn't previously been considered a suspect in the attacks, several days later, there came a loud knocking at the door. Gilles and Apolline looked at each other in surprise; they never had visitors. Gilles opened the door to two official-looking men.

'Gilles Garnier, Apolline Garnier, Pierre Garnier, Nicolas Garnier. You are all under arrest and will come with us immediately to be held in custody until your trial.'

'Trial? What trial?' asked Apolline.

'You are all suspected of werewolfery and witchcraft.'

All of them were silent, except de Rais, who was thoroughly revelling in their misfortune and thus a cacophany ensued:

'*Now you'll see. Enjoy these last moments with each other; I will be seeing you very soon.*'

'You are the Devil.' screamed Apolline. 'What did we ever do to deserve this? You ...' She was interrupted by her husband:

'What have you done to us?' he bellowed. 'I thought you were keeping us alive, but instead you've set us all up for death, even the children.'

'*As you've already discovered, children are the sweetest of all.*'

The shouting went on and on, and the boys started crying, but it made no difference; all of them were bundled into a cart and dumped in a cell underneath the Court. Gilles was stretched on the rack, a torture guaranteed to make anybody confess to anything, while his wife and children were subjected to ferocious beatings. The callous guards first beat Apolline while the children were made to watch, before beating the children in front of Apolline's eyes. She screamed and cried out her boys' names, feeling each blow as if it landed on her own flesh. She strained to reach them, but she had no chance against the strength of the guards.

'Stop it. Stop it.' she cried. 'I'll tell you what you want to know. Just don't hurt my children anymore.'

Apolline confessed that her husband was a werewolf. She further admitted that both of them had "conversations" with a person that nobody else could see; and that these were of greater duration when the moon was full. She also confessed that she and the children had eaten the human flesh brought home to them.

'I hated it, at first; I could barely bring myself to put it anywhere near my mouth. I had nightmares, that first time, that someone took my children away and ate them. What could I do though? It was there in front of us and I knew that if the boys didn't eat they would starve. I also knew that it fell to me to show them that it was good food.'

Gilles confessed at trial that one night, when he was hunting in the forest, he came upon a spectre.

'It was Gilles de Rais.' He announced to a stunned-into-silence crowd. 'I saw him as clear as day. He gave me an ointment, which he said would change me into a wolf to improve my hunting. I gladly accepted it; after all, both Apolline and I had been talking to de Rais for a long time and with his help we would be able to avoid starvation.'

He went on to confess to stalking and murdering at least four children, aged between 9 and 12, in early October. 'The girl you bit and clawed before being interrupted died from her injuries a few days later.' he was told.

'She would have provided a good meal,' said Gilles, 'with no loss to anyone as she died anyway.'

He also admitted to the strangulation and eating of a girl in early January 1573.

Garnier's trial, which was conducted by secular authorities because the Inquisition had no interest in matters of superstition, drew more than 50 witnesses, who testified that he had attacked and/or killed children in fields and vineyards. He was apparently seen eating raw flesh, sometimes in human form and at other times as a wolf. The crowd was angry and raucous; the families of the dead children had come armed with various weapons. They were screaming and crying as they attempted to reach Garnier and had to be ejected from the building. They continued to shout for their right to kill the accused and their tormented voices kept the crowd inside incensed. Judge Henri Bouget demanded, 'Silence in Court.' several times before the yelling and screaming in the Court died down to a dull muttering and he was able to speak.

Gilles was found guilty of "crimes of lycanthropy and witchcraft" and condemned to burn at the stake. Apolline and the children weren't tried, but such was the feeling of the people that Judge Bouget also condemned them to burn because of Apolline's testimony.

Apolline had paid no heed to the proceedings; she was too busy studying the crowd, looking for her parents. While the crowd jeered at her, thinking that her tears were because of herimpending death, she was crying because her mum and dad weren't there.

Judge Henri Bouget pronounced the sentence:

"Seeing that Gilles Garnier has, by the testimony of credible witnesses, and by his own spontaneous confession, been proved guilty of the abominable crimes of lycanthropy and witchcraft, this court condemns him, the said Gilles, to be this day taken in a cart from this spot to the place of execution, accompanied by the executioner, where he, by the said executioner, shall be tied to a stake and burned alive, and that his ashes be then scattered to the winds. The court further condemns him, the said Gilles, to pay the costs of this prosecution."

Apolline was still sobbing and now the children joined in; they were scared, still in agony from their beatings and didn't understand what was going on. Gilles tried to comfort them as best he could.

On the 18th of January 1573, Apolline, Pierre, and Nicolas were slung into a cart with Gilles and taken to the stake. Gilles was firmly trussed, and the pyre was set alight. His wife and children were made to watch him burn. The crowd roared and threw stones; they were eager to show their anger and of course they no longer needed to fear the people in front of them. After Gilles' final scream, the flames were re-stoked and Apolline was forced to watch as her children were thrown into the flames by the bereaved parents. All of the officials present felt that the parents deserved at least that much personal justice, so they stopped holding the group back and turned away.

Apolline was beside herself, listening to the screams of her children as the flames started to eat them; the stench of the burning flesh, so much like the flesh she had eaten, drove her to her knees. She could no longer stand and watch. The parents hauled her to her feet and turned her back to face the fire. She saw the faces of her boys and heard them screaming, 'Help Ma, please help. It hurts Ma.'

She saw their little arms reaching out to her and could take no more: she collapsed in racking sobs that seemed to come all the way up through her body from her toes. The children who had been a largely unwanted burden were now wanted, desperately. It was too late. Finally, Apolline herself was thrown onto the conflagration. She didn't fight the hands that grabbed and held her; she was a broken, wretched woman by then.

Even through the pain and the flames, Apolline's eyes searched for her parents, but it was useless. They weren't there for their daughter and grandchildren. The understanding of the depth of their hatred and abandonment hit her and knocked her sideways. She hadn't realised it until then; she'd always believed that they were only punishing her and that they would come and take her back.

Just before the flames finally consumed her, a single tear ran down her cheek and as the villagers began to return to their homes, a protracted howl was heard echoing through the forest.

There were numerous werewolf trials in Franche-Comte, and 30,000 cases of "werewolfery" were recorded in France alone, during the course of a century.

Gilles de Rais was re-tried in France in November of 1992, by the public, not by the authorities or any official sanction. The "court" was held at the
Luxembourg Palace and organised by a lawyer named Jean-Yves Goëau-Brissonnière to examine the material and evidence available from the original court.

Lawyers, writers, former French ministers, biologists, and doctors were presided over by Judge Henri Juramy. Gilles de Rais was found not guilty.

AGNES PORTER
(Died prior to 1603)

From the reign of Edward 1, until Henry VIII, at the foot of Ashey Downs in Ryde stood a religious house. It was connected to the Abbey of Wherewell, near Andover in Hampshire. Queen Elfrida had built the abbey in memory of her stepson, Edward the Martyr, who was murdered. Ashey Manor had the privilege of a Court Leet, and it is recorded that during the reign of Elizabeth I, a widow named Agnes Porter was brought before the court and charged with witchcraft. She was found guilty and sentenced to death by burning; the sentence was carried out on Ashey Downs. The exact dates of Agnes Porter's birth or death are unknown.

Tonight, You Burn

THE WIGHT WYTCH
Marisha Kiddle

Agnes sat by her window, looking out at the dark wet night, reminiscing about her past and watching the raindrops run down the glass. Life had dealt her a cruel blow so far and something needed to change. She had been born here, in this house, on this little Island and she wasn't sure how, but her life needed to alter for the better. A single tear ran down her face, matching a raindrop on the window, solitary and alone, just like her.

Agnes had married Thomas Porter in 1554, 10 years earlier in the parish of Newchurch, on the Isle of Wight. He was the love of her life, her companion in everything except one: they had never been blessed with children.

Thomas had constantly told her over the years that she was lucky to have her own home and an acre of land, reminding her that most women in the 1500's were not so fortunate.

— *Was that all he thought about?* Agnes wondered.

— *Does a child not matter to him? No heir?*

Agnes needed to seriously reconsider her future. She was old by mothering standards, being 30 now, but she knew it wasn't too late to have a child if she was quick. The problem was Thomas.

— Would he leave me so I could start again? It's his fault anyway, so surely he should grant me my wish.

She would need to have that conversation tomorrow when Thomas was awake.

The following morning Thomas sat down at the table, watching his wife carve bread and meat for his breakfast. She handed him a jug of ale to wash it down with and he noticed her face was sad and tired, like a woman who had the weight of the world on her shoulders. How he missed her beautiful smile and her love for life.

Thomas knew what the problem was, so didn't press for an explanation. It had been this way for about eight years, ever since she had failed to get pregnant after their marriage. Initially he had been there, consoling her like the loving husband, but he grew weary when he realised that nothing worked; her mood could not be lifted.

"I'm going to Newport today," he informed her, "And I won't be back till after nightfall."

The conversation had been started and it gave her the strength to continue her talk with Thomas. She spoke quietly, looking at her husband with all the love she could muster, to soften the following words that she knew she needed to air:

"Husband, may we talk for a moment?"

Thomas looked up from the saddle bag he was filling with food for his journey.

"What is it wife, I do not have long." Agnes sat on a stool beside Thomas and took his hand in hers.

"Thomas my dear, you know I love you with all my being, but I cannot continue in this predicament any longer."

Agnes took a breath and sighed as she looked at Thomas and said, "I wish to be free to marry another, so I may have a child of my own." There, it was said, Agnes thought to herself. Her pulse was racing; Thomas was looking at her, expressionless, still as a statue, and not saying a word. After what felt like hours, came his angry response:

"Who is this man you want to marry, wife of mine?"

Agnes shook, she had never seen her husband so angry.

"There is no one else husband. I just wish to be free, so I can find another to marry and have a child." Thomas carried on packing his bag, his anger building stronger at her words and eventually he turned to her and snapped, "No! You will not be free to marry another man. Not now, not ever! It is best, wife, if you get over your thoughts and start thinking about being a proper wife to me, and me alone!" Thomas grabbed his bag and stormed out the cottage as quickly as he could, before he did something he would later regret, or worse still, go to prison for.

Agnes slumped down on the floor shaking and sobbing; she felt broken and bruised. Why could Thomas not see? Why could he not admit that he was damaged and could not give her what she so desperately needed? Had she not given him the best years of her life? Had she not been dutiful and loyal? Had she not earned the right to be free?

Could he not see that she loved him above all others, but her need for a child was so overwhelming that it was suppressing her love of life?

So many questions were buzzing around in her head that it made it spin.

— *What am I to do?* Agnes blew her nose on her apron and, raising herself up off the floor, decided to go for a walk, find some mushrooms, and hopefully clear her head. Just after she had left the cottage, Agnes caught sight of old man Deacon repairing a stone wall.

"Morning Mrs Porter, nice day we be 'aving." Agnes nodded in agreement. "The steward up at Ashey Manor said, if I saw thee to say that he wondered if you'd go see 'im?

— *Me?* Agnes wondered.

— *What could the steward want with me?*

"Did he say what he wanted with me?"

"Nah, just asked me to pass on the message if I saw thee." Deacon smiled and carried on with his work. Agnes carried on walking but was now heading in the direction of the big manor.

Ashey Manor was an imposing building, having once been an abbey, before the Crown passed it on to Giles and Elizabeth Worsley in 1544. The current owner was their eldest, and only, son John.

The gardens were vast and beautifully kept, and Agnes felt very uncomfortable; she was not used to being surrounded by such splendour and elegance. As Agnes stood at the front of the manor, wondering if she should knock on the front door or find an entrance around the back, a voice came from behind her.

"Mrs Porter?" Agnes spun round to face the voice and saw Mr Hills, the Lord's steward, walking towards her.

"Mr Hills, I heard you wanted to see me?" Agnes replied.

"That I did Mrs Porter. Please follow me into my office."

They walked through the front door, towards a side room just off the main hallway. Agnes tried to take in the elegance of everything, but Mr Hills walked so fast she had to almost run to keep up. They eventually stopped in front of a large desk; Mr Hills pointed to a chair and told Agnes to "'Ave a seat."

"Lord Worsley is having some dignitaries come to stay." Mr Hills added, while searching for something amongst the clutter on his desk.

"He wondered if he could buy some of your stock for a feast?" Before Agnes could answer, another, louder voice came from the hallway.

"Charles? Charles are you here?" Agnes and Mr Hills both looked in the direction of the door to see who was doing all the shouting; a tall man with dark hair entered the room.

"Ah, there you are Charles. I've been shouting for you; have you sorted that ...?" He stopped short the second he saw Agnes; she wasn't sure, but she could have sworn he gasped in approval.

— *He has the most beautiful eyes.*

"Charles, who is this delightful lady?" Charles smiled.

"John, this is Mrs Agnes Porter. Mrs Porter, this is Sir John Worsley." Agnes reached out her hand to John and he gracefully kissed it.

A few hours later, Agnes was walking home with a skip in her step and a smile on her face. Her feelings of the lovely afternoon, spent in the company of John, made her heart skip a beat. However, the thoughts of returning to her husband, and their argument from the morning brought her back to reality.

— *Stop being a foolish woman. You are married. Sir Worsley has no interest in you.* That night, laying in her bed, the giddy excitement of the day surrounded her like a warm cocoon, but all too soon the sound of boots on the kitchen floor meant her husband had finally returned home. Agnes had no desire to strike up a conversation and so pretended to be asleep. Thomas clattered about, getting undressed, while Agnes lay still, growing increasingly tense and annoyed at Thomas' lack of consideration for her. He stunk of ale and what appeared to be a floral scent;

— It smells like that rose water Emily Worsley wears and the last thing I need is a cheating husband.

As Thomas started snoring, Agnes knew she could not go on anymore, something had to be done. She decided not to confront him although her pain and anger were raw. Maybe there was another way to solve her childless predicament, one that would provide her with a guaranteed way out of this marriage.

Agnes crept out of bed and quietly put her gown on, then she slipped out of the house and down the lane towards the harbour. If she were right, Jeramiah the ferryman would be on his boat. He was known to be able to get things that you couldn't find on the Island, having the daily opportunity to meet with foreign sailors in the taverns of Portsmouth.

Agnes found him curled up in a drunken stupor in the hold of the boat. She whispered in his ear "monkshood" and popped a shilling in one of his sweaty hands, while his other hand pointed to a shelf across from him; she found what she needed and promptly left before anyone could see her.

As usual, Agnes was up early preparing her husband's breakfast. Thomas sat down and Agnes presented him with a bowl of stewed fruit, which contained a small amount of the monkshood from the night before. He didn't acknowledge her, nor she him. Thomas ate and Agnes watched. There was a slight smirk on her face.

— *The start of a new life is about to begin,* she thought as she began her daily chores.

A few hours later when Thomas came home, Agnes naturally asked why he had returned so early.

"I'm not feeling good: I have had a gripe pain in my back all morning." he replied.

"Well, Thomas, you had better take yourself to bed. I will make a tincture and bring you some broth."

Thomas stumbled off to the bedroom as Agnes turned towards her stove. Fortunately, he was unaware of the smile creeping across her face;

— *Time to start phase two: the monkshood in the water worked, now to finish the job.*

Agnes looked at Thomas, lying in bed hardly able to move. He was vomiting and choking, and his breathing had rapidly become shallow and strained.

— *Looks like the monkshood has taken affect nicely.*

Over the next few days, Agnes gave Thomas small doses of monkshood in his food, enough to make him ill but not quite enough to kill him. Well not just yet, she didn't want to arouse his, or anybody else's, suspicion.

Agnes had met John several times since their initial meeting, and always on the pretence of sorting out the feast. John had been particularly encouraging in her attendance at his home, and Agnes was sure that he too was using the feast as an excuse to see her.

"Agnes, how is your husband now?" John asked, while they were sat in his parlour.

"Still bad, no matter what I try and use to help him. My tinctures are not healing him like they should; I fear it may be serious."

Agnes started to weep, bowing her head slightly and sneaking a glance towards John. John slipped his arm around her shoulders and gently pulled her towards him.

"Oh, sweet Agnes I am sure everything will be fine."

Agnes rested her head against John and silently wept; her plan to make John fall in love with her was working. Playing the devoted wife, riddled with worry, was gaining attention from John. The way he held her, the way their bodies connected, and the warmth she could feel coming from him made her feel safe, wanted, and above all loved. Agnes started to pull away, but John kept hold of her shoulder and looked into her tearful blue eyes. There was a slight pause before he lowered his head and brushed his lips against hers; perfect, Agnes thought, feeling the beating of her heart and the quivering in her loins, just perfect.

The same evening, on returning home, Agnes went up to see Thomas. He was still fading in and out of consciousness, and still covered in the same vomit and sweat from the first day of his illness: almost a week ago now. Agnes knelt on the floor beside him and offered a cup of water to his cracked, dry lips, "Here, drink." She commanded. "I have no use of you now; take more, drink. Your time has come to go to your grave, drink, drink, drink! Your sterile body is of no use to me; I want children and your body is too broken to achieve that, so drink." Agnes forced Thomas to take the water, tilting his head to pour the vile liquid down his throat. He spluttered and gargled until finally he choked on the last mouthful, his limp body giving way to the poison.

★

A few weeks had passed, a decent amount of time in mourning: long enough to stop the gossiping wives, who had nothing better to do, but Agnes was fidgety. She needed to get out of her house and see her beloved John; after all, that is what all this was for, wasn't it? Marry John and have children.

A million thoughts crossed her mind as she virtually skipped all the way to see him. The preparations for their wedding, the jealous looks on the villagers' faces, their future children playing in the manor gardens; pregnancy, oh, the joy of finally being able to be pregnant. John was a real man, unlike Thomas, he wasn't broken, and he needed an heir to his manor as much as she needed to be a mother.

John greeted Agnes, as she entered the manor house and led her through to the parlour.

"My dear Agnes, how have you been? I am so sorry about your Thomas; did he suffer at the end?"

"Why did you not come to the funeral?"

"I was called away: I had work to do in Newtown."

"You have sent no message to me in two weeks John; I was worried and alone."

"My dear, I did not want to cause you further stress with idle village gossip. You know how they love to talk." John took Agnes' hand and kissed the back of it.

"My dear, we have all the time in the world for me to prove how much I love you." He sidled up closer on the couch and rested a hand on Agnes' knee. She knew how to play him to get the attention she craved from him and he willingly obliged; the love they shared was strong and true. Months passed and the lovers kept their trysts going in secret, for fear of Agnes' reputation as a grieving widow being ruined. Spring was coming and Agnes was waiting for John to ask for her hand in marriage; she longed to come out of her grieving attire and start living again.

It was a warm day when Agnes set off from her cottage, down the lane towards the manor. Mrs Chiverton and

Miss Forde stood chatting, but as Agnes approached them and bid them good-day, they started whispering to each other and turned their backs on her.

— *How rude* she thought but dismissed them with the back of her hand. Maybe John has started preparations for our betrothal and gossip has begun.

Who cares about them anyway?

Her heart skipped a beat: she was now positive that her marriage to John was imminent. As always, John welcomed Agnes into his parlour and greeted her with his usual affection.

"Agnes, we need to discuss something."

"Yes John, what might that be?" Her heart was racing, and she had to control herself from screaming "Yes" before he had even asked her. "There has been some gossip about you my dear, that I need to ask you about. I am sure you are aware that I cannot marry someone who is at the centre of idle gossip."

"Well, of course John, I understand that. However, I expect it is mainly chatter among the peasants, who have discovered our secret." Agnes was still positive that within the next few minutes all this would be brushed away and she would be celebrating by teatime. Just then, Charles walked into the room. Agnes looked at him with disgust, for intruding on what should be a private meeting; John looked but did not say anything. Agnes looked at John with disbelief.

— *Why hadn't he asked Charles to leave?* Her disbelief quickly turned to anger and frustration, at what was clearly becoming a very awkward situation.

"Agnes, it is not about us. The gossip is about you: there are rumours about you being a witch."

John brushed his fingers through his hair and took a sharp breath, exhaling loudly. The way he snapped at her had put Agnes in her place rather sharply; the room spun, and Agnes thought she was going to faint,

— *What the hell? No-one knows; I'm positive that no-one knows.*

She took a deep breath, and tried to keep herself composed before she continued, lest they suspected she was coming undone and lying.

"Oh, John, it is all tittle-tattle and I really cannot understand why you are believing this utter nonsense." John looked at Agnes and sneered; the look in his eyes told her that he believed it. Charles took a step towards Agnes and John put his hand up to stop him.

"Tell me this then Agnes, what did your husband die of?"

"I told you, it was the bloody flux."

"I don't believe you Agnes." John started pacing around the room, his anger flashing across his face and his hands darting through his hair. He was trying to make sense of the situation, that much was obvious. Charles looked

at John and with a deep sigh, turned back to look at Agnes.

"I think ..." John stopped him from talking, walked back over to Agnes, and took her face in his rough hands.

"Do you know why I don't believe you?"

"No, I do not" Agnes replied in a hurt voice. She was starting to shake; this was not how today was meant to go at all. John stood up and nodded to Charles, who left the room for a minute and returned, followed by Jeramiah, the ferryman. "Agnes, this is Jeramiah, but I suppose you already know that. It's surprising what one finds out when a drunk wants cash."

The blood drained from Agnes' face, the world stopped spinning, and she became undone: a quivering wreck on the floor of the parlour.

"Wha ... What is the meaning of this? What are you doing to me? All I have ever done is love you."

"Oh, get up woman." John snarled at her; he had no compassion in his voice and acted like she was just an inconvenience. Charles pulled Agnes up off the floor and bound her wrists with rope. Agnes was frantic and began kicking and screaming for him to get off her. John walked over and squeezed her chin tightly between his thumb and forefinger.

"Your game, madam, is up. Tonight, you Burn."

89

"Don't be silly John; whatever this drunk has said to you is untrue and I have not been to trial."

"Ha! Trial? You forget my dear, I am Lord of the Manor and therefore I am the judge and jury." The room went quiet; John was still playing with his hair and getting his breath back after shouting. Agnes wasn't sure what John was saying to her, and it might be her last chance to ask.

"And what has all this got to do with you and I, John?"

"Agnes, my dear, there never was any you and me; it was all a ruse to get my hands on your land and property. You see, my sister Emily is very good friends with Miss Forde, who I might add, was sleeping with your husband Thomas. She told me all about your misery and how desperate you were to get away from him. Your conceit meant it was easy to make you fall for a simple scheme."

A few short hours later, Agnes was tied to a stake atop a pyre of logs and kindling on the top of Ashey Downs. The only people present were Charles and John. John lit the fire and said goodbye to Agnes, thanking her for all the fun. As the flames roared higher, the last thing Agnes heard was Miss Forde's new-born baby, crying in the distance.

AGNES WATERHOUSE
(1503-1566)

In 1566 Agnes was accused of witchcraft, along with Elizabeth Francis and Joan Waterhouse. They were all residents of Hatfield Peverel. Agnes confessed to being a witch and having a familiar, a cat or toad, called Satan. She was put on trial in Chelmsford, Essex in 1566, for using witchcraft to cause sickness and death, including the death of her husband. Agnes was hanged, becoming the first woman executed for witchcraft in England.

Satan's Widow

SATAN'S WIDOW
Scott Irvine

Agnes Waterhouse put another log on the fire to keep the cold at bay. The glow from the firelight made the small cottage, nestled deep in Epping Forest, warm and cosy. When the log had caught alight, the aging widow relaxed in her chair and her old white cat jumped on to her lap, as cats do, purring contentedly.

The fire flickered from a draught, and the room came alive with abstract lights and shadows dancing across the ceiling. A fierce storm was coming from the west and it shook the old building to its core, rattling its timbers, while heavy raindrops crashed against the wooden roof. Agnes was glad her outside chores were done and she could relax in the warmth and make plans with her cat.

Henry VIII's youngest daughter, Elizabeth, had recently inherited the English crown and, in doing so, increased the punishment for sorcery. This meant that Agnes had to be even more careful when practicing her craft.

The widow's white cat, currently sprawled on her lap, was called Satan; he'd once belonged to Agnes's neighbour, Elizabeth Francis, allegedly helping her to become rich over the past fifteen years. Agnes had received Satan in exchange for one of her 'special' cakes, which would help

Elizabeth find the true love that she sought. Agnes hoped the cat was a way for her to rid the village of its cheats, fraudsters, liars, wife-beaters, and those who did not respect the lives of their fellow human souls. She had discovered, through village gossip, that Widow Gooday had cheated a poor boy out of his cow, in exchange for what were said to be 'magic' beans. Mrs Gooday would therefore be the first mission for her new cat.

Since the reformation, Tudor England had become void of spirit, which was replaced with selfishness and cruelty. It invaded the latest generation's mindless souls, feeding the dark negative powers and creating pain and suffering for a great deal of the English population. Everything was about profit and gain; how did that ever create a fair society? How was it going to help the many homeless beggars the Queen's father had created with his Brexit? Agnes rolled her eyes, as she considered Henry's dissolution of the Catholic Church in England and the way he made himself the head of his new church, just so that he could divorce one queen and marry another. With her friend's cat, Agnes had the chance to make the light and dark even: Satan had worked well for her friend and came with good credentials.

Elizabeth Francis had Satan as a kitten and quickly 'acquired' 18 sheep for her inherited homestead. This allowed her to set herself up as a business supplying wool, hide, meat, and bone to those that could afford it. That was just a start for Elizabeth, who then lured the wealthy landowner, Andrew Byles, into bed; she saw him as the perfect husband. Using a fresh love potion, an offering to the nature spirits, and the earthly devices: fake hair, make-up, false hips, and high-heels Elizabeth tracked down her man. Byles gladly accepted her offer of wanton flesh after several drinks in the local alehouse, but in the morning he saw Elizabeth in her true form and quickly rejected any idea of marriage. Elizabeth was angry and, using Satan, had him killed very soon afterwards; his death quickly followed by the termination of the baby growing inside her. She was to be no single mother, as they were seen as the lowest of the low in the eyes of Elizabethan England; unless, of course, you were a mistress of a royal, which afforded privileges and power.

Soon after, Elizabeth found a husband: a farm worker, Christopher Francis, with whom she had a daughter. Her 'beloved' later turned out to be a fat, drunken liar and most unproductive in helping her become richer. Out of anger, she used her cat to severely cripple him and saw to it once again that her baby disappeared. Agnes also knew that her friend had used Satan to cripple the young child of her neighbour, William Auger, for refusing Elizabeth's advances.

The white cat pawed at Agnes, showing that he was ready to receive his reward for his evening's help in punishing Mrs Gooday. Agnes pricked her hand with a hatpin, between her thumb and fore finger, so that Satan could have his fill of her fresh sweet blood. Agnes would have to wait 'til morning to see if the cat worked for her too.

The storm had passed by the time Agnes awoke. Spring sunshine and fresh air breezed into the house through the windows that her eighteen-year-old youngest daughter Joan had uncovered. Agnes could hear her clattering away in the kitchen, preparing potions and tonics to sell in the village. Agnes could see Satan sleeping outside, enjoying the warmth of the new day, and felt a little excited at what the day would bring. She could not wait to get into the village to see if there was any news of Widow Gooday suffering any kind of misfortune, proving that Satan had done her bidding, and to hear any other gossip going around that she could make use of. Agnes was not to be disappointed: last night's storm had flooded the banks of the river Ter, and Gooday's cow had drowned after getting stuck in the mud.

During her visit to the village, Agnes learnt that her married neighbours, Richard Kersey and Emily Rose, were having an illicit affair. They had been meeting weekly, at the old druid fort in the woods, for the past six months. Agnes was not happy about that and told old Mother Percy so; adultery was so unchristian. Agnes believed that marriage should last until death: the constitution of marriage was a sacred union witnessed by God in sickness and in health, for better and for worse. If not, what was the point of it all? Family was important to the old widow; she had her values, and the family unit was top of her list. Agnes was very protective of her family and that of others. Without family values there was no community to speak of. Other gossip doing the rounds was the astonishing story of a giant beanstalk that reached up to the heavens, which had grown overnight somewhere in the forest, but Agnes believed that to be more of a fairy tale than a real story. Many strange things were happening in Elizabethan England at the time, with a lot of fingers being pointed in the direction of the Queen's astronomer John Dee, who it was said raised the dead and communicated with angels and spirits.

On her way home, Agnes came across her young neighbour Mary Fynee hanging washing in her yard and noticed there were some dark bruises on her arms. Mary told her they had been caused by a goat kicking her the previous morning; Widow Waterhouse had her suspicions but decided to accept the young wife's story for now. The next morning, Richard Kersey found three of his most prized hogs dead and Emily Rose discovered that three of her geese had fallen prey to a wild animal of some kind. Perhaps, thought Agnes, they'd think twice in future before making a mockery of something as sacred as marriage.

Some weeks later Agnes saw Mrs Fynee again; this time she was sporting a swollen black eye and more bruises on her arms and legs. Now, Agnes was convinced that all was not well in the

Fynee household. How Agnes hated wife beaters; she had seen it all before, with her younger sister Matilda. She had endured severe beatings from her violent husband for several years and it was always the alcohol that set him off. Agnes had felt powerless to help Matilda and swore revenge when her sister died at the hands of her drunken husband. Agnes's neighbour would not suffer the same fate: William Fynee would feel her wrath that very night.

That sunset, the gentle widow set out her charms and amulets, drew her circle, and summoned the dark lord into her home; she had a mission for him. At that same moment, twelve-year-old Agnes Brown happened to be walking past the cottage of Widow Waterhouse. She was on her way home from gathering red valerian for her mother's potions and witnessed a sight that could only have come from the devil himself. Watching unseen through an uncovered window, the girl saw the old crone on her knees, talking to her white cat in the language of the old Roman church. She could see and hear the widow and her cat clearly and could not believe what she was witnessing. After licking the face of the old lady, the old white cat transformed into a large black dog with devil's horns and the head of a monkey, wearing a silver whistle around its neck. It was the stuff of nightmares.

Young Agnes froze as she watched Widow Waterhouse place a dagger in the mouth of the hellhound, before sending it out into the darkness to do her bidding. Recovering from her initial shock, curiosity filled Agnes Brown and she followed the strange creature towards the village.

After settling out of sight, behind a parked cart, she watched intently, with bated breath, as the animal crouched in the darkness outside the busy alehouse. The demon dog ignored two men leaving the inn, before William Fynee left. He had his hands all over a woman that young Agnes didn't recognise and was staggering towards a quiet spot down by the river.

The dog tracked the couple out of the village towards the dark foreboding forest, followed quietly by Agnes, whose curiosity took precedence over fear. Suddenly, a woman's scream made young Agnes Brown freeze and moments later the woman was racing past her, up the hill and back towards the safety of the inn. She needed a few large gins and, of course, an audience to listen to her macabre experience of a dark shadow in the forest launching itself on poor Mr Fynee as she fled.

For a moment, the young girl wondered whether to follow her, but again curiosity quickly got the better of her and she crept forwards into the darkness. Agnes Brown was stunned and sickened by what she saw: William Fynee was dead in the undergrowth, his heart on the ground beside him and his throat slit from ear to ear, still spurting blood everywhere. On his chest sat the ape-headed demon dog, with the blood-covered dagger hanging out of its mouth. Agnes let out a loud gasp, catching the attention of the hideous beast; fear quickly returned, and she fled as fast as she could back home. She wished she could unsee what she had just witnessed; may the Good Lord protect her.

The gruesome murder of William Fynee was the talk of the village the following morning, after his body was found by men from the alehouse.

Young Agnes was too frightened to reveal to anyone what she had witnessed and for weeks she refused to go out after dark, for fear that the horned ape-headed dog was waiting for her somewhere. Life has a way of transforming fear into a disassociated memory, however, and one evening at sunset Agnes Brown was destined to face that fear once again. Late back from gathering herbs in the forest, the devil hound, with Widow Waterhouse's dagger in its mouth, rushed towards her. The young girl froze on the spot; she thought she was going to die. The beast told her that if she revealed what she had seen, he would thrust the dagger into her heart; he then vanished into thin air, leaving her alone with her thoughts. The following morning Agnes woke to find she was paralysed down her right side and knew that it was Widow Waterhouse's daughter, Joan, who had cursed her. Under interrogation from the priests who came to tend her,

Agnes revealed all that she knew about the events leading up to her being crippled.

Two days later, on 27th July 1566, Agnes Waterhouse, Joan Waterhouse, and Elizabeth Francis were arrested and tried at Chelmsford Assizes for witchcraft before Doctor Cole and Master Foscue. There was an excitable crowd of witnesses all calling for the death of the witches.

After two days the court decision was made: Agnes Waterhouse was found guilty under the 1563 Act of Conjurations, Enchantments, and Witchcraftry and sentenced to death, thus becoming the first witch to hang in England. Her daughter was found not guilty and Elizabeth Francis was ordered to spend a year in gaol for her troubles.

As Widow Waterhouse stood alongside the hangman, at the gallows, before a baying crowd, she sang out the Lord's Prayer in the cursed Catholic tongue. This just further convinced her accusers that she was guilty. Agnes died content in the knowledge that events had been put in place, with one last mission for Satan. He would bring about the end of the evil Tudor reign, with the Queen dying heirless and England being ruled over by a king born in Scotland.

That same year heralded in the Kingdom of the Stuarts under James I; surely, he could be no worse than any of the Tudors.

---
1 Authentic spelling of the time

AGNES COLLINS
(Dates unknown)

Agnes was charged with using witchcraft at the Court Leet, Arreton, Isle of Wight. Her alleged intention was to cause the death of Joan Amis, aged 10 days old. The child died on the 17th February 1580 and as a result, Agnes, a known midwife, was referred for trial at Winchester assizes. She was pardoned on 29th June 1582, having been found not guilty.

Redress

REDRESS
Donna Hayward

Agnes' heart was beating so hard and fast that it felt like it was going to burst out of her body; she thought everyone could hear and see it. She was trying to put on a brave face, but in reality, she was way past caring about the words she was about to hear or the consequences; she just needed it to be over.

She found it hard to focus on hersurroundings; her home village now seemed so strange to her. The people who were once her neighbours and friends were now just strangers, snooping and sneering; all of them waiting fervently for the verdict. She knew she was in trouble, as she was rarely seen at these Court Leets, preferring to keep to herself and mind her own business. The gossips' tongues wagged, even faster than a dog's tail when given a bone, in Arreton and the neighbouring village of Newchurch. Any news from local meetings reached her ears before the ink dried on the notes taken from the proceedings.

However, the gossips were quiet as to the exact reason Agnes was at the manor house today. There were whispers, but the people whispering always went silent as she approached. Only the children that she cared for, in her role as midwife and community carer, seemed to want to talk to her;

they loved Agnes and she loved taking care of them. They just chatted in their inane, childlike manner then went off to play. It was only Henry that was difficult: a loud, boisterous, cocky boy who would not listen to rules and constantly pestered her. She could not understand the way he spoke to her, the taunts he aimed at her: calling her a hag and a witch. Just because she was unmarried and could be considered past the marrying age; by now, she should have been settled down. She had no idea how to connect with him or get through to the 'spoiled nipper.'

— *It couldn't have been him that caused her to be here, could it?* She needed to clear her thoughts, racing at what he could possibly have said to cause her such trouble, *surely they wouldn't have taken the words of a child seriously?*

She was now just trying to concentrate on the table in front of her and the man in control of her fate. The Lord's steward, who was overseeing today's proceedings, sat with a grim face; his secretary sat to one side, at a separate table, ready to take the minutes of his employer's statement. The Lord of the Manor was sat at the front of the audience, as it was his home being used for the day's hearings.

As this was the summer Court Leet, there was a bustle of people waiting their turn to be heard and claim their share of justice. This was just for the parish, so it was never anything more than the pettiest of crimes: a pinched armful of apples, a little bit of lewdness from the drunken man in the street, disturbing the peace.

It was just a bit of entertainment for all those villagers wanting a little bit of satisfaction, should a comeuppance be due for a more despicable neighbour. This was a twice-yearly show, so grudges could be held onto, especially in the long winter months.

So, the list of misdemeanours and misdeeds were heard in front of the judge, arguments were resolved, fines issued, and local justice served. Then Roger Amis took his turn; he stood in front of the table of learned lawmen, a grave expression on his face.

"State your complaint, Master Amis."

"My Lord Steward, I 'ave a most serious grievance: many of the people in this room may know my wife was with child the winter last. Well, she did give birth in Febr'y to a beautiful daughter, which we named Joan, but our beautiful girl did not last a for'night even. She was taken ill and suffered terrible until the 17th, when she died at just 10 days old.

This was a tragedy to our family, made the worse for what I know to be the reason for 'er demise."

At this moment, Agnes' heart was lodged in her throat and she thought she would faint. She had been hearing the rumblings in the village, the people muttering to each other as she walked past. She knew the next words that would be coming out of Roger's mouth.

"Our child was bewitched. She was cursed by that woman."

He pointed firmly at Agnes;

"Agnes Collins. She did 'arm and cause our child to die by witchcraft." The gasp was both simultaneous and universal, followed by a deafening silence. This was beyond the bounds of the Leet: the little stuff was one thing, but an accusation of witchcraft was no small matter.

The secretary's pen stopped scratching the parchment and the Lord's steward sat statue-like for what seemed an eternity.

"Master Amis, the statement you have just made is a most grievous matter and it is beyond the jurisdiction of this court. We will have to pass this into the hands of a higher authority; their decision will be announced, and action taken in due course."

Agnes was confused: would she be arrested now, dragged to a prison, taken to the gallows, and hanged straightaway? Was there going to be a trial by ordeal? Although she knew the practice was dying out, the Island was always hanging on to tradition, so she fully expected to be dragged to the nearest pond and dunked until she drowned.

But nothing happened: the proceedings carried on until the day came to an end; people filed out and the room emptied. The steward and his secretary packed away their things and the manor house was returned to its owner. There were no further appointments until the winter, so the village went back to its usual routine.

The gossiping increased a little, and the stares were somewhat more intense. Agnes could sense the atmosphere when she walked through the village, going about her day. After a while, it all got too much; she knew she had relatives to the north of the Island in Ashey. It was still in the parish of Newchurch, but far enough from the gossips of Arreton.

She desperately wanted to run there and start again but knew she would have to wait for the assizes court ruling to see if there was a case to answer. More waiting ... More anguish ... More wondering if her life would be forfeit at any moment. This was going to be the longest time.

Summer blazed into autumn and the coloured leaves of the trees dropped like jewels, as they made way for the harsh, frosty winter winds. Still nothing happened and the villagers seemed to forget about the hearing, as they focused on surviving the cold, dark days. They were working all possible hours, to store enough food to stave off the growls of hunger in their bellies.

Spring came and went without incident; birds sang their songs of love and the farm animals produced their young. Crops were sown, with the hope of a good season, and enough food to harvest and store. Then summer came.

The trip to Winchester assizes was long and rough. The hours in the cart on the Island were bad enough, but Agnes had never been on a boat before. She thought she might fall into the water and succumb to one of the many monsters said to exist in the depths: unnatural beasts described in the tales told by passing fishermen on dark nights. It may have been entertainment for them, but it was terrifying for a young girl to hear. As she now saw the waves of an unimaginably vast stretch of water, she was afraid that nature would condemn her long before the justices. As the bow bobbed up and down, and lurched side to side, she began to think the appearance of a monster might bring some relief to the churning in her stomach. Ever since the start of the crossing she had suffered a sickness that drained the colour from her face and made her heave. The deckhands laughed at her fear, telling her this was a pleasant summer cruise, and she should be grateful she wasn't crossing in the winter. Agnes almost hoped for a guilty verdict, and even the execution that would follow if it meant she would not have to make the return crossing. She could see the mainland coast, appearing only a stone's throw away, but the crossing seemed to go on forever.

Finally, they berthed, and she saw the many buildings of Southampton.

So many people in one place; it was bustling and noisy, much more than she was used to. She was taken to a small cell for the night, close to the wharf; the remainder of the journey was to take place on the morrow. Little sleep was had; the night was as warm as a smithy's furnace, but the cold flagstones chilled her to the core, as if death already had her in its grip. Still the noises of the harbour remained constant; the tides waited for no man, ships had to be prepared at all times of the day and night in order to be ready to sail at the optimum moment.

From there, she was, bundled into another cart, bound for the county capital of Winchester. It would be another few hours' travel, bumping and bouncing along the ruts made by carts over the passage of time. Just when she thought she couldn't take any more, the silhouette of the cathedral came into view. Agnes was in awe of the massive construction: the western towers reaching to the heavens in gigantic supplication and the buttresses, with their ornate carvings, supporting the whole structure. She was not to see much more, as the cart turned in the opposite direction, towards the castle.

This was a less impressive building; although still very old, it had certainly seen better days. The stonework was crumbling but had not been deemed important enough to spend too much money on repairs. After all, as long as the cells kept the prisoners in for the short time they were held there, and the Great Hall could hold the Assize Court, it didn't matter if the rest was a little shabby. Agnes was led down into the dank gaol, torches barely lighting the way. A large, iron grille gate was unlocked and heaved open; Agnes was thrust through the gateway and the deafening clang of the gate jolted her further into the cell. She was not alone.

There were several others she could see in the gloom once her eyes had become accustomed to the lack of light. These were the men and women destined to be tried at the assizes with her, those wretched souls accused of the most serious crimes: murder, robbery, coining, vagrancy, recusancy infanticide, and, of course, witchcraft. Some were innocent, some definitely not so, but all could be led to the gallows if found guilty.

Sleep was impossible lying on the hard-stone floor. Her meagre, straw-filled mattress back home seemed a luxury now. Even the rats seemed to be bolder, coming right up to her, sniffing and squeaking before rushing away from her as she thrashed at them; better the rats approaching though, than the other occupants of her cell. She hunkered down with her back in a corner, so she did not need to keep looking around to see who or what might be approaching.

Morning came and in the Great Hall the dais was being prepared for the judges. A huge oak table was hefted into place by several servants, but it was dwarfed by the high vaulted hall and its tall stone columns. They supported the centuries-old wooden beam ceiling and divided the hall into three aisles. It was certainly built to impress and intimidate the worst criminals as they awaited their trials.

Agnes felt wretched; after little rest and no food, she once again just wanted her fate to be decided. Prisoners were being taken one by one up to the hall; some came back, their sentence to be carried out shortly, and some never reappeared. They were assumed to have been set free, innocent of their accusation.

"Agnes Collins." the gaoler called out.

She stood, her hands were bound, and she was led up into the courtyard. Would this be the last time she saw the sun, or heard birds singing?

— *Please, let me know my future if I have one, soon.*

The hall had an overwhelming effect on her: she gasped at the size of the room, and the amount of people present who had turned out to witness the proceedings.

The Leet back home was like a small family gathering compared to this. She hoped she didn't seem too afraid or give any signs that could be construed as guilt.

"Agnes Collins, you have been accused of the heinous crime of practising witchcraft on Joan Amis, aged 10 days, daughter of Roger Amis of Arreton. Your witchcraft caused the child to languish until the 17 February last, when she died. What say you on this?"

"Sirs, I was a friend of Mistress Amis and I looked after 'er while she was with child and in 'er confinement. I was with the family when Joan was born; she was a dear little thing. I so would not have wanted any 'arm to come to 'er. I do not know why Master Amis would say such a thing about me.

I knows I am practiced with 'ealing 'erbs, an' when little Joan took sick, I did make a brew to try and 'elp her fever, but all I wanted was fer 'er to be well."

"Well, we have the sworn statement of Mister Amis, and we are making enquiries about your character from reputable members of the village. We shall be making our decision in due course; do not stray from the bounds of your parish until we have passed judgement."

— *Again?*

— *Why was this so difficult?*

She had always known justice at all levels to be swift and carried out immediately. There was no use for gaols, other than to hold prisoners before their trial or execution. Why was she being tortured so? She still had to wait for the decision on whether she lived or died, and this was harder to take than any sentence.

The trip home seemed to take forever; the sea was just as stomach-churning on the return crossing, and every jolt of the cart jarred her weary body a bit more.

Agnes eventually arrived back at the village. She hoped her absence had not been noticed, or the reason for it, but the gossip soon told her otherwise:

"Agnes Collins is a witch and to be avoided, lest good folk be swept up in her Godlessness and end up going hand in hand with her, to the eternal fires of Hell."

She was pretty much shunned and barely spoken to when she greeted neighbours, and conversations ceased when she walked past.

When was judgement going to be made? How long would this wait be? Could she take it, or would she go mad? Even if acquitted, there was certainly no chance she could stay in this community: they had already made their judgment and carried out their sentence upon her.

The months came and went; season followed season: harvest, Michaelmas, All Hallows, and Yule. There was still no announcement when Easter came and went. May Day passed; Agnes remembered being chosen as Queen of the May as a child and loving all the attention. No such happiness this year, she stayed away from the revelry.

It was almost Midsummer when Agnes was summoned to the manor house. No Leet this time, but the Lord of the Manor, the Lord's Steward, and his secretary. This was almost more frightening than being in front of the village, or the Assizes assembly. It was too quiet. She waited. She held her gaze low, wary of what the Lords' Steward was about to say. He cleared his throat:

"Agnes Collins, there has been an accusation of the practice of witchcraft upon you. This is a most serious crime, which would carry the penalty of death by hanging should a guilty verdict be passed upon you."

She stared at a place on the table so hard, she felt it would smoulder and burst into flame, sealing her fate.

"By the Grace of Her Majesty Elizabeth, Queen of England, you have been granted Pardon of the offence and are free from all disgrace connected to the accusation. Agnes, you are innocent. Go with God's blessing and take up your life once more."

She stayed rooted to the spot. She had heard the words but was still trying to grasp their meaning.

Slowly, she stopped staring and looked around at the men seated at the table, the tapestries, the sumptuous curtains, and the light filtering through the leaden grid of glass in the windows.

Finally, she managed a tiny "Thank you m'lord." and found the strength to walk out of the room and into the sunshine. It had never felt so good.

Agnes had no belongings to speak of, so she just started walking. As she passed through the village, she did not stop to speak or take a backwards glance. She knew they would never change their minds about her, and her name was forever tainted.

On she walked, only a few miles to Ashey, not that far, but it felt like a whole new world: one that would not have heard the stories about her, one where she could start anew.

Her cousin answered the door and welcomed Agnes in. Of course, she could stay, if she couldn't find work, she could look after her *littl'uns*. And she remembered how good she was with the healing herbs, so Agnes wouldn't be short of people coming to her for a tonic or poultice.

The years passed and Agnes was happy. She never found a husband, and some considered it a little strange, having an old spinster in the village, but if that was the worst that could be heard about her, she was not worried. She was known for being a good carer and a fine midwife, which again was not usual for a spinster, but she was trusted by several families to keep their children in line and in return they loved her. She only briefly remembered her previous life: the struggle to clear her name, the anguish and fear of those months that had dragged into years. She always had little Joan in her heart: she did love her and grieved for her oh so-brief life. She had tried her best to soothe her fever, but the horrors of childbirth for both mothers and children were well known to every woman. She also missed the friendship of Mistress Amis.

That nipper, Henry Urry, she recalled, was a different story, however. He had tormented Agnes and called her so many names, including *'witch.'* He was a nasty piece of work and none of her ways would get any good out of him. Oh, he had vexed her something terrible. So, it was a good job the little bugger passed away, before he could let the spell she had put upon him be known.

URSULA KEMP
(1525- 1582)

As a result of an argument (it would appear more than a few times) with her neighbour Grace Thurlow, she was reported for practicing witchcraft.

At her trial reports of 3 deaths (Joan Thurlow, Elizabeth Leatherdale and Edna Stratton) were blamed on Ursula and she was found guilty of causing death by bewitching in Chelmsford on 29th March 1582 and hanged.

So, They Say

THEY SAY
Marisha Kiddle

My Name is Ursula Kemp.
I'm a midwife and a nursemaid:
I live in St Osyth
And I've never been afraid.

They say my neighbour Grace,
Was in a mood with me.
They say that she complained
To justice Brian Darcy.

They say that I am guilty,
That I'm the one to blame.
That Joan fell out her crib and died,
They say I have no shame.

They say me in law died.
They say that I'm a witch,
And that I put a curse on her
Just because she was a bitch.

They say I have familiars.
What do *they really* know?
That, I have some pets
And one is white as snow.

So here I am at fifty-seven
Sat in a dark, dank gaol,

Wondering how me boy is
With no hope of mail.

Talking of me son
Well, he confirmed *their* ditty,
So, now me days are done
And me only hope is pity.

Now me time has come
To tell the judge me tale.
I fear that I am doomed
To spend all me life in Gaol.

And though, I did confess
In the hope of being free,
The evidence was against me
Oh no! Alas! No Clemency!

GUILTY! They did find me
Which fills me with such dread,
For I'm going to the gallows,
To be hanged until I'm DEAD!

So, now me story's told
And I am flying free,
With no fear of growing old,
Nor a life of pain and misery.

I leave to you this wish
That you believe my strife,
I was truly not a witch,
Just a woman living life.

DOCTOR JOHN FAIN
(died 1591)

Dr John Cunninghame, also known as Fain, was a Scottish schoolmaster and known sorcerer. He confessed to having made a pact with the devil, but he subsequently recanted that admission. He was tried in North Berwick, Kirk: charged with using witchcraft against townsfolk, preaching witchcraft, and conspiring to cause harm to James VI and his new bride, Anne of Denmark. Fain was arrested on the confession of Gillis Duncan and further charged with conspiring to sink the fleet of King James VI, by conjuring a storm at sea, while the King of Scotland and his wife were sailing back from Oslo. He was arrested, along with several others, and tortured. This event would later be remembered as the *North Berwick witch trials.*

He also apparently attempted to seduce one of his students' sisters using magic; however, in this instance, the girl's mother was also a well-practiced witch and she re-directed the spell into a cow. The townsfolk claimed that the cow followed him everywhere.

Devil in the Detail

DEVIL IN THE DETAIL
Scott Irvine

I should never have trusted that bastard Irvine; I really believed I could rely on him to keep me safe until things had calmed down. I thought Alexander Irvine, the eighth Laird of Drum Castle, shared my concern over the king's plan to introduce new laws for Scotland: laws that would destroy all of us who use the supernatural spirits. The ancient crafts, I believe, should be available to all those who have the discipline to learn and good intent; nae solely for the church's use. The Laird himself is a witch and a high priest to a large coven in Drum Oak, east of Aberdeen. I really believed we were kindred spirits; that's why I ran to him when the North Berwick witches began to be rounded up. They were accused of a plot to assassinate the young king using Devil magic, as he returned from Norway with his new wife, Anne of Denmark. Gilly Duncan, the high priestess of Dunbar coven, was a woman of wisdom and a prominent healer in the East Lothian area, who was deemed to be acting suspiciously by her employer, David Seaton, the deputy bailiff of Tranent. It gave him an excuse to use his thumbscrews on her and a wet cord was wrapped tightly around her forehead so that it slowly crushed her skull as it dried. The pain quickly made the poor woman confess to belonging to a coven that had tried, through sorcery, to murder the king and queen. News of Duncan's testimony soon reached James VI, who took a keen interest in the interrogation and, after more torture, she was forced to name as many of her co-conspirators as she could. It woudnae have taken the king long to figure out that the mastermind behind it all was me, his stepfather: Francis Hepburn, the current Earl of Bothwell. When the doctor, John Fain, was taken to Edinburgh Gaol for interrogation, I knew it was time to get out of Scotland; a skilled torturer could loosen the tongue of any living soul. John Fain was a strong man, intelligent and honest, but I feared for his soul, I really did. Right nu, though, it is my soul that is on the line.

★

If it wasnae for Irvine's maid, who had an eye for me, bringing me notice that the laird had gone to alert the Royal Guard of my whereabouts, I would nu be in one of Irvine's dungeons. The only thing to look forward to would be interrogation by the king's men. I only had time to grab three days' supplies, enough to see me across the highlands to the west coast, na easy feat with January snow carpeting the land. I rode my horse Bess, following the Gormack Burn northwards from Drum Forest, to where I sit nu over a warming fire in the Pictish Cullerlie stone circle.

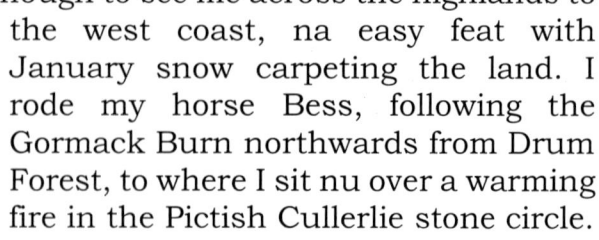

I am surrounded by the cold, darkness, uncertainty, and despair. My winter robe is wrapped tight around my frozen body.

I am 52 years old and for the first time in my life I feel vulnerable, but if there is one thing I am good at, it is surviving.

I am a Scottish noble: one of many royal princes descended from Robert the Bruce. I am privileged compared to most Scots, but surely that is God's will. It is a cut-throat world, where marriage or death can lead to sitting on the throne, and as things stand, James VI will wear the English crown when Elizabeth dies. There is a spirit that guides my actions, a fire burning in my heart from the mysteries and magic of the world we live in, an existence that is both physical and spiritual. I have discovered that the spirit world guides the physical realm, and that magic can influence the spirit forces that are always within all of us.

I wanted the king to pay for signing a treaty with that bitch Elizabeth, because it enabled the protestant queen to have my wife, the king's mother, executed in London three years ago. I had loved Mary from the moment she returned from France, to rule Scotland, after the death of her husband. Her marriage to the French king had been arranged when she was sixteen and, as soon as he died, Mary coudnae wait to return to her homeland. It was nae long after our first meeting that we became lovers; she was eighteen and I was a year

126

older. Of course, the Scots Guards and church bishops didnae see me as fathering a potential heir, so marriage was off limits from the start.

Three years later, it was arranged for Mary to marry the English Protestant, Lord Darnley, Henry Stewart, who forced himself on her on their wedding night. The head of the Stewart clan was cold, cruel, and ambitious; he feared those he saw as a threat to his lofty position. As his wife's lover, I was top of the list of those he needed to destroy. With the blessing of Mary, I had done what needed to be done: I had him killed. I had na choice; the maniac had already begun assassinating the Queen's counsel, which put a terrible strain on Mary and the people she served. I feel na guilt or shame in ending his life and can face my God safe in the knowledge that it was for the good of all and in the name of love, for my Queen. I was the main suspect and interrogated, of course, but I made sure na evidence came back to haunt me.

With an heir born to Mary and Darnley, we were reluctantly given permission to marry by the Scots Guards and bishops. Mary had to abdicate, and we had to leave Scotland, allowing James Stewart to become James VI of Scotland. He was barely one year old, so he remained under the supervision of the protestant bishops. While I went to Denmark to seek advice, Mary went to England to plead with her cousin Elizabeth for help to regain her throne; instead, she found herself under house arrest for eighteen years. She was eventually beheaded, without me seeing her beautiful, sweet smile, hearing her gentle laugh, or touching her fragrant skin ever again. When Mary was killed, my heart died, and I vowed to return to Scotland to avenge her ill-fated life and tragic death.

It is cold, and flurries of snow are drifting off the Grampian Mountains making my journey to Oban slow and very unpleasant. It is unbearable on my face and hands, but I have to keep going if I am to make the changing tide at first light tomorrow. I am grateful for my horse, ever-faithful Bess, carrying her master across treacherous terrain in hostile conditions for very little reward. She cannae come with me past Oban and will in truth be fit for nothing but dog food by then. Something spooks Bess, making her rear up, nearly unsaddling me. I see her ears prick up: she is alert; when she has settled, I gather myself and look around. I see and hear nothing in the thick Forest of Atholl that skirts the foot of the southern mountains, as far as Loch Ericht. I know of a lodge there, where I can get warm, eat, and rest for a few hours before I continue to the port and escaping Scotland for good. A few toddies of malt will help the blood flow back to my fingers and toes. Just as Bess calms down and I relax a little, an eagle swoops down after a mammal in the undergrowth; my heart stops for a moment and Bess snorts and stamps her feet. I pat her on the neck to reassure her, dig my heels into her side, and we continue slowly westwards, with each step through the snow taking me closer to safety.

★

So, my plan didnae work; admittedly, it was ambitious, but love makes people do crazy things. My Rosicrucian brothers put me in touch with Dr John Fain, who was an educated and honest Scot. He was a schoolmaster and family man in public, and a high priest of the North Berwick witch coven in private. The good doctor was vital for my plan to succeed. Ok, I didnae reveal I was the stepfather of the king, and Mary's widower. He would have heard of Earl Bothwell for sure, but he would have na idea who Francis Hepburn from Stirling was. I led him to believe that I was on a mission for the royal court, to prevent a bill being passed that would classify the use of science and witchcraft as treason. I wanted to put the fear of the Devil into King James VI, so he would take our power seriously; the doctor, I hoped, would take my proposal as a fellow free thinker sincerely.

My first meeting with the doctor was at the Beltane festival in Perth last spring. I put my plan to him, dangling the forthcoming prospect of increased witch-hunts against the likes of us as bait. I asked him outright if he believed in the power of witchcraft.

'I believe.' He replied after a little thought. 'At least, I believe in a force that is greater than anything we can imagine. It controls everything that happens on Earth, and I believe it can be controlled to do man's bidding.'

I cut in quickly:

'Is that force, as you call it, a power to benefit humanity, or harm it? I mean, would the world be better with the universal energy available to every man, woman, and child who cares to study hard? Who's to say the magic won't be used for wicked intent, as well as for good?'

The doctor rubbed the side of his face and looked me briefly in the eyes before replying: 'It's important that we, as humans, seek the truth that is the universe and explore the invisible realm now being proven to exist. Aye, the truth should be shared with everyone.'

'Everyone!' I countered. 'Everyone includes murderers, liars, traitors, and cheats. The world would be in chaos if everyone could practice magic. People would influence the spirit world for their own gain and take, without giving anything in return. The elemental world would soon collapse in on itself; then where would we be?'

The doctor responded, 'Nae everyone understands the workings of magic or would have the mind for doing their own magic. Most Christians are quite happy for the church to pray to their higher power for them.'

'Aye, but a murderer could, for example, cast a spell on you, your family, and your friends, to cause illness or even death if they so wished. Is that's ok, then?'

'Na, that is nae ok,' the doctor retorted. 'Magic and science take a lot of learning and part of that learning is nae to harm others.'

I thought he was a little naïve, so continued to weave him into my web. While he still pondered my questioning, I put to him: 'Do you believe that doing a bad thing to bring about a good thing is acceptable to God?'

He thought for a moment, unsure if doing wrong to make something better was moral or nae. It was na something he could answer right away.

'Let's put it another way,' I continued. 'What if you could change Scotland's destiny, and possibly England's too: heralding in a new age of science and technology, which would improve our knowledge of the universe and make our people wiser, healthier, and less reliant on the church?' The doctor remained silent, still unsure of how to respond.

'You have the power to change the future of your country for the better.' I tell him. 'You and your witches have the fate of the people in their hands.'

'What do you mean?' he enquired, always eager to improve the lives of his countrymen. 'What would we have to do?'

John Fain was nibbling on the bait; it was time to put my plan to him.

'I need a fierce storm to be conjured up in the North Sea, on the eve of this coming Samhain. A storm so violent as to put the fear of the Devil into the King and let him know of the powerful forces he is taking on.'

'The Devil!' spat Fain. 'What has he got to do with anything?'

'The Devil is the only force that the King is afraid of. He has to believe that the storm was created by the prince of darkness himself for the plan to work.'

'I'm nae sure,' gasped the doctor.

'The Devil is bad news; I cannae see my witches agreeing to do the work of the Devil.'

'But it willnae be the Devil's work; it would be the work of the Lord, in the guise of the Devil. God works in mysterious ways.' I reminded him. 'If the King goes unchallenged, all forms of magic would be solely the churches' domain. Those who practice it for themselves will, in the eyes of the law, be considered heretics and traitors. Our way of life will finish either on the end of a rope or burnt at the stake. Anyhow, I dinnae expect an answer nu; put the idea to your witches and remind them that it is for the good of all honest and decent people. They will be destroying an evil that will subject Scotland to terror and chaos; if the English Queen, likely as it seems, dies without an heir, the darkness would fall on England too.'

He agreed to put it to the witches, and we arranged to meet in Perth, on the next full moon, in three weeks' time. John Fain was hooked, noo he just needed to be reeled in.

It was close, but I made the ship sailing to Ireland in time. I set Bess free on the outskirts of Oban and prayed she would find another good soul to take her in, as I headed out into the Atlantic with Scotland slowly disappearing from view. I had time to reflect a little on the past few months and consider if maybe my plan was a mistake. Several innocent people had already been persecuted, tortured, and executed; my own life was now well and truly on the line. Was I wrong to try and scare the King into my way of thinking? James VI was young, but an experienced King. From the moment he was born, it appeared as if he were cursed with a darkness that would condemn every soul who went against his royal command to misery and torture. I am infuriated that the protestant swine is bringing in outlandish fire and brimstone laws that will lead to more slaughtering of God-fearing scientists and sorcerers in Scotland. His crown of deceit, twisting the truth, preaching nonsense such as the Earth is at the centre of the universe, orbited by the sun, planets, and stars, like our moon. The King's evangelising is an abomination of God's word and has been proven a lie. His own flock are cast down into the fiery pits of hell. Their bones are used to build God's heavenly kingdom on Earth if they dinnae seek redemption from the sin they are told they are born with. We are all doomed to rot in Hell for eternity if the bastard gets his way. Na, it was my duty to try and stop the King; I am convinced of that. His ways are evil. Since his birth he has been surrounded by advisers, teachers, bishops, and

diplomats, constantly reminding him that he is a direct descendant of Jesus. To question his absolute, divine authority would be to question God himself: blasphemy and treason punishable by death.

★

John Fain paid the price, as did Agnes Sampson and Euphemia MacLean. In the early hours of a cold January morning, Fain was dragged from his home, leaving his frantic wife and frightened young children behind. He refuted the charges outright, protesting his innocence all the way to Edinburgh Gaol, 20 miles along the coast. As soon as he was thrown into a cell, still protesting his innocence, the torture began: both of his legs were compressed by what was known as the "boot," a contraption similar to thumbscrews. It was gradually tightened, crushing his leg bones slowly and relentlessly, for days on end; Fain would have suffered badly. There would be just enough constant pressure, with each tightening of the screw, to stop him from passing out. After a week of screaming from unending agony and splintered bones, he finally confessed to being the clerk to those who served the Devil in East Lothian. He also revealed to his torturers how he sat beside the dark lord, at his left elbow, recording the meetings and administering oaths on behalf of the Devil.

The following morning, having been released from the "boot," he recanted his confessions, telling his gaolers that the Devil had visited him in his cell during the night, carrying a white wand. The "Evil One" told Fain that when he was dead, his soul would belong to him; then he snapped his wand in half and vanished into thin air. To save his own soul, John had nae choice but to recant his confessions, or else spend eternity in Hell's fires. Even after more torture in the "boot" and further excruciating torment, as needles were forced under his fingernails, the doctor still refused to admit any connection to the Devil. In frustration, his interrogators strangled him; his body was burnt on Castle Hill, above the city, one bitterly cold morning in late January. Agnes Sampson, Euphemia MacLean, and Barbara Napier were all found guilty of being in the Devil's service. Barbara Napier was later released, but Agnes and Euphemia were hanged on Castle Hill. They could hear the unearthly screams of misery and suffering coming from Fain's still smouldering corpse.

I was relieved when we reached Cork, in Southern Ireland; I dinnae make a good sailor. A rest, a feast, a beer, and a warm bed would soon have me back at full strength in both body and mind. It had been a difficult few days, leaving me devoid of much emotion or feeling. I was still a long way from being safe; the Scots Guards had a long reach, even extending to France, where I hope to arrive in a couple of days. But for nu, I have to keep my head down.

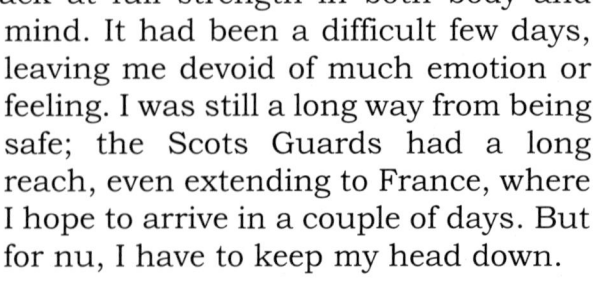

I had several meetings with Dr John Fain, organising the plan to frighten the King; his witches had finally agreed to participate in the Samhain ritual. They were all willing to stand up against the evil scourge that was gripping the land. Fain had put my plan to his coven first, then to the covens of Dunbar and Haddington. Gilly Duncan and Agnes Sampson were aghast at the idea of bringing in the Devil to oversee the ceremony but, with much argument, the doctor persuaded the high priestesses to understand what was at stake: nae only our country, but our very souls too. He had told me how his final meeting went with the high priestesses and their seconds:

John - 'Well, what do you think ladies?'

Gilly - 'Are you crazy John? Who is this man Francis Hepburn?'

John - 'Hepburn is a grand master of a society of free thinkers like ourselves, called the Rosicrucians or Rosy Cross. Their thoughts are based on spiritual development, with a mystical approach in marrying the elemental world with the spiritual realm.'

Gilly - 'Aye, ok, but why the Devil?'

Mary - 'I dinnae understand why we need the Devil involved in all this. What if we are found out?'

John - We wilnae be found out. we will only be making a storm far out to sea.'

Gilly - 'Aye, but we will be aiming our energy at a ship carrying our King and his Queen.'

Euphemia - 'And the captain and crew? What have they done to deserve our wrath?'
Mary - 'You mean Hepburn's wrath.'
Barbara - 'The Devil's wrath.'
Gilly - 'Shush, Barbara!'
Barbara - 'I am all for it: use the Devil to scare the Devil!'
Agnes - 'Are you saying the King is the Devil?'
Barbara - 'If what John is saying is true, then aye, our King is the Devil!'
Gilly - 'Don't be stupid Barbara, you dinnae …'
John - 'Stop bickering ladies. This is a serious situation and we only have two months to get it all arranged.'
Euphemia - 'What will we have to do? What do any of us know about raising a storm out to sea?'
John - 'Hepburn will give me the spells we need when I meet him next at the autumn equinox. It will be our last meeting before the ceremony.'
Gilly - 'I still dinnae like it.'
Mary - 'I dinnae either.'
John - 'We take for granted our way of life: our craft and healing ways, but our King intends to nae only stop it but make it illegal and punishable by death.'
Euphemia - 'You dinnae know for sure.'
John - 'I believe Hepburn; he comes across as sincere.'

Euphemia - 'Aye, ok, but how does he know all this?'

Barbara- 'Because Hepburn is the Devil.'

Gilly - 'Shut up Barbara.'

Agnes - 'But can we trust him?'

John - 'I trust him.'

Euphemia - 'You still havnae answered my question: how does Hepburn know what the King's plans are?'

John - 'He told me he has royal connections.'

Mary - 'He could be just saying that.'

Barbara - 'He is the Devil.'

John - 'To show he is serious Hepburn will be here at North Berwick to conduct the ceremony on the night.'

Mary - 'Dinnae prove a thing.'

Euphemia - 'What have we to lose? I am uncomfortable with having the Devil involved, but I think we have a lot to gain, if only the improvement of our magic skills. That is some powerful sorcery he wants us to use.'

Barbara - 'Aye, I'm in, if only to secure our way of life. The King is a threat and we all know that; it is in his stars. I vote to terrify him half to death.'

Agnes - 'What if the ship sinks or something bad happens to the King?'

John - 'He has his Lord to protect him and keep him safe. Dinnae forget, he is a descendant of Jesus, after all, and ships survive storms all the time. For Hepburn's plan to work, we all need to be in this together. Our intent needs to be synchronised and our faith solid, so the spirits will hear our call and do our bidding. Euphemia, are you in?'

  Euphemia - 'Aye, ok.'

  John - 'Barbara?'

  Barbara - 'Aye, I'm in.'

  John - 'Gilly?'

  Gilly - 'I guess so. Anyway, the Devil isn't real.'

  Barbara - 'He is real.'

  John - 'Be quiet Barbara. Agnes, you in?'

  Agnes - 'I dinnae like it, but you can count me in.'

  John - 'Mary, how about you?'

  Mary - 'Well if everyone else is, then I am too.'

  John - 'Great; then it is decided. On Samhain eve, we will assist Hepburn with his ceremony to raise a storm in the North Sea. It will frighten the King into nae bringing his new heresy laws to the people of Scotland. Thank you all.'

  Barbara – 'Who's round is it?'

★

  I had a safe passage across the channel from Cork to Brest, disguised as a French fisherman, two days ago. I felt a little safer in France, but the King had spies there and I still had a long way to go before I reached Italy. I had trustworthy friends and royal connections there, who dinnae support the Stewart cause. I had been living on my wits: hunting and gathering what food I could, sleeping in barns and ruined buildings. Nu deep in the enchanted forest of Broceliande, I am feeling more confident about my escape.

I am awestruck at the beauty of this ancient forest of oak, ash, beech, and lime; it dominates much of Brittany. Fate has crossed my path, bringing me to a coven from Huelgoat who practice their craft on each full moon. I found their camp by following my nose to the sweet smell of roasting boar on an open fire. My stomach rumbled at the prospect of a good hearty meal, and witches being witches, they na doubt also had a healthy supply of mead. I introduced myself, a fellow witch and Catholic Scottish noble on the run for performing sorcery against the Scottish King.

Sitting around a camp-fire with my new friends, my hunger abated and a goblet of mead in hand, I revealed the ceremony that had made me an outlaw. I told them when the new crescent moon had risen over the sleepy town of North Berwick, three covens of witches had waited nervously for the ceremony to begin. Magic was in the air that night: we could all feel it, me, the doctor, and the witches. Powerful spirits were gathering around the small church on the cliff, as darkness fell. Fain had broken in, with some of the others, and placed black candles around the church. On the altar was positioned a wax effigy of the King, wrapped in a cloth from the royal household, burning brightly in the dimly lit chamber of Christ. After the witches had left the church to meet the others at the edge of the village, I snuck inside unseen.

I had invited the East Lothian witches to an audience with the Devil himself and they coudnae wait to meet the dark lord of temptation, who was, of course, myself in disguise. I wore a hideous mask with burning red eyes and a beaked nose, a black robe, and gauntlets that looked like the hairy claws of a great bear. I hid out of sight, in the pulpit, waiting for the witches to return.

John opened the ceremony, calling in the quarters and their elemental powers and spiritual influences, allowing the two worlds to merge. Then he directed the attention of the coven to the pulpit, where I stood as the Devil. The worshippers gasped and then fell silent, waiting for the dark lord to speak to them. I allowed the silence to continue for a moment longer, before raising my left hand and calling for truth. I preached on the corruption of the protestant church and the danger Scotland was in from the King; witch-hunts had already begun across Europe and a war had started between religion and scientific truth. I remind the congregation of their duty to "science" to take the war to the king and church, when the King was sailing home from Scandinavia with his new bride, and vulnerable to the dark storm spirits of the North Sea. As the congregation roared with approval, I smiled, seeing my plan working perfectly. Nu it was time to end the ceremony, in honour of the demon Baphomet.

Hearing the chanting of Baphomet coming from inside the church, Gilly Duncan began playing her Jews harp, signalling her coven to light their torches and dance around the headstones. The witches sang and chanted as they danced:

'Goddess lead the way,
Sister go ahead, If you dinnae go first,
Then, Goddess, allow me instead.'

Seeing the torches dancing around the graveyard and hearing the music and song drifting out to sea after my Baphomet chants, Agnes Sampson was ready to perform her ritual at the cliff edge. Hekate was invoked to do their bidding.

An enchanted cat, with the privy member of a recently hanged murderer stitched to its paws, was baptised King, using full moon water. It was then held aloft, thrice calling to Hekate, before being thrown into the sea as an offering to the Dark Queen, already on her way to King James.

A loud rumble of thunder echoed in the heavens, as acknowledgment that the storm spirits had heard our call: almost immediately the wind picked up and the waves crashing against the bottom of the cliff began to gain strength. Our work was done.

An unnaturally fierce storm raged in the North Sea that night and if it wasnae for the brilliant seamanship of the Royal ship's captain and his crew, James and his Queen would have drowned. As it was, another ship was lost in the storm, with the loss of all thirteen crew, the ship's cat and its cargo of spirit and tobacco. The captain of the ship was Richard King from Southampton. The devil, they say, is in the detail.

★

The Breton witches tell me they work with the energy of an old Welsh wizard, Merlin; a druid who helped King Arthur, the great bear, keep the English Saxons out of Wales 800 years earlier. They also reveal how Merlin arrived in Broceliande on a quest for what they called the Holy Grail and how he became enchanted by the beautiful local fairy queen, Morgan le Fey. I was captivated by their story. She stole his powers and imprisoned him nearby, within a crystal cave in a hill, along the Valley of Na Return. They tell me that when a hero rescues the druid, they will be rewarded with great power and wealth, and have access to the fountain of youth forever. I decided I could afford to spend a little time here, especially as fame and fortune beckoned. On a full stomach, a good night's sleep, and with a sharp sword at my side I journey into the Valley of Na Return, with god on my side and honour in my heart.

ANNA MUGGEN
(died 1608)

In April 1608, Anna Muggen was accused of bewitching six people in her home town of Gorinchem. She was not tortured, having willingly confessed practicing witchcraft for thirteen years; having made a pact with the Devil as a young girl. On 29 May 1608, Anna Muggen was hanged after which her body was burned. Her remains were buried outside the city walls.

The following story was Inspired by the 'Wytches and Cunningfolk Album' by The Dolmen.

The First Drops of Rain

THE COBBLER'S CURSE
Diane Narraway

"I'll be back before you know it."
"Promise me, Johannes."
"I promise."

Anna hugged her husband as tightly as she could, willing him not to go. She knew it was useless though, and as much as she longed for him to stay, she eventually relaxed her grip. Her eyes followed him, as he headed off into the distance. He briefly turned, affording himself one last glance of his wife, a keepsake memory that would stay with him until he returned home. Anna, however, knew in her heart that he was never going to return. Her grandmother had called it a gift: saying that she was blessed with an inner sight. At this precise moment, watching her husband leave to fight for his country, and knowing he would never return, it felt more like a curse than a gift.

Anna and Johannes had been childhood sweethearts who had promised each other they would marry as soon as they were old enough, and at 15 they were married. Anna was a beautiful woman, and many commented on how lucky Johannes was. He too considered himself lucky: Anna was beautiful inside as well and he loved her with all his heart. They were very happy together and neither could've wished for a more idyllic life.

Johannes' mother had died in childbirth, and his father had contracted smallpox shortly after Johannes' and Anna's wedding. In spite of all Anna's efforts, he died: all the cold cloths, poultices, and small beer were of no avail. After his death, Johannes and his wife inherited the family farm and they were, in the most part, self-sufficient. He grew vegetables and sold them at the local market. along with Anna's home-made jams, preserves, and tinctures designed to treat variety of ailments.

The war, it seemed, had been going on as long as Anna could remember; every now and then new men would be conscripted, and this time Johannes was among them. She hated the war at the best of times and knowing that her beloved husband would never return made her hate it all the more.

She'd had an inkling that she was pregnant when Johanne left, and when her time of the month passed again, she knew she was definitely with child. She struggled: torn between the joy of having someone to remind her of her beloved Johannes and worrying whether all the chores that needed doing on her own would be too much for her. Of course, there would also be an extra mouth to feed.

Had she not had the gift of insight, she could, she felt, have struggled on, ever hopeful of his return. She did have insight, though. She patted her belly, hoping it would stir some strong maternal feelings, but it felt no different. Was it even right to bring a child into a world that seemed constantly at war; a world that ripped families apart? In short, she was afraid of many things: not being able to cope alone, miscarrying, or dying giving birth. Who would raise the child then? Johannes parents were dead, her parents were old, and any other family members had either moved away or died in this Godforsaken war.

Her heart was heavy; she had to make a decision, but it was not one she could afford to take too much time with, nor one she could afford to make lightly. This was the hardest choice she had, or would, ever have to make. She spent many nights agonising over the child slowly growing in her belly: tears poured down her face as she ground pennyroyal, wormwood, and rue to make the necessary tincture. She believed this was the right course of action, but that didn't make it any less painful. Her heart hurt and the lump in her throat, like her tears, seemed endless. Life was cruel and it hurt beyond any physical pain that would come later.

Sure enough, two days after swallowing the tincture, her stomach began to cramp. She wasn't too far into her pregnancy and this was to be a secret she would take to her grave. The pain of the cramps at times seemed unbearable and eventually, after several hours, she began to bleed. She watched tiny blood clots fall to the floor, mesmerised by the horror of it all. She sobbed all the more; there was no going back now, she thought, but going forward wasn't going to be easy either.

The pain of those few days never left her, and she spent many nights crying herself to sleep; even more so when the news of Johannes' death arrived. She despised this world for all it had taken from her. In sadness and despair, her once beautiful countenance and her cheerful disposition gradually became bitter and twisted beyond recognition.

Anna spent what seemed like a lifetime alone on the farm, working the land and hauling her produce to market. She still made jams and preserves but, like her, they too became bitter and her tinctures less effective; she began to sell less and less.

Every now and then, she would gaze into the mirror, no longer recognising the woman looking back at her. She let the tears fall: for the girl she used to be, for the love she had lost, and for the child she couldn't have; eventually they ceased to have any meaning. The winters seemed long and icy cold, but her heart had grown colder still. They say time heals, but it didn't heal Anna's broken heart, it just made it heavier and everything was harder to bear.

It was one of those nights: the wind was howling outside, the weight of her heart was even more unbearable than ever, and the tears flowed down her cheeks falling to the floor. On such a night she felt the icy sting of cold, as some of her tears landed on her feet, and she realised her shoes were worn and her clothes were rags. She could scarcely afford food, let alone clothes.

She barely slept that night, haunted by the same old dreams of lost love and the child whose life she had denied. All of which were compounded by her inability to afford the bare necessities required to survive another harsh winter. The only thing that prevented her from taking her own life was her staunch Catholic beliefs; she prayed every night for some respite from the heavy burden she carried.

Of course, when Johannes first left, she'd had offers from some of the younger, more eligible men in Gorinchem and some, of course, from the not so eligible men: mostly old beard splitters[1]. Now, however, when she needed help, she could neither afford it nor was she beautiful or nice enough to receive marriage proposals.

She gathered the last of her jams, tinctures, and preserves and headed into Gorinchem with the intention of selling enough to buy a pair of shoes. Unfortunately for Anna, her bitter and aggressive nature meant that many folks had learned to give her a wide berth. This meant that she made very little money and was just as cold and hungry as she was at the start of the day. She returned home, resolute that she would return the next day. She ate what little she had and spent another cold restless night. She was just 25 years of age, but her reflection and stature told a different story: the last eight years without Johannes had been hell and her bitterness, anger, and sorrow had shaped her into an old hag.

The next day was no better than the previous one, just colder with the need for shoes more desperate. Despite her lack of money, she headed to the Cobblers, hoping he had something cheap enough for her to buy, or perhaps she could offer him goods in exchange. Sadly, she was too proud to beg. The cobbler was busy working; everyone knew he was over-priced because he made shoes for the nobility who paid very well; he was not concerned with the needs of the lower classes.

"Excuse me please, Sir. I'm in dire need of some klompen[2]; what are the cheapest you have?"

He afforded her no more than a cursory glance.

"1 gulden[3]."

"1 gulden? That's ridiculous; I cannot afford that."

"Then your feet shall be cold."

"Please Sir," she begged, as much as she hated to do so, "Would you consider taking some jams and preserves in exchange? They are really good; I made them myself."

"And that is a recommendation is it? Go away, you old hag. I don't have time to waste. Either you have the money, or you do not; which is it to be?"

"I do not." she hung her head sadly and headed for the door.

Perhaps it was because she was tired, old before her time, hungry, cold; who can say? When she reached the door, however, she turned and, with all the fire in her belly that she could muster, cursed him and all his kin to hell.

"Damn you. I say damn you and all your kin. May you rot in the deepest recesses of Hell. May you perish in the fires of your damnation. I curse you, your kin, and your business."

He was so taken aback that the nail he was hammering slipped, going straight through his finger; such was his fear that he ran into the street, pointing at her and screaming that she was a witch.

"She's a witch I tell you ... cursed me she did ... witch! A witch!"

Such was his hysteria that others gathered around her, circling her, and preventing any chance of escaping. She didn't care: the only escape she really wanted was from this accursed life. She was arrested and six people came forward, claiming she had bewitched them too. She spent the night in a damp, dark cell reflecting on her life. For the first time in ages, she was fed and, perhaps, despite the damp, not as cold as she had been. The walls were thicker, and the wind didn't bite the way it did in her house. It wasn't a snap decision: the idea percolated in her mind throughout the long night before her trial, but for once she had a solution.

"You are accused of practicing witchcraft. The charges are that you did knowingly, and with all intention, curse Zeger Hendrix the shoemaker and that you did knowingly, and with all intention, bewitch Agnes Van de Berg, Jutte Dijksma, Kathrijn Mulde, and Yolente Tuinstra, along with her daughters Eva and Geertruyta. How do you plead?"

She looked around the room; she had grown up with these women. Jutte had been her best friend as a child and yet here they all were, pointing the finger at her. Didn't they think she had been through enough? Liars, every last one of them. She turned her head towards the accuser and in a loud, clear voice announced:

"Guilty to all charges. I have practised witchcraft for the past thirteen years, since I was just a girl of 12. The Devil appeared before me in the guise of a young man and I made a pact with him" If they couldn't see the absurdity of it all, then what did she care? As far as she was concerned, death would be a blessed relief; after all, she wasn't taking her own life: they were.

She was sentenced to death, and on the morning of May 29th her cell door was opened. The bright sunlight stung her eyes, and they began to water. Aged just 25 she was led to the gallows and the noose placed around her neck.

A crowd had gathered in Grote Market to witness her death and hear her last words. She looked around, catching sight of the shoemaker and those she had once called friends.

"I curse this city. All of you. My tears shall rain down upon you for all

153

eternity; the heavens shall open, and you will all be drowned in my tears."

With that, the trap beneath her opened, and as her body wrenched and shivered its last in the morning sunlight, the first drops of rain could be felt among the crowd.

---

1 Beard Splitter – Derogatory archaic term for a man who sleeps with a lot of women / also can be found as archaic term for penis
2 Klompen - wooden whole-foot clogs specifically from the Netherlands
3 Gulden – historical German and Dutch term for a gold coin

RICHARD WILKYNS
(died 1610)

Richard Wilkyns, was a farm labourer from Exeter, who had been fiercely accused of witchcraft for most of his adult life. He was eventually charged with killing two women, a man, and causing serious harm to another man and two women. He was also accused, whilst on trial of being responsible for the death of ten pigs, a cow, and a horse. He was, although it is not clear why, found not guilty of the charge slaughtering the ten pigs. He was first accused of witchcraft in 1600 for the death of a woman but was acquitted. His last presumed victim was in 1610, a man whom he had allegedly murdered in the centre of Exeter. He was tried on 9th July that year and hanged three days later.

The Noose Tree

A LIFE UNDONE
Rachael Moss

It was probably the last time he cried. He was 9 now and he'd soon be a man. This time it was a hole the boys had dug in the earth. He often walked this way back home after working with his father in the fields.

He liked the peace of the woods: the stream that trickled through it, the evening birdsong and damp scents bought him some sense of his own being. It was a piece of solitude away from the chaos of his home and of the city where he was often set upon; his body bore the scars of his attackers.

Tonight, they had distracted him by throwing a stone against the trunk of an old oak sending birds flapping to the sky, their alarm calls reverberating into the fading light. His attackers knew his right eye that stared blankly skywards had little sight, so, they always came at him from this side. The long scar that ran down his cheek, and his upwards-gazing eye which mocked the heavens, meant to many folk he looked as though he worked for the devil himself.

Two of them came at him from his blind side, how long had they been waiting there? A quick hard shove and he stumbled and fell into the hole they'd covered with branches, snapping them, cutting his face, as he crashed downwards. Searing pain caused bright light to flood to his vision as he was hit across the head, then battered with sticks as he grappled to stand up. It was always the same words they whispered to him, "evil-eye, devil-spawn," before leaving him, whooping as they ran.

Head hammering, sore, throbbing and bleeding, he staggered home – late, which meant a beating from his father and a scolding from his mother.

Somehow, his family had managed to avoid the plague that was so virulent in Exeter during the 1590s that had proved fatal to so many city-dwellers. He was the youngest of the four surviving children. He couldn't remember how many times his mother had lain in bed ill, but there were two or three sickly babies he remembered leaving this world, and his mother grieving: pale, thin, and sobbing. The cottage was already small and crammed with four children sharing a cold and draughty room. and his mother was always sobbing. She was often bruised also bearing the scars of another's ignorance; she had only borne his father one son, and he was cockeyed and stuck dreamily in a world of his own.

Jane, his sister who was three years his senior, was his friend, they'd talk and share their childish secrets. But she'd gone now, sent off as a servant to one of the big houses, along with his other sisters. He remembered the love his mother gave him when he was small stroking his hair, kissing him, treating his illnesses with rank smelling potions and her weak smile. He had vague memories of her teaching his sisters strange words; shaping objects from clay and adding hair before burning or burying them secretly. But her smiles left her the first time he came home swollen and bleeding, since then she had become distant towards him. As soon as he came of age, he began toiling the fields, fixing fences and buildings, and tending to the livestock on a nearby farm.

The animals were his favourite part of the day. He had a way with them, they trusted him, and unlike people, they would look him in the eye. He knew then the might and wonder of things; he felt their bewilderment, fear, and simple joy. He understood them and their way of being in the moment, the joy of the cattle grazing in a lush pasture, and the pig's squeal of delight at a scratch behind the ear. They were accepting of him, and they didn't judge; they were beyond that. Under Richard's care they bore healthy calves, strong lambs, and large litters of chubby piglets.

One day he caught a neighbour flogging his horse which had collapsed while heaving his master's cart along the road to St Sidwells; where Richard often walked on his way to his sister's. The man had over laden the horse and driven it too far and too fast. The poor creature had fallen, drenched with sweat, eyes rolling shaking in the dust. The man was shouting abuse at it, jets of spittle firing from his lips, lashing the mare with his whip, over and over: her legs kicking, as more and more stripes of blood crossed her flank. Helplessly she fixed her eyes momentarily on Richard, and he felt her frenzied fear and exhaustion; the sting of pain and confusion, and he felt the blood within his veins surge and seethe. He trembled, turning his good eye to look at the man, muttering to himself and in that instant he imagined himself throwing the man to the ground, smashing his face into the road, breaking his nose and crushing his legs with a rock. Richard, however, had remained still as the mare struggled to her feet, but still gripped with fury, she kicked the man to the ground and tugged the cart over his splayed out legs, breaking them. The man, his nose bloodied, broken, and gasping for breath, glanced up at Richard and flinched.

After that, the neighbours began throwing their slops at him, calling him a witch, the children became afraid, and the bigger teenage boys set upon him at every available opportunity. Stones were thrown through the windows of his home and his mother was tormented whenever she left the house.

Over time Richard grew up to be a tall, thin, but strong teenager. He began to try and fight back whenever he was beaten, but there was always more than one boy or man, and it was never worth any extra broken bones. He learnt how to sense when his attackers were nearby, and although his eyesight was bad on his right side, he could picture them in his mind's eye, and so he became more sensitive to their approach. His dark whiskers would quiver when someone was close by and his body would start to seethe and tremble; the scar on his face would burn every time an abuser taunted or threatened him. He would turn to look their way with his wild eye pointing skywards, muttering. In response, they'd stumble and fall silent. Some of his neighbours became ill, and he was accused of maleficium by the gossiping town and country folk.

He would often see folk wearing their Sunday best on their way to church, bound by rules based on fear: never to experience freedom of mind or able to discover their own way of seeing the world around them. He was reminded of the sheep on their way to market as he pondered his own freedom, within the vastness of his imagination and the unfathomable depths of his thoughts, despite the hardship of his life; his power came from within.

When he was 16, he thought he'd fallen in love: puberty and hard work had seen his body grow muscular and his desire matched that of a bull in a field of heifers on heat; uncomplicated with little more than a quick sniff of the genitals followed by sudden mounting and thrusting - it stirred him into an agonising frustration.

She was new at the farm, a niece of the farmer's wife, who had been sent to help out. She was prone to fits, so it was a welcome relief to her own large family to be rid of her and a great help to her aunt and uncle, whose remaining children were all under four years old. She'd milk the cows, and he'd watch, the way she sat on the stool, with her petticoats slightly raised, showing the top of her boots. He'd secretly watch her: her hair falling from beneath her cap, the steam from her breath entwining with that of the cow's, the sweet scent of cud and milk, and the tune of milk squirting into the pail as her fingers eagerly worked their way up and down the teats. It was unbearable. He felt compelled to watch; hidden in the hay barn and peering through the open door of the milking shed.

At night he'd think about her; her fingers, sticky and wet, rhythmically squeezing ... He would dream about her too, but the dreams always ended badly.

She was a bit older than him, perhaps 18, a woman, not a gawky teenager like some of the girls he saw walking down the streets who'd scream and run as soon as they saw him, nor was she like the older women who struck at him with their bitter tongues. She smiled at him once. He'd fed the pigs and was returning to the fields when she came to collect eggs. She had smiled at him, nobody since his mother when he was a child had smiled at him.

It was after that he came to see her one morning as she was milking. Sunlight was bathing her in a pink glow, and he could almost feel the softness of her skin. He bid her a good morning as he entered, suddenly casting a shadow, which startled her and caused her to spill the milk. She looked up at him, a tall burly figure silhouetted against the light. It was the same handsome figure she'd seen from a distance working in the fields and with the animals, and although she tried she was unable suppress a wide-eyed smile. His heart sang; he longed to kiss her lips. He bent to help her rescue the milking pail and the sunlight caught his face, illuminating his upward tilted eye. She screamed, threw the milking stool at him, called him a monster, and shouted at him to get out. He ran off, humiliated.

He could feel the overwhelming repulsion she felt towards him and he felt that hatred cutting him to the bone. He swore that night that he was done with humankind and their wickedness, instead he stayed out late working, or talking to the pigs that looked at him without fear or hatred. He'd sleep in the fields with the cows and avoid going home to his father's anger and his mother's tears. He couldn't help them, beyond giving them his wages; they were stuck in their life of woe.

He avoided the milking barn whenever he could, although occasionally he'd see the woman, and each time she would insult him, every word piercing him, like a dagger to the heart. He'd had enough of being shamed, which was only made worse by the hot pulsing desire he felt for her.

He knew he must have some part of her, and eventually found some of her hair on the flank of the cow where she had rested her forehead. That night he took it with him and wandered into the woods, along the trickling stream, and into the fields where he slept a little, dreaming, under a dark moon.

Next time he saw her he smiled awkwardly. She turned away and fell, muddying her dress, which got her into trouble. The next time, she spilt the day's milk, then the butter curdled. This was followed by dropping the eggs, smashing them, and two days later, after he had bid her good evening her face became covered in acne. She couldn't get this disgusting boy out of her mind. She couldn't sleep, and if she did she had nightmares about his leering face and wonky eye. She stopped eating, she became too frightened to milk the cow or collect the eggs; she was afraid and tormented. She suffered an unbearable stomach pain after he had waved at her from afar, and three days later, she died: twisting in agony and all the while, ranting incoherently. Two days after that, they came for him. Someone from her household must have accused him of causing her death through enchantments.

He was brutally wrenched from his bed early one morning and flung into a rat infested, dark and filthy gaol already occupied by mad, foul smelling men. No open sky or wind in his face, no beasts to find comfort in other than the rats. He became ill and weak, but that wasn't the worst of it. He was stripped naked and strapped to chair shaved and checked for witch marks. Although, he had quite a selection of scars from the beatings he had endured over the years; it was agreed that none of these were actual witch marks.

He was starved, deprived of sleep for 36 hours, and forced to continuously walk around the room. Still, determined, wilful, and escaping within himself, he would not confess.

He was eventually tried around midsummer.

The parishioners at his trial called him an abomination of God: pure evil. They told how he'd beat the boys when he was young and how they'd come home bleeding and battered: how he'd cause folk to fall in the street by glancing at them, and how their children became sick after seeing his upward turned eye. They told how he'd been seen copulating in the mud and faeces with the swine's in their pen, and how they suckled on his blood. He pleaded his innocence in court, amongst all these men with their airs and graces. He said he'd barely spoken to the girl and possibly because of lack of evidence, but more likely, because he was a good worker. The fields and farm flourished under his hand, and the landowner, his employer who had gone along with the court case out of courtesy to his wife's family, had much influence, and so, Richard was acquitted.

After his time in goal, Richard, sickly and depressed, was taunted all the more, and driven from the streets time and again. His mother perished; the strain of constant harassment by her neighbours, ended her sad life. At last, for her, it was over with. Their rented cottage festered without a woman to take care of it.

Richard was burdened with resentment and anger after his imprisonment, torture, and trial. However, he would still collect water, brew beer, and do what he could with curing, salting, and preserving, so that they at least had something to eat and drink.

His father sunk into depression, money became scarce, and they were forced to live on grain and water.

Richard avoided human contact as much as possible, sleeping out when the nights weren't too cold or wet, and sometimes when they were; only returning to the city after dark, leaving before it was light. He burned with anger at being driven to live as an outcast.

He would often imagine causing great suffering or death to those who had wronged him. Sometimes he would have nightmares, where occasionally he'd see shadows moving through the trees or walking across the fields towards him: other times, flashbacks to the prison cell or the endlessly walking back and forth.

So, his life continued. To the animals he'd confide his resentment and they listened unflinchingly. The seasons changed, over and over, likewise his workload: the dance of life and death, new beginnings and endings chasing each other in life's spiral. He became intimate with the movement of the planets across the sky, he learned how they affected the crops and animals. Often, at night he'd sit quietly or wander by a stream, or along the river Exe, drawn there by some potent desire or understanding. The water had always called to him silently, drawing him to it, purifying, clarifying, meditating; although he would avoid the conduits and fountains within the city where people would be.

His only dealings with people were from the brief conversations with his distant father, rare visits to his sister Jane or taking orders at the farm and working with other labourers in the fields; he avoided people on the street. The world of trees, sky, field and river, were the play within his own mind and emotions materialised in the world outside.

In 1603 the plague hit Exeter again, and everal families of the dead or dying would blame Richard and his supposed maleficium.

Then, one spring, another woman came into his life. She was recently widowed; a spinner for the wool industry, and glad to be free of her husband and his demands. She would watch Richard working in the fields, following him home as he lived near her own. His strength and relentless energy and his powerful walk, would have her transfixed. She knew about his supposed bewitchment of the girl and her death, but it only made him more exciting. She stopped him one dusk as he was finishing his day's work, he knew she'd been watching him, and at first this made him jumpy, but her voluptuous figure stirred his unquenched lust.

And so, she took him into the woods, and like the bull in the field, he was upon her. His passion and fury made her weak at the knees; his frustration and anger had found an outlet at last. She'd meet him night after night; her untamed beast.

Despite his mistrust of mankind, he became fond of this woman Mary and she was neither abusive, nor frightened of him. She'd press her hands upon his right eye and grin in satisfaction.

She would love to watch his big-callused hands upon her white skin, and she was always ready for him. Rather than being repulsed, she'd clutch him tightly, pulling him into her. Occasionally they'd be seen together, and Mary would pull away from him, but he thought that this was due to her modesty. His loneliness was abated, and he now had human contact, more physical than companiable, but it was more than he'd had in a long time, and he fell in love.

He'd look forward to their meetings and would hum to himself, his step was lighter, and, for the first time, he felt happy: the nightmares eased, and the anger and resentment mellowed. He became gentle, and eventually he asked her to be his sweetheart; to marry him. After this she didn't come anymore, she'd lost interest in her wild animal now that he had become domesticated.

He searched for her, suffering the torments of passers-by, freezing them with a glance. Wretched and bewildered he combed the streets, bribed children who would take his money, visualised her dwellings in his imagination, until he found her in her dismal lodgings. He stood there forlorn and pleading and she shut the door on him, hard, trapping his fingers. He yelled pushing the door open to free them, and she mistakenly thought he was forcing his way in. This suited her fine, but once he was inside, he grasped her hands gently, knelt on the dirty floor, and like a lost boy asked her again to again marry him; telling her that he didn't want to live without her, and he'd do anything he could for her. She laughed at him, the weak wounded animal, spat in his face, and told him she'd rather marry one of his pigs.

He was hurt by her spite, he felt her abhorrence of his unfurled heart, which was now as bitter and painful as it could be. He turned and walked out into the rain splashed streets, maliciously gawped at by her neighbours, even stung by some boy's catapult; he was broken.

He worked harder to blot out his bewilderment and anger, only finding solace in the natural world around him. The songs of the birds with their different meanings, their flight patterns, what they meant and the voice of the river singing its way downstream: ever in motion and ever changing.

However, his anger and resentment seethed.

He would crave the warmth of a woman's body but wake to the cold damp earth and his own emotional pain. He would see faces in the pale light of dawn and dusk, but when he turned around, he would find nothing there.

One Sunday afternoon in late summer Richard walked to the village of St Sidwells, he visited there as often as he could. The springs which provided water to the city, were a place of great energy. The waters from deep within the earth which bubbled up to the surface, gave him a sense of power, and he was able to forge a strong connection to it: weaving and moulding its relentless vitality. It was here, also, where the springs pulsed upwards, by the East gate, that St Sidwell had been beheaded with a scythe by her father's farm labourers, and this always captured the imagination of Richard.

There was a farmstead, with a sow and 10 piglets that Richard passed on his way home. A girl came past and threw them some scraps. This caused much delight and grunting from the sow, and high pitched squeals from the piglets, who had been hungrily suckling at her teats but were now disturbed as their mother scrambled to her feet. The girl went back in the house taking a quick glance at Richard, before closing the door behind her. A streak of brown fur appeared from the copse, bounding into the pig pen, driven by some primal instinct, and triggered by the high-pitched squealing. Within seconds a thin dog pounced upon the piglets, massacring them. The sow screamed and charged: it all happened in an instant and Richard hurried on his way, knowing it would be blamed on him if he hung around.

A month later, as the sun was lowering in the sky and the blackbirds were crying their evening song, Mary came to him as he was finishing work in the fields. She was weak and sickly with black circles under her eyes, belly swollen, and obviously very ill. She begged him to lift the curse he had surely put upon her, promising to marry him if he did. However, his heart was dead to the world of people, untrusting, unforgiving, and hardened. He told her that he had not knowingly caused her any harm; she staggered home and three days later was dead.

Richard was moved from duties and reposted further away from the estate buildings by the landowner, who was even more suspicious of Richard after Mary's death, and was concerned in case a household member should catch his evil eye. Having been banished to the outskirts of the expanding property meant that he no longer had access to the pigs and was further deprived of comfort or companionship.

Late summer gave way to the chill and damp of autumn, and with it the promise of winter.

All the seasons held beauty to Richard, but perhaps winter most of all; the cold would blot out everything but the essential need to work and stay alive. He would watch the delicate ice crystals as water turned from liquid to solid, then back again as it was freed, and released back to life. He'd admire the glittering frost, the pure white blankets of snow, and the starkness of the naked trees; when the world was in darkness, he was alone under the breath-taking wonder of the shimmering night sky. He felt at home in the infinity of it all, its predictability and perfection.

Life continued, the fields were ploughed, sown, and harvested, more hedge banks built, more areas of land cultivated on the steep hillsides, channels dug, exhausted men would till the land with mattocks, and tired horses were used to further break up the red Devonshire soil: fields were harrowed, fertilised, buildings fixed, and new labourers employed for the expansion of the farm. In June and July, the countryside would be thick in a haze of burning earth, where fires would destroy the weeds.

One night Richard had to fetch a neighbour who was known as a wise woman, as his father had been taken ill and he had been up all night tending to him with the help of one of his sisters, and the next morning he returned to work leaving his sister with his father. The wise woman, who had been one of the few who had been kind to Richard, was sent away by his sister who insisted she could heal him herself; four days later his father passed-away.

Richard's eldest sister moved into the cottage with her family, and the tension there was un-nerving. The children taunted him and his brother in law tried to drive him from the house.

Late autumn he was returning to the pastures to check on the bull's progress with the cows, when he heard the mournful sound of their cries echoing from the vale. Hurrying along, he arrived at the northern top of the hilly field where he saw that the cattle were breaking out, stampeding through the woods, wildly thrashing their back legs, snorting; snot flying from their nostrils as their hooves churned the ground into ruts. A figure stood by the gate. The man glanced at Richard, who felt a sudden unexplained shock, and then whistled as he briskly walked away. Richard was struck by the way this man held himself, the confidence he exuded, the way his greying hair wound tightly into corkscrews down his back, and the strange way he briefly held his gaze. He jolted and fear wound tightly cross his chest. His fear was realised as on the ground, by the gate lay the body of a cow; Richard ran to her. Her wild eyes stared blankly, and her soft mouth was open. He crouched down next to her and whispered gently to her.

Two labourers, hearing the commotion from the cattle, came rushing. They saw Richard leaning over the body of the cow and swore at him. Eventually, with his help, the cattle were returned to their field and Richard filled in the gap in the hedge bank where the cattle had escaped from the field.

His relationship with the other labourers was not at all friendly, but they mostly gave him a wide berth rather than physically confront him. They tolerated him because he did a lot of their share of the work; they would shout abuse at him, and he would ignore it. However, the next day four of them ambushed him, kicking, and punching him, breaking his teeth and ribs, accusing him of sending the cattle into a frenzy, and killing the cow.

A few weeks later, his body still aching, he was ploughing a field using the old chestnut cob and another gelding, when the stranger reappeared out of the trees, waving his hands. The old horse, usually calm and steady, suddenly reared his head, and strained at the reins, whinnying. The creature staggered and swayed, and Richard had to soothe the beast, whilst the other horse snorted and tossed his head, although appeared otherwise less perturbed. The man once again disappeared.

Ploughing was slow progress after that with the old horse twitchy and nervous. It was after dusk by the time he returned the horse to its paddock and the other labourers were returning home, hurling abuse his direction. He stayed with the horse that night, in the cold listening to owls crying their sorrowful tunes into the darkness. Towards the dawn a fox slinked by, edging closer, grey, and indistinct in the fading last quarter of the moon. The poor old horse fell to the ground, still.

Two creatures were dead after the stranger had appeared, and also the labourers were angry, for they believed Richard had killed the beasts with his wicked enchantments, in revenge for his banishment to the edges of the estate. They complained heartily until Richard lost his job, and when he turned up for work the following morning, he was badly beaten. Without his work and the animals, Richard was lost. On top of which he could no longer pay the rent on the cottage, so responsibility for it fell onto his brother in law and eldest son. The younger two children would beg or steal in order to make ends meet.

He would only sleep at the cottage with his sister's family when the nights were freezing; their displeasure at his presence was too much for him. Other nights he would sleep in the woods, creatures snuffling around him. Sometimes, in the flickering light of the moon, he thought he caught glimpses of the mysterious stranger sneaking through the trees, but when he blinked, he was gone.

During the day he searched for work at neighbouring farms, but the door was always slammed in his face; the frightened eyes and bitter tongues of the householders drowning in their fear.

Desperate, he returned to his former employer, intending to ask him for his job back: a servant answered the door and refused him entry. Beyond dejection, hunger, frustration, and weariness, Richard shuffled off, ridiculed by the stable boy who passed him on his way back to the city.

He had little to live for, but he had known some joy in his work and in the presence of the creatures with their honesty and understanding, and in the patterns found in the world of nature there was meaning and purpose. In the waters of the stream there was continuation, change and immense power. He needed to return to the fields and the farm before he starved.

Anger bubbled away inside him and he sought revenge on the stranger who had taken away what little joy and comfort he had.

The winter was bitterly cold, and Richard was forced to spend the nights with his sister's family. One of her children died, which meant there was one less mouth to feed, but another was on the way.

Then the news came that his employer had become sick. The doctor had been called, and rumours had spread accusing Richard of maleficarum. He decided to leave the city, and all the misery it had caused him, behind.

It was a mid-winter's day when he once again walked to the village of St Sidwells, carrying a small box containing his belongings. He set off to visit the springs, and his youngest sister.

Jane was the one person in the entire world where he really knew love. He'd visited her from time to time, after he had been to the springs, but what with the work on the land and her being busy with her children and home, his visits were always fleeting. This time he was hoping that her husband could find him work.

They were short of labourers on the land: the recent outbreak of the plague had taken four men and replacements had not yet been found. The gorse fields needed men to harvest and process the firewood. When the ground thawed there would be much work to be done making new hedge banks, and when spring came new workers would be desperately needed.

It was a risk. While the surrounding farmland of East Devon, was further away from the city, and may not know of Richard's reputation, there was always the chance someone would. And there was of course his unusual eye, which had caused him so much trouble in the past. Jane suggested he tried to wear his hair so that it flopped in front of his right eye, hiding it a little. Following her advice, he found work in the fields north of St Sidwells and squeezed into the cottage with his sister's family.

Apart from his short affair with Mary, these were probably the happiest times of his life. He celebrated mid-winter and Yule there. The children liked him, and he developed a close friendship with one of the little girls who he'd make toys for, playing with them in the long winter evenings. Unlike adults, young children didn't judge him, and he devoured their openness and innocence.

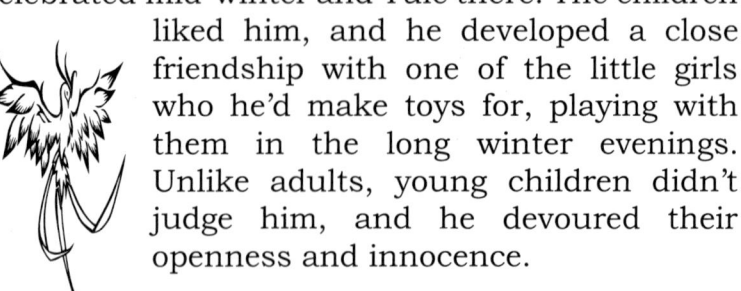

Winter turned to spring, the primroses threw open their pale yellow faces, lambs frolicked, buds burst; the world became pregnant with longing and potential. Seeds, full of infinite possibilities, were sown, and unfurled into manifestation.

Light, and hope flourished. Richard worked hard and kept himself to himself as much as possible. The days grew long and hot, then shorter and cold, as the seasons changed once more.

The other labourers thought Richard odd, as he'd spend time with the animals, talking to them and would never speak to other workers unless necessary. He had a strange manner about him: the way he walked, his atmospheric presence, and the way he would regularly sleep out in the woods and fields or be seen wandering in the moonlight. These things unsettled them, and, once again, rumours began to spread about him. Witchcraft seemed to become more widespread, and it's punishments more severe since King James came to the throne three years earlier. By this time, the new, harsher laws against it had sparked more unrest and Richard's life began to get more difficult again. He was watched closer and more talked about. Some people saw him by the springs and accused him of spoiling the water that flowed into the city. He caught glimpses of the strange man he'd seen near the dead cow and before the old cob died and his nightmares started up again.

One morning he thought saw the stranger standing in the shadow of an elm tree, with a dead ewe lying on her side, by his feet and crows pecking out her eyeballs. When he glanced up the stranger had gone.

The woman who had been throwing the pigs, the slops at the time the piglets were killed by a dog, heard the rumours about Richard and began to gossip about his presence there that time. He, according to her, killed the pigs with his bewitchment.

His sister's family were threatened, and his relationship with the children altered, they became wary and resentful of him. He'd been to see the woman with the pigs and explained that a dog had killed the piglets, begging her to believe him, but she had slammed the door in his face, screaming obscenities at him.

Richard held onto his job, once again because the land and animals flourished with him there, but his nightmares were increasing. He would see the hangman's gallows looming over him, the curly-haired man would flit between the trees and smirk at him from the shadows.

At night he would go to the springs with their primal swirling and speak to the waters.

The following winter the woman who had accused him of killing the pigs fell ill. She lay in bed with a fever, writhing and hallucinating. Her illness dragged on until the spring, when finally, she recovered. During that time, another woman in the village become ill with the same symptoms. Richard, an easy scapegoat was blamed. Richard's past had caught up with him, gossip had spread from Exeter and he became widely spoken about. As far as they were concerned he was responsible for numerous illness, deaths, and more specifically there was the man with the horse and cart who was injured all those years ago. Then, there was the woman who had milked the cows on the previous farm, the death of Mary, the death of the pigs, the cow and the horse, the illness of his previous employer, and his general reputation and oddity. Now, there were two more women who had become very ill.

He became a poor, lonely, feral creature.

Humanity had disowned him. Even his sister had begun to wonder at the rumours about him as before he left her home he had become more and more agitated and prone to tempers. The children, who he had grown to love, especially the youngest girl, were now frightened of him. He spent much of his time muttering to himself. Having known happiness, it was harder for him to have it snatched away, as any joy in his life had been.

He was driven out of the village, and the farm, and forced to live, banished, to the surrounding countryside: hunting partridges, rabbits, hares, fishing, and foraging. Sometimes his tall lone figure would be seen walking the hills, gesturing. At times, men would try and hunt him down but somehow he managed to evade them. Always the man with the ringlets would haunt his dreams and waking hours.

Winter was especially hard for Richard. He managed to catch a few hares, as their prints would show in the snow, but he was always hungry, and desperately cold. His hair and beard had grown matted, his clothes were tattered, and both his eyes looked wild. He lived by instinct, like an animal, and thought only of revenge upon the man who shape-shifted in the shadows.

By the time spring came around again, Richard was weak and half-starved, but a few plump baby rabbits, hares and even a fox cub, gradually began to rebuild his body. He returned to the springs in the early hours, before dawn most mornings, to draw upon the strength that the waters gave him.

One morning, as shoots thrust from the Earth, buds burst from the trees, the ground was soaked with dew, and the creamy pink light of dawn had begun to break through the night, Richard was leaving the springs and heard carriage wheels rattling along the cart road towards Exeter. Crouching in the half-light he watched as it trundled by. Suddenly he was jolted in shock when from inside the carriage he caught sight of a long strand of ringlet hair tumbling over the shoulder of a man. It was him! The stranger who haunted him.

Richard jumped up and ran after the carriage, leaping onto the back and clinging on. He steadied himself as the carriage bumped its way down the road, edging his way towards the right side door. Grabbing the handle, he managed to fling the door open so that it crashed against the side, the driver pulled up sharply, and the motion threw Richard to the ground. The passenger was truly startled, as the face of a wild creature with an eye pointing skywards loomed down at him through the suddenly wrenched open door, and although Richard was silhouetted he saw enough of his face to be absolutely terrified; the look of a savage animal intent on its kill stared him directly in the eye, only for a moment, but more than long enough to stir terror in the man. This was no ordinary bandit. Richard felt his fear and feasted on it.

Richard leapt up like a cornered animal just as the driver was getting down with his whip, slicing it through the air. The end of it caught him across the shoulder and another across the chest, he fought back ferociously, trying to punch and kick the man, but the whip was long. Richard was lashed mercilessly, leaving long crimson gashes across his flesh beneath his ripped clothing. Still he wouldn't stop fighting. The driver, who was worried about going too far and killing him, quickly leapt up onto his seat when Richard stumbled, and sped the horses on.

Richard spun himself round after his stumble to see the carriage jerk away in a cloud of dust that stung his eyes, choking him. On the side of the carriage was wording he recognised the shape of. It was a wool-merchants in central Exeter. At last he knew where to find him. His body burned with pain, but he limped away triumphant. He remembered the look of total fear in the man's eyes as he held them for that brief moment, and he vowed to make that image burn in his mind forever.

Richard managed to heal his wounds with plantain, woundwort, and yarrow. He was being searched for by men on horses and dogs. He hid during the day in badger sets, fox dens and sometimes in trees; he would follow streams where possible, to mask his scent from the dogs.

At night, he harvested plants under the dark moon: speaking into the gloom he would bind them together.

When midsummer was approaching, Richard walked to Exeter one night as the moon was beginning to fade, with the scent of honeysuckle in the hedgerows, and meadowsweet in the pasture, filling his nostrils and fuelling his wild desire. His destination was the headquarters of the wool merchants. He was hunting down his prey. He arrived in the city just as dawn was breaking amidst the cacophony of birdsong. He skulked down the quiet streets where vagrants lay in the filth and passed a couple of prostitutes who were trudging wearily home after their night's work. Eventually, he reached the headquarters - the wool merchants in St Mary Arches Parish. He hid down a side alley and waited.

As the sun rose, a brazen yellow, heaving from the grimy rooftops, and casting deep shadows across the cobbled streets, as people started to appear; market traders with their wares, young boys with thieving fingers dashed across the roads, and the stench of fish from fishmongers swarmed the air. Still, in the shadows, Richard waited.

A carriage came trundling along and stopped in front of the wool merchants. It bore the same writing as the carriage on the St Sidwell's road. He waited. The door was opened by the driver and a man stepped out wearing a green apron with red strings, he was short, and his hair was limp. It wasn't the man he wanted. The man walked into the building and disappeared.

Richard continued to wait, agitated, as the streets became busier and noisier. Eventually, another carriage pulled up outside the building with the same writing on the side. Richard held his breath. The driver opened the door, and a man was helped down onto the pavement. He also wore the green apron with the red strings; he was frail and weak, thin, and pale. He had corkscrew hair. Richard leaped from his hiding place, knocking down a woman in his way and confronted the man whose eyes were now wide-open in terror. He dropped dead right there on the pavement and was caught by the startled driver.

A sudden fear gripped Richard as a realisation coursed through him. He ran, and he ran, towards the river, sending cartloads of wares tumbling as he went, his strength and size enabling his passage. He ran and ran like a hare chased by hounds and ended up on the marshes. He waded slowly through them under the blazing sun, sending birds, shrieking, into the sky. He was exhausted but trudged on, sinking deeper with each step.

Eventually he came out onto drier land and headed to the trees, where he sat, shaking, against the trunk of an oak; comforted by its shade. He was frightened and bewildered. The man outside the wool merchants wasn't the man who'd been responsible for the death of the cow, the horse, or the ewe. He wasn't the man who flitted in the shadows or who he glimpsed in the lonely moonlight. He wasn't the man who stalked his dreams, but it was the man on the St Sidwells road, and the driver was the same. He had made a mistake. He howled into the copse; sunlight flickering through the trees in a confusing dance, and he wept.

He slept from sheer exhaustion. When he woke the shadows were longer, the wood pigeons were calling from the branches. He loped off, directionless.

They found him the next day, further up-river, wandering through the trees in a small wood. Five of them felled him and dragged him, for a mile, until he gave in, resigned to his fate; they took him to the goal.

His trial didn't last long. He barely spoke and didn't bother defending himself. He was broken and accepting, although the fear and powerlessness he felt at his fate was unbearable. He could already feel the rope about his neck, rough and thick, and the moment when his body will fall, the snap when his neck will break and how his body will shudder and jerk, as his life slips away from him.

He was convicted of the death of the milk maid: the death of Mary, a cow, a horse, of bewitching his ex-employer, the woman with the pigs and the other woman who had become ill just after, and finally, the death of the wool merchant. Two days after sentencing he was dragged helplessly to the gallows, to the sound of the cheering of the crowd below. As his neck snapped and his body danced, his right eye turned downward towards the crowds. There he hung, until the eye that had caused him so much grief in his life was pecked out, and swallowed by a crow who soared off, out of the city, and into the blue skies: high above the toiled land, tangled woods, and meandering, shimmering river to be returned once more to the raging sea.

JOAN, MARGARET AND PHILLIPA FLOWER
(Died 1618)

The events surrounding the deaths of Henry and Francis Lord Ros happened between 1612 and 1620; there was little evidence of foul play, never mind witchcraft. In fact, the Flowers women were tried five years after leaving the service of the Earl of Rutland at Belvoir and Francis lived for a further two years after. Therefore, in the spirit of keeping the narrative consistent, some of the dates have been changed to represent a shorter time frame, but all events still lead up to the recorded date of the trial: 11th March 1618 in Lincoln, which was documented by J.Barnes in his pamphlet "A Wonderful Discovery of Witchcrafts," published in 1619. Excerpts of this text have been included for authenticity.

The Flowers of Bottesford

THE FLOWERS OF BOTTESFORD
Esme Knight

SUMMER - THE KINGS VISIT – 1612

The castle was abuzz with people; far more people than Katherine had ever seen at Belvoir before. Maids, cooks, and footmen darted from place to place airing drapes, polishing silver, and scrubbing floors in preparation for the Royal visit next week: everything had to be perfect.

Katherine's father was Francis Manners, 6th Earl of Rutland, and he was good friends with the King, or so he told Katherine and her brothers. He had many fancy titles and was always being called to some far-away country on royal business when he was not at court. It was seldom that she got to see him at all; most of the time it was just herself, her two brothers, (well, stepbrothers) and Lady Frances, her father's new wife. Katherine had been told to address her as 'mother,' but only did so to avoid getting into trouble. It was even worse now that baby Francis had come; her father doted on him and spent any spare time he had with him. It was bad enough when Henry had come along three years ago, but now there were two boys in the household; she barely got a look in and could not see it improving as she got older.

She rested her chin on her hand and stared out of the window; a team of gardeners were tending the lawn and chipping away at the hedges. She had been told to keep out of the way. Even her nurse was busy – somewhere – Nanny was helping the tailors and seamstresses with new clothes for all the children. She was bored and feeling left out so she jumped up from the window seat, found her shoes, and decided to go for a walk to occupy the time. She wandered along the oak panelled corridors, hazed with dust kicked up from all the furious cleaning, until eventually she reached her father's study. She peered through the open door, but he was not in there. Disheartened she carried on through the house; Belvoir was a big rambling place, and even though Katherine had lived there all her life, she still had not explored all of it. What better time than now to start when no one was paying her any mind? And so, it was that eight year old Lady Katherine Manners spent the next hour creeping in and out of rooms, poking in cupboards, and generally going unnoticed until she stepped through a small wooden door and found herself in the bright daylight of a courtyard unlike any she had seen before.

It wasn't the wide and clattering courtyard where the coach and horses were kept, but a stony square yard with a well. Half barrels cluttered the small space, spilling dirty water and grey suds onto the cracked flagstones and the air hung sharp with the scent of soap. Three women were arguing while they washed bedsheets and table linens in the soapy tubs, twisting and squeezing them, before draping them over a rope which had been strung between the narrow walls so that they billowed and drew like sails in the gentle summer breeze.

Katherine shrank back into the doorway and listened. The youngest of the three, named Pippa, had a new suitor: Thomas Simpson, whom she had loved since she was a girl, but it was only this spring that she learned he loved her too. Both of them had to end their courtships with others before they could be together and were now understandably besotted with one another. It was all very romantic thought Katherine.

The other two women were cautious of this new romance, to say the least. The older woman who was doing most of the berating appeared to be the girls' mother, while the third woman, the elder sister Maggie, mostly tried to stop the bickering.

"Another young man? What will people say? Really Pippa, you should be more considerate and think of others too." snapped the old woman, gesturing at herself and her other daughter "Folk tattle and it's hard enough as it is to find work."

"You find it hard to get work" Pippa retorted "'cause you're so nasty all the time. I never have any trouble getting work and usually it's not as back breaking as this." She put her hands into the small of her back and leant over her elbows.

"Oh yes, we all know how you find work, you slattern!" Joan Flower had been taken ill with a strange sickness last winter and, ever since, her manner had completely changed. Where before she had been kindly and well liked, she was now generally rude, envious, and ill-tempered. The sickness had altered her face as well as her mind, giving her a strange countenance. The left side of her cheek slumped, affecting her speech which, when it did make sense, was full of oaths and curses. She had gone from being a competent woman to an afflicted crone overnight.

"Mother!" Maggie interjected, "That is not true; Pippa might be flighty, but she has always been sweet on the boy and you know it. They were both just too proud to tell one another for fear of rejection or embarrassment; I think it's lovely." She smiled and nodded at her sister in approval, who beamed back at her, jigged on the spot, and clapped her hands. Turning to her mother Maggie continued,

"And don't use words like that. If folks hear you say it about your own girl, they'll think there's merit in it."

"She casts a bad name for all of us, why do you always stand up for her? The shadow of it falls on you too." said the old woman, shaking her finger at Maggie.

"Because she's my little sister and it's my job; now stop belly-aching, the pair of you and get working or you'll be losing this job too." Maggie huffed off to a tub and dunked another sheet into the suds as the women sulked in silence.

Katherine had been watching all this through the narrowing and widening gaps in the line of linens as they were blown by the wind; suddenly the sheet was drawn back with a wet flap, startling Katherine who let out a yelp, echoed by a similar cry of surprise from Maggie who had just discovered the girl peering around the doorframe. Their squeals drew the attention of Joan and Pippa: their previous quarrel forgotten, they halted their work and stood to wind their way through the washing lines to see what had caused Maggie fright.

"Lord, mercy me!" exclaimed Maggie, clasping her hand over her mouth. She softened her tone when she saw the girl was startled too. "What are you doing there? You gave me a fright."

"Ooh, a little girl; she's so pretty, and clean." cooed Pippa, bending down. "Where did you come from little one? Are you lost?"

"I'm Katherine; I live here." said Katherine. All three women drew back with a low gasp as apprehension flitted across their faces. Katherine continued in the hope it would put them at ease:

"It's alright, my Father owns this house; he's the Earl." This didn't appear to help as the women recoiled even further and began to talk amongst themselves in hushed tones.

"What is she doing down here?" said the old mother.

"She must be lost." replied Pippa.

"Shouldn't someone be looking after her?" Maggie asked. "Surely she's not all the way down here on her own?"

193

"We'll be in trouble for this, mark my words." grumbled mother, taking a furtive look around at the empty courtyard, checking for traitorous gossips who would tattle.

"Let's just take her back up to the house proper; there might even be a favour in it for us." said Pippa.

"We should take her to the house because that's where she belongs Pippa, not because you might get a pie for your trouble." Maggie scolded. "You stay here and carry on with the whites; I'll take her. Neither of you can be trusted to talk to the kitchen staff, ne'ermind Housekeeping."

Katherine furrowed her brow while the women tossed back and forth what to do with her; it occurred to her that she could probably do mostly what she pleased, and three washer women were not going to stop her. On the other hand, if a servant had to drag her home and tell that she had been found wandering around by herself, everyone would be in trouble and she'd be in bed with no supper for a week.

Katherine piped up "I can hear you, you know."

Phillipa, Margaret, and Joan Flower halted their talk mid-sentence, and all turned to look at the girl in unison. In that moment, the familial resemblance was striking, and Katherine thought they looked a little like the waterfowl she had seen on the lake, as they all craned their necks to face her at the same time. She giggled, she couldn't help it;

it broke the spell and Pippa giggled too, followed by a chuckle from Maggie. Joan however just gave a loud disgruntled snort and shuffled off back to her wash tub.

"Don't say I didn't warn you." she chuntered as she disappeared between the flapping cloth.

Maggie turned to the girl. "Are you lost?"

Katherine shook her head. "I'm exploring." she replied.

"Do you know where you are?"

"The ... Laundry?" Katherine's eyes matched her guess.

"Do you know how to get back?" This time the girl shook her head, looked down at her feet, paused, and then turned her gaze back toward Maggie. For a second, Maggie thought perhaps she saw a flicker of fear in Katherine's eyes, and her kind heart melted.

"Would you like me to take you back to Be'voir?" This time the girl nodded, and a shy smile twisted at her lips.

"Thank you, exploring is hard work." Katherine told her, looking back down to her shuffling toes. "And if I'm not back for tea, then Nanny will miss me, and I won't be able to go exploring anymore."

Maggie sighed; she felt for the girl. Who wouldn't want to ramble around a beautiful place like Belvoir Castle? Though she reckoned that if the girl's parents, the Earl and Countess, knew she was having as much fun (as any girl her age should), unsupervised too, poor little Lady Katherine would be confined to a room and not let out until her wedding day. She wiped the suds from her elbows on her apron. Maggie looked at Pippa, raising an eyebrow, and gave a nod towards Joan. Pippa recognised that look; she sighed heavily and rolled her eyes, then turned, ducked deftly under a sheet and was gone from sight. Knowing that Pippa was keeping her eye on her mother, Maggie then turned back to Katherine and with a little curtsy said,

"Come on then, m'lady. Let's get you back in time for tea." Off the pair went, headed through the small wooden door, out of the yard.

★

It was the day of the King's visit and the frantic buzz of activity had been condensed to a stressful hum as the household staff quietly moved about the castle, adding finishing touches. Fresh flowers in every room, clean linen on every bed whether it was to be occupied or not. Katherine was standing on a footstool in front of the huge mirror in Lady Frances' dressing room, her hair tied in rags, while Nanny tugged at the buttons on her bodice. She felt ridiculous. The cloth was stiff and bulky, restricting her movement and making her fidget; Nanny scolded her to keep still but the starched collar scratched her neck. Katherine wriggled her shoulders, resigning herself to a quiet sulk, while her stepmother reeled off a list of what to do and what not to do in the presence of the King.

"Now, now child. We cannot be having long faces today." snapped Lady Frances, noticing the sullen look on Katherine's face from where she sat across the room, drinking a hot cup of the very new and fashionable China Tcha.

"It is vitally important that we do not embarrass your father in front of the King, so remember, smile coyly, be polite, don't stare, lower your gaze once you have shaken hands, don't fidget with your clothes, or shuffle your feet. Keep your back straight, don't chatter, and don't interrupt. In fact, don't speak except to greet His Majesty. If he asks you a question, keep your answer short, and to the point, and stay with Nanny at all times. And lastly, curtsy just like I showed you. Do you think you can manage that? And no wandering off; do not think I have not noticed." Her stepmother brought the delicate cup to her lips and narrowed her eyes over the top if it, peering at Katherine as she took a sip.

"How many children do you think get to meet the King of England? Remember just how lucky you are."

Katherine did not feel lucky; she felt hot and itchy: a perfect captive audience for Lady Frances as she carried on with her little speech.

"A Lady does not sour her face, and that's what you are Katherine, a Lady. Someday, if you do well, you will have a husband with your own family and household to tend to, then you will understand what duty is and you will be grateful for this advice." Lady

Frances smoothed down her skirts and shuffled in her seat, ironically as uncomfortable in her dress as Katherine was in hers. Why was it so important to meet the stupid King anyway? Her father only cared about her brothers. She had recently found out from her new friend Maggie that girls could not be an Earl even if they were the eldest. It didn't seem fair to her, but it was suddenly starting to make sense why her stepmother wanted her to act a certain way: girls were only good for looking pretty, being quiet, and waiting to be married to someone rich and important. They could never become rich and important themselves and you wouldn't be able to 'catch a match' as Lady Frances put it, 'If one did not deport oneself correctly.' She wasn't sure what that meant exactly, but she did know it meant a whole world of boredom: no exploring, no fun, and no friends. Just being quiet and still for hours on end while wearing horribly uncomfortable clothes.

    She had visited the small stone yard every afternoon over the last couple of weeks and watched the Flower women wash whatever the housekeepers brought down to them, listening to them chatter. They spoke about their lives away from the castle and always made sure she was back in time for tea. She felt envious of the freedom of the simplicity of their lives. She understood that they were poor, but the kind of wealth they shared through family and love, even despite the bickering, was something she had never experienced with her father and stepmother. Nanny and her other nurses were kind and affectionate enough, sure - but she did not feel close to them.

Maggie asked her things about herself that no one had ever bothered to find out before, and she enjoyed talking with her. She told Maggie how she liked marmalade for breakfast and loved to watch the sunset from the high window of her nursery. Maggie squirmed with her when she told her that she had once found a big frog by the pond but had been too scared to touch it. She talked more in the little laundry yard on those sunny days before the King's visit than she had to anyone else in the castle, ever; it was wonderful.

She watched the enamoured Pippa sing and dance about her love, skipping between the washing lines as she worked and began to realise that her life was destined for something entirely different. Perhaps not servants' work, but servitude of another kind, that of a Lady of high society: dutiful, polite, and subdued. Constantly at the mercy of decisions made by men like her father. She would never be able to laugh, sing, and chatter freely as these women did.

Yesterday Mother Flower was griping on about one of the other women who worked at Belvoir. A house maid had snubbed Joan, causing her to tell the maid to mind her manners. The maid had complained to the Cook that the old laundry woman had spoken to her in a tone that was not fitting for a washer woman who was only here for the Royal visit, while *she* held a permanent position. In turn the Cook had gone to the Butler, who had spoken to the Housekeeper. She had scolded Joan Flower about her unfavourable disposition and said that if she heard of anything like that happening again, she would be dismissed.

"I don't see why you are surprised." said Pippa, "This always happens; everywhere you go, you say summat nasty to the higher ups and they tell you to sling your hook. Why can't you just be nice for a change?" Pippa frowned and scrubbed the cloth harder against the ridged metal washboard half submerged in the tub.

"Well I got respect for myself, haven't I?" Mother Flower drew herself up, jutting out her chin. "I won't be spoken to like that by a mere girl. Who does she think she is, Duchy of Rutland?"

Once again Maggie stepped in "But you didn't have to cuss at her." She exchanged glances with Katherine, as if to teach a lesson.

"If she'd've minded her manners and asked me nice, I would have tol' her the an'imacassers were next after the tablecloths. But no, she had to call me a lazy crone." Joan bristled with anger. "There's a lesson for you, my little Lady. It dun't matter hoo y'are, born high or low, dun't matter – manners cost nuthin. Even if you've got nowt – you've got your digni'y."

In fairness Katherine could see her point: the women had been working hard from first light until dusk every day, and at this time of year that was late into the evening, just to make sure that every piece of fabric in the whole castle was clean for the stupid King and his royal visit. The pile in the laundry just kept growing as more linens were brought down. Her father was anxious about impressing King James and constantly barked orders at domestic staff left and right to clean this, and wash that; no wonder the women were getting overwhelmed.

All this fuss for one stupid King. Nanny tugged at the knotted cotton rags in her hair, pulling her out of her reverie and back into the moment. She stared at herself in the mirror; was this all there was? That was the moment it began: the anger, the determination, all the things that drove Lady Katherine to eventually become the richest woman in England outside of the Royal Family remained with her until her last days. Many years later as she lay dying of plague in Ireland, in the home of her second marriage, it was this moment that she remembered. In this moment she had made a choice, with the ringlets falling about her face, in the first of many awful dresses she would wear throughout her life. She locked eyes with her reflection in the gilded mirror and clenched her fists, resolving that she would never be just somebody's wife, she would be *Somebody*.

What happened to the Flower women was only more evidence of how easily women can be disposed of. Was it because they were her friends? Because they stood up for her, or because they taught her to stand up for herself? She never truly knew; what she did know was that they did not murder her brothers by sorcery.

★

The King's visit came and went. James I was at Belvoir for a total of five days and nights, though Katherine only saw him a handful of times during his stay. He mostly spent time with her father and the Duke of Buckingham, a man named George Villiers; the three men cavorted like they were boys again. George was softly spoken and unassuming in comparison to the King and the Earl, but kind and generous. He even took the time to talk with Katherine at repast most afternoons. He too had an overbearing mother, something which they immediately bonded over. She had not seen her father laugh and jest this much before; it was clear that he and the Duke were the King's friends as well as his devoted subjects.

However, Katherine was eager to return to her own newly made friends: Maggie, Pippa and even Joan, as soon as she could after the King had departed. The very next day she hurriedly snaked her way through the castle to the wash house and the little stone yard. She burst through the open doorway calling out "Maggie! Maggie!" but in the yard stood two women she had never seen before. She froze and her heart sank into the hollow pit of her stomach. Katherine opened and closed her mouth, but no words came out. Tears prickled her eyes and she was about to turn tail and run, when just at that moment Maggie stepped out of the laundry door at the other end of the yard, her arms full of white sheets. Katherine ran to her and flung her arms about the woman's waist.

"Maggie, I missed you."

Maggie Flower looked apologetically at the new laundry maids, pulled the girl off her, and set down the linen. She looked down into the expectant face, wide eyes rimmed with tears, and placing her hands on Katherine's shoulders she softly spoke "What are you doing down here, girl? Won't you get in trouble?"

"Where's Pippa, and Mother Joan?" she asked, shooting a dark look over her shoulder at the other women, who were failing miserably at pretending to not pay attention to the Earl's daughter hugging a scullery maid. Maggie took her to one side, ducking under a line of wet sheets, where they sat on a wicker hamper. Katherine was starting to get nervous; she could feel bad news coming.

"Mother and Pippa have been dismissed from Belvoir. They have been sent to the poultry." Maggie said quietly.

"Mother got into another argument."

The poultry was the dairy farm that supplied Belvoir with fresh milk, cheese, and eggs, and also meat when there was no game. The pay was half of that of the laundry, and no accommodation either. If they couldn't find lodgings in Bottesford, they'd be in with the cattle or out on the moor.

"No!" shrieked Katherine. Maggie quickly shushed her and continued.

"This time it wasn't really her fault. Yes, she did cuss the man, but he was ... " Maggie trailed off searching for the right words to explain what was, in fact, a quite horrific event to an eight-year-old. "He sort of ... grabbed Pippa and tried to hurt her. Pippa screamed for him to let her alone and Mother Joan went over to stop him and tore his coat ..."

"Tore his coat?" Maggie was right: Katherine didn't understand, but she could see that her friend's face was serious and sad instead of the relaxed smile Maggie usually wore She was also clever enough to know that there was more that Maggie wasn't telling her.

"It's a bit more complicated than that, especially for a nice young Lady like yourself, but when you're older you'll understand." Maggie didn't know how else to say it. How do you tell a young girl that it wouldn't matter if you were high born or not, if a man wanted your body, he could take it and you had no way to defend yourself? If you did, then it would be you who was punished, not he. She was grateful that her sister and mother had only lost their jobs and not their lives. Maggie had been retained since there was no just reason to dismiss her other than family connections. She had neither seen the assault nor the altercation that followed; neither had she been in any trouble before, so she'd been able to keep her wage and bed at the castle.

"I'll talk to father and tell him that the man was wrong, that he should go, and they should come back here, to the laundry, so I can see them." Katherine offered. Deep down she knew that it wouldn't work, she may be the Earl's daughter and a Lady, but she was still a little girl who no one took seriously.

Maggie took her hand and gave her a kindly look.

"Thank you, my sweet girl, but it's best we just try and forget about it, and ..." She paused, torn between self-preservation, her family's safety, and this poor lost little girl. Katherine's brow furrowed, her eyes pleading Maggie not to say what was coming next. "And I think it would be a good idea if you didn't come and visit me anymore." She saw the tears welling in Katherine's eyes and fixed her gaze on their interlocked fingers instead. Her voice was small and barely audible, "I don't want to get into trouble and lose my job too. If folk found out that you'd been playing down here, well, I don't know what could happen, but I'd rather not find out"

Katherine slumped against Maggie's shoulder, pressing her face to the rough cloth of her dress to scrub away the tears.

"But you're my only friend." She sobbed, "No one else talks to me. I'll be all on my own"

"I know, darling girl, I know." Maggie hugged her tight and kissed the top of her head. "But it's for the best." She lied. The edges of her own eyes were beginning to fill with tears now too. Quickly blinking them away she uncurled the girl from the tight embrace. "Now, now. We must be strong. For each other and for Mother and dear Pippa too … understand?" Katherine nodded. "In a while, this will have blown over and you can visit again, but, not now, at least, not until the autumn. Then we'll see." It was the height of summer and a good couple of months before autumn. Maggie hoped that Katherine would have forgotten about the maids she befriended, and it would become no more than a curious tale she would tell at court about the folly of her youth, and hopefully keep her family safe.

AUTUMN - DEATH OF AN HEIR - 1612

The months passed slowly for Katherine without the company of her friends; only visiting the laundry on a handful of occasions, and then only for a short time. After a few visits, Maggie suggested she waited until after church on Sunday when the staff were given a half day. She would meet Katherine at the groundsman's gate to the gardens, where they could sit for a while before she took the path to the Poultry to visit her family with whatever provisions she could scrounge wrapped up in a knotted apron. It was not as good as spending each afternoon in the laundry yard with them all together, but it was better than not at all. Katherine felt lonely most of the time, and her afternoons with Maggie were the highlight of her week.

As the nights drew in and Autumn crept up around Belvoir Castle, the light summer drapes were replaced with heavy tapestry curtains. Furs, rugs, and quilted blankets were scattered about every room. She wondered what extra comforts the servants were being afforded, if any. Did Maggie have a winter coat or a dry pair of shoes? She had not visited the laundry since the summer but that afternoon as her breath hung in the frosty late September air, she once again made her way through the corridors and hallways down to the laundry, with a parcel tucked under her arm in the hope that Maggie would be there.

Katherine peered around the frame of the small wooden door into the stone yard trying to see who might be about before entering. The cold air among the wet linen created a freezing chill, and yet still there were the women up to their elbows in soapy water. She almost didn't recognise Maggie as she stepped out of the laundry door, wooden bucket in hand; it was more than the low sun that cast the shadow upon her, painting lines of sadness and hardship across her face. Maggie tipped the boiling water into the tub and the steam hissed as it rose. She leant into it, taking comfort from the warmth, and swept her forearm across her brow. Katherine saw she was wearing a thicker pinafore over her usual simple cotton dress, but it couldn't have offered much protection against the biting air. Her down cast eyes looked out from her withdrawn face as she pressed her thin lips together with the effort of scrubbing the cloth along the washboard. Katherine felt a knot twist her heart, but she swallowed the rising lump in her throat and waited a few moments until the other women were distracted. They were chatting absently while each twisted one end of a long sheet in the opposite direction until grey water dripped and pooled on the flagstones. Katherine seized her chance.

Maggie!" she whispered, "Maggie! Psst! Over here!"

Maggie lifted her head, hair plastered to her face with soap and grease and looked about her. Her eyes fell on the little doorway and the girl, and her face lit up. The child awkwardly shifted her weight foot to foot, beckoning Maggie to come to her so she could keep her presence discreet. Nervously looking over her shoulder at her colleagues, Maggie quietly moved towards Katherine.

"Katherine, my lamb! What are you doing here?" Maggie exclaimed in a hushed voice. "Is something wrong?" she continued as concern flashed across her face.

"Oh Maggie, no not at all. I have something for you." said Katherine excitedly, throwing her arms around her. She could feel the bony edges of Maggie's shoulders through her clothes; she was not much more than a skeleton and so cold to the touch.

"You're so thin, and it's so cold down here."

"Oh, it's not so bad," Maggie shrugged. "There's a fire in the laundry and the water is warm. Don't you worry about me." But her eyes said something different. "Anyway, why have you come all the way down here on this frosty day?"

Katherine held out the bundle she had been carrying. "It's for you." she said, "And Pippa, and Mother Joan." Maggie's gaze flicked between the parcel and the girl quizzically.

"Go on." urged Katherine, pushing the gift into Maggie's arms.

"They were going to be thrown away, so I saved them."

"What on earth is it?" asked Maggie turning it over in her hands.

"Open it and see!" Katherine was almost bursting with anticipation. So, Maggie checked that the other washer women were still engaged in their task, and assuming that she was still at the tub and hidden by a line of frost-crisp sheets.

Maggie found the end of the bootlace tying the badly rolled up bundle of cloth and pulled: what unfurled were three woollen shawls, a thick winter bonnet, and a pair of fur lined gloves. She looked at the clothes and then at Katherine, who was eager eyed and rosy cheeked. Maggie was torn; she knew the girl meant well, and that she and the Flower women were in dire need of these things. However, she also knew that the girl had no concept of what could happen if someone noticed that they were missing, or worse: someone noticed they were wearing them. She shook her head and began to bundle them back up. "I can't, Katherine. I ... I just can't take these from you. It's too much."

There was confusion and hurt on the girl's face.

"But ... but why not?" Her wide eyes looked up at Maggie and she went on, "I brought them for you; they are mine from last winter. Father brought new ones from London this week and Nanny put these in the hamper to be taken to church for the poor. But they are mine and I can give them to whoever I want, so I pulled them out again and saved them for you. Please take them." Maggie couldn't refuse the girl for such a selfless act, and she did say that they had been put aside for charity.

"You are the kindest child, Lady Katherine, thank you. I'll make sure that Mother and Pippa get them on Sunday." She took the child's hand and gave it a squeeze. It was plump and warm and soft in contrast to her bony, icy fingers.

"Go now, child. It's nearly dark and you'll be missed."

Katherine wrapped her arms around Maggie's neck once more and held her tight.

"I'll see you on Sunday then?" It was a question. Maggie nodded, then, with tears stinging her eyes, Katherine turned and ran back into the house away from the little stone laundry yard.

★

The drapes had been drawn for days. An eerie silence fell on the halls of Belvoir Castle, broken only by the creeping footsteps of the servants as they sombrely went about their duties, wearing a melancholy that matched their black arm bands .Lord Henry Ros had died. The sickness affected the whole family and many of the staff too. Raging fever, hacking cough, and vomiting accompanied a clammy pallor of the skin and the need to sleep for days. Lord Henry, aged four, and the Countess were particularly stricken with it. Nanny had taken baby Francis away to the nursery so that he might not worsen as her mistress and the boy did. The Earl and Katherine, while sickly, were not so troubled by it. In fact, Katherine was relishing the time she and her father were getting to spend together during her stepmother's confinement. It was something she had missed terribly over the last couple of years since his duties at court had increased. It made her hopeful that perhaps she could have the affection she saw in abundance between Maggie and her family. Katherine and the Earl sat together in his study, wrapped in blankets, playing chess, reading books, and telling stories while supping hot broth and laughed till their bellies ached. She and her father had never laughed like they did the winter that Henry died; after that, she never saw her father laugh again.

    A wail so heart-breaking it curdled the blood sent several people, including the Earl and Katherine, to the Countess' bedchamber. Arriving at the open door, Katherine saw the Countess clutching the lifeless body of her eldest son to her breast and rocking him; her face twisted in the agony of her grief. The Earl pushed on into the room while Katherine stood wide eyed in the doorway. The adults rushed about her; some hands clasped across their faces, some still and silent. Her father had collapsed on the bed next his wife, burying his head between them. She could see from the lurching movements of his shoulders that harsh sobs wracked his body. Katherine was numb and more than a little frightened by the horror unfolding before her, yet she remained frozen to the spot.

Nanny was on her knees by the washstand, bent over double with her head in her hands. Every so often she would glance up to take in the scene, and then just as quickly look away, shaking her head as if to remove the image. To see her hurting, upset Katherine much more than witnessing the Countess' pain. Perhaps it was just a way to cope with what was happening, not just her brother's death, but from that moment onwards, she knew everything would change. Her blossoming relationship with her father was now gone as she watched him with his family, a family she no longer felt a part of, if ever she truly had.

Cautiously she stepped into the room

"Father ..." her trembling voice was small but cut through the silent tension like a falling goblet shattering on tile. All heads snapped round to look at her.

"Take the girl out of here!" barked the Earl at Nanny who, hastily smudging her tears on the back of her hand, gathered her skirts, and rose to hurry the girl out of the room. Nanny swept Katherine up, by the collar of her dress, along the corridors towards her own room.

"What's ... What's wrong with ... is Henry ..." she stammered, unable to bring herself to say the word.

"Dead?" finished Nanny. "Dead? Is that what you want to know? Yes ... Yes, he is, poor little soul. And no thanks to you, young lady." She did not even look at Katherine, her red eyes and wet face stared straight ahead. Servants parted like waves in the wake of her glare as she continued to march the girl along the hallways by the scruff of her neck.

"Me? What? Why? I haven't done anything." Katherine cried. As she skipped her steps to keep up with Nanny's pace, she noticed for the first time that her own face was streaked with tears. The old nurse came to a sudden halt and turned Katherine to face her, gripping her shoulders.

"Haven't done anything, have you?" she scolded. "Don't think your sneaking off has not been noticed. I turned a blind eye, because you're a child, and life becomes too hard too fast, but I should have known it would mean misfortune. And that's what you've brought my lady, tragedy. Tragedy upon your own family – how could you?" She shook the girl, her bony fingers digging deeper into her small frame.

"Associating with dirty peasants, from the laundry no less! With their cursing and pestilence and common ways. See what you have done, brought disease into this house. Now our little lord is gone forever, and the Earl and Countess' hearts are broken. And for what?" With that she released her claws with such ferocity that Katherine stumbled backward, landing so heavily she bruised her sitting bones. "I hope you are pleased with yourself, child." Nanny turned on her heel and with the same brisk pace walked off, leaving Katherine to pick herself up under the watchful eyes of the staff who had scurried into the corners like rats in a cellar. She felt their curious eyes and gossiping mouths all around her. The longer she sat there, the longer her humiliation would be, so she took a deep breath, lifted her head, and clumsily got to her feet. She wiped the tears from her cheeks and stuck out her chin, then looked around at the loitering staff. Setting her gaze, she made sure every servant present knew they had been seen before she strode off towards her rooms as confidently as she could muster.

Later that evening, when her father came into her room, he found Katherine lying on a fur, under a blanket in the gloom of the fading winter sunlight. He sat on the floor next to her and stroked her hair to see if she was awake. When she rolled over to meet his gaze with eyes as swollen as his, he asked her if it was true: if she had been spending time with the servants in the laundry. She told him about Maggie, Pippa, and Joan, and how they enjoyed her company and made her laugh. She told him that she had been lonely.

Katherine could see the Earl was uncomfortable with the idea that his daughter, a Lady of the British realm, was consorting with common peasants hired from the village as servants. They were not even skilled enough to be kitchen staff. The grief of his son's death was still a fresh wound and the Earl was unable to contain his disgust. It did not make any sense that women who spent their days elbow deep in carbolic soap could have caused his pain, but he needed someone to blame right now and these anonymous women were as good as any. He vowed they would be off the estate by dawn. Katherine pleaded with him not to dismiss Maggie, or at least to send her to the poultry so she still had work and the Flower women could stay together. All this did, however, was inform her father, that mother and daughter, though not at the house were still in his employ and he wanted them gone. Katherine begged and even in his heartbreak, he could not ignore his daughter's distress. A compromise was met, and the Earl agreed to offer Margaret Flower severance pay of forty shillings and gift the family a wool mattress and bolster pillow on the condition she left her lodgings at Belvoir, taking her family from the Poultry and off the property immediately.

  The rumours started the same day. At first, just a whisper on the cold November air. *Witch.* Whether it was Nanny's frosty tongue or gossip among the staff gathering weight as it passed from lip to lip, but by sunset Maggie Flower had poisoned the boy and as for Mother Joan: they all knew how sour she was; she had placed a curse on the family. Witches, the lot of them.

WINTER - COMING OF AGE

Time passes and young Lady Katherine, now eleven years of age, has already been betrothed. She will marry the Duke of Buckingham once she has turned fifteen. It seems like a lifetime away to the child, but no doubt it will come around soon enough. For now, though she is still somewhat free to play and go about her daily life as she pleases. A new tutor has been brought into the castle; she has to learn her letters, English history, and music: all subjects deemed suitable for a woman of the gentry, along with making time for arts such as painting or embroidery. It fills her time and Katherine finds herself less bored than she had been as a younger child. The curiosity to explore was mostly replaced by her accruement of knowledge, and the corners of her that still remain curious were quickly filled with fear from the horrible sequence of events that her previous actions had caused. A feeling gripped her chest, from time to time, when she wondered what had become of the Flower women. Once the tableau of her father and the Countess upon the huge oak posted bed, holding the small limp body of her dead brother, had faded from her mind she allowed herself to remember Maggie and that wonderful summer she spent laughing and playing in the laundry and sitting on the grass by the groundsman's gate.

That is, until the shame crept back in and she pushed it back down inside.

Katherine rarely saw her father anymore. When he was not at court or on a diplomatic envoy for the King, he was with his wife and their son. When they did meet, he could not look at her; it was as if he had blamed all the pain and loss on her and to escape it, all he had to do was escape her. It appeared that she was almost a footnote in his life and the sooner she was Buckingham's problem the better. Besides, he had become crazed with the same obsession as the King, who was convinced that witches were everywhere. The Earl had become paranoid and even the staff had been instructed to participate in mandatory daily prayer, both morning and evening, to prove their godliness. Witches could turn your milk sour, control the weather, fly upon a broomstick, speak to devils who took the shape of animals, make you fall in love, give you the madness, bring sickness and even death.

It seemed a little ridiculous to Katherine, who discovered just about anyone could be a witch: no evidence was needed apparently, just hearsay. If you failed a promise, or an informed guess was correct, or simply if someone did not like you, you could be accused of witchcraft and hung. At first, she assumed it was just her father and Buckingham being dramatic; many fads came and went at court that the rest of the people never even got to hear about, let alone experience. However, the hysteria had swept across England like wildfire, already reaching Bottesford where earlier this year nine women were hung at the Tyburn. If anyone could be a witch, thought Katherine, why was it she only ever heard of women being accused and executed?

★

More years pass. It is November and Lady Katherine has just turned fifteen. The household is preparing for her forthcoming marriage to George Villiers, Duke of Buckingham, in the spring of next year, but among all the excitement Katherine falls ill with a fever and sickness. Other members of the household too are afflicted, namely her tutor, with whom she spends most of her time, and of course her brother Francis, who also has lessons. There is tension throughout the whole of Belvoir as family and servants alike dare not even think of what happened the last time the children were sick.

Katherine was sweating and shivering in her bed, the cold moonlight spilling into the room from where both the drapes and windows were open in an attempt to try and abate her fever. She wrestled with her thoughts, unable to sleep. She was so tired from the sickness: her bones ached, and the pressure in her face and stuffy nose made her head swim with every movement. Katherine no longer often thought about the Flower women, but here and now in her delirium, memories of Maggie and the way they parted following Henry's death came flooding back, stronger than the moon's silvery light into her bed chambers. Francis was sick and, God forbid he should die, would she be blamed? She was not entirely sure why she had been to blame before. That cranky old nurse of hers blurted out her secret and it cost a poor woman and her family their livelihood. Perhaps it was just because it all happened on the same day. Her mind was fuzzy right now; it was such a long time ago and the memories of Maggie were all jumbled up due to the fever. *The fever.* That was it: a memory rose to the surface.

One day she had seen Maggie picking wildflowers on the road to the Poultry and ran to catch up with her; Katherine had commented on what a nice posy it was. Maggie, on her way to visit Mother Joan, had said, oh no they were medicine. Mother Joan had a fever and the flowering herbs were to be steeped into a brew to calm the heat and relieve the pain. She had not thought of this day since it had happened, but now she recalled it as clear as if it were yesterday.

Without a second's thought, she unsteadily rose from her bed, grabbed a robe and slippers, and left the bedchamber. The chilly darkened hallways were striped by moonlight from the castle's tall windows and she did not need to light a candle.

Katherine padded through the silence, her feet retracing a path she had forgotten she knew: past rooms, down staircases, through the kitchens, into the gardens, to the back gate leading away from Belvoir toward the Poultry.

Half asleep, by the moon's light she searched for the blooms she remembered so vividly; sure enough, there they were. After gathering handfuls of fragrant herbs that she did not know the name of Katherine stumbled back toward the house and into the kitchens. Searching for a kettle, the clattering woke one of the Butler's servants, who burst through the door in his shirt tails. He quickly lowered the poker in his hand as he saw her Ladyship in her nightgown, rummaging about the copper pots. She explained that she needed hot water, a pot, and cup brought to her room immediately; yes, she was awake, and no she did not require any further help.

Twenty minutes later a light knock on her bedroom door stirred Katherine from where she had dozed off, curled up in the old chair by the fireplace. A sleepy and dishevelled looking maid entered the room, sheepishly set the tray on the table, and left. Katherine carefully picked the buds and petals from the flowers then dropped them into the pot; she let them steep a few minutes, until the water was a drinkable temperature, then drank the lot.

★

Katherine woke with warm light from the open windows on her face. She felt light; the weight of the fever had lifted, leaving her smaller somehow, cleaner. The was a distant clatter and the murmur of hushed voices, but not from outside. As she slowly became conscious, Katherine realised that is was coming from much closer, from inside the room. She lazily rolled over to see if she could discover what had disturbed her slumber. It was the dishevelled maid, head bowed and hands trembling as she set Katherine's breakfast on the table and cleared the cup and pot under the scornful eye of Nanny. In her half waking state Katherine could not make out what they were saying, but the maid was shaking her head while Nanny pointed to the leaves and broken stems littered around the pot.

"What time is it?" asked Katherine, sitting up. Nanny's head whipped round, her face dark as thunder. The maid scurried out of the room, closing the door silently behind her. "Is that breakfast already?"

"It's two o'clock, m'Lady; you slept all day. I had the kitchen bring you some warm milk, bread, and jam." Nanny bristled. "But it appears you have already had some." Katherine did not understand the tone of her voice; something was wrong. It was the voice Nanny used when she was in trouble, but she had not heard it in a long time.

Now that Katherine was grown and about to be married, Nanny had had to change her manner and address her as a Lady of the house, rather than a child under her care. She was still having trouble adjusting; it was a visible struggle for the old nurse and caused her much conflict. For once, Katherine decide to use it to her advantage.

"Thank you, Nanny. That was thoughtful of you." said Katherine, in a detached tone. She watched Nanny shuffle uncomfortably for a moment, then continued, "I woke in the night thirsty for a warm drink, so I went down to the kitchens myself and had the maid bring it up. However, I'm feeling much brighter today, thank you." Katherine offered no more information and Nanny was no longer in a position to demand it.

"That will be all, thank you Nanny. I would like to enjoy my breakfast now." she said, with a glance at the door. The old woman dropped her gaze and made an awkward bob of a curtsey before drawing herself up, hands clasped tight under her bosom, and sweeping out of Katherine's bedchamber.

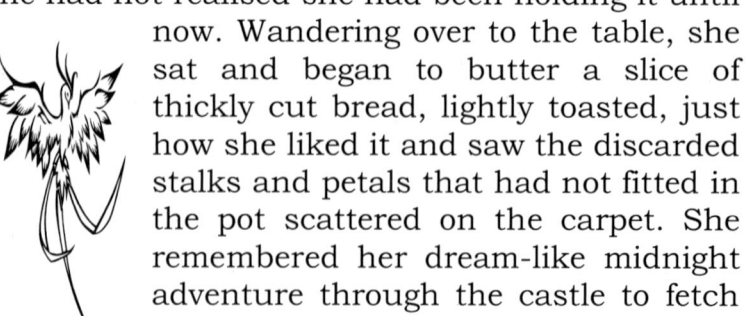

Katherine let out a long slow deep breath; she had not realised she had been holding it until now. Wandering over to the table, she sat and began to butter a slice of thickly cut bread, lightly toasted, just how she liked it and saw the discarded stalks and petals that had not fitted in the pot scattered on the carpet. She remembered her dream-like midnight adventure through the castle to fetch the healing herbs that Maggie had shown her all those years ago. Her fever was gone: no shivers or aches; she still had a cold nose, but there was no burning pressure behind her eyes. Like a flash, she realised she must take some of the brew to her brother. If she could save Francis with this medicine, she thought, then perhaps she would be redeemed for whatever blame her father placed on her for Henry's death.

Later that afternoon, when the sun had set, Lady Katherine Manners put on her shawl and returned to the path. She picked more of the fragrant flowering herbs by the light of the rising moon and stopped by the kitchens to ask that another pot of boiling water be brought to her rooms. When the brew was steeped and still steaming, she carried the tray through the gilded corridors of Belvoir Castle to her brother's room, where she hoped he would drink it and be well by morning. What she did not expect was to find both her father and the Countess standing over Francis' bed wearing grave expressions, accompanied by a very stern and smug looking Nanny.

SPRING – THE FLOWERS OF BOTTESFORD

It was now March. Katherine was to have been married in two months' time. However, all preparations for her wedding had been halted and her nuptials postponed until only God knew when, lest it overshadow the trial. Not that anything could. It had been the most sickening four months of her life: beyond anything that had happened to her when Henry died. Her father had become consumed by the notion that Margaret, Joan, and Philippa Flower were in league with devils, had cursed his family and caused Henry's death by sorcery and foul witchcraft.

At least today it would be over. She sat in the public gallery of the courthouse in Lincoln, beside her father and stepmother. A rope had been hung to section off a private space for her family to sit. Below them, the courthouse was packed with jeering onlookers from the surrounding villages, come to see a witch hang. Most times the sentence didn't disappoint, and the crowds would flock back again as soon as another poor soul was condemned, paying tuppence to squeeze themselves inside and catch a glimpse of the woman before she was dragged into the street and up on to the gallows. Worst of all was the smell. Katherine kept her handkerchief close to her face; it hid her tears.

The grey faces of her parents were lined with grief.

The examinations had been gruelling enough just to listen to, so she could not begin to imagine what Maggie and Pippa had endured. While her family had the people's sympathy for their lost children, they had experienced nowhere near the torture and hardship that her friends had, nor had they been so reviled in their suffering. However, now Maggie sat alone in the dock, slumped on the small wooden stool in a white cotton smock. Hollow eyes stared out at nothing from her tear stained and bruised face. Cuts and burns could be seen all over her body, where the examiners had searched for a witch's mark. Katherine was grateful that at least Pippa had escaped. Gossip said that she had bewitched a guard with her lewd ways and promised him the reward of her sinful flesh, and he, being too enamoured by the spell to resist, had let her go. The more likely truth was that her husband, the same Thomas Simpson who she had loved all these years and had borne three children with, had come to fetch her. Maggie, who was a spinster, had no one; not even her mother.

Joan Flower had not even made the journey from Bottesford to the Lincoln Gaol. She may have talked harsh but underneath she was an old woman who had been ill several times over the past few years. If she had been subject to the same examination as her daughters, it was not surprising that she had not recovered. The transcript read aloud by one of a number of pompous righteous men in wigs and stockings claimed she had choked on bread and water after requesting Holy Communion: a clear sign that she was a witch, for she could not receive the host and it curdled in her throat. Katherine knew that Joan was atheist in her belief, sacrilegious yes, but witch, no. She would never have requested taking communion, and it was likely that she died from the examiners forcing it into her mouth. They hadn't brought her body to Lincoln, or even taken her home to Bottesford; instead, they buried her at the next crossroads they came to, for fear she may rise again.

It was so frightening how quickly a woman's life could be thrown away. Katherine's palms were clammy, the heat and smell in the room making her nauseous. She wanted nothing but to grab Maggie's hand and run out of there. She would forsake her title, her lands, her marriage, just to live a simple life washing clothes with Maggie every day. Bile rose in her throat as her heart broke; what had they done to her? The woman who had been more of a mother in one season than the Countess, Nanny, and all her nurses put together, now sat alone and afraid just out of reach. Dirty bare feet, tangled hair, dried blood crusted her seeping wounds and she trembled from head to toe as the accusations against her were read out. One of the wigged men rose and read from a paper.

"That by most wicked sorcery Margaret Flower, with her sister

Philippa and her mother Joan Flower, did foully conspire to cause harm to the most honourable Earl of Rutland and his Countess, by wishing sickness and death upon the heirs Henry Lord Ros, and Francis Lord Ros. Which they did by means of vile sorcery and witchcraft." A jeer went round the crowd and he turned to face the rabid onlookers, "Here in my hand I hold the confession of Margaret Flower, that she did join with her mother and sister in these foul deeds and not only caused the death of the Earl's sons, but also cursed his good lady wife the Countess of Rutland that she would bear no more. A Confession, I say." He waved the paper in the air for effect.

"If I may indulge the court, I shall now read to you what His Grace George Manners, brother to the Earl, and the very Reverend Samuel Fleming found." The Judge nodded and Henry Hobbart, the man under the wig and Chief Prosecutor drew himself up ready for his big finale. Then in a deliberate and dramatic voice, he began to read.

"She saith and confesseth, that about four or five years ago her Mother sent her for the right-hand glove of Henry Lord Ros. Afterward her mother bade her go again into the Castle of Belvoir and bring down the glove or some other thing of Henry Lord Ros, and she asked what to do? Her Mother replied to hurt my Lord Ros: whereupon she brought down a glove, and delivered it to her Mother, who stroked Rutterkin her Cat with it. Then the cat

was dipped in hot water, and pricked often, after which Henry Lord Ros fell sick within a week and was much tormented with the same. ... About four years later the Countess gave her forty shillings, a bolster, and a mattress. She bade her lie at home, and come no more to dwell at the Castle, which she not only took in ill part, but grudged at exceedingly, swearing in her heart to be revenged ..."

The crowd hissed and booed with all the relish of children watching a street puppet show. Katherine, astounded, could not believe the lies they had put into her mouth. She *gave* Maggie those gloves, she didn't steal them, and saw to it that she got the forty shillings. It was plain to see that the woman had been beaten as well as tortured for days on end: it's likely she would have said anything to make it stop.

"... She further saith, that her Mother and she, and her Sister agreed together to bewitch the Earle and his Lady, that they might have no more Children ..."

Katherine phased in and out while Lord Hobbart continued to read the alleged confessions that were also attributed to Pippa and Joan. The words began to drone in her ears as she kept her gaze fixed on Maggie. Maggie kept her gazed fixed on something far in the distance, or deep inside her thoughts. The effect was the same, staring blankly from behind dead eyes.

"... whereupon she took wool out of the said mattress, and a pair of gloves, putting them into warm water, mingling them with some blood and stirring it together. Then she took the wool and gloves out of the water and rubbed them on the belly of Rutterkin her Cat, saying the Lord and the Lady should have more Children, but it would be long first."

Nonsense!

After what seemed hours, without any defence presented on behalf of Margaret Flower, the sentencing came. It was inevitable, but in those few moments Katherine hoped, prayed some miracle would shine upon them and Maggie would be cleared. For a heartbeat she thought her prayers had been answered because, in the quiet before the judge read the verdict, the broken woman lifted her head and looked directly at her. Katherine's heart leapt to her mouth and she scooted forward on the edge of her chair to lean into Maggie's eyes over the balcony. She did her best to convey her love and how sorry she was for all that had happened with just her face. They held their breath and each other's gaze in the syrupy silence.

"GUILTY" rang out throughout the courthouse and the people stuffed into the court room below erupted in a great whoop, sneering, and bellowing like animals at the spectacle of another witch tried and convicted. She felt an arm across her lap slowly press her back into her chair; it was not proper to be seen sympathising with witches. Her father turned to her; he had not looked at her properly for a very long time.

"I hope you have learned that your actions have consequences." was all the Earl said, before he stood and escorted his sobbing wife from the room, leaving Katherine to follow behind.

★

The sun was bright in a blue sky, but the air was cold. Margaret Flower was led barefoot and shackled up the rough wooden steps to the gallows. She shook her head when asked if she had any last words: there was nothing she could say that would make any difference, so she just stared at the beautiful sky until the bag was placed over her head and the rope was tightened around her neck. The last thing she felt was the cool breeze on her dangling toes.

---

1 The earliest record of tea being drunk in the British Isles, was in high society coffee houses, only the very rich could afford it and it was reserved for the gentry, often kept under lock and key. As confident to the King it is very likely that the Earl's household would be well stocked with the finest "Tcha[1]," as it was known, straight off the merchant ships of the East India Company

THE EXAMINATION OF MARGARET FLOWER, SISTER OF PHILLIP FLOWER &C. ABOUT THE 22. OF IANUARY. 1618.
(The wonderful discouerie of the vvitchcrafts of Margaret and Phllip Flower, daughters of Ioan Flower neere Beuer Castle)

"She saith and confesseth, that about foure or fiue yeare since her Mother sent her for the right hand gloue of Henry Lord Rosse, afterward that her mother bade her goe againe into the Castle of Beauer, and bring downe the gloue or some other thing of Henry Lord Rosse, and shee askt what to doe? Her Mother replyed to hurt my Lord Rosse: whereupon she brought downe a gloue, and deliuered the same to her Mother, who stroked Rutterkin her Cat with it, after it was dipt in hot water, and so prickt it often, after which Henry Lord Rosse fell sicke within a weeke, and was much tormented with the same.

She further saith, that finding a gloue about two or three yeares since of Francis Lord Rosse, on a dung-hill, she deliuered it to her mother, who put it into hot water, and after tooke it out and rubd it on Rutterkin the Cat, and bad him goe vpwards, and after her mother buried it in the yard, and said a mischiefe light on him, but he will mend againe.

Shee further saith, that her Mother and shee, and her Sister agreed together to bewitch the Earle and his Lady, that they might haue no more children: and being demanded the cause of this their mallice and ill will; shee saith, that about foure yeares since the Countesse (growing into some mislike with her) gaue her forty shillings, a bolster, & a mattresse, and bad her lye at home, and come no more to dwell at the Castle; which she not onely tooke in ill part, but grudged at it exceedingly, swearing in her heart to be reuenged. After this, her Mother complained to the Earle against one Peake, who had offered her some wrong, wherein she conceiued that the Earle tooke not her part, as shee expected, which dislike with the rest, exasperated her displeasure against him, and so she watched an opportunity to bee re/uenged: whereupon she tooke wooll out of the said mattresse, and a paire of gloues, which were giuen her by Mr. Vauasor, and put them into warme water, mingling them with some blood, and stirring it to/gether, then she tooke the wooll and gloues out of the water, and rubd them on the belly of Rutterkin her Cat, saying the Lord and the Lady should haue more Children, but it would be long first.

Shee further confesseth, that by her mothers commandement, shee brought to her a peece of a hand/kercher of the Lady Katherine the Earles daughter, and her mother put it into hot water, & then taking it out, rubd it on Rutterkin, bidding him flye, and go; whereupon Rutterkin whined and cryed Mew: whereupon shee said, that Rutterkin had no power ouer the Lady Katherine to hurt her."

GOWANE ANDERSOUN
(died 1626)

Gowane Andersoun was tried for witchcraft in Aberdeenshire on the 14th of December 1626. His death is believed to have occurred in the following weeks.

Witches and Devils on the Wind

'THE FATES OF MEN ARE THEIR FATES ALONE'
Tarn Nemorensis

Swirling, effervescent mists circle my feet as I wander through the woods, roots curling and reaching up to me. The world sounds hollow, but also full, whisperings and natterings, echoing through the leaves and branches. My spirit form can see with fiery eyes in ways that my shell cannot. The spirit world filters through and bleeds into the realms of men, I move between them, seeking answers. Tree spirits lay mostly dormant at this time of year, but they still hum at my presence, recognising a kindred soul as I step through this land of eternal twilight.

My footsteps are silent, passing through the ferns and grass like a dragonfly through air, as I make my way towards the mortal village of Broombae. My fetch walks close behind, in sync with my thoughts as I carefully make my way up to the treeline, his form is evasive, as undefined as the fog clinging to the mountains. A shimmering coalescence of colours flocking and gathering gradually becoming human.

He makes no sound as he follows me: my fetch, my watcher, my familiar, my guardian, my guide.

The village too, seems quiet; the farmers out in their fields turning in the rest of the crops in order to provide compost for the following year. Nothing but the odd child running from house to house, and a few stray cats roaming the streets. No obvious wandering spirits, and no familiars to tell their masters of our approach: it is well known that witches live here. My fetch leans in close behind me, resting his fingers upon my shoulder he points to a barn at the back of the main house.

Sure enough, the flocks that had gone missing from Alford were now residing in the neighbouring village's barn; much as we had suspected. The months spent rearing and feeding these sheep to provide food and wool for the coming winter were now here, stolen. All the hard work my son had done, from their birthing to their feeding and care. I feel a deep anger rise in me, but my fetch grasps my arm and dips his head, so it rests alongside mine.

'Soon.'

I nod as I turn away from the misdeed, anger still scorching through my veins. My fetch tuts at the scene, clearly as displeased as I was. We prepare to go back home, to tell the others what we've seen and to decide the best course of action.. I wanted to return to my family, hoping they would bring some levity back into my day. My fetch slowly and gracefully steps into my spirit form, merging us back together like a whirlwind of song and shadow before we emerge as a swallow, soaring high above the treetops. Our feathers vibrate in the wind, as we look across to the edges of the snow-capped mountains.

The trees blur as we speed on past them to Alford, over the brooks and hills- and there's a chill in the air as the year comes to a close. Suddenly, we feel a tug on the cord that binds us to our witch fire and our master. It is new, unfamiliar- a magical scent unlike that of our coven, no bloodline is as yet established to this wandering aura.

Intrigued, we curve in flight. The villages and mountains rush past us: past Craiglich and the Cairns, past Leochel Cushnie, past Mortlich and Queen's Hill until we recognise Aboyne, with its beautiful lochs and rivers. The whisper of the witch flame beckons us down to a house, where a woman sits with her husband at the table. They sit in companionable silence, but we can feel the stirrings of the cauldron's fire beneath her skin; her soul is eager to leap free and dance in ecstatic harmony with the essence of the land. She seems more vibrant and alive than the man she sits with, even though they both sit still and silent. My fetch separates and we shift back to our natural states, and the woman senses the disturbance. My fetch moves closer to her, and sees what I do not,

'Margaret ... Margaret McConnochie.'

Names have power, and I let her name slip over my tongue as my enchantments shimmer through the air. My silent suggestion entangling with her thoughts, I lead my fetch outside, passing through the walls of the house. I hear Margaret make an excuse to her husband and she joins us outside. She clutches her shawl tightly around her shoulders to shield herself from the wind as her eyes search for us,

"I know you're out here, spirits! Don't make me grasp my iron and banish you!"

I chuckle as I solidify my spirit body so she can see me through the haze of the veil,

"No need for that, sweet Margaret"

She startles at the sight of me, clearly confused and asks, "Are you the devil - or some lost wandering spirit?"

"Do I have cloven hoof, or the wailing of the dead? I'm neither spirit nor devil" I reply as I walk slowly towards her, "although you could say I'm here, in spirit"

She appears to have become less suspicious of me, her face now showing more curiosity than fear. However, my own suspicions rise, and I ask-

"You too have been in places, in spirit? You have walked, scampered, run, or flown, to places that are here, and yet, not here? To places that look like here, but when you are not within yourself?"

She does not answer, but also does not deny my queries. My fetch starts to circle the woman, clearly intrigued- his form sizzling and sparking as he paces.

'This one could be perfect. She falls into the dreaming and

shimmers to other realms as easy as sinking into sleep. Her spirit skims the veil and seeks to stretch out from her skin.'

I nod in agreement with him and I push further –

"You have travelled to the realms of the good folk, and to the places within the caves, to the twilight lands, and to the moon when she is full?" Margaret holds her shawl a little tighter as she nods. I step forward and take her hands in mine, her hands warm under my gloves.

"Fear not Margaret, your secret is safe with me. Would you like to learn why you can do these things that many others would call unholy, even when their own saviour and saints practised such things?" I gesture at the plants around her garden before taking her hands in mine again, "Why you grow wormwood and ragwort in your garden and keep heather by the door?"

A blush spreads across her cheeks, and she lowers her head, caught out in her sin of healing the sick. I squeeze her fingers until she returns her gaze to mine, and I softly carry on, "I can show you these things and can teach you many others. There are others like us. Just like you. You could be so much more, if you are just brave enough to wonder and daring enough to claim your rightful power." She bites her lip but does not shrink back from my grasp.

She steels her shoulders as she replies, "I am no fool good sir, with your words so cunning and sly- I know of the one you serve."

I smile as her eyes drop to our hands. Her voice wavers slightly, "Will he ask me for my soul? Will he force me to do unspeakable things?"

I laugh, lean forwards conspiratorially and whisper, "He asks for no such thing that you are not willing to give, and he forces no one to do his will. He asks, but the fates of men are their fates alone. People can cast blame upon him, but he has none in his heart. But you may find what he offers encourages you to a greater offering and price. But once you have promised, it is best you deliver."

I remove my hands, take off my cap, place it in her grasp, and watch as her fingers curl instinctively around the rim. "When you wish to meet with us, throw this hat to the wind." I say, "And meet us on Tombreck Hill"

I look over to my fetch and he cocks his head, his form fizzing with anticipation and his eyes ablaze.

'She'll need something more to not run to her priest like she's done her whole life. Give her more.'

I pause for a second, and consider his words, evaluating the best course of action.

"Do you want a taste of what's to come?" I coax feeling the energies of the land gather within me as I settle upon a plan. She hesitates and then nods - a slight dip of her head, as if it somehow lessens her acceptance and absolves her of any sin. I could feel the approval of my fetch as he places his hands on her back, his fingers passing through her skin like sand, touching her spirit. I bend down, and as my thoughts weave enchantments I kiss her forehead. Her spirit flies, in an ecstasy of colour and light.

Over the next few days, I make sure to return to normality. I venture out only to work or secure meats and milk from the market to take back to my family. The Priests of Aberdeenshire have been seeking any excuse to accuse people of witchery. Ever since the cries of Popery were flung about, the priests seem more determined than ever to prove their new protestant faith.

★

I return home from my day's working as a record keeper, my fingers ink stained and my eyes weary. The warmth of the house is welcoming, and I can smell stew cooking on the hearth as I scrub my hands, desperate to remove the day's toil. I greet my wife in the kitchen, hold her close and kiss her on the cheek. I tangle my fingers into her hair and let my days troubles just fall away in her embrace.

"Is Johnne back yet?" I ask, breaking away to move into the warmer part of the house. Isobel follows me to the living space and returns to her spinning, her basket of wool growing smaller by the second.

"It's a big night for him tonight" I added, warming my hands by the fire.

"He's still tending to the cows, he'll be back soon" she says smiling at me, her fingers looping in and out of the wool. Her smile never fails to warm my heart and make the day's work seem worthwhile. I smile back, and readjust my coat, "In which case, I'll be useful, and go and pick the herbs for tonight"

"Don't take too much of the Mugwort, my darling. I need it for the neighbours, their youngest has been struck down with a terrible blood sickness, so I'll need it for healing: one for the burning and one to sew into their bed clothes." She chimes in, and I laugh.

"Always thinking of others, my love. Tell me, how did the gardens fare once you had worked on them the other day- when you sprinkled mint powder over the land?" I ask, and she smiles knowingly; a private joke, only we share.

"The mint spirits were more than happy to start at work, they'll ensure a good crop for the village and sweet fruits come harvest" she grins, proud of her accomplishment.

"Your work as always is stunning, my hen" I place a kiss on top of her head on my way out to the garden. The air is cooler as the sun sets and the mountaintops darken the sky early. I reach inside my coat, take my knife, and cut back the hawthorn and ragwort. I leave fresh breadcrumbs scattered at their base, to give thanks for their help. I whisper to the Mugwort spirits as I cut the leaves and stems, sharing stories of my day, and discussing with them what will take place tonight. Promising them blessed water from the streams on the mountain, and songs of praise once the night over. I stand up to return indoors, but I am distracted by a hushed muttering coming from the trees. My eyes scan the pines for the source of the dampened cacophony, but no spirit shows itself, and no animal steps out into the twilight. I feel a pressure behind my eyes as my fetch focuses on me and whispers.

'It's the Corpse Road.'

I walk over to the line of beech trees, the ones that mark where the coffin road connects church to church and graveyard to graveyard- where spirits wander after their bodies have been laid to rest. This network of trees had an unfortunate second purpose that the church had failed to recognise: the spirits of these trees were always more than happy to pass along messages to all those who spoke their language. I walk carefully up to the trees, taking care not to slip on their rolling seeds, place my hands on the trunks and lean in, curious to decipher the message. Images flash through my mind, sensations, and smells. I see a harbour, thatched cottages and can smell fresh fish and the sea. It's the village of Futtie, where Agnes Durie lives on the coast. I calm my mind and bring my thoughts to surface, images of the mountains and grain, of Gallows Hill and the cows, the lands around humble Alford. I send these impressions back to her through the roots and branches of the trees, as one spirit passes it along to the next, a web of information. Recognition worms its way back to me, identification of coven blood. Next, a warning flickers across my sight- Aberdeen is host to a witch hunt.

'Guard yourself.'

I sigh and reply that we are aware of the increase in tension and can feel the underlying fear. Whilst there, I pass along the news of the rite tonight, the initiation of my adopted son.

'I shall be there in spirit flight to welcome you and Isobel ... and Johnne finally to the circle. Take care, Gowane, and be safe.'

I remove my hands from the trunk and whistle a spell of good fortune for the spirits of the Beech trees. I head back to the house with my bundle of herbs, and upon opening the door can taste the soot of the fire on my tongue. Johnne appears in front of me with a grin and a bowl of stew in his hands. He still has smudges on his face from a hard day's work and his blonde hair was as scruffy as a bird's nest.

"That was a long time for some ragwort" he smirked, waiting for me to drop the herbs on the side.

"The Corpse road had a message from Agnes" I reply, taking the stew, "She warns of the hunts in Aberdeen" Johnne's face dropped slightly and I carried on, "and how she's also looking forward to meeting you."

His grin appeared again, and my boots scuff the hearthstones as I sit down in front of the fire with him. My fingers defrost in the warmth as I gaze upon my son, knowing that this night would be life changing for him. I hope it does not bring up things hidden from him, things long buried, scattered memories of his childhood before us; memories of pain.

"Tonight, is a special night for you, son." I say, raising my eyebrows at him, taking a breath to calm my own nerves. "A sacred one. Have you thought what you're to offer him, and what he might ask of you?" I inquired, spooning hot stew into my mouth, "you're above age now - you know what life can give and what it can take away."

"I have," he assures me, "and I'm sure I'm certain ... but what did you offer, and what did mother?" He replied, picking up his own bowl. I grunted, stirred my food around in the bowl for a bit, feeling inevitability of a difficult conversation dawning.

"Your mother, she offered him a yearly feast, of breads and sweet berries. It's why we have such beautiful raspberries and brambles about the gardens and forests." I took a pause, stirred my bowl some more as I thought of a way to broach the next subject.

"And he asked for her ability to bear children. It's why we had none of our own" I leant over and took his hand in mine, "But it's also why we were blessed with you. He is not cruel to those he works with. He is not overcome with jealousy, nor does he anger when we weaken. He knew how desperate we were to have a child; it's why the initial ask was so high. But the price was fitting for the rewards he gives, we can protect our home and heal the sick. We bring crops and good fortune to those in the village. When your mother cried to the stars for answers as to why his demand was so great, he answered with the falling of his star, and he led her to you." I place my stew down and bring my hand to Johnne's face. "He led us to you because he could sense our pain. He gave us a child. And we have never regretted it. You are more my son than any other could be" Johnne brought our hands to his forehead as he contemplated my words, his energies to-ing and fro-ing as he pondered.

"And from me he asked for continuous small tasks, things that he doesn't have time for, smaller pieces for larger plans. I offered him my soul and he took it, and I trust no other's hand more with it. He had proven himself to me even before we were in contract. He could sense the witch fire in my soul and bestowed me powers. Powers to protect those I love, powers to bring the crops and plants to flower" I recounted and smiled as he raises his eyes to mine,

"He will force nothing from you. You know of him, you have sat at his table and drunk the wine he gifts us. You saw him when he taught your mother to weave magic in the same breath as she weaves at her loom"

Isobel came into the room and sat down beside us, tucking her long skirts under her legs, a vision of beauty.

"And he gives us such gifts. No need to have such doubts, child. This is going to be a sacred moment; one you'll remember for your whole life. The coven will sing for your ascension, and the spirits of those who came before you will arrive." She promised, dragging her hands through his hair as if he were still a child, and not a grown man.

"What if I have no want to see those who came before?" Johnne hinted.

"He'll banish them before they ever set foot, never you worry" She replied, her face aglow from the fire, confident in her words.

Johnne seemed to accept this, I could feel his frenetic emotions slowing as he re-centred himself. Hopefully, that would be all his worries quelled.

"Eat up your stew, we have plenty to prepare for!" I finished, raising myself from the floor.

The next few hours were filled with the chopping and blessing of the herbs that we had brought back, and the bundling of the straw. We wash the floors with a lavender water, made with blessed mountain water, and burn rosemary to chase out any spirits that sought to endanger our rite. We lay the herbs on the floor in sacred symbols in front of the hearth and throw the mugwort into the flames. Bundles of straw are placed in front of us as we kneel in front of the fire. The air hums as we prepare our ritual; magic can be tasted upon the tongue. I give the ragwort to Johnne, a plant spirit that has always worked well with our lineage.

"This will be your guide through the forest" I remind him. "You have no spirit flight yet, so take caution as to who sees you." He nods as he bundles up in coats as he prepares to leave the house.

"We'll see you there, and don't be shocked as to what you might see when you arrive. It's not so much different from our feasts with Him" I say, as he laughs, muttering something about wildness and drunkenness as he shuts the door behind him. I seal the door with a ward cast through the space.

"He's going to do so well" I say to Isobel and she agrees, and in that moment by the fire I see her, youthful as what she once was when she first came across Johnne that night, when her hair was not speckled with grey. Her splendour still shines through, and it comes out with every spell and every smile. Her soul never ages, it's still so vibrant and free. I truly could not have asked for a more beautiful family, I realise, sitting amongst sacred herbs in a warm home, surrounded by memories of laughing nights and hardships we have lived through. My joyful memories fuel my witch fire, empowering my surroundings, sinking my magic deep into the walls and wards. Thank the master in all his guises for bringing me this. Isobel grins at me, her excitement growing as she feels the lick of the witch flames, as the night grows darker and the hour approaches.

"Don't go dreaming with the fairies, love. We have work to do" She reminds me with a kiss on the cheek. She settles back to her space, rubbing herbs into her hands and I refocus, brought back to the present by her insistence, not to be lost to enchantment this night.

Isobel begins her reel of spells as I start to shift through the veil, her voice soft and effortless, a beautiful harmony to work to as I sprinkle herb dust around the straw. The rosemary smoke flows around us, and I can smell the mugwort as it sizzles, their spirits aiding me. I take some straw from the bunch, keeping one hand on the bundle,

"Up Hors, Up Hattock" I declare to the room as I throw the pieces of straw upwards, they drift into the air and my spirit form follows them as they float in the currents.

We arrive to the clearing on Tombreck Hill, still hand in hand with the flight of the straw spirits, the stars alight and burning in the sky. The pine trees bend in the wind, and the fire pit sparks in blue and red; the fire sprites form their own dances amongst the logs. I become aware of the other's spirits gathered around, witches, fetches and familiars, the spirits of the dead and long forgotten gods. There's already a low chanting happening amongst some of them, unholy words of rhyme. It echoes around the hilltop, combining with the howling of the wind through the mountains. It is a thing of beauty. I recognise the Spirit form of Agnes across the circle, and Isobel goes to her so they can catch up, their energies intertwining in joy as they embrace. I turn to my fetch, his form resembling stormy clouds with red lightning streaking through it; he's excited for tonight.

"I take it Johnne is not here yet?" I murmur, looking at all the spirits gathered in companionship.

'No, but he is close by. Not long now.'

I feel a sudden distinct shift in the circle. Margaret appears, clutching my hat between her fingers.

"I'm glad you made it" I exclaimed, "please let me introduce you to the others."

I place the cap on my head and take her around the circle as I make the introductions. Isobel comes over to us, joy emanating off of her.

"This is Margaret, from Aboyne. She's natural at spirit flight and the ways of the healing herbs" I praise and turned to my wife "and this is my wife, Isobel, talented in many a thing" Isobel giggles and smacks my arm teasingly before we fall into pleasant chatter.

It wasn't long before Johnne appeared, his strides purposeful as he joined the group. Pride swelled in my chest at the sight of him being so sure of his own power, his own place in the world. He looked slightly ragged as his trek through the woods was undoubtedly long, but his determination obscured it. His eyes lit up at the sight of me and Isobel.

We go over to him, praise him for making the journey so quickly through such windy weather and smother him with assurances. We bring him close to the fire side, closer to the spirits that were now kin to him. The music starts to ramp up as more spirits filtered through to the gathering, their forms appearing like a fine mist in the darkness. Isobel started to lose herself to the song of the coven, joining in, her hips swaying as the ethereal charm took root. The stomp of the trancing spirits creates a heartbeat, like unearthly witch drums that echo through the mountains. I put a hand on Johnne's shoulder, worried about how he's settling in, but his face is nothing but awe as the energies start spiralling out.

Suddenly, a vibrant echoing commotion fills the air, silky smooth but powerful, like the waves hitting the shore, the enthusiasm of song or the slow rumble of thunder. It was all at once a deafening cacophony and a silent hush. Black smoke starts to gather around, and I felt the witch fire surge inside me. A pure, vital light that infuses my very being, the sublime shock of it still brings me to my knees. I can taste the embers in the air and feel the very earth move beneath my hands as the veil shifts.

A disorientating reverberation that causes the air to swirl and the land to spin. Then it is like the earth sighs, and things return almost to normal as He appears from the flames, tall and horned. Gazing upon him is like gazing into the night sky, his skin translucent and iridescent, as though he exists in between all worlds. His face shifts, flitting between beast, man, bones, and darkness. His eyes are like gazing into madness itself, ephemeral yet endless, beautiful beyond all measure, likely to capture your gaze and never let you look away if you stare for too long. It's easier to focus on his long black coat and the clicking of his boots upon the stones. I sneak a look over to Johnne and he was transfixed, lost in reverence. The Witch-master takes a liking to him, first placing his hand under Johnne's chin.

'Rise'

He stands, silent. The Devil's voice slides through one's mind, alluring and sweet. I remember my own time before his feet at initiation, the feeling as though all of your thoughts just fall out of your head and when your soul has never been so excited nor so much at peace. The sheer radiance of his power permeates your being as you stand there, and you're not quite sure how you can still breathe.

He cocks his head and leans in close.

'What have you brought to offer me?'

Johnne takes a shuddering breath.

"I offer you my services in enchantments of the land. Name your enchantment, whatever you wish to create, and it shall be yours."

There is no emotion on the Devil's face; none that are easy to decipher, but he seems to take a moment to consider while his eyes rake the man in front of him.

'That is acceptable.'

His eyes narrow, and he brings his face in closer, right next to John's ear- as though to whisper even though his voice carries such resonance that it's felt in the heart of all men.

'I offer you many things. The gift to feed your family, to dress them in fine clothes. You shalt want for nothing that you cannot fix. You shall have my blessings and my words of power. I bestow upon you these things, as well as that which I promise the coven.'

His head rears back, almost snake like, a fluid action that is clearly not mortal. The devil starts to pace around his newest witch, gloved hands clasped behind his back. My own heart thuds as I hear the clacking of his boots, the beat syncing with the rhythm of my thoughts, running amok with wonderings of what he will ask of my son.

The silent contemplation of the Devil ended, ***'... And what do I want to ask of you?'***

He raises his hand to his chin as though deep in thought, his coat swishing as he turns to complete another lap.

'Your soul is an obvious choice. As are your skills in the rearing of creatures.' His eyes take on a wholly unearthly glow before he announces his suggestion.

'But I have ... a better idea. You will be tasked to work with the spirits of the dead.'

Johnne's face pales, and his apprehension is palpable. Suddenly, I am far more worried about his task than I ever was my own. Our earlier conversation flickers through my mind and my own thoughts of the time we found him, broken and hurt come to the surface. Of those monsters he had killed to survive, his own blood kin, now amongst the spirits of the dead he was being asked to work with.

The Devil tuts and narrows his eyes, impatience seeping out to his physical form, coiling like serpents in his skin.

'Such immediate resistance to my calling. Fear not, child I will not task you too hard. If you work with the enchantments of the land and life, you too must work with that which lies below. Why do you hesitate so?'

The Devil trails off and pauses, shifting to look at me. Understanding crosses his face before rolling his head to gaze back at Johnne.

'You will not have to work with your own bloodline. Not for three generations ... Is that acceptable?'

Johnne nods eagerly, and I'm surprised he does not pass out from shock. The Devil sneers, whether at Johnne's initial refusal, or his own bending to suits Johnne's desires.

'Such leniency I give to you for your new kin. But I am known for fulfilling desires, so why not another? But there is an addition for my leniency in such a matter.'

I feel as though my heart is about to burst and my fetch twitches uneasily beside me, his fingers jerking skittishly.

'You shall keep a book of our enchantments. Your father is a record keeper for the mortals, and I wish for you to be mine.'

I let out a breath I didn't know I'd been holding. It was a fair ask. I am glad in that moment, that I spent many a month teaching him to read and write, his fingers spilling ink and breaking fine nibs. How many black stains in the wood that still have yet to leach away, despite weeks of scrubbing? Hard work that comes to fruition. Johnne looks as though he has regained his earlier confidence; a glimmer of a smile touches his face as he meets the Devil's eyes. The Devil smirks at Johnne, taking his face in his hand, as though inspecting a horse.

'I will enjoy having you amongst my witches. Such witchery and sorcery you shall perform in my name. Such power I shall grant you, and how mighty you shall grow. Kneel, Child. And swear over yourself to me, pledge your oath.'

Johnne kneels and the Devil places one of his hands upon his head and a boot between Johnne's feet. Once again, I'm overcome with memories of my own time, the power coursing through my skull with his touch; the overwhelming essence of his being intermingling with my own. Like being set on fire, drowned in a sea of ice and being reborn all at once, while your soul sings in harmony.

"Everything betwixt the crown of my head, and the soles of my feet belong to you" I hear John whisper, "I revoke my claim to any other."

Pleasured energy radiates out and I can feel my fetch curl in bliss, making my breath catch in my throat. The Devil is clearly more than satisfied of Johnne's worthiness as a new initiate. His fanged teeth showing, as he removes his hand from Johnne's forehead.

'And now the book.'

His Book appears on the ground before Johnne: ancient and sacred. The pages rustle as hot air passes over them, but the embers do not touch it.

'It is such a pleasure to have a witch who can already write.'

John signs his name into the book, taking care to write it as clearly as possible. The ink does neither runs nor bleed, nor does he smudge it with his hands. His name, black and bold. The Devil hums a sound of approval, before directing his gaze towards me.

'Such elegant penmanship, you taught him well, my favoured Gowane.'

Euphoria wraps itself around my heart: a rapture within itself; intoxicated with elation at having pleased him, and how my son continues in my tread. The book vanishes when we look away, and the

Devil steps back, deeper into the shadows away from the fire.

'*Lay your body on the ground. It is time you were bonded with your fetch.*'

Johnne follows his instruction, his skin aglow from the flickering flames. The Devil catches my eye and I understand his silent instruction. It's my turn to start the reel. Magic and rhymes fall from my mouth, a poetic meeting of chant and song: charm, and spell. It flows, the true song of the earth, guttural yet soft, like the snow on the hilltops. The others gathered, soon join in, an unholy congregation, a hymn for the Devil and his good folk.

The Incantation rouses the spirits, and many more gather to share in the experience. Many of the witches lose themselves in the dance, their fetches riding the winds whipped up by the rite, a howling tornado of limbs. The ethereal chorus continue their unhallowed melody as the Devil removes his gloves. His hands are like claws, scaled, tipped and sharp and he places one upon Johnne's chest. I change the rhythm and lead the gathering toward a crescendo. Everything is heightened, on edge of a precipice, waiting for the final spark that will lead us to bliss. I can feel the Witch Master reach in deep into our raised power, joining with it, channelling it through Johnne's soul, coalescing all his pieces together. And then there is a calamitous crash, as though worlds were ripped apart and then smashed back together. I see

Johnne's fetch and spirit form appear briefly on top of his body, radiant and opalescent- purely magnificent, before they all snapped together in a thundering roar that echoes across the gathering - merging forever.

Silence falls amongst those present; the hushed swishing of Witch's clothing as they slow their maddened dance. Many fall to the ground, spent, riding out their ecstasies. The Devil raises himself and gloves his hands. Johnne lies on the stone, unmoving, his eyes staring beyond the realms. I become aware again of the smell of the fire and the steadiness of the ground beneath my feet, the world is no longer swirling and twirling.

'Gowane, Isobel, return to your shells. You may have to come and fetch him. This is his first flight ... he may have trouble adjusting to his new gifts.'

I approach Johnne, place a hand on his shoulder, to assure myself of his safety. He is strong, and so he will not fall into madness. I turn and take the Devil's hand and kiss it, relief coming over me.

"Thank-you"

'Your supplication is truly the prettiest of things.'

His eyes glitter as he smiles.

'Before you go back, know that your troubles with Broombrae are being seen to. I shall ride in a week, be sure to join me then.'

It was fortunate that Johnne recovered fast from his initiation and that madness had not set in, as it allowed us to pass off his whereabouts with the excuse of a fever to some of the other villagers. They for the most part accepted this, far too pleased by their own child's recovery after administering Isobel's medicine. I remember Isobel's initiation - a much different story, the paralytic convulsions and spirits keeping her up all hours of day and night, gibbering to things that appeared to not be there. I'm thankful that his ride was easier.

However, someone obviously noticed, and soon enough, Broombrae decided to take advantage of his disappearance and took the cattle that he normally tended, breaking apart our wards on the barn. Johnne was distraught when I told him, but it was no matter, I decided – they would soon get their comeuppance. I pull up a stool by the hearth of our home, chalk in my hand to draw new protective seals on the stone surround. Isobel brings in heather to tie to the corners, hoping that an extra ward would be welcomed.

"I am glad that we ride tonight" I confess to her, beginning my work "We won't have many animals left if we wait too much longer"

"I only wish Johnne had longer to prepare" She replied, tightening the knots that hold her magic, perhaps a substitute for the hand wringing that her hands sought to do.

"It is but unfortunate circumstance. Too many of us have been accused in the last few years, and even though their spirits live on and attend our rites, there are still things that only us mortals can do."

"I know," she laments "but it still does not ease my heart. They have witches of their own, those who tie themselves to other creatures not of our master, and they have those who follow Christ but still ride the winds. They broke through our wards before, and it makes matters complicated." I sigh, as she did Indeed, speak the truth.

"Johnne is very talented, and he will do just fine. He rides in spirit as though he were fae. The skills the master gave him are great and numerous" I say to her, to reassure her as much as to reassure myself.

She makes the small noise of a disgruntled mother, and I know nothing I say will ease her concerns. I place an arm around her and stare into the fire, content in being in the moment just for now.

My flight that night was different - atop a horse that galloped through the stormy clouds, and with each beat of their hooves, thunder rumbles across the mountains. The Devil rode at the foremost, his figure as black as the night, eyes as red as blood, a golden bow across his back and a silver whip by his side. With a crack of his whip, the dead rose from their graves, stiff even in spirit as they merged with the throng. As he raised it to the heavens, lost souls, normally captured by the light of the moon came to join us in our quest. With the whip striking the dirt he called to the fae to come out of their mounds to join their spectral flight. Soon enough, there were witches and ghosts upon the wind, riding through to the village of Broombrae. The Witch master had given me the finest of bows to use on this night, with elf-arrows a'plenty to use in defence of our village.

The horde fell upon the village, shouting and howling, to find the thieves and swindlers. Thatched roofs were set alight and the fires made us a ghastly sight. It didn't take long for their own witches to cast their hats to the winds and challenge us. Tangles of bodies, as we were all thrown across the clouds.

Soon there was a frightening battle in the sky, ugly and bloody. Arrows sailed out of my bow, to sicken those who took one to their flesh. The Devil's whip rained fire upon the souls he caught, damning them eternally. The witches of this village had not merged with their fetch, resulting in less cohesiveness with their own attack: wild and fleeting. I aimed my bow at a fleeing witch and struck her dead with my arrow. Her fetch went into a wild rage, and it was next to be put out of its misery.

My fetch rode behind me, casting enchantments over the fields to blacken their crops. I rode up next to Johnne, also on a steed.

"Animate that witch's corpse, her body could still hold use to us yet, even though it is without spirit" I ordered.

Johnne nods as he rides down to her home, his own fetch going to work on the protective spells that surrounded it.

I had no time for praise or pride, but I felt both in that moment as I rode on further to the barn. I land my horse upon the roof, hooves scattering on the wood and thatching. I approach the animals, coaxing them out of their hiding spaces, their eyes wide and afraid.

I turn to my fetch, "Take them back to Alford, ensure they are secure and stay put to make sure that none of the thieves escape us and cause harm to our village."

He flits off, his form melting in with the shadows as he guides the animals back home. I return to the fight, spells crafted by the movements of my fingers and with whisperings of sacred words. I smile as figures fall from the sky, brought down by my hand, my village's revenge, and justice almost complete. A sudden force comes at me from the side, knocking my spirit form into the stone wall of a nearby house. Momentarily stunned I gaze up at the sky above me, the glittering stars, glowing spirit forms, fiery whips and dying souls, all merging together to form a warped but beautiful image as the colours merged together like paint on the canvases of the rich.

Another blow to my stomach as the witch was upon me, fingernails scratching at my face. She is here in her shell- her physical body, her iron jewellery enchanted to keep her spirit locked inside. I can smell the pigs' blood under her nails and know that she is trying to curse me. I hope my offerings to the heather spirits have been ample this year as I evoke their spirits and powers, rubbing the heather over my wound before I backhand the witch. The Witch stumbles back, screeching. She prepares to cast another curse, grabbing iron nails from her pocket, whispering banishing chants, before, quite suddenly, a pitchfork runs her through. I hear the wail of her fetch as she dies. Her body falls forward, revealing Johnne and his reanimated corpse, still holding the pitchfork. Gone was the child I once knew, and Oh, how he had grown into something so fierce and wonderful.

"Sometimes mortal problems require mortal solutions" he says, concentrating at the situation at hand.

Isobel descends from the sky, her crimson hair floating with her flight, eyes fiery with channelled fury.

"The Master says that the priests are coming, we should head back before they get here."

I close my eyes for a second and will my shell to open its eyes. I see my fetch holding guard over me. He tilts his head as he crouches down.

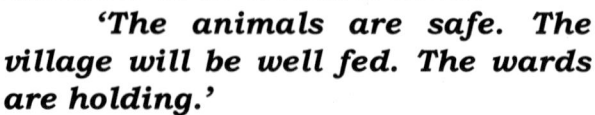

'The animals are safe. The village will be well fed. The wards are holding.'

I snap back to my spirit body and whistle for my horse.

"The animals are safe." I say as I kiss my wife, "Burn down the barn."

She smiles a crooked smile as she summons fire spirits from the bowels of hell, her arms moving to a dance none of us could hear. Soon enough, the fires that provided light for the barn grew hotter until their sparks set the wood ablaze. A ferocious splintering, and creaking groaned out from the timbers as it started to collapse in on itself. I pick her up and place her on my horse as she cackles to the wind, and I grin as I hold her close. There is majesty to her ecstatic madness when she is in flight. It is another part of her that I love.

'You both have such passion for your craft.'

His voice slithers across our shoulders as the Devil rides alongside us.

'You exalt in all I have to offer you. You cherish it. When you finally are called back to the flame, you will find such peace there. Your family is glorious in its worship.'

Johnne finally catches up to us, and the Devil turns his head.

'And you, my child. Your words reach the heavens and drag them down to walk again. It's magnificent how you use my gifts.'

We ride across the cairns and the hills and into the night before we return back to our shells, our souls in need of rest, but our work done. It was maybe less than a week after that, while my wife was weaving, and my son was fixing the barn that the men came with their iron shackles and their torches. They were mortal men and priests, and we professed our innocence, claimed that we were good children of God. We were honour bound Protestants, and good unto the Word. The villagers rallied around us, those who we had healed and nurtured, whose crops we brought into being. However, somebody from Broombrae must have seen us that night, and ran to tell their saviours, presumably leaving out their own sins as the priests called us by name.

Isobel hissed and spat as they beat her with fire irons and sliced at her skin. And she groans with pain, as she misses her son, her warm fire, and our nights together. They tore at my clothes to find witches marks, and when they found none they decided to make their own. I start to gibber and lose my mind as they keep me awake for nights on end, my head hurts, and I'm never sated of thirst. Their nasty iron implements scratching and gouging, causing my flesh to mould and rot. I know nothing of what happened to Johnne, as either his cell was too far away, or perhaps, as I hoped, had escaped.

My heart longed for the latter, my only point of sanity. My fetch stays by my side the whole time. Uttering soothing words, taking messages to the others so they know of our fate. He returns one day and kneels by my side. I look at him over the top of my knees and it hits me how emaciated I am, my shin bones shining through my skin. He purrs comfortingly.

'The Master knows of your state. He asks if you wish to leave your

shells behind and join his hunt? We'll still be together, you and I. As he made it to forever be.'

"Is your fetch here?" Isobel's voice, weary, but the softest thing on my ears comes out from the darkness, "Has he seen our son? Has he seen Johnne?" My fetch remains silent, his colours are muted as if in a deep despair.

"I don't think so, my love" I stuttered, "He has spoken to the master, he asks if we wish to leave our shells behind and join his hunt"

She screamed and cried at the lack of news, a mourner's wail, as I hear her sobs catch on her dry throat.

'There are guards around this place, laid by mortal men. Tamed iron and wards hold him away- I am only here because I am bound to you, probably not a small consolation.'

A small smile reaches my lips as my sweet familiar still tries to hold my spirits high.

'But he works a plan to rescue you. But it may take time. He suggests that you may prefer something ... simpler.'

I breathe deeply, and my ribs splinter, pain across my breast. It was, as ever with the master, our choice in the end. My words to the fair Margaret echo across my mind as I try to keep my eyes open, my body falling to delirium.

He asks for no such thing you are not willing to give, and he forces no one to do his will. He asks, but the fates of men are their fates alone. People can cast blame upon him, but he has none in his heart.

It was always decisions, always choices. Always a barter, always a gamble. How simple it must be for men of God, to have no choice. To always follow and be certain of their actions. To work within their four walls of plain stone with no richness and texture. How simple. How tragic.

I listen to my wife's ragged breathing and the sound of iron on stone as she drags her arms, trailing shackles behind her.

This was no place we should be, unable to fly. Unable to dance with the stars and drum around the fire. To never smell burning rosemary and chatter with the spirits of the forest. Unable to help the sick and curse the wicked. Locked away, unable to see our kin and unable to let our souls gallop on the winds and laugh from the mountaintops.

This was no place we should be; unable to fly. And now we had our choice, and it was ours to make alone. My fetch leant close to me and my masters voice left his lips.

'*You are never alone.*'

ELIZABETH CLARKE
(1565 – 1645)

Elizabeth Clarke was the first woman persecuted by the Witchfinder General, Matthew Hopkins in Essex, England. At 80 years old, she was accused of witchcraft by local tailor John Rivet. Hopkins and his assistant John Stearne took on the role of investigators. Elizabeth was later tried at Chelmsford assizes and sentenced to death by hanging.

Matthew Hopkins
Witch finder General.

Matthew Hopkins: Drunk on Power

AN UNREMARKABLE LIFE
Issy Ballard

Elizabeth Baxter had always been an extremely imaginative child. She would constantly tell her mother and father wild stories about the people who lived in the rural village of Essex. One such story, that particularly stood out to her mother, was one that later proved too realistic to be the work of a child's imagination. Elizabeth's mother, vividly remembered standing in their bakery kitchen when Elizabeth stormed in red faced, puffing, and shouting something about missing children.

"Elizabeth, you must calm down before you try to speak, or you'll never catch your breath," her mother was not an unkind woman but had little patience for her daughter's shenanigans.

She stood still for a moment, trying to steady her breath before launching into her story.

"Jaime and Amelie were playing near the water, and they got swept away by the current. Neither of them knows how to swim, and they're drowning about a mile downstream. I could hear them gurgling water, it was a horrible sound, like a drowning cat" She finished her story with a sigh and collapsed into a nearby chair.

"How do you know all this? And how on Earth could you hear them gargling water if they were a mile away?

Did you see them getting swept away?" her mother was beginning to panic, thinking of these poor children on the verge of drowning.

"I saw it in the water like a dream. I was looking into the well and instead of my own reflection I could see Jaime and Amelie splashing around by the stream. Then Amelie tripped over a rock and landed face first in the water, Jamie held onto her leg, but the current was far too strong, and they were both swept away." Elizabeth said this as if it was an everyday occurrence for everybody.

Her mother groaned, grabbed her by the arm, and pulled her to the door.

"How many times have I told you Elizabeth, I am extremely busy, and don't have time to listen to your lies!"

Elizabeth tried to protest, but her mother could be stone cold when she wanted to be and pushed Elizabeth out of the door slamming it shut behind her.

Sobbing quietly from her mother's reaction, Elizabeth walked along the edge of the stream, tossing pebbles into the water and watching them get dragged downstream. She heard a twig break and looked up to see who was there. To her horror the mother of Jaime and Amelie was looking around in the woods beside the stream and stopping every now and then to lean over the water as far as she could. Elizabeth put her head down and tried to walk past without being seen, but to no avail and she heard her name ring out through the silence.

"Elizabeth!" she looked round to see Jaime and Amelie's mother over.

"Have you seen Jaime or Amelie? I told them not to go any further: to just stay here."

Elizabeth stood motionless, fear coursing through her veins at the thought of having to tell a mother her children were dead. The mother looked at Elizabeth expectantly for a few moments but got no answer and so she turned back around and continued her search deeper and deeper into the trees, calling out her children's names as she went.

As soon as Elizabeth was sure the mother was out of sight, she sped back home and vowed to never look into the well again. That night she quietly cried herself to sleep, all alone in her home while her mother Matilda worked in the bakery and Branwell her father fetched supplies from the neighbouring town.

★

Elizabeth woke to the sound of her father returning home. It was late in the evening and the full moon shone, dazzling in the sky: the candle had burned away, and Elizabeth's room was pitch dark.

Elizabeth wanted to say goodnight to her father, and so she stole out of her bed and crept downstairs. However, the scene that met her was grave: her father looked tired and devastated, his thick, dark hair was ruffled and messy, and his, once shining eyes were dull. Her mother too was white as a sheet. Elizabeth froze, and craned her neck, straining to hear what they were talking about.

"Their mother has not stopped worrying for hours, their father is still at the forest hoping they will appear. Their children are too bold, wandering into the forest with wolves and bears and the like stalking around."

"I'm not so sure they're in the forest," her mother said in a hushed voice, her eyes filled with fear.

"What do you mean by that?" her father replied sharply.

"Elizabeth told me something earlier, I didn't listen properly but now its caused my blood to run cold. She said, she was looking into the well and had a ... well, a vision of sorts. She claimed the children had fallen into the stream and were being swept downstream. I believe their family might be looking in the wrong direction." An uncomfortable silence settled around the room, as the significance of her mother's implications became obvious.

"I hope you're not trying to imply my daughter is a Wytch," he eventually replied laughing.

"Matilda, please tell me you're not hysterical."

Elizabeth didn't stay to hear another word, she rushed up the stairs, and climbed back into bed. Although she was unable to sleep, constantly going over what she had overheard. She wasn't sure what a Wytch was, but she was sure it wasn't a word she wanted to be associated with. She swore to herself that she would never do anything out of the ordinary again, and that from here onward she would lead an unremarkable life.

5ᵀᴴ JANUARY 1583

This was the day of Elizabeth Baxters' eighteenth birthday, and the festivities began as soon as she was awake. Her mother had lined her room with brilliantly coloured flowers, and had laid perfume soaked cloths around her bed, so upon waking she would feel as though she were lying in a beautifully scented meadow watching the sunrise.

She opened her eyes with the biggest smile on her face, as long as she could remember her mother had promised an eighteenth birthday so heavenly that even God would be envious.

Elizabeth had recently taken up the brunt of the family business, as her father had been taken ill with polio and was on strict bed rest until the symptoms passed. She travelled to the neighbouring village once a week to pick up baking and general household supplies. She met with the other business owners once a month to discuss business, and although they rarely, in fact never took any notice of Elizabeth's ideas, she was grateful to be invited to the meetings.

Elizabeth heard a gentle knock on her door, followed by her mother appearing in the doorway carrying a range of gifts. She entered and sat on the edge of Elizabeth's bed.

"Happy birthday, sweet Elizabeth. Here are some gifts from me, your father, and the neighbours too as it's a special birthday."

The gifts included pressed flowers preserved in small jars to brighten her room, a variety of herbs as Elizabeth loved their scent, beautiful fabrics, sweet breads her mother had made, and birthday notes from all the neighbours.

"When you're ready to come downstairs, your father will be waiting to wish you happy birthday, perhaps I'll even braid your hair before we light the bonfire."

She gently stroked Elizabeth's face before leaving the room. Elizabeth got dressed into a fine, brown silk dress with jewel embellishments around the collar and sleeves: the only dress she owned.

As she came downstairs, she saw her father, frail and delicate sitting in a makeshift wheelchair, but beaming with the strength of a thousand suns. Her heart soared seeing her father once more finding his inner strength, and she thought that absolutely nothing could go wrong.

Her mother carefully braided her hair weaving small flowers in and out of the soft, chestnut strands of hair. Wearing her best dress and with her hair done, Elizabeth felt almost beautiful; a feeling completely alien to her.

"You should get some fresh air while I'm preparing the bonfire," her mother suggested. "Just be sure to be back before dusk."

Elizabeth obliged, and wandered through small town. She took in the beauty of her surroundings; something that she had never noticed before, how the birds arranged themselves when they flew, the sound of the rustling leaves, the light reflecting off the water in the well.

Elizabeth had avoided the well like the plague since that fateful day the Jamie and Amelie died. However, today she looked, and the water was so still she could see her reflection as clear as day. Her reflection was as beautiful as she felt, she had grown into a fair-complexioned young woman, with rosy cheeks and bronze skin from the sun. Some of her hair had escaped the braids and hung in wisps framing her face, shining in the winter sun that was flooding the town.

At the bottom of the well embers seemed to flare, floating to the surface, before disappearing. Elizabeth squinted her eyes to try and make out what was happening down there. She managed to make out a great flame rising up from a pile of wood stacked as high as a house. People were dancing and laughing around the fire, and she recognised herself and her mother among those enjoying the fire.

She watched with a smile for a few moments before the scene dramatically changed. The fire turned black and rancid. The smile dropped from Elizabeth's face and she wanted to turn away, and although she suspected something catastrophic was about to happen, she still couldn't stop herself from watching. Her mother, smiling, went to step over a stray log, but instead tripped, landing directly in the fire.

Elizabeth immediately jolted, standing bolt upright clasping her hand over her mouth; she let out a whimper. She stood frozen for a few moments, trying to take in what she had just seen, before sprinting back home, leaving a trail of scattered flowers behind her.

By the time Elizabeth got home the bonfire was already ablaze she stared in horror as her family and neighbours were already grouped around the fire and dangerously close. She froze, desperately wanting to drag her mother away from the fire, but unable to move her feet.

"Elizabeth!" she had been so lost in thought, she hadn't realised her mother had been calling her.

"Come here." Elizabeth replied, desperate to get her mother away from the fire. With a confused look, Matilda broke away from the group to talk to her daughter.

"What's the matter? You look terrible? Oh no! What happened to your hair? Matilda tucked a stray strand behind Elizabeth's ear.

"Don't go near the fire," Elizabeth begged, with tears in her eyes.

"Why not?" Matilda asked. She had the same look on her face, as she did when Elizabeth had come to her as a child with her 'wild stories.'

"It's so dangerous," Elizabeth pleaded, she grabbed her mother's arm and attempted to drag her further back from the fire.

Matilda groaned and shook Elizabeth off.

"You're being ridiculous, I have organised this for you, so come over and enjoy it." she hissed.

Elizabeth started to cry, which made others take their attention away from the bonfire, instead looking over to see what all the fuss was about. "You must stop this." Matilda yelled, pulling Elizabeth towards the bonfire. Elizabeth tried to keep her feet firmly in place, but her mother was too strong, and she began to stumble forward.

"NO." she screamed.

In a fit of panic, she yanked her arm back, causing Matilda to lurch backwards. In what seemed like slow motion, she tripped over a stray log. A look of terror passed her face as she fell backwards, desperately grasping for something, but there was nothing but air. Within seconds she was in the fire: a terrible scream rang out amongst the crowd.

People stopped laughing and dancing as they realised what had happened. More and more screams could be heard as people frantically tried to rescue Matilda, but the fire was too hot to get close to. The smell of burning flesh filled the air, thick and nauseating.

While those gathered were panicked, frantically trying to rescue Matilda, Elizabeth stood stationary, unable to tear her eyes away from the horror of her mother's mutating body. Blood rushed to her ears, her skin went cold, and her hands began to jitter uncontrollably. She could barely hear the crowd screaming; all she could hear was her mother's awful wailing swimming around inside her head.

Elizabeth hadn't even realised she was motionless, until somebody grabbed her arm and pulled her away from the awful scene. She barely even cared to notice who was leading her away until she realised she was by the well. That awful well that had shown her nothing but death and suffering.

She finally focused her eyes on her surroundings and realised Jaime and Amelie's mother, Faye, was walking with her, gently holding her hand. She wanted to speak but her voice caught in her throat.

"I am so sorry Elizabeth. I can't imagine the pain you must be feeling." Faye said softly, at this point they were at the edge of the forest.

Elizabeth just looked at her, still unable to speak.

"I know when they found the bodies of Jaime and Amelie, I didn't find the energy to get out of bed for a fortnight. It was incidentally your sweet mother who led me to eventually find them, she'd had some kind of idea they might have been swept downstream. Even though I lost my babies, I can't imagine the pain of watching your mother die, and in such a violent way."

It was clear Faye thought she was helping, but each word felt like a knife stabbing into her head.

"I ... I'm sorry," Elizabeth finally managed to choke out.

"Elizabeth this wasn't your fault, it was a terrible accident, but you can't blame yourself." Faye said kindly, taking her hand again.

Elizabeth just nodded, gulping back tears loudly.

"Why are we here?" she asked, her voice thick with emotion.

"I thought you may like the calm here. I come here a lot to talk with Jaime and Amelie." Faye said.

"Sorry?" Elizabeth asked sharply.

"Jaime and Amelie, this is the only place they'll talk. It was their favourite place to play." her voice was full of glee, the kind of glee a grieving mother feels when she finds a doll that looks like her child. Elizabeth looked at her strangely for a minute, but Faye's smile didn't falter.

"Jaime and Amelie are dead." she said flatly, she couldn't muster the energy to be kind.

"Yes, their bodies have perished, but their souls live on and they visit me here." Faye explained.

Elizabeth began to back away, not wanting to associate herself with this. It sounded far too much like devil worship.

"No, no, don't leave" Faye begged. "I can show you."

She closed her eyes and wrapped her arms around herself. After a few moments she began to laugh, a laugh that although sweet on the surface made you want to run away as far as you could.

"I can hear them. Their voices are so sweet" she laughed, tears streaming down her face.

Elizabeth took this as an opportunity to escape and she ran the entire way home, tears flying out behind her.

As she got home she realised the door was ajar, and candlelight was pouring out. She crept inside and saw her father was sitting in his wheelchair, his back to the door. She tried to pass by him as quiet as possible, but he sensed she was there.

"She's passed." he said flatly.

"I know," Elizabeth whispered, her voice seemed loud in the deathly silence of their home.

"What were you and her arguing about?" he asked, in a monotone voice.

"I thought the fire was dangerous." Elizabeth explained timidly.

"Was it another vision?" his voice picked up, and Elizabeth could sense his anger bubbling beneath the surface.

"Yes." Elizabeth admitted, seeing no point in lying.

There was silence for a moment, and Elizabeth considered walking away, thinking her father was done.

"FREAK" he exploded. "You're a freak and a Wytch, and you're no daughter of mine. You are never to speak another word to me again, and before the year is out you will have found a husband and you will be gone."

Obediently, Elizabeth held her tongue and crept past him to go to bed. She lay in her bed, in her sweetly perfumed, beautifully decorated room, and cried the entire night: the next day, and the day after that.

27ᵀᴴ MARCH 1590

A lot changed for Elizabeth Baxter in seven years. For a start she was no longer Elizabeth Baxter, she was now Elizabeth Clarke. She was married to a tailor's assistant named Alistair Clarke, in a shop owned by a tailor named John Rivet. Mr Rivet was younger than Elizabeth and Alistair. At just twenty years old his father had died, leaving him the family business.

They had met when Elizabeth was meeting with the tailor in order to make her father a new jacket. Although she hadn't spoken to her father in seven years, and despite him not attending her wedding, she still bought him a new jacket every year, ever since his polio had left him paralysed.

He could still speak and the very few times Elizabeth tried to visit him, after her banishment, he had screamed at her for consorting with the Devil, demanding she leave. His neighbours would check on him when they found the time. However, his condition, and the horrific death of his wife had made him extremely angry about his condition, and everybody dreaded seeing him as he treated them appallingly.

Elizabeth didn't much like John Rivet, any time she had entered the shop he would tut, mutter, and cast her dark looks. Elizabeth assumed he must have heard the stories which had spread through the town like wildfire. Hardly any of them contained little, if any truth, the most popular one was that Elizabeth had cast a dark incantation, causing the fire to reach out and wrap itself around her mother, dragging her into the flames.

Many of Elizabeth's neighbours, those she had once called aunts, were the people spreading this fabricated tale. It seemed the once tight knit community, was coming apart at the seams.

Over the past seven years many seemed to have forgotten, but there were still a few people who remembered her mother's death and as a result Elizabeth had become rather reclusive. She stayed at home most of the time cleaning, cooking, and waiting for her husband to come home: wondering where the confident business-woman in her had gone.

One thing that Elizabeth enjoyed doing was making medicines using the herbs Alistair sometimes bought from the market. She would grind the different herbs together and blend them with water to form a paste. She could heal burns, cure colds, typhus, and malaria. Keeping some of them under the bed could also cure diseases of the mind, including depression and hysteria.

Originally, Elizabeth just made them to cure her and her husband's maladies, but once people learned she was making them they began paying to be cured. This didn't help her image, but it did give her a taste of being a business-woman again; and she couldn't get enough. She would make batches upon batches to cure a variety of ailments, the most common of which was hysteria. This was caused by the dramatically increased death toll; the Black Death was something which Elizabeth sadly couldn't cure.

On Tuesdays Alistair finished his work at four in the afternoon, making this Elizabeth's favourite day of the week. She would cook his favourite meal and lay flowers on the table, ready for his arrival. This particular Tuesday Elizabeth heard the door open as usual and ran to greet her husband.

"Welcome home, how was your day?"
Elizabeth smiled; she loved the sight of her husband. Alistair sighed, rubbing his temples, and completely disregarding her question.

"What's the matter?" Elizabeth faltered slightly. Alistair looked troubled.

"Come and sit down," he said, not looking at her. Elizabeth obediently followed him to the table and sat down opposite him.

"So how was your ..." she started, but Alistair cut over her.

"... I have to go to London." he said flatly.

"Great! I would love to go to London we could go to the Globe Theatre, and look around the markets, and take in the culture it'll be amazing." Elizabeth exclaimed, her heart jumping at the thought of leaving the small town and going somewhere where nobody knew her.

"No," Alistair said sharply. "I have to go to London. Alone."

"I don't understand, how long are you going for? ... A week?" she asked, her heart began to sink, as she knew the words she never wanted to hear were coming.

"I'm going to live there. There's nothing left for me here." he explained bluntly.

"So, I'm nothing?" tears started to pool in Elizabeth's eyes, her ears started to ring, and blood began to rush to her face.

"Yes, you're nothing Elizabeth," he declared nastily. "You have utterly destroyed my life here in Essex. Not only do people avoid me when I am out with you, but you're barren. You have spent so much time talking with the devil that he has taken both your soul and your womb. A woman who can't bear children is not a woman. She is worthless." With these final words he packed up his bag, taking it and his coat and left.

Elizabeth felt as if she had been stabbed in the stomach. She could barely stand up to clear the table. She recalled how when she had found out she couldn't have children she had cried for a full six days. It was her husband's strength that had helped her to move on. Now everything was crashing down around her.

She grabbed the largest jar of hysteria mix she could find and placed it under her bed, in order to slow her tears. Unfortunately, she couldn't quiet her mind long enough to drift into sleep.

It was several hours later, when the candles had burned down, and the night was black as pitch that Elizabeth's tears finally stopped; she felt almost peaceful, yet her mind was still churning over the days event.

She got up, having decided to take a walk through the empty town. It was almost silent outside and for the first time in her life she felt completely alone in the world; it was a nice feeling.

When Elizabeth reached the stream, she took her shoes off and waded into the calm water. It was extremely cold, and she shivered violently, but the cold helped clear her mind. Despite the cold, she continued her walk, and as she grew nearer to the forest, Elizabeth could see a small figure hunched over at the entrance; she felt no fear and approached.

"Who's there?" She asked loudly, causing the noise of the forest to quieten for a moment. The figure looked up and to Elizabeth's surprise it was the mother of Jaime and Amelie: their eyes met, and it was as if no time had passed since that fateful night when her mother died.

"You're Jaime and Amelie's mother," Elizabeth whispered.

"I think we know each other well enough for you to call me Faye." she muttered, her eyes darting around madly, as if she was searching for something.

"What are you doing here?" Elizabeth asked, sitting herself down on the ground opposite Faye.

"I'm talking to my sweet Jaime and Amelie."

"Still?" Elizabeth enquired in a hushed voice.

"They talk to me every night, they never grew up, so they sound the same." Faye had tears streaming down her face, but she was laughing.

"Can I hear them speak?" Elizabeth shivered, but with excitement; she no longer felt cold or afraid.

"They would love that. They've been asking to speak to you for years."

"They have?" Elizabeth asked cautiously.

"They have." Faye was no longer smiling, although tears continued streaming down her face.

Elizabeth waited patiently as Faye lit twelve candles and placed them around the pair in a circle. A haze appeared to fill the circle, and the air sweltered around them. It felt as though they were caught between worlds. She could hear various whispers but couldn't make out any actual words and couldn't see any faces.

"Jaime! Amelie! Follow my voice!" Faye cried.

The voices got louder and louder, and closer and closer. The words they were saying became clearer and clearer until Elizabeth could hear what they were talking about, as if they were beside her.

"Who's this?" the voice of a young boy asked.

"This is formally Elizabeth Baxter, presently Elizabeth Clarke." Faye answered smugly.

"Mother, you did it," exclaimed a young girls voice.

"What does she mean?" Elizabeth demanded.

"Be quiet!" snapped Faye, her eyes filled with anger and her voice filled with hate.

"What are you talking about?" Elizabeth screamed, as the voices around her became louder and louder.

"You let my children die!" Faye bawled.

"No, I didn't. It was an accident!" Elizabeth began to cry, guilt crashing around in her mind.

"You're right, you didn't do anything!" Faye shouted accusingly.

The wind grew stronger the candle flames whipped furiously but were never extinguished. Elizabeth could barely hear but Faye who was still screaming accusations at her.

The wind seemed to die down as quickly as it came, and the soft voices of the children spoke.

"You saw us. In the water ... falling in." Jaime started.

"In the well. You saw it in a vision, yet you let us die." Amelie continued.

"You could've saved us, but you held your tongue." Concluded Jaime.

"You killed my children." Faye whispered, pointing a shaking finger at Elizabeth.

Elizabeth sobbed loudly and put her hands behind her to steady herself. She accidentally knocked over one of the candles, and in doing so, broke the circle and the connection.

"What did you do?" Faye shrieked, desperately trying to grab the candle to reinstate the circle.

She also tried to grab for Elizabeth, who had already leapt to her feet and was on her way home.

She raced past the stream and the well, not bothering to check if anybody saw her.

As soon as she got home she slammed the door behind her and stood panting, desperately trying to compose herself.

18ᵀᴴ MAY 1604

For the most part, Elizabeth led a solitary life, she had no friends, no family, and no husband. Her father had died in 1595, but nobody had realised for a full month: not until the flies were so thick that people couldn't see through the window, and the smell of death began to escape the house.

Following the wishes of her father, Elizabeth had excluded herself from his funeral. She was also strictly prohibited from visiting his grave; knowing that her father hated her even in death devastated Elizabeth. However, nobody could really stop Elizabeth from visiting his grave, and once a week after midnight she would sit by his graveside, and sing sweet songs trying to guide him into Heaven.

Sadly, there was another, smaller outbreak of polio in Essex, and Elizabeth was severely ill. It was one of the worst cases the doctors had seen. Most people got mild symptoms, like that of a common cold lasting anywhere from a few weeks to a year. Equally, most people fully recovered. A few people had been confined to using wheelchairs for a little while; at least until they regained the feeling in their legs. In Elizabeth's case it seemed as though the disease had disconnected her leg from the rest of her body, have eaten through the muscle. The village doctor recommended amputation, which Elizabeth was totally against, until the pain got so unbearable she would do anything to alleviate it. In 1603 the surgery was completed.

As expected, the amputation was painful, but Elizabeth reduced the pain by swallowing herbal tinctures, and using various poultices on the wound. By 1604 the wound had completely healed, and Elizabeth appeared to barely notice it anymore. However, she refused to spend her life constricted to a wheelchair like her father, so she fashioned a pair of walking crutches out of a branch, from a large oak tree in the forest.

Elizabeth found herself walking in the forest daily. Faye no longer frequented it, as when Elizabeth knocked over the candle that night she broke the bond between her and her children. As a result, Jaime and Amelie were no longer tethered to the world of the living; perhaps they had finally found some peace. That same night when Faye realised she could no longer talk with her children, she poisoned herself in an attempt to reconnect with them. Her death was just one of many tragedies.

The reason Elizabeth spent so much time walking in the forest was that she was trying to build up the courage to do what Faye had done so easily; communicate with the spirits from the other world.

This particular night Elizabeth had finally plucked up the courage enough to take candles, which gave her the necessary strength. She sat down on the earthy ground deep in the forest, making sure nobody saw her, and laid her crutches down beside her.

Carefully, she lit each candle and set them in a circle around herself. Immediately the air seemed to shimmer, and she felt the voices of hundreds, if not thousands of spirits whispering.

"Matilda! ... Bramwell!" Elizabeth called for her mother and father.

She heard a soft voice come closer and become clearer.

"Mother?" Elizabeth whispered.

She felt her mother's soft hand stroke her cheek, and she began to sob. It had been so long since she'd felt any affection it felt completely alien to her.

"I'm here," her mother said kindly.

"Please forgive me," Elizabeth gasped.

"There's nothing to forgive, you tried to warn me, and I didn't listen. You've done nothing wrong."

"I wish I could see you." Elizabeth desperately wanted to hug her mother, but her mother wasn't really there to hug.

"I'm glad you can't see me. I look exactly how I did the moment I died. I am burned to the bone, and my hair is gone and my eyes liquified. What little skin I do have is red and blistered." Matilda's description made Elizabeth shudder.

"Where's my father?" Elizabeth asked, after a moment of silence.

"I don't know, I haven't seen him. There is so many spirit's. It's like we are all cramped together in a box." She replied, a tone of melancholy in her voice.

"That's horrifying." Elizabeth began to cry again.

"It's not so bad." Elizabeth felt her mother's hand reassuringly touch her face again.

"Does this mean Heaven isn't real? Has God abandoned us?" Elizabeth asked.

"I have no answers for you Elizabeth, all I know is that I always tried to follow the word of God and now I live in Purgatory, it's hard to tell what in life matters any more. However, I would advise you to follow the path that is right for you. Don't base what you do while you're living on what might happen when you die." Her mother's voice began to get further and further away, until it was gone completely.

Elizabeth sat for a moment, hoping that her father might hear her pleas and that he would speak to her, but he didn't, and so instead, she broke the circle and headed home.

Over the past few years Elizabeth had gathered more and more herbs; not just locally but from more distant, if not exotic places, until she could do much more than heal. People would visit from all over for Elizabeth to grant wishes for them, and they would pay handsomely for her services.

Sometimes they sought luck in love, other times marriage, or even lust. Sometimes they wanted Elizabeth to make pouches of herbs for them to take home and use against those they believed had wronged them. Sometimes people just wanted to buy small amounts of the more exotic herbs in order to create their own concoctions.

However, whispers had grown commonplace around the neighbouring towns, claiming that Wytch hunters were coming into the towns and slaughtering women and even young girls whose behaviour was out of the ordinary. In fact, many of them would simply refuse to leave a town until they had killed at least ten women and children. These rumours didn't worry Elizabeth, since Essex was such an unimportant village unlike the larger places such as London and Suffolk, which were so large it seemed unlikely the Wytch hunters would ever make it to Elizabeth.

9TH NOVEMBER 1645

Elizabeth was old now 81 years old and one of the oldest people to ever live in the village of Essex. She still sold herbs and tinctures, but old age and infirmity had rendered her unable to leave the village, so it was difficult for her to obtain the rare herbs that people came from far away to buy.

Elizabeth was also becoming increasingly worried about Wytch hunters, although the trend seemed to be dying out; Wytchcraft had apparently been eradicated in large villages and towns. As a result, Wytch hunters were finding their way into the smaller villages.

It was said two avid Wytch hunters: Matthew Hopkins, and John Stearne, had received news of a Wytch in Elizabeth's own village and were making their way to Essex and would be arriving in around four days. Elizabeth disposed of all of her herbs and tools used to communicate with spirits. However, there was nothing Elizabeth could do about her appearance or reputation and knew the Wytch hunters investigations would lead them to her.

In fact, people seemed to be trying to frame her; several times she had found chicken bones on her doorstep and blood smeared on her door. Elizabeth was sure her days were numbered, and it would probably take less than a few hours for the Wytch hunters to determine she was a Wytch.

She didn't see herself as a Wytch, she used no special powers, cast no spells, and did not consort with the devil: she used natural herbs and sold these along with her remedies and flowers in order to survive. She lit candles in order to communicate with spirits who travelled easily between the worlds of life and death.

13TH NOVEMBER 1645

On the 13th November 1645 Matthew Hopkins and John Stearne arrived in Essex. It took them less than half an hour to for them to hammer on Elizabeth's door. She tried to ignore it, but they were so persistent, leaving her no choice but to open the door.

"How may I help you?" Elizabeth inquired.

"Save the formalities," one of them said, as they both pushed past her and sat down.

She sat herself down opposite them. They were as different as night and day. Matthew Hopkins was tall, lean, dark, and mysterious, with a hat that covered his brooding eyebrows: his black eyes stared out from under it accusingly. His hair was silky and dark as midnight and rested on his shoulders weightlessly. He wore a long black, trench coat, which bore the mark of Rivet Tailors on the sleeve, where she had met Alistair. Hopkins clearly had some Mediterranean heritage which was apparent from his tanned skin and eye shape. He sat bolt upright with a look of disgust on his face that only an Englishman could have. He couldn't have been more than twenty years old, full of youth and excitement of life, that only one who hadn't lived very long could feel.

John Stearne, on the other hand was short, with straw coloured hair cut almost down to the scalp. His eyes were stormy like the sea, but there was an undertone of kindness and understanding, although Elizabeth was certain she would get no kindness from this man. He wore the clothes of a poor man, although it was clear by his demeanour that he had more money than he knew what to do with.

Elizabeth allowed the silence to reign for a few more minutes, before clearing her throat and initiating the conversation.

"I'm not going to pretend I don't know who you are, but I'm also not going to pretend I know why you're here," Elizabeth said loudly, trying to establish dominance early in the conversation.

"Mrs Clarke, I think you know full well why we're here. In fact, the supplier of our information seemed very confident you know exactly what you are." Matthew Hopkins said coldly his eyes fixed on Elizabeth.

"Well, who is the supplier of your information?" she asked.

"I don't have to tell you, but I will. John Rivet. He says he saw you casting enchantments many times." Matthew smirked.

"I'm not sure what you're talking about," Elizabeth jittered nervously.

Matthew leaned forward, till he was almost within an inch of Elizabeth's face.

"I would like for you to stop talking," he hissed. "The fact is Mrs Clarke we have witnesses and proof of your despicable acts, and in a few days' time a rope will be sucking the sweet air out of your lungs." He laughed loudly, repositioning himself once more.

Elizabeth silenced herself, and her eyes dropped towards the floor, unable to meet the eyes of either man anymore.

"What happened to your leg?" John asked pointedly.

"Polio." Elizabeth answered simply.

"You know, there is some scientific that proof polio is a punishment from God for consorting with the Devil." Matthew laughed again, it seemed he was drunk with power; people's lives were nothing more than a joke to him.

"Mrs Clarke if you would just confirm that you have been practicing Wytchcraft your pain will be over. You are old now, clearly infirm, with no husband, and no income. What kind of quality of life can you have?" John said, it appeared he was trying to be kind but each reason she should die wore out Elizabeth's heart more and more.

"I'm not sure I understand what you're saying to me" Elizabeth repeated.

Matthew grabbed Elizabeth by the arms and dragged her, screaming, towards the door. He continued to drag her all through the town, making a show of her to the neighbours, who had come out of their homes to see what all the noise was about.

Finally, he dragged her into an old building the two were using for their investigations. Inside there were six cells, only maybe 3 feet square, and four feet high; neither big enough to stand in, nor big enough to lie down in.

Matthew threw her into one and locked the door as soon as she scrambled up to try and free herself. He brushed the dust and dirt off of his trousers and left, closing the door behind him, and plunging the room into darkness except save for a few candles placed outside the cells.

Elizabeth sobbed and looked around to see if anybody else had been captured and to her surprise most of the other cells were already occupied. The cell at the far end of the room contained a sickly young woman, white as a bone, slim as a stalk, pretty as a flower. She was slumped over, her chest rising and falling rapidly, and her eyes fluttering open, then closed.

The cell next to the sickly woman contained, to Elizabeth's horror, a solitary new-born baby gurgling quietly. The baby didn't seem to have enough energy to even cry, and Elizabeth didn't want to think about what might happen to him.

The cell next to the baby was empty and the cell next to that, was home to a black cat, desperately howling and trying to scrabble up the bars. In the cell next to Elizabeth were two young girls, twins, crammed into the same cell. They both had their eyes closed, and one was resting her head on the others shoulder.

Elizabeth could feel her heart shatter at the devastation of it all. As she cried the sickly woman opened her eyes and began to look around. Her face was shining with sweat and her clothes were soaked, she was clearly extremely sick.

"What happened to you?" Elizabeth asked in a hushed voice.

The woman opened her mouth to answer but nothing other than a low gutteral noise came out. She let out a sob and curled up on the floor. Elizabeth didn't know what to do, this was hell.

The door opened and Matthew Hopkins appeared with a sheet of paper in his hand.

"Beatrice Draper," he declared loudly. "You have been found guilty of the crimes of Wytchcraft and are sentenced to death by hanging, to take place on the afternoon of the 13th day of November."

Beatrice didn't even open her eyes. She just groaned and moved her head slightly.

"Which is now," Matthew added.

He crossed the room and unlocked Beatrice's cell and waited for a moment to allow her to stand of her own accord, but she was both incoherent and too weak to move. He impatiently scooped her up in his arms and in the process banged her head against the metal and caught her ankle in one of the bars.

An instant later, he was slamming the door behind him.

Elizabeth shuddered at the thought of what was going to happen to her. In all of the noise, one of the twins had woken up and was looking fearfully at Elizabeth.

"What's going on here?" Elizabeth asked, she desperately wanted an answer.

The girl took a few moments to reply.

"That man ... Matthew Hopkins, took us from our homes, apparently two children with identical faces are not children of God but children of the Devil. He says we are to die later on today, but as we confessed it will not be such a painful death." she whispered back fearfully.

"You confessed?" Elizabeth groaned in a hushed voice.

The girl nodded, tears building in her eyes.

"What are your names?" Elizabeth asked.

"My name is Edith," she said. "This is Marjorie." she pointed at her still sleeping sister.

"My name is Elizabeth," Elizabeth said kindly. Edith opened her mouth to speak again before the door opened slowly and Matthew Hopkins crept in. He stopped outside Elizabeth's cell and knelt on the floor in front of her.

"Look at the little bird locked in the little cage," he laughed nastily. "Just confess, and your pain will be over."

"Never." Elizabeth spat.

"I think you will," Matthew Hopkins said, standing back up and brushing himself off.

In horror, Elizabeth realised he had another piece of paper, another death warrant. Matthew strolled over to the cage where the baby was lain, still gurgling, still unable to cry.

"Godwin Payne. You are accused of Paganry and are sentenced to death by drowning to take place immediately." He opened the cage and picked up the baby.

To Elizabeth's surprise he was quite gentle, rocking him in his arms slowly and cupping his face with his hand. He hummed Greensleeves to him, and the baby quietened sighing heavily and sleepily.

"I believe I might have to keep you," Matthew whispered. "I'm not sure I can bring myself to execute a baby." He seemed very paternal with Godwin he even laid a kiss on the child's forehead before exiting the room with the baby sleeping in his arms.

He was only gone for thirty minutes before returning, alone. As soon as he entered the room he headed straight for Elizabeth's cell.

"Elizabeth. Confess." he hissed. Elizabeth hadn't realised until now that she might have the upper hand, as it was becoming clear that Matthew didn't really have enough evidence to prosecute her.

"Why do you need me to confess?" Elizabeth asked smugly.

"Let's put it like this ... John Stearne has had slightly more experience than me in Wytch hunting, and so, when we kill a Wytch it goes down that he has found the Wytch guilty. I am then written in the book as having assisted him. You are to be the first Wytch I have prosecuted alone, the first Wytch that people will see I have found guilty." Matthew was clearly passionate about this; he looked almost insane.

"But I'm not a Wytch." Elizabeth said through gritted teeth.

"We shall see," Matthew sighed, leaving the room.

Elizabeth groaned. She knew she couldn't keep this up for much longer.

17ᵀᴴ NOVEMBER 1645

These past few days had been the worst days of Elizabeth's life. Worse than when her mother had died, worse than when her father had died, worse than when she had been accused of letting Jaime and Amelie die.

The Wytch hunters had strict instructions to not let Elizabeth sleep, until she had confessed. So, every hour or so, somebody would come and ring a bell in her ear. On top of this, everyday members of the town were encouraged to come and throw things at Elizabeth accompanied by jeering and scornful comments.

The lack of sleep caused Elizabeth to become delirious and nauseous. She began to experience hallucinations: imagining flowers growing out of the dusty stone floor, or her father with maggots crawling from his rotten skin, emerging from the shadows and throttling her.

Matthew Hopkins opened the door for what Elizabeth knew was the final time, the twins had already been hauled out of their cells a couple of days earlier, and the cat had fortunately managed to scramble out of its cell, escaping through a small window. She knew she had to confess. She couldn't continue to live like this.

"Ready to confess?" Matthew asked, reaching through the bars, and wiping a bead of sweat from Elizabeth's face.

"Yes," she mumbled, unable to focus her eyes on him or even shrink away from his cold touch.

"I couldn't quite hear you," he said, his eyes full of glee.

"Yes," Elizabeth groaned, slightly louder.

"We have a confession!" Matthew shouted.

He never bothered to read her warrant, instead he just grabbed her and dragged her outside.

Directly outside was a makeshift gallows, with a wooden podium, a bar, and a thick rope already tied into a noose. Matthew continued dragging her. A small crowd had gathered around the podium, but Elizabeth's vision was too blurry to make anybody out.

"We have the last Wytch in this village!" Matthew yelled as he hauled her on to the podium.

The crowd applauded. The very same people who had been willing to accept medicines and herbs from Elizabeth, now gathered to watch her die without batting an eyelid. Elizabeth groaned loudly, unable to stand unaided and leaning all her weight onto Matthew, who was only as supportive as he chose, allowing her to fall to the ground every few steps.

Eventually they reached the podium where Matthew made his well-rehearsed speech.

"For the crimes of Wytchcraft we sentence you, Elizabeth Clarke, to death by hanging. To take place immediately!"

The crowd applauded.

Elizabeth finally managed to find her voice and let her final words ring out as Matthew placed the noose around her neck.

"I wish for the seas to flood every village in England. The clouds to rain fire. The sky to open up and for God's blood to wash everybody away. I wish that every child be stillborn. Every animal be barren. Every plant wilt. I wish for death, destruction and decay to settle on the shoulders of every man, woman, and child ... and may the Devil take our souls."

The last word had only just left her lips when Matthew shoved her off the podium. The crowd screamed, Elizabeth's brain briefly lit up inside her head, and then nothing.

ISOBEL GOWDIE
(Dates unknown)

In Auldearn, Nairnshire, during the spring of 1662, Isobel Gowdie, a cottar's wife in her forties, was arrested on suspicion of witchcraft. She gave a series of four voluntary confessions in front of a panel of local dignitaries.

The unconventional, eerily poetic, and explicit nature of her confessions has been a source of inspiration for poets, historians, musicians, scholars, and witches alike for the past three hundred years. She has been the subject of novels by writers such as J.W Brodie-Innes, Jane Pankhurst and Grahame Masterson.

Closer to us, in 1990 James McMillan wrote her a symphony, "The Confessions of Isobel Gowdie," and pagan musician Damh the Bard paid homage to her poetry in his anthem "Fifth Fath Song".

The reasons behind Isobel's apparently voluntary confessions are unclear. The nature of her narrative; a mixture of faery lore and demonic belief, differs widely from the expected structure of witchcraft confessions in the 17th century.

Her influence on modern Wicca is also remarkable: she is the first witch to mention the existence of covens of 13 members, led by an officer and a maiden.

Her shape shifting song is also widely used in pagan circles to this day. Although the text of her confessions has survived the centuries, we have no record of her execution, further adding to the mystery surrounding her case.

The Second Coming of the Hare

THE SECOND COMING OF THE HARE
Lou Hotchkiss Knives

APRIL 1662 - MID-MORNING

The heat in the steeple has become almost pleasant. Through the interstices between the tiles, the blinding April sun is pushing rays of light into my gaol. They fall onto the floor in pools of gold, shimmering dust hanging and dancing in the oblique beams; a reminder, if anything, of the omnipresence of the invisible world. I have no idea what today's date is. I've been here for a week. Twice a day Reverend Forbes sends one of his servants with a bowl of oats and a fresh pitcher of water, but that's it. Nobody's allowed to talk to me but every time I hear the door below creak open and footsteps make their way upstairs, I imagine it is them and persuade myself that all hope of release is truly lost. That way, when they come for real, it won't come as so much of a shock. At least I like to think so.

My back and legs hurt. I shuffle about the dusty floorboards in a vain attempt to get comfortable. The ceiling is so steep I can hardly stand up, let alone walk from one wall to the other. As a result, I spend most of my days sitting down or lying on my back, my mind torn between resignation or anxiety about the future.

When they came to arrest me, I put up no resistance. To be honest, I had been half-expecting them for almost two years. Ever since that Samhain ritual under the Faery Hills, there had been a multitude of signs, subtle at first, then gradually more ominous: a certain worry in the flapping of the wings of wild birds; and carefully tended flowers, in my garden, mysteriously dying whilst in bud. The dried up toad that had appeared on my doorstep, one misty January morning. The raven that I saw dropping dead mid-flight, one day in Lochloy. For weeks after that I could not brush the terrified warning I had heard in its last, mournful cry.

I wonder who else has been arrested. I know Janet Broadhead has, and since her whole family also belongs to the coven, it is highly likely that John and his mother have had a dawn visit from the Elders as well.

Twenty years ago, we may have gotten away with a fine, banishment at worst; but times have changed. Witchcraft is not an activity the authorities turn a blind eye to these days. We all know what happened to that Bandon woman, of Dyke, who was arrested a few months ago. She was burned, and so was her sixteen year-old daughter, and both had only admitted to ruining a neighbour's crop, whereas we have spent the past twenty years gleefully and actively trying to rid our communities of the bastards who oppress our kind.

They will use torture, for sure. And the minute someone pipes up, and someone most certainly will, we will all go down.

For twenty years I have lived in a twilight world where beauty answered beauty, where love was freely given, and rules were routinely broken; a world whose language was song and where revenge itself had the accents of poetry.

I have lived in a dream, and now the wake world is catching up with me, irons and all.

THE NEXT DAY

It is raining hard outside. The constant hammering of the rain on the tiles above prickles my soul like the needles of a witch hunter looking for the Devil's mark on a woman's body.

My back is killing me. I barely slept last night. The cold kept me awake till the early hours, and on the heels of discomfort came doubt and the subsequent terror which I had so far managed to keep at bay. Curled up in a ball on the floor of my prison, wrapped as tight as I could in my shawl, I spent hours trembling like a leaf caught on the Autumn wind. Back home, in the hut I have shared with my husband John all these years, I have always kept, even during the most devastating winter nights, the comfort of a dying fire. Here I have nothing - no hay bed, no blanket, no sheep skins to act as a barrier against the cold.

The bastards. They know exactly what they're doing, leaving me holed up in this forsaken place. An exhausted woman will confess to anything. They have it all down in writing in their witch-finder manuals. The evidence compiled over decades of methodical interrogations has provided a method to their madness. They know a hungry, thirsty, sleep-deprived woman will, inevitably, give in and betray her own kind, especially when faced with a sinister crowd of interrogators dressed in official black gowns standing around a table covered with torture instruments.

I feel sick. Fear tightens my throat, tenses my arms, and sends shooting pains down my legs.

How did I end up here? Who denounced me? Janet? Another neighbour? Does it matter, since we are all, most likely, going to end up sentenced to death, and burned alive in a barrel of pitch? Already, I can imagine the unbearable heat, the smell of my hair going up in flames, the pain of my body engulfed in the blaze, the scent of my flesh bubbling and charring like bacon. How much does it hurt, and for how long? Does one scream, choke on smoke and cough wildly, or stay silent, stunned by the agony? How does it end? What happens to the heart to finally stop it from beating? and does that hurt more than everything else?

Suddenly I can't breathe. I attempt a deep breath, try to inhale, first bending forward, then lying on my back, but to no avail. My palms are clammy with sweat, and my vision blurred. I can't even raise my arms. My body starts to jolt and writhe helplessly on the floor. Never have I felt like this. This must be the end.

You're dying, Isobel, I tell myself, you're dying, and you are absolutely alone, an accursed witch, a wretched soul, abandoned by all, even by God.

God.

God was supposed to love me, and yet I spat, in his face.

What have I done with my life?

ANOTHER DAY

Is there an end to this torture? I can't eat, or drink, or even piss. I stink, and the odour follows my every move like a menacing, olfactory shadow. I swear I have started rotting already. Perhaps I am already dead? Or not. Maybe there is no death? That's what they say. The soul is eternal. Or is it ? For twenty years I thought I knew better than them and all their sermons. Now I'm not so sure.

I am to burn, that is certain; but will my ordeal be restricted to this world, or will my agony last for all eternity? Is this the wage I am getting for my sins? Could it be that the Kirk was right all along, about life, death, God, Jesus Christ, and we were wrong?

I feel torn. From the bottomless pit of my terror, forbidden Catholic prayers from my childhood spring to my lips, faint echoes trembling like orphaned sparrows. Blessed Saint Catherine, have mercy upon me.

"I beg you, blessed Saint Catherine, assist me in my darkest hour. I don't know who I am anymore. My wounds are sore, and I will do anything."

As I jerk on the floorboards, choking and weeping, I can almost feel her presence faintly beaming from behind the wall of my torments. It is her it seems; light, eternal, ethereal; yet she never fully extends her hand. Why? Am I that filthy, that she won't help me? Or does the renouncement of my baptism put me far beyond any Christian mercy?

Or am I being deluded again? Or is she, as the Kirk elders claim, naught but a flight of popish fancy?

"Blessed, Saint Catherine, are you there? My whole being screams for you from the chaos that rages beneath my skin, yet you don't answer."

I am alone. Nothing exists now, bar the unbearable silence.

"Saint Catherine, were you ever here? Do you even exist?"

Terrified and bewildered, I reluctantly decide to turn to the very one whom I had sworn to forsake forever.

"Jesus, are you all that remains? Or am I sinning again by even daring to utter your name?"

Long minutes pass desperately searching infinity for an answer, but it's all in vain. Nothing. Not even the faintest speck of light.

Suddenly I feel ashamed. You are a fool, Isobel. What are you doing, praying to the God of your enemies? There is no point to last minute contrition. It is too late, woman, don't you get it? So why are you now turning away from He who once favoured you so much? Can't you see He is your only hope?

Wringing my hands in desperation, gazing at the shadows lurking in the steeple above, I call His name out loud.

"Devil, are you there?"

After a moment I hear a voice in my head, but, in my torment, I am at loss to know whether it truly Him, or just a figment of my imagination. The voice is deep, soft, reassuring, like that of a father.

"Of course, I am Isobel. I am the only one who ever truly cared for you. I claimed you as mine before you were even born. Do not deny me, child. Do not surrender."

DAWN

After hours passed in the throes of madness, my body finally succumbed to exhaustion, and I slipped out of consciousness and into the twilight world of dreams, that blessed, unexplored land which lies beyond the prison of the flesh and the tyranny of human logic.

I find myself descending the stairs of the old, ruined tower that stands on the estate of the Laird of Park. Below me, I can see the daylight entering through the opening where the door once stood. A strange breeze is blowing, soft like a warm shawl, and such is its musicality that I am compelled to join in with it's with its song. I know the song. I composed it myself and I have sung it many times: in my dreams and under my breath, in the wake world; on those wild September nights when I would escape the dread of my marital bed and run to the solace of the hills and the companionship of the coven.

> *"I shall go into a hare,*
> *With sorrow and sigh and mickle care,*
> *And I shall go in the Devil's name,*
> *Aye 'til I come home again."*

No sooner have I reached the entrance of the building than I feel my body shrinking, and I let out a scream of delight as my skin turns to fur and my legs to brown with wiry paws. I am a hare. I am free. I dart out of the tower, a possessed beast returned to the familiar exhilaration of Nature. I run like I have never run before, through thickets of heather and gorse, over rocks and under verdant shrubs of fern, leaping over brooks, my mind delirious and elated. Another song then enters my mind.

"Horse and hattock, in the Devil's name!"

Suddenly I am lifted up in the air, riding the wind on a horse made of clouds, its mane a haze that dissipates in tenuous filaments as we gallop through the sky. Below me stretch the moors, drowned in misty hues of mauve and dark green. My heels beat the flanks on my mount, my hair whips at my face, and I realise I have resumed the shape of a woman. My eyes are weeping from the cold wind, yet I carry on singing.

"Horse and hattock, horse and go,
Horse and pellatis, ho! ho!
Horse and Hattock, in the Devil's name
Aye, 'til I come home again!"

My last words swell like a wave, suddenly crashing across the heavens, and echoing throughout the infinite landscape. Above me, the moon is rising; next to it, one star tentatively twinkles in the dimming light. The vibrations of my song still resonate across the twilight, growing gradually fainter. The next second, there is a shock, as if my horse had been shot by a spear and was collapsing beneath me. I yelp and plummet to the Earth below, but before I can hit the ground I realise the scene has changed again, and I am back on the moors, shaken, lying on a bed of heather. Above me, the firmament is impossibly blue and strange music is playing although it has no identifiable melody, it is eerily beautiful despite its lack of structure. Before me stand several unusually sized cairns with open entrances. Looking around I see a crowd gathered around large tables laden with food, all basking in the comforting light of several bonfires. My heart leaps as I recognise the familiar faces of my fellow witches: John Young, of Mebelstown, our ritual officer; the ruddy complexion of Bessie Wilson, who was there at my baptism, and her daughter Jean Marten, our Coven Maiden, Isobel Nichol, from Lochley, John Naylor, and Elpseth Nishie, John Mathew's wife; who else is there? The crowd is dense, colourful; some are leaping, some dancing, some laughing. In the midst of them are dark silhouettes, the denizens of the Faery hills: black skinned, pointy-eared, long fingered. Some of them I know - Mac Hector, Swein, Rorie, Thomas the Rhymer and the Roaring Lion; the familiar spirits whom we were assigned as personal companions on the day of our baptism. Others I have never seen before. My eyes search for the Red Riever, my own familiar; but he is nowhere in sight.

I get up and make my way towards the merry crowd of revellers, but immediately sense something isn't right. I appear to be moving forward, yet the distance between me and my friends remains the same, as though I were walking on the spot. I call out their names, but no one seems to notice me. I shout louder, wave my arms, but to no avail. Why? I am becoming more agitated by the second. Why can't anyone hear me? Why can't I join them? This is all too much. Falling to my knees, my hands clasped upon my bosom, tears of frustration roll down my cheeks, I bow my head, hair covering my face as I adopt our ritual posture in supplication. My voice is broken.

"My beloved, why have you forsaken me?"

I close my eyes in anticipation of an answer, but the world falls silent. My body dissolves in an immensity of white, an insubstantial sea of nothingness. For a brief moment, I feel suspended in time, floating in between realities. This becomes that, life becomes death, above is below, that which is full is empty. I cannot comprehend this, and, realising I am teetering on the edge of madness, I empty my mind and let the White ocean of light overpower me. Is this the end?

Time passes, and I am still breathing; gradually I am returned to the dreaming, where I am standing in the biggest room I have ever seen. It is semi-circular, with steps going down towards a platform. Hundreds of people are gathered here, talking, and laughing excitedly drinking from beautiful tankards and intriguing transparent jugs, basking in the bluish light that seems to emanate from strange circular candles attached to the ceiling.

Never before have I seen such beautiful people. These must be Lords and Ladies, or possibly Kings and Queens, but whether they belong to the race of men or faeries is difficult to assess. Some have pointy ears, like the inhabitants of the hollow hills; some have horns like devils, or long fingernails of multiple colours. Some have faces, that shimmer with pearlescent dust, some not; some have black skin, others are white. Whose court is this? Where am I?

I start walking amongst the crowd, but no-one notices me. The women, for the most bare-headed and adorned with jewels, are clad in such extraordinary, luxurious garments I find myself gawping in amazement. There are impossibly long sleeves of black velvet, gloves of brightly coloured leather, and dresses made of iridescent fabrics that change colour as they catch the light. I notice some of the women are wearing breeches, like men, which shocks me. Who are these people? Young and old, they all exude health, wealth, and refinement. What is this place? On the wall is a banner of purple and black, with writing I recognise as letters; as I cannot read, I am none the wiser. The script appears both familiar and alien. I scrutinise it for a minute, intensely, as if to force meaning out of it, but my concentration soon falters, and the letters retain their secret.

I startle as the assembly suddenly erupts in a cheer. A man has appeared on the platform below, carrying what appears to be a musical instrument, one I have never seen before. He smiles, bends towards his audience as if to curtsy and begins to play. The sound that in ensues is louder than thunder, louder than anything I have heard before. Instinctively, I wince and bring my hands to my ears. A second later, I freeze.

I know the song he's playing.

It's my song.

"I shall go like an Autumn hare,
With sorrow and sighs and mickle care,
And I shall go in the Devil's name,
Aye, 'til I come home again."

His accent is not one I am familiar with, but these are unmistakably my words. He's not the only one singing. The audience around me has started swaying, joining in with my tune.

"And I shall go like a Winter trout,
With sorrow and sighs and mickle doubt ..."

As I stand, rooted to the spot, transfixed I suddenly become aware of a tug on my sleeve. I turn around and am greeted by the large, familiar smile of a small, elfin-eared man dressed in black.

My heart leaps. After weeks of loneliness, the relief of finally being acknowledged by someone is overwhelming. Without thinking and driven by an irrepressible impulse of elation, I fall into the man's arms and kiss his cheeks with a joyous cry; but, to my surprise, he immediately recoils. Puzzled, I pull away, only to be struck by the paralysing realisation of who he is.

Reality grinds to a halt. Crushed by the enormity of what just happened, I smack my lip in disbelief.

I've kissed a faery, an absolute taboo in our circles; and not any faery, but the Red Riever, my very own familiar spirit.

We stare at each other in silence, realising the enormity of what just happened.

"I'm sorry" I mumble, my voice lost in the tumult of the music and the chanting of the crowd around me.

What have I done?

The blue light above us turns a mournful mauve. The Red Riever's grin has melted into a sweet, melancholic smile. His voice, resounding in my head, momentarily quietens the roars and cheers of the assembly, as if relegating them to another reality. His tone is kind, calm, but tainted with sadness.

"You did it, Isobel."

"I'm sorry" I repeat, shocked and despondent.

We both know what this means. A witch can only kiss a faery once - on her baptism day when the kiss of her appointed familiar spirit bestows upon her a gift to celebrate her initiation. On that blessed day, Janet's gift had been Beauty, Bessie Wilson's laughter, whilst I, Isobel Gowdie of Auldearn, had been awarded the blessing of poetic inspiration and song.

Yet, on that same day, we had all been warned that, should any of us kiss a faery again, we would condemn ourselves to an early and brutal death. Such are the rules of the covenant that exists between the Realm of the Hollow Hills and that of humans; as peculiar and arcane as they may appear, when those rules are broken, the sentence that ensues cannot be overturned.

Another minute passes in silence before I finally muster the courage to ask the question that has been torturing me for days; the words escaping from my lips like a flock of terrified birds.

"So, ... does that mean that they ... ?"

For an instant, in my mind's eye, I watch the birds, my words circle around me before disappearing in the distance like wild geese, heading West. Here one moment, gone the next.

Like me.

The Red Riever kinks his head to one side with a wan smile.

"You are to burn, Isobel."

His reply echoes inside my head like a bell tolling, the shock knocks me sideways. My body goes limp and sinks into the floor, life escapes my being with every breath I take, and one by one, my senses cease to be. Gone are the crowd, the music, the noise. Suspended in space, my soul looks down, incredulous, at the creature of flesh and bones called Isobel Gowdie, an empty shell crumpled on the floor far beneath me like a discarded item of clothing. Is this what dying feels like? No, it is not death, not yet. This is only terror.

"What am I to do?" I beg with the last of my breath, my exhausted lips unable to utter another word. I sense his command even before it reaches my ears, and such is its preposterousness that I gasp, and am immediately returned to my senses.

He wants me to admit to everything. This is bewildering, unfathomable. How could I? Such a deed would, in effect, sign the death warrants of the entire coven; at the mere thought, my soul, like a hounded hare cornered by dogs, scuffles in horror. This cannot be. For the past twenty years, the coven has been the closest thing I've had to a family. Why ask me to betray them now?

The Red Riever takes my hand, his touch familiar and reassuring. Gradually, and with incommensurable relief, tension leaves my limbs, but all the sorrow in the world is now flowing from my eyes.

"I do not understand" I reply, utterly broken under the grasp of his loving fingers. His arm extends in a wide gesture.

"Look at them" he replies softly, his gaze embracing the colourful crowd whirling around us, those fantastic people clad in fineries and amidst whom we are but mere ghosts.

"Who are they? Why did you take me here?"

Inexplicably, his grin returns, illuminating his dark features as he gives me one of his long sideways glances, his black eyes sparkling like precious stones.

"These are the children you birthed with your songs, long, long before they were even born."

"What do you mean?"

The Red Riever's grip on my fingers tightens.

"This," he declares, gesturing at the revellers, "is a vision of the centuries to come, should you decide to confess and offer yourself and your songs in sacrifice, when the judges come for you."

None of this makes sense. I shake my head in disbelief. What about the coven?

Nodding as if he had read my thoughts, the Red Riever continues, his eyes locked into mine, his expression solemn.

"Your songs are all that matter, Isobel. Your songs are the key that can open the hearts of people to our ways again, long, long after you have all ceased to exist. Your songs have the power to birth an era when witches will finally be free. But for this to happen, for your words to survive the centuries, you must speak, and the thirteen of you must die."

The floor opens beneath my feet. This is surreal, incapacitating.

I shake my head again.

"But how? I am just a cottar's[1] wife." I sob, shaking from the shock.

"One was a mere carpenter, and his death changed the face of your world. Why not you? Besides, you kissed me, and thus sealed your fate, my friend. All living things eventually die. The same is true in the spirit world. What have you to lose?"

His smile is warm, his gaze insistent and purposeful.

His words shake me to the core.

"Do what you will."

I feel faint.

The room is spinning, the colours mingling, the lights blinding. Another universe is swallowing me, dragging me away from the vision and the clutch of the Red Riever. For a second my whole being revolts, struggling desperately, to resist the force that is ripping me from him, then the lid of the world is slammed shut, and my oniric journey abruptly ends.

I awake a bolt upright, gasping for air. I am back in my steeple, it seems, yet something has changed. The place is bathed in a soft glow, like that of dawn.

Am I still dreaming?

A sense of awe surrounds me. Something is here, unmistakably; something of such tremendous nature and power that my eyes fill with tears. Shuffling around I kneel in the eerie light, and without thinking, put one hand on the crown of my hand, and the other on the sole of my feet, as I did twenty years ago, on the day I gave myself to the Devil before the assembly of my fellow witches.

Time stops. The air fills with gold, fills with void, fills with stars. The cold and the heat touch my tentative fingers in the space betwixt the empty and the full. Within becomes without, sparkle, obscurity, breath, un-breath.

Music and silence dance to one rhythm. A curious sound, like that of a drum, playing in unison with my heart, beats its way through my awareness, getting progressively louder and louder. It is a thud, regular, predictable, inescapable; an immemorial dance; one I've known, one that has existed since the essence of manifestation was awoken at the beginning of the world. This thud is the sole reason for my existence. It has guided me through infinite space. I have heard it throughout every life I have ever lived.

It is the thud of several footsteps going up a flight of stairs.

The morning sun greets me through a broken tile, and from the nearby woods comes the symphony of an orchestra of birds saluting the new light. It must be a beautiful day, outside. Whether I'll live to see the light again, after today, is another story.

Any second now, they will open the door.

---

1 Cottar - In Scotland, a peasant or farm labourer who occupies a cottage, and sometimes a small holding of land, usually in return for services.

LISBETH NYPAN
(1610 – 1670)

Charges were brought against Lisbeth and her husband, Olé, in 1670, after they sued in the courts for slander. After their petition was turned against them, they were interrogated in Leinstrand and later in the Lagting Hall, Trondheim. The trial lasted for six months, with various witnesses testifying that Lisbeth had been known as a healer since her 30s, and that many had gone to her for help. It was well-known that her remedies included a combination of Christian practices, dark arts, and natural medicine. She also practised an old folk tradition of 'reading in salt,' which involved reciting a prayer over salt to be eaten by the patient. Most witnesses admitted to feeling better after being treated by Lisbeth. Both she and her husband Olé refused to plead guilty, despite torture and imprisonment. Lisbeth was considered more guilty than her husband and as a result was sentenced to death by burning. She was one of the last people burned at the stake in Norway.

On 17th May 2005, a sculpture designed by Steinar Garberg was erected to commemorate Lisbeth at Nypvang Primary School, Leinstrand. There is also a road in Kattem named after her.

Lisbeth Nypan

THE LAST WITCH OF TRONDELAG
L. N. Cooper.

*'Three times burned. Three times born (again)
Often not seldom. Yet still she lives'*[1]

— There was I, tied above the pyre as the flames rose higher. I felt my legs prickle and sear, yet through the haze of heat and smoke I saw my sisters dancing. Soon I would be joining them; I could feel it. But as the fire consumed my body, the cries of the townsfolk were all I could hear. Distorted shrieks of "Burn witch, burn."

— The last sound I recall: a shrill scream, a cry almost. Or was that I?

— I felt my face starting to melt, and searing heat turned into whispering cold.

— Everything went black. Then there was I, with my sisters, dancing merrily, encircling the fire. Celebrating the release; release from all the hatred, the torture. Finally, free.

★

Her blue cloak swept the forest floor, as she glided towards the gnarly oak tree, beneath which wood sorrel grew in abundance. Her day of foraging was complete, and she smiled as she glanced at her basket, now brimming with wildflowers and herbs. This wonderful hoard would prove most useful in her workings over the coming months. She looked up, gazing through the tree canopy and brushed her long silver hair away from her face as she whispered her blessings to Sunna.

The short stroll back to the village was accompanied by the sound of birdsong and rustling vegetation, as the animals, indeed all of nature it seemed, were preparing, and storing in readiness for the winter. Here, the summer months were short and the winters long and harsh. As she entered the village, Lisbeth was greeted by the hustle and bustle of the villagers, as they eagerly prepared for the evening's celebrations: it was Midsummer's Day.

Arriving at the Inn, she opened the side door and called to her husband Olé. There was no reply from him, so she made her way along the narrow stone passageway to the kitchen, where she began preparing and storing the herbs she had gathered. She sang as she washed, dried, and tied them; her thoughts drifting back to her morning wander through the woodland. Just as she was reaching up to hang the last bundle, Olé arrived with their children who were now adults. Cheerfully they embraced and chatted for a while: small talk mostly. How their day had been and reminiscing about days gone by, with many a Midsummer tale being told.

Together, they left for the evening celebrations; it seemed the whole of Leinstrand had gathered in the village square. The village was brightly lit with lanterns and lavishly decorated with summer foliage. The deep tones of the

Glarr horn filled the air, signalling the start of the festivities: merriment, dancing, and feasting ensued.

Lisbeth and her family joined the crowds and of course, the mead flowed.

She smiled thoughtfully to herself.

— *Later, when all the festivities die down, that's when my true workings can begin.*

— *Later, much later ... in the hidden room.*

★

The months passed from summer to autumn too quickly, and as the days grew darker and colder, the busier Lisbeth became. She was healer to many, wise woman to some, and witch to a few.

The local villagers came and also some of the townsfolk from Trondheim: all seeking cures for their ills, or something to soothe their spirits. Angelica for infections, sorrels to heal, and the chewing of Willow bark for pain. Lisbeth's other speciality was 'reading the salt,' empowering it by chanting a rhyme over the grains. The rhyme she used was a curious mix of Christian prayers, black arts, and herbal medicine; it had served her well for some 30 years now. Those afflicted would then eat the salt and be cured of their ailments. This particular day, a young girl from the village named Helda was in need of Roseroot to boost her immunity, as the time of the flu was upon them. Whilst Olé ran the Ale house, Lisbeth beckoned Helda into the small side room.

"Have a seat dear." Lisbeth smiled. Helda was taken aback by the heady aroma of herbal and floral tones filling the room: they smelt delicious. As she inhaled the fragrance, her nostrils tickled with delight. She practically slid onto the bare wooden chair and gazed around the room in wonderment at the array of bottles and jars filled with herbs, tinctures, and potions. Here she waited, while the crone balanced precariously on an old milking stool, in an attempt to reach the bottle of Roseroot. Having successfully obtained it, which was no mean feat at her age, she administered the dosage. While squinting at the bottle, she noticed the tincture was running low.

Helda paid with coins; Lisbeth charged for her services, though only what she deemed fair. Exchanges were commonplace: a gift for a gift. Lisbeth knew her supplies would continue to wane as the winter months progressed and more ills came forth. She hoped she had enough to last. Her thoughts were interrupted by a terrible din from next door. She peered into the passageway as Olé bellowed:

"Just you remember to whom I am married. Now get out, be gone with you."

Young Helda dashed out nervously, avoiding the ruckus, while Lisbeth shook her head disapprovingly at Olé.

He liked his drink, had a temper, and whenever someone angered him, he liked to remind them of his wife's talents.

She smiled wryly, knowing it was a good job they couldn't see what happened in the hidden room

★

It was nearing 3am as the four cloaked figures shuffled quietly along the passageway. They quickly glanced around, before a hand pushed against the faded brick in the wall, which groaned as it slid sideways. The figures disappeared into the opening and the wall closed behind them. Upon entering the dark, dank room, they were greeted by the familiar scent of stale incense, the remains of wax effigies, candles, and fetishes. Chattering excitedly, they removed their hoods, entered the sacred working space, and lit the candles which cast eerie shadows of the Altar upon the walls. From the north came Maja, from the south, Nora, Olga from the east, and their host, of course, who dwelled in the west. They came together to commune with the spirits of their ancestors and honour the old ways on the night of Samhain.

"It's so wonderful to see you all again." said Lisbeth.

"It's so good to be here again." said Nora.

"My favourite time of year." smiled Olga, spinning with excitement.

"It's been a long journey," said Maja, "and it's getting more and more difficult to meet up nowadays."

"Decidedly so." agreed Lisbeth. "Right ladies, are we all ready?"

Together they cleansed and cleared the darkness, before casting the circle and invoking the ancient ones. They joined hands, danced, and chanted; they raised the Power. For tonight, they were free to work their rites and make their magick. Intents were spoken, offerings made, and spells were cast unto the flames. They toasted, boasted, and honoured their dead, and felt the cool silky breeze as they embraced their manifestations. The blue swirls of spirits brushed past their faces, as they danced with their ancestors long into the night. Although the time of betwixt was upon them, none were ready to leave.

But it was time so leave they must, quietly and carefully. Tired, but with a sense of fulfilment, knowing that their works were wrought, they exited the safety of the hidden room. Unseen, the three cloaked figures slipped quietly out of the side door and disappeared into the dawn light.

★

So busy was Lisbeth with her healing, that Midwinter passed her by almost unnoticed. Her husband, as usual, amused himself in the Ale house, drinking excessively throughout the winter nights.

More often than not, his temper would fray and frequently he would boast about his wife's prowess as a healer and wise woman.

Lisbeth was surprised to find that springtime was nearing and with it came a slight skip in her otherwise old, creaking bones.

However, rumours were spreading about Lisbeth's practices and Olé grew drunker and angrier.

"Gossip and tittle tattle." she would reply dismissively. But in this day and age one could not be too careful: many a woman had been killed for much less and some for nothing at all. These were dark times. So, after much discussion, the couple decided to sue for slander, especially as the local gossip against Lisbeth had turned from 'tittle tattle' into a wave of imaginative lies. Accusations of her 'putting the sickness' on people were becoming more widespread and the villagers had decided that having to pay for her services was suspicious. And so, they took their petition to the court-house in Leinstrand.

"Miserable peasants," blared Olé, "after all the people you've helped."

They filed a petition for lies and slanderous allegations that had been made against them; they were, nonetheless, ill-prepared for what was to come.

The light had returned to the land and it was a glorious day; Lisbeth clattered around the kitchen, whilst Olé sat slumped over the table, mumbling about his head hurting. As this was pretty much a daily occurrence, Lisbeth slammed the herb-infused cup down in front of him then grabbed her basket and cloak. Today the woodlands awaited her: she sensed the earth had awakened and she could feel it beckoning her.

A sharp knock on the door startled her and the basket fell to the floor. Olé groaned and held his head in his hands, as his wife answered the door.

"Elizabeth Pedersdatter Nypan?" asked the official-looking young man.

"Yes." said Lisbeth.

"And Olé Nypan?" said the man.

Olé appeared in the passageway and grunted. A parchment was unravelled before them, and he began reading.

"You are hereby summoned to appear before Judge Willem Knutssen, in the court of Leinstrand, upon this day. The court officials are here to escort you."

"Ooh, this must be about our slander petition." said Lisbeth cheerfully.

"Let's go and sort the buggers out then." grumbled Olé.

They locked up the Inn and followed the officials to the courthouse. As they climbed the courthouse steps, Lisbeth gasped; she could feel an icy coldness rush through her body: a sense of foreboding.

"Something is decidedly not right." she whispered to Olé.

They sat on a small, uncomfortable wooden bench in the hallway of the lavish court building and waited for what seemed like hours. Lisbeth became fidgety; her feelings were seldom wrong, and she felt very uncomfortable. Finally, they were called into the courtroom before the Judge, who looked exceptionally stern and gloomy. As he spoke, Lisbeth became distraught: the realisation of what was happening was suddenly all too clear.

Their case for defamation of character was never going to be heard; instead, it had been turned against them, in a trial for witchcraft. Olé became argumentative and had to be removed, but Lisbeth spoke calmly and clearly, describing in detail her healing methods. She swore she used only God's name to heal and had not intentionally caused any harm to anyone. The more Lisbeth insisted that she and her husband were victims of lies and gossip, the less the court believed her. They claimed she was soliciting help from Satan and not from God. Young village girls and townsfolk were called upon, who gave fantastical evidence against Lisbeth, stating that she had made them sick in order to gain money for curing them.

— *But how had it come to this?* Thought Lisbeth.

—*I should be in the woods, not imprisoned in this dark dungeon.*

The parish priest of Leinstrand, Olé Mentsen, and the bailiff, Hans Evertsen Meyer, were her only visitors. They tried to persuade her to confess, but Lisbeth refused to confess to something she had not done, and no amount of torture would change her mind. As the months rolled by, sad and weakened by the constant interrogations, she let her mind drift back to the woods and to the beauty of nature as she stared through the one small window in her cell. It allowed the sunlight in and sometimes the moonlight shone too. Shivering from the cold buckets of water thrown over her to keep her awake and sleep-deprived, and so hungry, she wasn't sure if her old bones could take much more. Yet still she protested her innocence.

Finally, they were moved to Trondheim and taken before Superior Judge Hans Mortensen Wesling. A ferocious fellow, he was known for his hard sentencing, which was particularly sadistic for those accused of witchery.

Her voice now harsh and raspy, she retold her story one last time and spoke the verse she used to heal:

> *"Jesus rode over the moor*
> *He stood forth, and made the leg*
> *Lord in flesh, skin, bones*
> *Ever since as before*
> *God's word Amen"*

It seemed, however, to fall on the deafest of ears. The Superior Judge had already decided, upon her lack of confession and the testimonies of the townsfolk, that Lisbeth had indeed called upon Satan and not God.

Therefore, on September the 5th in the year of 1670, Superior Judge

Hans Mortensen Wesling, in the court of Trondheim, passed sentence upon them. The Nypans never admitted any guilt, even after imprisonment and torture. This was regarded as contempt of court and most likely contributed to the severity of their sentences. The verdict stated that it was impossible to obtain the right confession because of their close links with the devil. Lisbeth, as the female, was considered the most dangerous and therefore, sentenced to be burned alive. Olé, although also found guilty, was sentenced to execution by beheading.

Thin and haggard, after her months of imprisonment, the cool wind sweeping through her hair felt wonderful. She barely heard the shouts of the townsfolk, as the cart whisked her towards the city's west gates and her awaiting funeral pyre. She did, however, notice the trees and leaves: it was autumn. The realisation of just how long she had spent incarcerated was surprising: it had seemed a lot longer; those six months had totally drained her. As they shoved the coarse sack over her head, she thought of her home, and how it would be sold off by the courts. However, in the privacy of her face covering, a weak smile crept across her face as she stumbled up the steps to the awaiting pyre.

No one ever did find that hidden room.

---

1 The Poetic Edda, Volume I
Lays of the Gods: Stanza 21 Voluspo

MADDALENA LAZZARI
(Died 1673)

In Bormio in the year 1673 Maddalena Lazzari was accused of witchcraft and subjected to various kinds of torture for four months. Despite which without success. Eventually, the City Hall she remained resolute of her innocence. As a result, the board made the decision to sentence her to fifteen hours of Judas Cradle liable of adjournment. This was a particularly lethal form of torture consisting of a wide and rough-hewn wooden pyramid on top of a stake.

Maddalena was stripped naked and ropes were roughly tied around her before lowering her straddled onto the tip. The tip of which was so positioned to enter her vagina. This form of torture was long and slow and designed to gradually rip its victim in two. The agony was unbearable, and she confessed to being a witch after just three hours. Despite her confession they left her for another five hours, in order for her to confirm her earlier confession. With the guilty as charged verdict Maddalena Lazzari was sentenced to death by beheading, her body then burned on the stake and her ashes scattered.

The Judas Cradle

THOSE EYES
Diane Narraway

I still remember his eyes; how could I forget them? They shone like black obsidian, little pools of sorrow and compassion. They drew you in, pulling you ever closer until you were completely lost in them. They portrayed his life: the scars of a plague survivor, the loss of those he loved, his overwhelming desire to help those less fortunate. His eyes lured and enticed you; so beautiful and yet so desperate. It was as if something was missing, something he needed: approval? love? It didn't matter what, I was captivated by him; I felt he was the most beautiful man I had ever seen. Father Benedetto Odescalchi, but to me he was my Bene. I felt blessed to be in his presence and eventually we became lovers.

I too had lost many I loved to the plague and, like him, I had somehow been spared. I had made the long journey to Rome to seek work and a fresh start, away from the harsh memories of those I'd lost, including a man I had been betrothed to. The pain of these memories had led me here, but jobs were few and far between, so I took the only work I could get. I was one of the girls in Senora Lucrezia's bordello; an establishment frequented by the more discreet members of Rome's male population. This included money lenders, members of the senate, and of course the clergy, especially those from the conclave. Bene was one such man; he was a favourite of Pope Innocent and was destined for great things, or so he believed.

I remember the night he came into the bordello. It had been a quiet night and we were all desperate for some earnings. He looked nervous and unsure of himself. We all adjusted what little clothing we wore; hitched up our petticoats, puffed our breasts out, and pursed our lips to maximum effect. All of us vying for custom. If I'm honest, I was shocked that he picked me, as Gianna, with her flaming red hair and creamy skin, was by far and away the popular choice with most of our clients. Still, he chose me, and I led him by the hand to the chamber upstairs. That was where I first looked at his face, and I caught my breath at the sight of those beautiful, despairing eyes. At that moment I forgot I was a whore and I loved him in the way that all men long to be loved: passionately and with all of me, including my very soul. Oh, how I hungered for him, as night after night he visited me.

Eventually, he bought a residence in Rome and set me up as his maid. I was no longer a whore; I belonged solely to him and I lived in his house. He was climbing ever higher in the church, and this meant he was often away from home. I did not mind; I just longed for his return. I ignored the knowing looks from those in the marketplace; the sneers and jeers from those in my previous employment. Jealousy is an ugly thing. And the time we had together when he returned to Rome outweighed being spat in the face by Gianna or cat calls from the other girls. I had my Bene and one look in those eyes and my heart would melt. I knew that he loved me, a woman can tell these things, and I honestly believed nothing could come between us.

By the time my Bene became Cardinal, we had been together many years and were, I thought, just as much in love as ever, and it seemed my Bene was right: he was destined for great things. The jeers of the bordello had long since stopped as newer and younger girls replaced older ones. Lucrezia had died a few years back and Gianna had taken over as Madam. After all, my Bene wasn't the only member of the conclave to have had a mistress, many even had children. Some acknowledged their bastards, others did not. I had always taken care not to get pregnant and the chances of me doing so were fading fast.

"Isobella." I heard a voice I recognised; while my eyesight was fading fast, my hearing was not. I turned around to see Gianna; the years had been less kind to her. Bordello lifestyle is not easy: the bruises from disgruntled customers, the heavy face powder; it all takes its toll and I felt for her. More than anything, I was grateful to my Bene. I may be a secret, but I am a healthy, well-fed secret. I wasn't sure why she had stopped me, but I suspected it wasn't going to be to pass pleasantries;

how right I was. There had been many whisperings that Bene was to become Pope and I was, in my secret way, so very proud of his achievements. That was all about to change.

"Meet Maddalena." I looked at the young girl, a child by comparison. I even managed a smile, although I could feel my world beginning to crumble.

"Ciao." was the best I could manage, trying to swallow the lump that was beginning to form in my throat.

The girl stood rooted to the spot, unsure of herself and mostly avoiding eye contact.

"She is with child," Gianna hissed, "and who do you suspect the father is?" I sorrowfully shook my head, knowing already who the father was.

"You didn't think it was only you, did you?" she sneered.

"He started coming back years ago; this one just didn't take the right precautions. Did you, slut?"

The girl shook her head as Gianna gripped her arm, shaking her aggressively. The years hadn't changed her temperament any, she was just as unpleasant as ever. I wasn't sure of anything at that moment, the lump in my throat was now accompanied by a knot in my stomach and the pricking of tears.

"What do you want from me?" I finally asked. "Money?"

"Of course, money; she needs to be rid. What use is she with child?" Gianna shook her again, just as aggressively.

"I will come back tomorrow with some herbs to remedy this." I wasn't even sure which herbs I needed, but I wished and needed to talk to my Bene. Was he even mine anymore? I headed home as fast as I could and, once inside, I allowed the tears to flow. I sat there for what seemed like forever sobbing, unable to shift either the lump in my throat or the knot in my stomach, both of which were growing by the second. When Bene returned, I explained the whole thing, between sobs: the girl whose name I had forgotten, and that she was with child, and Gianna's demands.

"Oh, is that all?" was his reply. He looked confused, "I thought something really awful had happened."

I looked up at him through the tears.

"Something really awful *has* happened." I protested, relaying the whole thing to him once again. He laughed.

"Did you think you were the only one? Are you that naïve? Really?" At that point I wasn't sure what to feel.

"She is with child." I added, just in case he hadn't grasped the gravity of the situation.

"I heard you."

"Gianna wants rid of it."

"So, get rid of it. I don't care how. I can't jeopardise my chances of becoming Pope, which means no child and no inconvenient whores."

When had I become so blind to the true nature of the ambitious man? When did my Bene change into this power-driven monster? Desperate to make sense of the chaos unfolding before me, I took myself to my chamber, hoping it would all be gone by the following morning. It wasn't.

I took the girl from the whorehouse the next day, telling Gianna that I would return with her when the child was gone. We went by carriage, taking all that I either held dear or, more importantly, all that I could sell. I was angry, bitter, and my heart had been shattered into a thousand pieces. I wanted to blame this child, Maddalena Lazzari, but Bene had made it clear that she was just one of many. I had given my life to him: I had gone without children to save his face. Gianna, likewise, had tormented me for years, all the while knowing that he was one of their valued clients. I felt betrayed, hurt, lost, the list goes on ... One hopeless emotion tumbling after another.

I travelled with Maddalena to Bormio; I still had some family there, who I hoped would help me. To be honest, I had no plan, just a whole lot of chaotic emotions and a 17-year-old pregnant whore. It was a few days before we reached Bormio and I passed off Maddalena, how her name burns into my very soul, as my niece. We arrived and just as I had hoped, my family greeted us and welcomed us into the family home. I think I intended to let her have the child and get it adopted, but the more I thought about it, the more *I* considered adopting it. After all, it was my Bene's child too, although he felt less and less like my Bene with each passing day.

★

Maddalena resisted the idea of having the child adopted, having decided, rather foolishly I thought, that she could bring it up.

"How will you provide for him?" I inquired.

"There are no bordellos here; you will be a common streetwalker and that is no way to raise a child."

"Perhaps I shall return to Rome ... Perhaps I shall ask Benedetto to help with money; he is a Cardinal after all."

I was enraged and slapped her hard around the face. How dare she? Go to Rome and take my place as Bene's mistress? I hated her even more than I hated Bene. It became uncomfortable, us both being in the same house. Maddalena gave birth on 13th March 1673, both myself and my cousin Juliana were in attendance. It was a long, arduous labour, and many times we thought we were going to lose either mother or child. She was very slight of frame and her body was not equipped for childbirth, but she was resilient and eventually, after several hours, she gave birth to a baby boy. He had those beautiful black obsidian eyes and it unnerved me.

Here was this helpless child, the image of his father, and in that moment Bene was all I could see. All the betrayal and hurt was once again raging within me. Would my heart ever find peace?

Maddalena was pale and needed to rest; as I pulled the cover over her, I noticed a mole upon her breast. I remember reading about witch's marks and third nipples and wondered if this may be a way to be rid of the mother and keep the baby for myself.

But those beautiful eyes lured me in, and I could not settle. My heart was fractured and the following night, in a fit of rage, I smothered the baby whilst his mother slept. Come the morning, it was I who found the lifeless boy and I screamed in anguish: I hated myself for the monster I had become. My scream brought my niece and her maid running, as well as waking the mother who, on seeing her beautiful boy lying there still, began screaming too. I nudged my niece and pointed to the suspicious mole. If life in a bordello all those years ago had taught me anything, it was how to be a convincing liar. I had heard so many stories of witches and their evil doings that it was almost too easy to bring a convincing charge against her.

She was arrested and her child buried in a shallow grave on un-consecrated ground; after all he was an unbaptised bastard.

His mother was taken to the gaol for torturing; I went to watch the torture. I wanted, or perhaps I needed, to see her suffer as much as I had.

Her existence had broken my heart and ripped my world apart. It didn't matter that she screamed at me as loudly as she could, and neither did her desperate, rasping screeches of, "There were others." Likewise, her despondent pleas of, "All men have other women." or even her venomous, "Did you really think you were enough for him?"

Her words fell on deaf ears, either I didn't believe her, or I didn't want to believe her. And so, I watched as they fitted her with the bridle designed to wake the witch. Sharp spikes pierced her mouth as she was chained to the wall; it was her turn to be in pain. I didn't care about 'others,' why would I? She had brought his bastard into the world. An abomination with the same beautiful eyes that would lie and betray anyone who loved him. My soul was in torment. I was consumed with rage. She was chained to a wall and deprived of sleep for several days; I don't really recall how many. I would watch her struggle, suffer, and cry till her eyes were dried up, and at the end of the day I returned home to my chamber. Occasionally I would wrestle with my conscience, but I had cried more tears than she ever could; the spikes of her bridle were nothing compared to the ones that pierced my heart.

For all that, she still didn't confess to witchcraft. Over the coming months she was subjected to a variety of different tortures, yet she always remained resolute in her denial. I began to despair that many were starting to consider her innocent. I heard a tale in the town market of a young Witchfinder in Milan, who had a device he guaranteed would extract a confession out of any witch. He called it the Judas Cradle. A curious name, but as everyone knows, witches are the scourge of the earth: opposers and betrayers of our Lord, so perhaps it is a fitting name after all. I contacted him and he arrived in Bormio; Witchfinders are always happy to ply their trade. I have to admit, the Judas Cradle didn't look anywhere near as terrifying as I had imagined, but then I wasn't the one on trial. I petitioned the City Hall, who were all set to free her, with the backing of my newly acquired Witchfinder, who explained to them:

"The need for caution in all matters concerning witches ..." pointing out in no uncertain terms that, "... one can never be too careful."

City Hall agreed and Maddalena was sentenced to 15 hours of Judas Cradle. I watched as they stripped her and, using ropes, hoisted her up before lowering her onto a wooden pyramid atop a stake. She was positioned so the tip of the pyramid would enter her cunt and she would be gradually split in two.

Now I felt sure she would confess, and I left, spitting my parting words to her: "Filthy witch whore!"

The look in her eyes as I left still haunts me. I knew she was guilty of nothing other than being a young girl like I had once been, trying to make a living in a harsh world. She fell for the same pair of eyes I did and got caught out; I could easily have been her. I could have been her many times over. The look of betrayal as I left her to the mercy of the Witchfinder and his Judas Cradle was the same look I had seen in the looking glass many times over. I heard she confessed after only three hours: having endured all those months of torture, she was broken. I also heard the Witchfinder spent an additional five hours torturing her before she was condemned as a witch. I didn't go and see her beheaded; I didn't need to, and I could smell her burning flesh from my home. I even felt the ash upon my face when they brushed away her final remains, although that may just have been my own twisted imagination.

I am here now though, belladonna coursing through my veins, waiting for death's sweet release, and as I write this, I hope that those who read it will feel compassion for us both. You, Maddalena, who underwent so much physical pain, and I, whose anguish was too much to bear – both tortured because of those eyes. Those beautiful eyes.

May our sorrow be remembered

Isobella De Luca

TEMPERANCE LLOYD
(1603-1682)

Temperance Lloyd was born in Devon, England and was baptised in Hinton St Mary 11/02/1603, Temperance was charged, tried, and acquitted for witchcraft at least once before. At the age of 80 years old she was tried again for witchcraft based on wild accusations of hearsay and image magic. This time, Temperance Lloyd openly confessed, stating that the devil, in the form of a short black figure would beat her if she did not do his bidding. (A more accurate and detailed historical account can be found on the internet.)

Temperance, along with her 'accomplices': Susanna Edwards and Mary Trembles were all hanged at Heavitree, in the summer of 1682.

> THE DEVON WITCHES
> IN MEMORY OF
> Temperance Lloyd
> Susannah Edwards
> Mary Trembles
> OF BIDEFORD DIED 1682
> Alice Molland
> DIED 1685
> THE LAST PEOPLE IN ENGLAND
> TO BE EXECUTED FOR WITCHCRAFT
> TRIED HERE & HANGED AT HEAVITREE
> In the hope of an end to persecution & intolerance

The Bronze Plaque

THE BRONZE PLAQUE: ROOTS OF THE MOTHER
Defoe Smith

Clouds of various forms sink low in the skies today, and on the occasion that the sun shines through, it seems weaker than normal. Although it'd burn your eyes, you can almost stare at it; then comes an instant darkness, as a mighty rain cloud sheds some weight in order to climb over the rolling hills; bringing a dip in the temperature which causes the hairs on her bare arms to stand on end.

As the big dollops of rain leave splat marks on her green sack cloth dress, she knew that today was going to be one of those days. You know, the type of day where it's muggy one moment, then blustery and cold the next. She had so much to do and so many errands to run; there was no time to worry what the weather sprites were up to.

From an early age, following the death of her mother Temperance had followed her father around the village, helping him where needed - or not. From soothing the sick, to providing comfort for the dying. T'was a dangerous time for such activities; the chances of becoming ill by tending to the sick were significantly high, as was the likelihood of being accused of witchcraft. Either way, a premature death was the inevitable outcome. It was not even that folk were scared, well certainly not when they needed help, and everyone at some point or another needed help. It was more a case of human unkind, and the fact that they soon forget what has been done for them. There are, of course, a few kindly folk that fall outside that category. It is also easy, for one who has been kind and helpful all their life to suddenly get drawn into the evil that we do.

Today, like any other there was work to do. During the evening meal previously, her father had reeled off the names of people that needed help around the village, then finished off the list by saying:

"Fix what you can Temperance, and gently, but surely cast aside what ye can not."

She never fully understood that statement, up until her last days, but it always stuck with her – 'Fix what you can Temperance, and gently, but surely cast aside what ye can not.'

Temperance walked down the lane with purpose to her first house call: an elderly lady who whilst milking her cow, had her foot crushed resulting in a deep cut across the tendons on the top of her foot, and a deep sea blue bruise that wasn't going away on its own. The lady struggled to keep it clean, due to the fact that she still had her cow to milk and chickens to feed, there was no one to help. The local quack had said that infection would set in and at best she would lose her foot, at worst and more than likely she would die. However,

Temperance knew a thing or two about wild herbs and other healing methods and would do all she could to see the old woman right. She cleaned the wound, that in all honesty did not actually look too bad and repacked it with a green-brown paste before bandaging it back up. She then produced what looked like a sheepskin bucket, turned inside out: fleece on the inside with a bit of rope threaded through some holes at the top.

"I made this for you last night. It will keep your foot padded and cleaner than not, whilst tending your animals."

The lady said nothing, but slightly smiled and nodded as she took the young healer's hand in silent gratitude.

Temperance left the house and had taken only a few steps down the path when she felt a presence as if she was being watched. As she continued to walk she scanned her peripheral vision to see if it was her overactive imagination, or if someone was indeed snooping, when she heard the voice of a man.

"You would do well to stay away young miss: meddling in the affairs of others will do no good you know!"

Although she knew who it was from the voice and from previous threats, she couldn't see where it was coming from, and a confrontation would serve no positive purpose. It turns out, that down the way, Temperance was accused of cursing a man: that he should become unwell and die. This man was a wealthy land-owner who had approached the old woman with the damaged foot about acquiring her small holding and land; he was counting on the fact that the old woman's foot would get worse and worse, and she would have to move out or perish during the oncoming winter. Either way, he did not need a healer coming around to hinder his plans; something he held with him until the bitter end, when on his death bed he uttered those condemning words:

"T'was her, that Temperance, is a witch! She cursed me."

As time went on, the old lady managed to heal and the rumours around town became more frequent, about how young Temperance and her little group were in league with something dark and sinister. More and more people with the slightest reason jumped onto the blame game: from jealous ex-lovers to those folk who were simply envious of the kind and compassionate young woman Temperance had become over the years. All of which added to the hearsay.

This continued for many years: past the death of her father, throughout the times of civil war, during the sickness and plague. Over time, Temperance did not care much for the town or its inhabitants. Instead, she favoured a small animal shack and woodlands just west of the river; people could come and see her if they needed or wanted her. She was old and had seen enough cruelty and death, including the hanging of many friends over the years. There was no sudden drop, and an instant broken neck, no jig like the highway men and pirates in the famed journals of the time. After being pushed from the step of ladder, they would go rigid and do more of a walking motion in the air before going limp, as the last bit of waste drips from them.

One rainy night, just as it had got dark, Temperance had bedded down for the night, and was drifting off to the sounds of the wind and rain battering on the roof of the shed, she began dreaming of a girl in a time different to hers She was laughing and had a brightness about her features ... one of hope.

The girl was running and looking behind her as she raced towards a mighty oak tree and as she reached the bottom, the girl stopped and turned before shouting in a voice that did not match either the girls stature or gender.

"TEMPERANCE!"

Temperance startled herself awake; eyes opened wide.

"Temperance Lloyd, you are wanted for the crimes of witchcraft." The voice exclaimed.

As the old lady attempted to focus, a fist came out of the darkness, like a wave of silence and Pain ... then darkness.

Time has a way of leeching fact.
Behold the beaten, the burnt and hacked.
The tortured, the bullied and compelled.

The mighty have fallen, the oak is felled
If you wasn't guilty beforehand, you sure are now.
It matters not the reason or indeed the how.
A witch ye now know, they said, it must be true,
But what complicit acts can the pin find on you.
Look for a mark, a blood spot or tag,
There's no wood to bite on nor muffle of rag.
The snap of a finger, numbness comes too late:
Done for, broken, exceptional fate.

She sleeps now, she has earned that. She has slept for a mighty long time, but every so often her spirit will awaken, not to seek vengeance for the cruel way things ended up. She will return to remind folk that people still need helping, even the cruellest among us.

330 ODD YEARS LATER...

Young Sally, had just moved to Bideford from west London and although she struggled to make friends locally, she had no problem taking herself off on little adventures; exploring the nooks and underbelly of the town she must now call home with a familiarity as if she had been here before.

She would make lunch and stay out all day from early morning until the streetlights came on. She always had her phone on her, so if her parents needed to get hold of her, or vice versa, there was the safety of modern technology.

Now, Sally wasn't a tomboy by any means; she loved all the girly stuff that one would expect a fifteen year old to like. But she had an air of fearlessness about her, which, coupled with the fact that she was intrigued with the local history of witchcraft compelled her to explore. It was as if there was something out there waiting for her and only her to discover.

Sally wasn't particularly interested in the hocus pocus of what is perceived of witches and Wiccan folk on television. She was more interested in how people could be so blindly cruel, and how people who were healers, or believers in something different other than the church could be rooted out and persecuted for no other reason than they were different.

It all started, when Sally and her family visited Rougemont castle in Exeter and she chanced upon a bronze plaque that read:

"The Devon Witches,
in memory of
Temperance Lloyd,
Susannah Edwards,
Mary Trembles
Of Bideford Died 1682.
Alice Molland,
Died 1685
The last people in England
to be executed for witchcraft
Tried here and hanged at Heavitree.
In the hope of an end to persecution and intolerance."

Temperance was such a beautiful name, Sally thought. She thought a lot. She thought about what Temperance Lloyd was like, but short of her imagination, there was no way to know for sure; in a way that bothered her to the point of obsession. She had read all the books and pamphlets she could find and studied everyone's opinions on the subject: through various google searches and forums. She even had some pretty scary dreams after reading about Witch Finder Generals: Hopkins and Stearn. But still, there was that one thing out there, almost calling her name: to come, search, discover and be a part of that particular history.

Today, Saturday to be precise, was like no other. Sally awoke to the sound of the front door closing as both her mum and dad departed for work. They ran a curiosity shop down one of the little alleyways; a quieter life than London but equally as busy it seemed to her.

Getting dressed and easily parqouring from the banister to the unreachable window ledges, then hopping to the next stair levels bannister and slip! Missing her step, Sally fell a full flight of stairs; landing on the back of her head as she hit the ground between the hallway and the cupboard under stairs. Blackness.

"Come now dear girl, are you still with us? That's it young missy open those eyes, let's take a look at you. You took quite a fall, and to be fair it has been many years since I have seen anyone climb that far up the mighty oak. Come on that's it, do not be fearful."

Sally opened her eyes and was understandably confused, the last thing she remembered was her teeth smashing together as she hit the ground, and now she was ... She was?

As se focused she could see a kindly woman's face looking at her, smiling, but beyond that there was nothing, not black, not white, not dark not light just nothing.

"Am I dead?" Sally asked.

The old woman laughed as she lowered herself onto a seat beside what Sally was laid on. She did not say much else straight away, just smiled gently and passed over a simple drinking vessel.

"Who are you? And where am I if I am not dead and not at home?" Sally croaked.

"Just drink some water, I think you know who I am, you dream about me. You live in the footsteps I have travelled, and you know my story more than most care to understand. I know not where we are, but I know you are not dead and neither am I as such, thanks to the likes of you. You are safe dear girl, and apart from the wound on your lip you appear to be unharmed. How on Earth you managed that after falling from the top of the tree, someone must have been watching over you. Gain your strength and come outside, I am sure you have lots of questions. Do not fear."

Sally's new-found friend walked over to the door that was in view of that she cared to see it, and as the door opened a blinding flood of warmth and sunshine came washing in, which added to the mystery as to where she might be? The light that came in illuminated nothing. All that could be physically seen was a beam of sunlight, the silhouette of the old lady shuffling along with a walking staff, out into the light and obviously herself.

After checking herself over to make sure all her limbs were intact, she shimmied to the edge of the stretcher, and stood up onto what appeared to her as a simple flagstone floor littered with straw; with that thought, walls and a ceiling appeared. She was inside some sort of animal shed. Gently and very bewildered, Sally walked over to the door and pulled it open. The pain in her eyes was almost unbearable. No matter how hard she tried to close her eyes, it felt as if an unknown force was prising them open, and tipping scalding hot swimming pool water onto her eyeballs. She relaxed her eyelids, took a deep breath, then gently opened them again.

This time she could see fields, with corn and wheat waving in golden splendour and beautiful blue skies with distant white puffy clouds giving depth to the light; there sat stroking a black goat was the old lady, still smiling gently. Sally, amidst the confusion and unanswered questions knew who the old lady was, she was exactly how she imagined her to be. Now was the time to confirm that. She walked over and sat next to her before beginning.

"Temperance? ..." she queried.

"Sally? ..." Temperance replied with a cheeky grin.

"How are you here? Where is here? They hu ... they ex ... You died long, long, ago. I have read all of your trial papers and have examined everything related to you and your friends that perished."

She continued ...

"People all over the world talk about you and learn what you did, I've got so much to ask you Temperance ... please Te ..."

Temperance interrupted by holding her crooked bone thin finger up to her wrinkled and leathered face, then took hold of Sally's hand with both of hers. Sally looked down at the old hands, they were barely warm but were real: every finger on both hands looked warped as though at some point in time they had all been broken. She found herself gently running her thumb along Temperance's index finger.

"My dear, do not worry about these old bones, long before they did for me, they were pulling and punching at my flesh in an attempt to break me down ..." Temperance uttered whilst examining her own hands.

Sally, still in a whole world of confusion and bewilderment fired back a volley of questions unintentionally abruptly.

"Are you a witch? Were the other two part of our circle? All those things you admitted to!" She stopped as abruptly as her questions came across.

Temperance thought for a few seconds, and again with a cheeky grin. she replied equally as abruptly.

"Yes, No, And? ... There is no time as you need to be on your way soon; before it gets dark for you. All I know is you fell from the top branches of the mighty oak over there, as for where you are? You are where you want and need to be at any moment. As for me, I am well aware of what happened, it was not pleasant. I confessed as I did and received their punishment which I knew would end my days ... I am old and had, had enough of the hounding and accusations."

She kissed the goat on the nose and set it loose before continuing.

"I no more sent ships to the bottom of the ocean, or cursed those people dead than anyone else did, and as for my two apprentices: Susannah and Mary were my friends who I dearly loved. We learnt stuff together, from reading to the natural world, from boys to our own bodies. When we were together we had no restrictions on what we could learn ... or do. If that be a Circle or coven then so be it; be it true or not and by saying so, I was in their minds, in their books and in their thoughts. The sad part, for me was listening to what they did to those poor girls before they confessed. I still hear those cries of help that the rector twisted and used for his own purpose, as though they were calling out for the Devil. Their questioning was so gruesome that it caused one witness to faint at what he had seen. I bet that is not in your history books though, they more than likely said it were a possession."

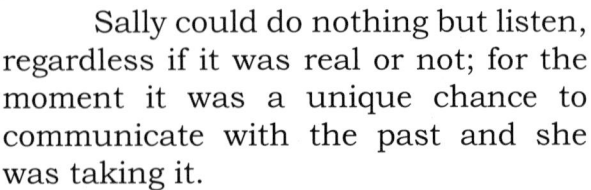

Sally could do nothing but listen, regardless if it was real or not; for the moment it was a unique chance to communicate with the past and she was taking it.

Temperance continued with a slight chuckle and a smirk on her face, which made her appear more youthful. Before Sally's eyes, Temperance had gone from the wrinkled and leathered face of an eighty-year-old from the sixteen hundreds, to a face of beauty; a youth of someone half that age, and back again.

"The lovely story of cavorting with a short black man was partially true, but he was no master of evil, or a shape shifter; merely a man from distant shores was he. He doubly served his purpose both physically and in legend I believe. You see, I've always healed those that needed it. Through my supposed deeds, all these things has kept my name alive and as those that are kindly folk think of me, the more I am me. You, dear, have found me as I am: a healer. In your real world I only exist in thoughts, but through the thoughts of other healers I am part of the energy that helps those still practising the arts."

Temperance slowly stood and looked up toward the tree.

"You must go back the way you came now young lady, and remember me, for it is through that, that our memory lives on through you.

Before Sally could reply there was only the brilliant light burning her eyes, and the portly branches of the mighty oak. She could not think how to climb the branches that appeared before her, but instinctively one after the other, she climbed for all she was worth.

As she continued upward, the air became thinner, and the light began to fade to nothing again, until eventually the silence turned to beeps and other chattering: "She's waking up, nurse. Sally can you hear me sweetheart? Oh, thank goodness!"

Sally awoke in a hospital bed with her mum and dad beside her, she had been unconscious for three days but was otherwise miraculously uninjured. She kept her experience to herself but always remembered the words that Temperance had said to her. Still, to this day, Sally wanders and explores searching for the place she dreamt of whilst being unconscious; although some places seem similar, but her search continues whilst thinking of Temperance Lloyd of Bideford, tried and hung for witchcraft; not dead as long as people remember her.

338 YEARS AGO —

"Fix what ye can and gently but surely cast aside what ye cannot,

I wipe the blood and tears from my eyes; swallow my cries,

I refuse the hood and watch as the hang man ties my knot.

I have fixed what I can, but now cast myself gently aside:

Although I am broken, I have lived this life, through trouble and strife.

Now the devil is here to take me, and in his carriage I will ride."

A note from the author

From the very first moment of writing and learning about Temperance Lloyd, something actually sparked in my mind. I repeatedly dreamt of an old Bideford and surrounding areas, as well as the townsfolk of the time.

Within the story, if you read in between the lines and know how to join the dots, there may be cryptic hints of past life regression or even some weird possession.

One thing is for sure though, I shall never forget Temperance Lloyd, and this fact alone will ensure her memory will live on.

Defoe Smith, July thirtieth, twenty-twenty.

TITUBA
(Dates unknown)

Tituba was the first woman to be accused of practicing witchcraft during the 1692 Salem witch trials. Tituba confessed to witchcraft, whilst naming several others which may be what saved her from death. She was later released when her bail was paid. Her origins, date or whereabouts of her death are unknown.

Obeah Magick

OBEAH MAGICK
Diane Narraway

'Hush Mama Tiwa, dunnuh fret so ... I's here now.'

It was a warm summer's day and the old woman began to calm at the sound of her granddaughter's voice.

'Lemme sing for you.' Luysa cleared her throat and began to sing; as she did so, the old woman calmed enough to speak a few soft words.

'You knows Luysa, I is named after me Gran'na Ma an jus' like you, she was a preencess an shoulda been a Cacique ... but for them Kalingo an them eenvadus, conq'rors an settlers: ev'ryting change then ... an no for the better.'

Even though the old woman was struggling to speak and had precious little time left, Luysa could hear the disdain as she practically spat the word "settlers."

'Is a 'kay Mama calm youself. I's gonna call this liddl'un Tinima after yous an Gran'na Ma; an she'll be a feerce, min'ful gal an a wize woman.'

'Oh, you's 'ave it all feegured out, does you? Well, that's a good thing: chile should cum inta this world with a pu'pose.' She patted her granddaughter's stomach: 'This liddl'un will goes dahn in hist'ry an her name will be eternal ... sing for me, Luysa, you knows the song? The true song.'

Luysa could hear the crack in her grandmother's voice, in the way that those weary of life sound, and she knew this would be their last conversation. Mama Tiwa had been there at her birth and so, traditionally, Luysa should be there at her grandmother's death. It was the way things were done. Taking her grandmother's hand, Luysa began to sing: no ordinary song, but the ritual for the dying:

> *"Oh, Baron Samedi take her hand,*
> *Lead her to the gates,*
> *Oh, Papa open the gates for her,*
> *Show her the wondrous land,*
> *Gather her up, warm her soul,*
> *Let her spirit now fly free,*
> *Papa open the gates I say,*
> *Open the gates for she."*

She watched her grandmother breathe her last and, as she did so, a warm smile creased the old woman's face. She seemed as happy in death as she was in life.

★

Luysa's child was born in the fall that year: a baby girl they named Tinima and even though the island they called home had been invaded, for the time being Luysa's family, once feared Carib royalty, were still among those privileged enough to be called "free."

That was soon to change, when a slave woman named Fortuna leaked information of a plot to overthrow the settlers: a rebellion, that had taken several years of planning, was over before it even began. Several slaves were imprisoned or executed, and while Luysa's daughter escaped with her life, Luysa and her husband were executed as an example.

The young Tinima was taken in by a wise woman the locals referred to as Karina because she spoke both the masculine and feminine languages of the Carib and Arawak tribes. This, and her knowledge of local herbs and medical prowess, meant she was of far more use alive to both slave and master alike. She had been a close friend and adviser, as well as healer to Luysa's family and would have done anything for them, so was more than happy to raise their child.

Like the wise woman, Tinima's bloodline was an interesting mixture of fierce warrior Carib, Arawak, and Yoruba; and she would grow to be well- versed in the mystical Obeah and Voudon traditions: blood rituals, including the importance of the blood sacrifice when honouring the ancestors and Loa.

Despite her knowledge of the dark arts Karina had a softer side and sang to the child each day. Songs of hope, beauty, love, and ancestral songs that praised or lamented those now beyond this realm. Under this guidance, Timina grew to be a strong and capable priestess. She could cure and she could curse, she could heal, and she could harm. She understood the ways of the Loa, and she danced to channel the ancients prior to sacrificing an offering to them. Little was hidden from her and she grew to be more powerful and knowledgeable than even Karina could have predicted. But the one thing she was powerless against was love.

★

John was a handsome young man, a skilled hunter and trapper. Unlike hers, his blood was pure Arawak and like most Arawak men, he had a peaceful way about him. Karina was old and had little time left, and although she would have been happy to see Timina married and settled but John was not the right man.

'Sum trappah! 'ims the one whose trapped ... *im's a slave Timina* ... What life'll you 'ave slavin' away for white folks ... It no right ... Yous ancestrus them were caciques ... Yous free why put youself in bondich? Why?'

'But Mama Karina, I's luv 'im ... he's a warm an kind; an who'll look after me when yous gone?'

'Oh chile ... I's can see yous luv 'im, but you is a gonna be a slave with him ... an what if it's his Mas'ser you needs protecshun from?'

'But I's luv 'im mama ... reelly I does.'

This argument went on for days, going around and round, with neither willing to see the other's point of view until finally: 'Reelly chile yous be a death of me ... Go go. Go head marry the bugga ... I's give up ... Jus promise me yous gonna be 'appy.'

'I's will ... I's will ... I promise, an I's luv you Mama honnes' I does.'

Timina was just 13 years old when she married John and set up home with him, and it was only a few weeks later that the wise old woman who had cared for her took to her bed. And, like her mother before her, she sat at the side of the bed holding Karina's hand as she sang the end of life ritual song to Papa Legba and Baron Samedi.

'You knows chile,' the old woman interrupted, her voice weak as she struggled for breath, 'It's been a pleasure to sees yous growin'; an always beleeve in youself an luv that man chile ... you promise me now that you'll allways luv 'im as he luvs yous.'

'I's will,' Timina replied, 'hush now Mama ... hush.' Tears had begun to stream down Timina's face, but Mama Karina had already breathed her last by the end of the song.

— *Pull yourself together Timina, you have a husband to tend to and the mistress needs her coat fixing, not got time to be mithering over the dead.*

Sure enough, Mama Karina was right: it was only a matter of time before the master sought Timina out, and *masters* don't take no for an answer. And all the begging and pleading Timina did got her nowhere; just like every other pretty slave girl on the island she was "fair game," and this was to be their "little secret arrangement" – call it what they liked. It was violent and abusive: rape, pure and simple, and that was exactly how John saw it when he found her crying and eventually found out why.

All the devils known to man raged inside that man as he marched straight into the drawing room and laid the master out cold with one blow. The mistress screamed for assistance and several other slaves arrived on the scene.

'Fetch help ... fetch help ... hurry.' The mistress was yelling hysterically: demanding that John be hanged for this crime, while John, restrained by his fellow slaves, desperately tried to point out that this "son of a whore" had just brutally raped his wife. The master began to come around at this point, with his wife still trying to decide whether she should be relieved he was ok, or angry that he'd sexually and violently abused *yet another one* of the slave girls. The only difference between Timina and those the master had previously forced himself upon, was John Indian who was currently restrained by other slaves, while the rich white folk decided on his fate.

Fortunately for John and Timina, the master had a guest staying that weekend: a kind and God-fearing man, by the name of Samuel Parris, who gestured to the other slaves not to fetch assistance, instead offering what he believed to be a reasonable solution.

'Why don't I take him and his wife?'

'He should be hanged.' Protested the mistress of the house.

'Well, that's as maybe, but what's to be gained by everyone knowing his crime, other than everyone will know his master's crimes too ... and there seems little to be gained by that, besides the looks of others as they walk past you in the street.' He paused for a moment to decipher the look on the mistress's face: a mixture of anger and shame.

'They will look upon you with pity ...'

'Oh, as if their husbands behave any better

'Why should I care what *they* think?' she hissed.

'You shouldn't, but I can see from your face that you do.' Tears began to roll down her face as she knelt beside her husband, who was now beginning to stir.

'Why is that slave still here? He assaulted me. Why hasn't he been punished?'

'Shut up George!' the mistress spat back at her semi-conscious husband, 'You have brought shame on this house ... and me.'

She began to sob whilst the master, George, attempted to console her, protest his innocence, and demand justice be sought for this (as he put it) unprovoked attack by this "vicious nigger."

Samuel Parris viewed the whole scene and fast reached the conclusion that were it not so tragic, it would have been quite farcical. Fortunately, he was a rational man and had a solution that would solve everything, except their marriage.

'As I began to say a moment ago, I believe I have a solution which I think you will find agreeable.' His words immediately gained the attention of those present and clearing his throat he continued, 'As I said earlier, why don't I take the nigger and his wife? I was hoping to procure a couple of slaves on my trip; this way you won't have to endure any further upset.'

'He should be hanged for what he's done.' protested the master.

'Shut up George!' the mistress interjected once again, 'Take him, take the pair of them, but take them now lest I change my mind!'

So, Samuel Parris returned to his home in Boston, Massachusetts with two very relieved slaves and his purse just as heavy as when he left.

★

The year was 1680, and a fresh start for Timina and her husband John. However, she, still reeling from the rape and concerned that her husband viewed her in some way as responsible, changed her name to an old Yoruba word meaning "to atone": Tituba.

The years in Boston were good enough: they were both well-fed, well-kept, and had no complaints. Samuel Parris married and had three children: Thomas, Elizabeth, and Susannah. Tituba grew fond of the children and while she often prayed alongside them, she never forgot her own shamanic roots and still performed her own rites when none were present. She gave thanks to her gods, as she knew many a slave was a lot worse off than either her or her husband John.

Tituba had never told anyone, not even John, that she had been in the early stages of pregnancy when their previous master had so savagely raped her, the result of which was that she had lost the baby. She hated him so much for that it was hard to bear, and even more so now as she looked upon the beautiful Parris children, day after day. Who knows what drives someone, but she had just tucked Miss Elizabeth into bed when the idea came to her: revenge!

She waited until John was asleep, before creeping out into the moonlight to petition her gods:

> *"Baron Kriminal, Hear me feerce,*
> *Baron Kriminal, Take from 'im spirit,*
> *Take from 'im soul,*
> *Bury 'im deep, an bury 'im whole."*

She drew a sigil in the earth with a stick.

> *"An when Mas'ser George be dead an gone,*
> *an buried deep beneath this earth,*
> *Rainbow Serpent,*
> *let for me body to then give birth."*

Sure enough, in the summer of 1689, a year later when the family had moved to Salem, news came of Master George's death. Master Samuel said it was a tragedy and that he had been a good man, but his eyes said he knew better, and the rest of the family weren't the type of folk to speak ill of the dead.

Master Samuel had become the minister of Salem Village, and the first thing Samuel Parris did was to ensure Tituba and John had a legal and proper Christian marriage; even slaves, niggers, or otherwise should abide by Christian laws.

Obviously, this took place in the house, as slaves were only permitted in white folks' church once a month and even then only right at the back. Master Samuel believed all should be just and proper in the eyes of the Lord. It had all been acceptable back in Boston, but now he was Minister Parris things were different. He even wanted to give Tituba a "proper" Christian name, but he compromised, being appeased by the fact that it meant "atonement." After all, only sinners get raped: God protects the righteous.

Tituba struggled with all the "God-fearing" and "good Christian behaviour" that was bandied around Salem Village. She was sharp and observant and saw far more than she let on. John on the other hand, embraced Christianity: often hushing his wife when she spoke of the "devils work," as he now put it. She began to feel isolated and lonely; she wondered if he saw her as a sinner, something tainted and unclean. She kept her mouth shut and learned to keep all she saw to herself.

Tituba was lonely and felt isolated: her husband was present in her bed but not like before; she could feel the disappointment in his touch. The child now growing in her belly: the child she had so desperately longed for might as well have been Master George's for all the love she felt from John these days. She recalled mama Karina's words to love her husband as he loved her but didn't think she could be that disinterested in another human being. In short she was sad. She would walk alone in the forest at night and talk with the ancestral spirits, and on special days, her special days she would collect mice from the traps and sacrifice them to the Loa. It was these small rituals that calmed her own spirit and fed her soul; in these moments she knew peace.

Her child was born in the Spring of 1690, exactly nine months after the news of Master George's death. She named her "Violet," after the colour of the sky that evening. John never cared much for his daughter any more than he seemed to care about his wife these days; he was distant, preoccupied. As soon as she was able, she resumed her nightly excursions to the forest to speak with the ancestors: to once again calm her spirit.

It was during one of these nightly excursions that she stumbled across Miss Betty and Miss Abigail in the woods laughing, and Miss Abigail was kissing Miss Betty and touching her in the same way that Tituba remembered John touching her.

Miss Abigail had moved from Boston to Salem at the same time as the Parrises but had only recently moved in with them after both her parents had been killed during a recent Indian raid. Miss Abigail was not much more than a child herself, yet there was already talk of finding her a suitable husband before "wilfulness" set in. By the look of things, Miss Abigail had no interest in a husband, and "wilfulness" as the puritans called anything they deemed unacceptable behaviour, had most definitely already set in. Miss Betty was younger still, and while their actions seemed very inappropriate, on the surface, neither girl seemed especially unhappy.

Tituba stood frozen on the spot, torn between her "moral obligations" as Master Parris put it, and the fact that she had only been a year older that Miss Abigail when she married John. And how some of the girls back home were contracted to be married when they were several years younger than Miss Betty. In the only way Tituba knew how, she began to ask the ancestors for guidance. She began scratching at the ground, and in doing so she startled the young girls. Tituba could see the fear in the girls' eyes at being caught and they too could see fear in hers.

Betty was the first to speak:
'Please don't tell father … you know how he is.' she whimpered.

Generally speaking, Tituba saw Master Parris as benevolent: he doted on his wife and children and was far kinder to his slaves than most men, but she knew that he would see their actions as shameful and sordid.

'If you don't tell, we won't.' sneered Miss Abigail. Abigail had never much cared for Tituba, although it wasn't clear why the child was so hostile towards her: now, however, it seemed obvious. Abigail was jealous of the relationship between Miss Betty and the slave girl. They were close, like sisters: Miss Betty was far easier to get on with than her sister, who was younger and prone to melancholy – a sickly child who would often take to her bed. And Master Thomas spent a lot of time studying the scriptures and preferred his own company to others. Tituba and Miss Betty had spent a lot of time together, prior to the arrival of Miss Abigail.

Abigail's words echoed inside Tituba's head:

'What yous meen, yous not gonna tell? ... Tell what?'

'Well, whatever you were doing, it wasn't the practice of a good Christian woman, now was it?'

'Oh, you wouldn't Abi,' Miss Betty piped up, 'Tituba would be beaten for such things ... You weren't doing anything, were you Tituba?'

'Yes, she was, she was conjuring the devil ... consorting with him ... weren't you Tituba?'

The contempt in Miss Abigail's voice was a bitter pill to swallow and

Tituba was growing increasingly aware that she was damned, whatever she said.

'Troofully, Miss Abigail I's doin' no such thing, an I's thank yous to no say els'wise.'

'Like I said, I won't if you won't ... Slave!' Tituba could hear the hatred in her voice, as she hissed the last word with all the venom of a deadly viper.

'I's unnerstan Miss Abigail ... I's unnerstan,' Tituba could see she was beaten by this slip of a girl, but figured she could resolve the situation later, this time with magick. She hadn't used magick since she left Barbados, and even then it had only been because John had begged her to after the rape incident that nearly cost him his life.

"Use whateva majik yous has Tima, just doncha let we be sep'rated, no through death or els'wise ... I's couldn't bear us to be apart ... not ever"

And Tituba, being a good wife had dutifully obeyed. She loved her husband passionately, but was equally aware that at that point if John had hanged, she would have been a lot more vulnerable as a single woman. Now, however her magick: Obeah magick, would be used to silence Miss Abigail and, in doing so, protect Miss Betty.

★

Tituba waited till the house was sleep; John was in a deeper than usual sleep, having had his drink laced with Barbados rum and laudanum, which had been prescribed for Mistress Parris when she had the bloody flux the previous spring.

She had decided to bake a witchcake and had sneaked out to the storage shed, in order to search for the rye she had collected earlier that year; rye that she knew carried the spores of "daw'ers bloody fire," as they called it back home. In the early hours of the morning, the small slave moved stealthily through the yard, and with her apron pockets, full she headed back to the house.

The house was in silence as she baked her cake, chanting as she added urine to the mixture, using molasses, and fruits to mask the taste. And all the while she chanted, cursing Miss Abigail, putting a jumbee on her. And amid the pleasant aroma of cake baking, she stood on the porch gazing up at the dawn sky. Black clouds swirled tempestuously above her, and she knew there was a storm coming, and unlike any other storm, this one carried with it Obeah magick. This storm would carry her curse straight to Miss Abigail.

Tituba served the children breakfast and this morning, on the surface was no different to any other, except Miss Abigail's rye cake was laced with all the curses Tituba could muster.

'This is delicious ... here Betty try some, its lovely, and uncle says we should share.'

'Ooh yes please, it smells lovely ... thank you.'

As Betty took her first bite, Tituba was frozen to the spot, powerless to prevent the inevitable jumbee that was now heading to both girls. If she spoke up, then she would surely be tried as a witch, and in any event the storm was coming and there was nothing that could stop it. The "daw'ers bloody fire" would take effect soon enough, and as it came with added jumbee, the symptoms were sure to appear much faster. Not only did the symptoms appear faster, they also took a much stronger hold on the girls.

The date was January 20th, 1692; a date that Tituba would not forget in a long time, and one that history would never forget.

Predictably, Master Parris was convinced the devil was at work when, after only a few days, the girls were twisting, writhing, and contorting in such a way that he could only explain by demonic forces. Mistress Parris was beside herself with worry and unsure what to believe. In the early days no one knew what to expect, but Tituba knew in her heart the storm was upon them, and she had summoned it. She, of course, wasn't the only one.

'Yous done this Tiba? Yous bring a devil upon these girls an this house?'

'No 'usband no me Sir ... How's you think such a thing?'

'Hmmm ... I's knows you Tiba, an I's knows Obeah when I sees it.'

'No, me Sir ... No, me.'

'Mighty fishy Tiba ... Far too likes them girls back in Boston them years back ... Lord have mercy upon yous, wife.'

'No 'usband, I's tellin' yous, NO'

Despite her protests and her denial of either event, John remained unconvinced that Tituba had no part in the chaos that was unfolding around Salem Village, or the incident concerning one Goody Glover several years earlier; without a doubt there were similarities. John was far from stupid, but she knew he had a weakness for rum, and his loyalties lay where there was access to the Parris's wine cellar; Barbados rum was a different kind of devil, but a devil, nonetheless.

That said, John Indian knew his wife and he knew that when Tituba cursed, she cursed fierce. Of course, what he didn't know was why she would curse Miss Abigail, and especially Miss Betty as she was so close to her, nor did he know of the goings on between Miss Abigail and Miss Betty. It was with bitter anger towards Miss Abigail that she had summoned a storm equally as angry and the sky, which Tituba had watched swirling angrily above a few days previous, was nothing other than the reflection of her own angry spirit currently raging within her.

The house was in chaos with Master Parris and the Mistress keeping a constant vigil over the girls, but all the praying and fasting was to no avail; there was nothing that could undo the Obeah magick of the once fierce Warrior Priestess.

Eventually the Parrises were forced to seek medical advice: Tituba's husband John was sent to get Doctor Griggs.

'Mark me words Tiba, this'll cum back upon yous; I's knows it.' John shook his head, knowing that sooner or later Dr Griggs would realise the girls were beyond all earthly help. Tituba knew it too; she wasn't sorry for what she'd done as such, but she was devastated that Miss Betty had been affected. That was something she did regret, and between bouts of hoping Miss Abigail suffered tenfold, she even feebly attempted pleading with their God for Miss Betty's recovery. John was wrong, their God didn't listen to slaves after all, and Miss Betty showed no signs of recovery. Of course, as John had predicted Dr Griggs' eventual conclusion was witchcraft.

'It breaks my heart Samuel, to see your children suffering this way and whatever ails them is beyond any medical help ... I feel a more spiritual approach may be required.'

'What are you saying, Sir? That my children are spiritually sick? How can that be?'

'I fear it is similar to the Goodwin girls in Boston.'

'Witchraft? Are you implying the daughter of a preacher is possessed by the devil?'

Griggs shook his head sadly, desperately seeking a preferred word, but none came, and eventually after a short, but uncomfortable silence he concluded, 'I fear that is exactly what I am saying, and it is with great sadness and regret that I say it.'

Parris sat down ashen faced and shaken to the core. The very thought that the devil was active in his house was hard enough to comprehend, but that his daughter and niece had been taken possession of was just too much. Dr Griggs made his apologies, excuses, call them what you will, and left Preacher Parris trying to find the right words to explain it to his wife. Elizabeth Parris was not the strongest of women and could take to her bed with news that the hens had only lain three eggs instead of four. How would she cope with news that the two little girls in their care were possessed by the devil: worse still, as a result of witchcraft?

'No, no, NO. This is too much.' was her response, followed by a bout of severe melancholy, which resulted in Mistress Parris taking to her bed for the following week.

★

Samuel Parris was not the most popular preacher and had only narrowly escaped his parishioners not paying him any wages, especially angering them by buying what they viewed as trivial trinkets: gold candlesticks and new vessels for the meeting house. In fact, it was only the girls' affliction that was standing between him and poverty. Some may have called it divine providence. Tituba certainly saw it as such, and it appeased her conscience slightly, as she believed Master Parris, despite his unyielding puritanical beliefs, was underneath it all a good man. Above all, she still hoped Miss Betty might recover from this unfortunate affliction. And if she had to hear her husband say, "This all yous doin' Tiba, I's just knows it." one more time, she might just call a jumbee on him too.

February 24th the Master got ready for church as usual, Mistress Parris accompanied him as did John, while Tituba remained home to watch over the girls, whose demonic writhing and contortions had now turned to hallucinations and accusations. With the house all but empty, Miss Abigail turned on Tituba calling her out as a witch.

'Hush now, Miss Abigail, don't say such things; I's no weech.'

'Witch! Witch!' she continued, pointing, and screaming at the slave girl. Fortunately, by the time the rest of the household arrived back, Abigail had fallen asleep yet continued to writhe and contort even whilst sleeping.

'Tiba,' her husband began in a hushed whisper, 'I sees Mary Sibley at church an she says yous need to bake a weechcake.'

'Why?'

'To fine out if this weechcraft, she says it would 'elp them girls. I's knows yous can fight Obeah with Obeah; yous can remove that curse yous bring upon them girls.'

Tituba sighed, she could fight Obeah magick with more Obeah magick, but in doing so she would be admitting her guilt, and she wasn't about to do that. And although she was curious as to how Mary Sibley knew about such things, she decided against pursuing that line of enquiry either.

'I's tells yous what John Injun, yous make them a weechcake if yous think it'll help. If there is a jumbee upon them girls, I's dinna put it there!'

'Tiba wife, yous bake a weechcake, or so help me I's will cuff you dahn in front of the Lawd.'

So, rather than take a beating, under John's instruction she collected the girls' urine, and baked a witchcake, which John fed to Mary Sibley's black dog. No one except Tituba herself expected the following outcome: it was the crash of broken crockery that led Mistress Parris to the girls' room.

'She is the Witch! Witch! Witch! Witch!'

'I's no weech; please stop sayin' that, Miss Abigail.'

Tituba was stood rooted to the spot, with the bowl she used to mop the girls' brows in pieces on the floor. Abigail was sat bolt upright, arm outstretched, repeating the word "Witch" over and over.

'It must be that feever M'stress 'Lizbeth; I's no weech.'

Fever or no fever, Samuel Parris had fetched the local magistrate and Tituba was arrested. For whatever reason, perhaps it added further proof that the devil walked among them, maybe he was playing for sympathy, looking for compassion among the villagers, Samuel Parris informed both villagers and the magistrate that it had been his daughter Elizabeth who had accused Tituba.

Perhaps the word of a preacher's daughter was more believable than that of an orphan; especially someone who had lost their parents during a native raid, and whose judgement could be clouded, and their rage fuelled by a native slave. Either way, his testimony was confirmed by both his wife and Tituba's husband.

Tituba was only in her cell a few short hours before she saw two other women being dragged by their hair and brutally thrown into the cell opposite. She shook her head muttering under her breath, 'Even in gaol, we's still no eq'al.' Tituba was angrier than ever before and inside her spirit burned with fury; Salem would pay for what it had done to her. The royal blood of her warrior ancestors raced through her veins as she drew shapes in the muddy floor of her cell.

'Call me weech.' she spat on the mud *'Call me hag.'* she spat again.

'I's willl see yous perish in the fires of yous lies,' she spat once more, before hitching up her skirt and pissing on the muddy shapes.

'Let yous chil'en be yous judges an fine yous guilty.'

All three of the convicts, whether guilty as charged or not, were all guilty of being controversial and nonconventional in the eyes of the rest of the villagers. Tituba knew the other women well enough: Salem village was small, and gossip travelled quickly. Sarah Good was a pauper, generally viewed as a scrounger by puritan and slave alike. "Lidd'l more than a pow white gal" was how many of the slaves referred to her. Tituba scowled at the two women, as she recalled how Sarah Good had kicked her when she had fallen over a few days ago, and how Sarah Osbourne, now also in jail, had added,

'Best place for that nigger trash.' She was happy they had been arrested and relished the fact that Sarah Good's husband and neighbours added fuel to the fire, by stating that they had feared her a witch, albeit for different reasons. Unlike Sarah Good, whose husband claimed she was frigid, Sarah Osbourne was considered a fornicator and Jezebel by slave and mistress alike.

The following morning Tituba travelled with her cellmates to Boston, where Master Parris arranged to interview Tituba. Up until now, Tituba had viewed her Master as a fair and just man; she may not have understood his religion, but he certainly tried to live by its teachings. Everything now was different.

'You filthy nigger,' he screamed, slapping her so hard around the face she feared her jaw may break. It did not, but nonetheless this once kind man was raging with a fire in his belly she'd never seen before.

'Who was with you? You witches always exist in covens. Do we have a coven in Salem?' He administered a sharp kick in her lower back, and she screamed.

'So, tell me how many of you are there exactly?' Tituba had no wish to feel any more pain, and there was no love lost between her and the Puritanical hypocrites of Salem Village, and although she had no idea how many witches were in a coven and neither did she care; she reeled off a few names: those she could remember. He hauled her up by her hair in order to throw her hard against the wall, and punching her repeatedly, he continued, 'And what animals and familiars did you see? Were there black dogs, hogs, birds? Did you conjure them too, nigger girl?' Tituba sobbed; she had no idea what he was talking about and just wanted the pain to stop.

'Yes Mas'ser, there was a huge black beast, an a dawg, an a hog ... hungry for blood it was. Could scarce control it; them feerce creachers Mas'ser, honess' them is.' Desperate to stave off the beatings for as long as possible, she continued, 'there was birds, yeller 'uns, an rats both red an black.' She could see that she had his total attention now and, at least for the moment, he wasn't punching, kicking, or slapping her'What else?' he gestured for her to continue and she did so, widening her eyes, fixing his gaze, and with all the drama she could muster:

'There was cats, fritenin' 'orrible black cats, an a fox, sly as sly can be he was, Mas'ser. An a woolf, ungry, ungry woolf, with them big ol' teeth an feerce 'im was; jaws all drippin' with saliva, jus' ready to ...' At this point Parris was mesmerised and his eyes were nearly as wide as Tituba's, 'STRIKE!' she growled, causing him to jump.

Flustered and embarrassed, he composed himself and punched her hard, this time breaking her nose. She hit the floor, banging her head against the wall. Through bleary eyes she watched her blood dripping onto the floor. She hated him now, as much as the rest of them.

'What else do you whores of Satan do at your gatherings? Do you ride sticks? Eh, nigger bitch?'

Tituba was weak; her head was spinning, and Parris was kicking her with every question.

'Y... yeah, I's rode stix I's has ... rode stix, you say Mas'sser? Yeah that's what I's done.'

Parris could see he had gone too far: Tituba was in no fit state to offer any further information, so he turned to leave. As he did so, Tituba called out as best she could:

'Ask the chil'en Mas'ser, they'll tell yous.'

And sure enough, by the time he returned to Salem more children had become afflicted, and as more and more people were accused, Salem was in chaos. Tituba watched silently, as the jail filled with the terrified residents. Their conversations, confessions, and night terrors gave her as much `ammunition as she needed to bring Salem to its knees, and every time they brought her in to court there was uproar. She confessed to being a witch, and her performances whilst testifying were some of the most dramatic ever to grace a courtroom. Her husband was often present and whenever she appeared he would throw himself to the floor, feigning the symptoms of the Parris' girls. It mattered not to Tituba, in fact, it all added to the drama. The crowd that gathered to watch the trials gasped in horror as she announced, 'That Goody Good, she did have a creecher that was neither man nor beast: it has the 'ead of a wooman an the legs of a beast, an it has wings it do. It were ... ungodly, I's tells you.'

All these dramatic performances and her confession, irrespective of how it was obtained, secured her life; she happily watched as 20 left the jail, never to return, and 4 died whilst awaiting sentence. At night she smiled to herself in the dark hours, safe in the knowledge that Salem was suffering. Most of those who had not been arrested had children who were afflicted, those whose children weren't affected lived in terror that theirs might be next, and those without children lived in fear that Satan was among them. There wasn't a family in Salem Village that hadn't been affected.

★

Tituba's glory was short lived and by the time a year had passed, it was all over, and she had seen plenty of those who had been arrested freed and found not guilty. As the last of her jail-mates were led out to freedom, she couldn't help but feel a deep sense of injustice. Wasn't it she who had pointed out many of those accursed witches? Hadn't she alone described their satanic activities: their dances with devils and their naked cavorting? Why were they free, while she remained cooped up in a tiny cell in perpetual darkness?

Drastic action was required or, rather, needed: she was owed her freedom; she was owed a debt of gratitude that needed to be redressed. She began to scrabble around for a loose stone, stick, or bone, in fact anything she could scratch in the dirt with.

'Dunna do it Tiba.' the familiar voice of John Indian cut into her and her train of thought.

'Wotcha doin' 'ere usband?'

'I's paid yous bail, now get up an' let's go. Don't got all day.' She was up and ready; she didn't need telling twice.

Outside, the sunlight hurt her eyes: she'd been in that dingy cell for far too long; her legs were shakey too.

'I's been all cooped up in that ch'ck'n shed.' she whimpered, as John took her arm to steady her.

'Where Vi'let?'

'She good wooman ... she good.'

'Where Vi'let, usband?' he could sense her determination.

'She's a good I's says. Nows drop it.'

'Where's mi daw'er ... tell me now John Injun, less so help me ... '

'You'll what?' he snapped, tightening his grip on her.

'Leggo ... leggo of me arm. LEGGO' But he just tightened his grip, dragging her behind him; the more she protested, the tighter his grip became until in the end, she stopped arguing and just stumbled along behind him. Eventually, he stopped deep into the woods, slammed her full force to the ground and, positioning himself on top of her, reached under her skirt. Tituba flashed straight back to her rape in Barbados, and although she tried to scream, John placed his hand forcefully over her mouth.

'Husha wooman!' he growled, as she felt him force his way inside her; the best she could do was close her tearful eyes and hope it would soon be over.

The pain of him thrusting into her, harder and harder, obviously wasn't enough for him: he accompanied it with a tirade of insults.

That's right nigga beech ... stay still now ... let ol' John has 'im way now. Yeah, like that ol' Mas'ser back in the Carib ... that's right, jus' like yous put out for 'im.'

Tears streamed down her face and it seemed like forever till he was done with her; she hoped he was done, at least for now, as she just longed to get back and see her daughter.

John finished but kept one foot on her as he buttoned up his breeches and all she could do was lay still with her skirts up, and tears rolling down her cheeks. John knelt down, keeping his knee positioned firmly on her stomach.

He reached into his coat, pulled out a knife and before she had time to realise, he had slit her throat. He looked down at her blood mingling with the warm earth.

'See nigga beech: that's what yous get for messin' with the Lawd's people; them is good folks, no nigga weeches. I's knows you called that jumbee, I's knows Obeah when I's sees it; stoopid nigga beech, burn in them fires of hell you devil's whore.'

He spat on her body, the same body he had fucked not five minutes ago, and with a parting 'Nigga weech,' he left her to the mercy of the wolves and other creatures that inhabited the woods around Salem Village.

'Is done, Mi'stress.'

'Thank you John; you are a good man.'

'Thank yous, Mi'stress.'

Elizabeth Parris may have been a sickly woman who took to her bed at the drop of a hat, but all those days she missed church alone in her bed gave her plenty of time to ruminate. Of course, John Indian could be a pleasing distraction, should she feel up to it: John Indian being a well-built Arawak man in all the places it counts, whereas her husband was, she felt, lacking in that department. Besides, she wasn't the first Puritan woman to hop into bed with a slave and would doubtless not be the last.

That aside, her ruminations had led her to consider the obvious: that despite Tituba's protests, the fact remained that two God-fearing fine, young puritan girls had accused her of witchcraft. Naturally, she should believe them, and once Tituba confessed she had hoped for her to be executed along with the rest. When that didn't happen, she decided to take matters into her own hands, or more accurately, the hands of her slave lover. She knew that her husband was stupid enough to let Tituba back into their house, and aside from the fact that she didn't want "that witch" anywhere near her house and especially not her children, they were also incredibly short of money. She drafted a letter to her husband, addressing it from one Noyes Corey. He had no reason to suspect it was anything other than genuine, and although the signature wasn't of anyone he recognised he was happy enough to accept the money that accompanied it. He replied, but it mattered not whether the address was real; he had enough money to pay off some of his creditors and his wife would be happy that Tituba was not returning. The plan was fool-proof: it worked; in fact, it worked a little too well. Happy that he had received so much for Tituba, he decided to put John Indian up for sale: he fetched a good price too.

When Elizabeth heard of her husband's actions, she once again took to her bed: only this time she remained alone and nursing her broken heart; life was never how it should be. The aftermath of the jumbee curse had taken its toll, and even though she lay cold in the ground, her curse lived on.

Eventually the pain became unbearable and Elizabeth took to her bed with several bottles of laudanum. Only two of which were needed.

★

The sun dripped through the bearded trees and many heads turned as a beautifully dressed woman stepped onto Indian Bridge. With the untimely and inexplicable death of Minister Parris's younger son, this woman, whose skin was slave, but her clothing Mistress, had become the sole heir to a Barbados property. White folk balked at the notion of a slave girl owning such a fine property and Samuel Parris's other children wondered why he had not sold the property during their poorer times. They also wondered if the Indian girl who had grown up alongside them might actually be their half-sister; she wasn't.

She was the daughter of the once beautiful and proud Timina and John Indian. The blood in her veins was a lethal blend of Arawak, Taino, and Carib. Her mother had called her into being using Obeah magick and now she, Violet Indian, was home.

GILES COREY
(1611 – 1692)

English-born American farmer who was accused of witchcraft during the Salem Witch trials. After being arrested, he refused to enter a plea of either guilty or not guilty. He was subjected to pressing in order to force him to plead, but he died without doing so after three days of this torture.

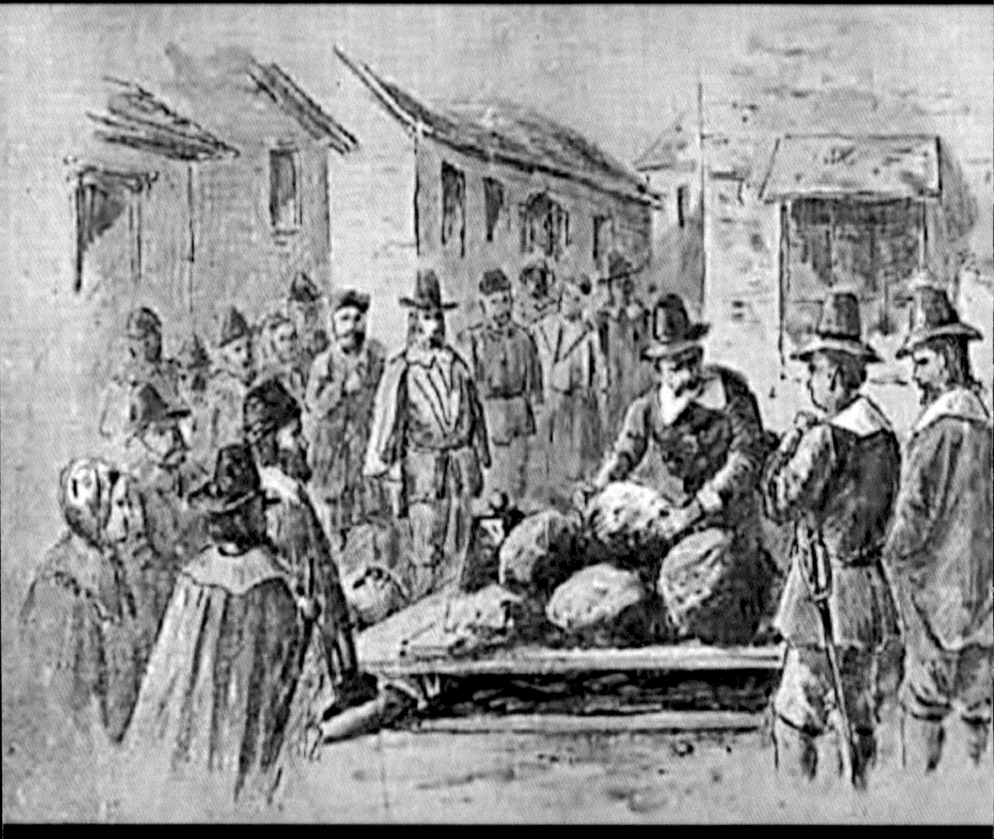

MORE WEIGHT
Diane Narraway

I guess my story really begins when I was thirteen. My mother had what they call a chequered past: I was living proof of that. See, the colour of your skin only matters when there is a colour of your skin. And I had a colour. The response to that was varied, largely depending on whether my mother was within earshot. It was definitely 'nigga' if she wasn't, and more often than not it was accompanied by a whole variety of imaginative adjectives. On top of this, my mother had the lousiest taste in husbands, and the latter of them was the worst of all: Giles Corey, a wealthy farmer from Salem Village. He had a five-year-old son that needed a mother and my mother, likewise, had Thomas, my five-year-old younger brother who needed a father. And me? Well, I was, to all intents and purposes, their mulatto slave. And Giles Corey treated me as such: he barked orders at me, only ever referred to me as 'nigga boy' and beat me regularly.

Salem Village was for me a living hell. I was stuck in a house with a violent, bad-tempered bigot and a mother who had no love for me whatsoever. I was their slave and nothing more. It was, and had always been, a lonely existence, now it had become frightening as well. The only shining light in my life was Tituba, Minister Paris's slave girl.

Obviously, my mother and stepfather were good 'God-fearing white folks,' so, when they was at the meeting house, I would sneak over to the Parrises and steal a few moments with Tituba. She was a few years older than me and it was like having a big sister, even if it was only on a Sunday. Tituba was a beautiful person, both inside and out, and I adored her. She would tell me stories of her homeland, her childhood, and what it was to be free. "We don't never knows what we got til' it gone." she would say, shaking her head sadly. I had no idea what freedom was, but it sounded fantastic. The time I spent with Tituba, drinking small beer, and sharing our stories, made life in Salem Village slightly more bearable.

Tituba confided in me, and I in her. She was so loyal to the Parrises, especially their daughter and it was obvious she was far kinder than her husband. I asked her once about the bruises on her arm and she shook her head, "Pay no never mind to them, they is nothin,' Mas'ser Ben."

They obviously were something, but I could spend time trying to prise it out of her to no avail or I could just enjoy her company. If I'd been a man instead of just a child, I would have rescued her and loved her as she deserved. I was, however, too young, and immature for such things, but I did love her, very much. She was the only person who had ever shown me any kindness.

★

"Where's my ale, nigga boy?" I sighed ... just once my real name would be nice.

"Hurry up! I don't have all day." He had more time than I was taking, but there was no point in saying so; instead, I dutifully handed him his ale and braced myself for a beating. Beatings nearly always took the form of a whooping with a switch, but I could never have braced myself for what was to follow. As expected, I felt the switch strike me, unexpectedly across the back of my knees and much harder than normal. I crumpled to the ground and he kicked me hard in the ribcage; I heard a crack as I struggled for breath. It was at this point I felt his boot slam between my legs; I remember nothing after that. I must have been unconscious for some time, as one of the farm hands, under my mother's instruction, had dumped me in the hay barn. The beating obviously continued after I passed out and when I came to, every bit of me ached. I could scarcely see through my swollen eyelids. It was a struggle to get to my feet, but I managed it. Giles Corey was a clever man and already had experience of beating a slave to death; even in a rage he knew when to stop.

It was a bitterly cold Sunday morning and the family, thankfully, were all safely tucked away in the meeting house, redeeming themselves in the eyes of their Lord. Their god was cruel and dispassionate. He; was not benevolent and merciful, at least not to slaves. I stumbled across the icy, cold ground to see Tituba.

"Oh! My Lawd, what 'appen Mas'ser Ben ... what 'appen? who done this tebble thing?" She didn't wait for me to answer, "Did Mas'ser Giles do this dre'ful thing to yous?"

I didn't need to answer her, she already knew.

"Dunna worry Mas'ser Ben, they get there's ... is a cumin." I had no idea what she meant but nodded in agreement. She sat nursing her baby daughter as we chatted some more. Time always passes too quickly on a Sunday morning, but on this occasion it seemed to pass quicker. Time had run away from us, and I raced back to the house as fast as was possible, given the state of my battered body. By supper time I knew something was wrong: there was much talk about the Parris household, and I strained to hear as much as I could. I cared not for the minister or 'his holier than thou' family; I just wanted to know that Tituba and her baby were safe. It appeared that Abigail and Elizabeth had been taken ill; the relief was immense. Had I trusted their Puritan god, I would've given thanks; instead, I just slept easier knowing my beautiful friend Tituba was safe and well.

★

Over the following few weeks, I noticed a change in Tituba. She confided to me that she was "Mighty worry 'bout Miss Betty," as she put it, "Miss Betty gotta bad bloody flux ... mighty bad."

As the girls grew weaker, the change in Tituba was apparent: she looked as though she carried the weight of the world upon her tiny shoulders. For 'God-fearing, charitable, love thy neighbour' white folk, they did a whole lot of gossiping, and could be right spiteful too. Minister Parris's home was a favourite topic of conversation, especially after Dr Griggs diagnosed Miss Elizabeth and Miss Abigail as being bewitched. Mr Parris's sermon in the meeting house, when he announced the devil was among the good folk of Salem, fuelled much debate among his parishioners. Curiously, my mother, or Mistress Martha, as I was made to call her, was the voice of reason, largely denouncing the notion of witchcraft.

I tearfully watched my only friend, the only person who ever gave a damn about me, dragged out of Minister Parris's house under arrest for witchcraft. My mother said it was a farce and that her only crime was the colour of her skin; oh, the irony! Being part of the crowd that gathered to watch Tituba, Mistress Osborne, and Mistress Good get arrested was both a shameful and a heart-breaking experience. I didn't care one iota about the white folks being dragged off: the devil could take them and be damned, but Tituba, my beautiful, wonderful Tituba, for her I wept.

For all my weeping and sobbing over the loss of my friend though, there was a small part of me that couldn't help but wonder if maybe, just maybe, there was some truth in it. Her words echoed in my head: 'Dunnah worry Mas'ser Ben, they get their's ... is a cumin.' Is this what was coming?

Surely any witch smart enough to curse would be smart enough to not get caught.

The following weeks can only be described as insanity; the whole of Salem was in chaos. There was sheer panic as folks began to believe that the devil walked among them, bewitching their children. Neighbour eyed neighbour with suspicion and parents lived in fear of their children either being bewitched or, worse still, accusing them of being witches.

As I said, my mother's approach was, given the madness around us, surprisingly rational. She did not believe in witches and viewed the whole sordid affair as the hysterical ramblings of teenage girls, pulling the wool over the eyes of every arsworm[1] and swill-belly[2] in the village. This was an unpopular view of the situation with just about everyone but me. I was actually impressed by my mother's take on things, although it changed nothing within our household. In her outspoken defiance of the whole situation, she refused to refer to it as anything other than a 'ridiculous affair;' having attended the first examination of events in Boston, she deemed it 'not worthy of her time' and attempted to persuade her bastard of a husband likewise.

"These accusations and so-called examinations are a mockery, and this good God-fearing household shall have no part of it. I'm telling you Giles, stay well away."

"That, wife, will only serve to make us look guilty and wives do not tell their husbands what to do; would you like me to remind you of that?" He screwed up his face in anger "Is that what you want woman?" She lowered her gaze, sheepishly retreating.

"No, I didn't think so." I thought that was that, but no; my mother, at times, was as foolhardy as she was rational and as soon as he had left the room she collared me.

"Hide his saddle, boy." Seriously. She thought *that* was a good idea. I was damned either way. If I disobeyed her, she would beat me and if I obeyed her, Master Giles would beat me harder. Perhaps foolishly, I obeyed her. There was no perhaps about it, not only did I get the beating I expected, but he, Master Giles. Oh, how his name leaves a bitter taste in my mouth, began to view my mother with the suspicion that she may be bewitched herself.

★

I never saw Tituba again after she was arrested. I knew she had been jailed in Boston and I kept my ears open for news. I expected to hear that she had been hanged but took solace in the fact that no news was good news. I missed her desperately.

Then it happened: two men knocked the door one evening. It was I who opened the door to them.

"Fetch your Mistress, nigga boy." As always, I dutifully obeyed and then remained close enough to hear the conversation, but far enough away not to be beaten for eavesdropping. She spoke before they had a chance to greet her or exchange any pleasantries:

"I know what ye are coming for; ye are come to talk with me about being a witch." The tone of her voice was remarkably self-righteous, given that there were three women already in jail and that my mother, at least, believed them all to be innocent. To use that tone of voice, she had far more faith in the justice system than I did, but then again, she was white.

"That's right," they retorted, slightly taken aback, but continued before she could say anything else, "Ann Putnam and her girl Mercy Lewis say you bewitched them. They say you visited them and attacked them while they slept."

"And pray tell me, how was I supposed to have done that when I have been home all day?"

"They say you flew in."

"Really? And you believe them? This wouldn't have anything to do with Ann Putnam being your niece would it, Edward?" One of the men looked slightly sheepish, but the other was still determined.

419

"Now look here Goody Corey ..."

"No, you look here, both of you. Has it occurred to either of you to ask Ann Putnam or, for that matter, Mercy Lewis what I was wearing when I supposedly attacked them?"

"Yes, it has." the other man, Ezekiel Cheever, swiftly retorted.

"And did she tell you what clothes I had on?" My mother was mocking them, and they weren't happy, to say the least.

"Yes, actually. We did indeed ask her that very thing, and she claimed that you temporarily blinded her, so she couldn't see you, but then you know that don't you? Which is exactly why you asked us that. Is it not?"

"Exactly!" piped up Edward Putnam, regaining his confidence.

"This is utterly ridiculous," she said, rolling her eyes, "utterly ridiculous and I'd thank you to leave."

"This isn't the last of the matter, Goody Corey." piped up Edward Putnam, who was positively triumphant in the outing of my mother as a witch, "No Ma'am, not the last of it."

The two men left and by the end of the day, my mother was the talk of Salem Village, probably Salem town too. My mother was an evil, sanctimonious bitch, with disastrous taste in menfolk and a cruel streak as wide as a creek, but she wasn't a witch. For all her 'God-fearing, church going, and bible-reading ways,' folk were quick to point the finger. No one, not even that vile husband of hers, considered the girls to be anything other than victims of my mother: the witch.

At no point did my mother look bothered by any of it, if she was, it was only in the privacy of her bed chamber. Word had it that a warrant had been issued for her arrest late on Saturday, but it was too late for it to be effective. So, my mother, who was as proud as she was self-righteous, marched defiantly into the meeting house on Sunday and sat amidst the pious. She didn't even bat an eyelid at all the not- so-hushed whispers and pointed fingers. She was still a member of the church and, as such, had as much right as anyone to be there, as long as her arrest warrant went unserved. No one, but no one, had stopped to consider that perhaps she had been tipped off in advance about the clothing conversation; the only reasonable conclusion was that she had used supernatural forces to learn such information. However, as much as I hated her, in this instance she was innocent. However, there was a distinct irony, in the fact that she, who had shown such disdain for the whole sorry affair, was now part of their circus. She was still vehemently protesting her innocence when they arrested her Monday morning and promptly took her to the meeting house, to be examined by Judge Hathorne. Master Giles left shortly after, but not before taking his anger out on me.

"It's all your doing, nigga boy. You and that nigga slut from the

Parrises house; you have cursed this house. Nothing but an embarrassing little nigga boy." Every insult accompanied by a kick or punch. I lay curled up in a ball, wondering if I could muster the energy, and get past the pain, enough to sneak in and watch the trial. My ribs were so sore I could barely breathe and by the time I reached the meeting house, the trial was in full swing.

"Why did you ask if the child told what clothes you wore, Martha Corey?"

"My husband told me Ezekiel Cheevers and Edward Putnam were intending to ask me that when he seen them earlier."

"Who told you about the clothes? Why did you ask that question?"

"My husband because he heard the children told what clothes the others wore. Sarah Osborne, Sarah Good, and the slave girl."

"Giles Corey, is that true? Did you tell her?"

All eyes were fixed on the old bastard who staring directly at his wife, shook his head;

"No Sir, I did not."

Judge Hathorne looked perplexed, "Did you not say that your husband told you so? If not you, then who hurt these children? Look upon them, now Martha Corey."

"I cannot help them. I did not do it. I am not guilty."

"Did you not say you would tell the truth? Why did you ask that question about the clothing? How came you by such knowledge? Is your husband lying? Are you?" He fixed his gaze on the old man. He was lying and I knew it.

"No; I did but ask Edward Putnam and Ezekiel Cheevers."

"Which one of you dares to lie to all in this assembly? You are now before authority, so, I expect the truth, which you promised to do. Speak now and tell me who told you what clothes?"

I left before either of them answered. I needed laudanum for the pain in my side: that bastard Corey had broken my ribs; I was sure of it. Not that it mattered, the only escape from chores and beatings was death. I know it's wrong in the eyes of God, but I hated that man with every fibre of my being.

I returned to the trial just in time to hear Judge Hathorne encouraging my mother to find God's mercy through confession.

"Only the Lord God can redeem you and surely you wish forgiveness for this evil. I would urge you, Martha Corey, to repent in front of God and the good folk of Salem."

"And I would urge you, Judge Hathorne, not to believe the rantings of hysterical children nor hollow-mouthed rogues." She stared directly at her husband and my heart hit the floor. A ripple of laughter went around the meeting house, and the look on that old bastard's face suggested someone, me, was going to pay; she opens her mouth and I get injured.

"Perhaps," Judge Hathor added, loudly enough to quell the stifled laughter and murmurings, "you would like to explain why you chose to hide your husband's saddle to prevent him attending the trials in Boston?"

"I did not know of what benefit it would be."

"She wants to stop them finding witches!" Thomas Putnam blurted out loudly which was followed by further disruption.

"Indeed." Hathorne offered, trying to resume order.

"Perhaps then, Martha Corey, you could tell me if you know there to be any other witches in Salem?"

"None that I know of, but then I am not in the business of knowing witches."

"She's lying!" came another voice from the crowd.

"Yes, yes can we get on?" Judge Hathorne seemed anxious to get the whole thing over with.

"When did you turn away from God? Did you ever worship the Lord our God? Just how long have you served the devil?"

"I am an innocent person; I never had anything to do with witchcraft since I was born. I am a gospel woman."

At this point, Mercy Lewis began mimicking her movements, followed by Ann Putnam; a few other girls joined in. Mercy then hollered "She said she had no familiarity with any such thing she was a gospel woman: a title which she called herself by; but the afflicted persons told her, 'Ah! She must be a gospel witch!'"

It was chaos: someone, one of the girls, I can't remember who, claimed they saw a yellow bird flying above her head, while another saw a man whispering in her ear. She recognised this man as the devil. My mother was right in one thing: it was a farce! She was charged and taken to join the others in Boston jail. That was the last I saw of my mother.

★

Would that I would have willed it any better, but on April 13th my bastard of a stepfather, who had beaten me daily since my mother's arrest, was himself arrested. He was accused of being a wizard by the same girl who had accused my mother. The beautiful irony of that remains with me, ever present, a constant smile; sometimes hidden, sometimes visible, but always there.

Since my mother's arrest there had been several women accused of witchcraft, along with little Dorcas Good, who was scarcely more than a babe, and only two days previous, John Procter had become the first man accused. He, unlike Master Giles, was a good man undeserving of such a fate. In fact, the majority were good people compared to Giles Corey.

The knock at the door and even the familiar "Get the door nigga boy." lingers in my memory, to be cherished for all time along with the following conversation:

"Giles Corey, you're under arrest."

"Really? On what charge exactly? Is your niece seeing things again?" He sneered at Edward Putnam, who'd become a dab hand at arresting people. I actually think that was the single most stupid thing I'd ever heard the vicious old bastard say. Even the men arresting him looked bemused.

"Witchcraft." the other man, whose name I can't recall sneered back.

Needless to say, he was right, in as much as Ann Putnam was behind his arrest. Once again, she and Mercy Lewis had experienced Giles Corey visiting them with the intention of harming them. And not only Giles Corey, allegedly the ghost of a man who had died in this very house attacked them too. I couldn't help but wonder what madness was gripping Salem Village that all these 'godly white do-gooders' were now being accused of the very thing they were opposed to. Tituba's words rang in my head, 'Dunna worry Mas'ser Ben, they get there's … is a cumin.' By the look of it, it was here! I kind of hoped Tituba was behind the chaos; I, for one, would feel much safer if she was.

I never saw Giles Corey's examination, but there was plenty of gossip in the following days about how the afflicted girls had all been affected by his presence: falling unto seizures and squealing, as if pinched. Apparently, it was so bad Judge Hathorne called for Corey's hands to be tied. And even when his hands were tied, the slightest movement of his head affected them.

Most in Salem were outraged or feared his demonic powers. I thought the man, himself, was demon enough.

Over the following months, the children of Salem pointed their finger at several others: too many to name. Some of them deserved it: my mother and that bastard, Giles Corey. I cannot fully express my joy at his arrest; I hated that man with a passion. Before my mother married him, I didn't think I could loathe anyone more than her. But I could!

By June, they had assembled a thing called the Court of Oyer and Terminer, allegedly to determine a person's guilt or innocence, with proper evidence, as opposed to, one could only assume, improper evidence. There was no 'proper' evidence; it was all hearsay and conjecture. The whole thing was conducted using the Witchfinder's Bible: 'Malleus Maleficarum,' along with extracts from the actual Bible; what a circus it was.

I heard later that year my mother had been found guilty; needless to say, I wasted no tears on the heartless bitch. I was far more interested in hearing whether that evil bastard Giles Corey was going to be found guilty. As far as I was concerned, even if he was innocent of witchcraft, he deserved to hang. The bruises on my body were a testament to his evil and brutal nature.

It was a seven hour walk from my home to the meeting house, where the trials were being held and, generally speaking, I had no interest in watching many good folks being sentenced to death for something they hadn't done.

Giles Corey's trial was a whole different thing. I didn't care what he was sentenced for, I just wanted to watch the bastard hang. On the ninth day of September, I made the journey to Salem courthouse in the hope of witnessing Giles Corey's face when he was found guilty. I wanted to look him straight in the eyes, as they sentenced him to death.

"Giles Corey, you stand before these good folks accused of Witchcraft. How do you plead to this?"

"I do not plead."

"Don't be ridiculous man!" a member of the crowd shouted, above the murmurings of the crowd.

"Quite so. Quite so. Let's hear what the girls have to say on the matter, as they were the ones afflicted by your alleged witchcraft." I'm not sure Judge Hathorne believed for one moment that Corey was innocent; after all, the others were all guilty.

I sat on the edge of my seat, listening to the various accusations made by the girls who had accused him. I hoped and prayed that there would be enough to convict him.

"May I remind you of the testimony you gave in court, stating that you were stopped in prayer by your wife. Are you sure it was she who stopped you and not the devil you serve? Pray elaborate."

"I cannot recall what stopped me with any certainty. My wife came towards me and found fault with me for saying 'living to God and dying to sin."

"And you mentioned another incident took place in the barn. Pray tell the court what it was that scared you in the barn?"

"I know of nothing in there that frightened me." The old bastard was beginning to look worried. Good. I only came to watch him suffer.

"Why, there are three witnesses here today that heard you say as much, as plain as day. Thomas Gould has, himself, made a testimony that you knew enough against your wife to do her business. I'm sure the court would like to hear what the knowledge was that you spoke of."

"I presume that of living to God and dying to sin."

"As I recall, both Marshal George Herrick and Bibber's daughter corroborated this claim. How say you to that?"

"I have said all that I can say to that." Corey snapped and it was obvious to all present he was beginning to feel the strain.

"And what was it about your lame ox that caused you such concern?" asked the Judge, referring to the statement in front of him.

"I believed he may be hipped."

"And what was the ointment your wife had when she was seized? You had said it was a potion she had made under Major Gedney's direction."

"If I said that, then truly I was mistaken, for the ointment you speak of most assuredly came from Goody Bibber."

"I see. I think perhaps we should hear from one of the afflicted. Who will speak, among you girls?" At this point, several of the girls present began to wail and moan, throwing themselves, as if possessed. All of this was accompanied by cries of "Witch! Witch!" from the rest of those present. Fortunately, before the whole thing descended into absolute mayhem, Mercy Lewis stood up bold as bold could be and delivered her well-rehearsed statement on Giles Corey's activities.

"I will speak, if it pleases the court." Judge Hathorne indicated for her to continue.

"Well, Sir, I saw the apparition of Giles Corey come and afflict me, urging me to write in this book he had. The pain was unbearable, but he continued most dreadfully to hurt me. Sometimes, by times beating me and I feared he might break my back. This was a regular happening till the day of his examination, being the 19th day of April just passed. And then, even during the time of his examination, he did afflict and torture me most grievously and also several times since. Always he is urging me vehemently to write in his book. I do verily believe in my heart that Giles Corey is a dreadful wizard. For ever since he has been imprisoned, either he or his appearance has come and most grievously tormented me."

I could easily believe that Giles Corey would be more than happy to beat anyone: man, woman, or child, we are all inferior creatures that needed nothing more than a good thrashing. I figured if Mercy Lewis' testimony didn't seal his fate, nothing would.

"What say you now, Giles Corey? Are you guilty or not guilty? And if guilty, do you repent in the eyes of the Lord?"

"Neither Sir. I do not plead either." Giles stood tall, as if untouchable.

"Are you telling this court that you will not enter a plea?"

"No Sir I will not."

Corey was an old man, but he stood tall and defiant. I sighed; was he about to be freed? The thought of that brutish man being released filled me with terror. I was considering fleeing Salem and taking my chances elsewhere, although one white master was much like another, when Judge Hathorne saved my life.

"If you will not enter a plea, then I have no choice but for you to be taken to the empty field, adjacent to the Salem jailhouse on Howard Street, where you shall be stripped naked save for you privy parts and pressed until you answer to the charges."

None of us had seen that coming. Various murmurs ran around the courthouse. In Corey's defence, such as I would award him, Judge Hathorne had decided the old bastard was guilty from the beginning. I had heard as much said back at his examination in April. Not that I cared whether he was guilty or innocent, I just wanted rid of him.

★

I awoke early on the seventeenth day of September; truth to tell, I'm not sure I had slept at all. Sherriff Corwen was due to administer the torture as set by the court eight days previous. I had never seen a man "pressed," but it sounded horrendous, and I wasn't going to miss out on seeing Giles Corey get his due.

I watched as he was brought out of the jail to the field and I had to remind myself how much I despised this pitiful wretch. He was brought out on a leash and stripped down to his undergarments, which hung loosely on him; prison portions were much smaller than the gluttonous bastard was used to. I was glad he had been surviving on scraps; he'd fed them to me often enough if I was lucky. He carried the board that would be laid on him. I half expected Sherriff Corwen to put a crown of thorns on his head and, as ironic as that would be, there was nothing to compare this beast of a man to the Jesus Christ our saviour. The only soul Corey would save was his own.

Watching Corey laid upon the warm September grass with a board placed over him, I felt a tinge of pity. He was a wretched creature in life and now a pitiful wretch in death. At least, what I hoped would be his death. Although I fully expected him to change his mind, to plead guilty, and swear to repent, but the only words any of us heard were "More weight. More weight."

Two days this torture lasted, and I never shut my eyes to sleep the whole time. I just sat there watching and listening. After twenty-four hours or so, a church official appeared to witness the old man call out, "More weight. More weight."

No sooner had the words come out of Corey's mouth than I heard Master Parris, with Bible raised aloft:

"In the name of Our Lord and our saviour and according to the will of Christ, you Giles Corey, who have until now enjoyed the privileges afforded to a member of our church and congregation, are hereby cast out of the said church and congregation and delivered unto Satan."

It was a truly horrific form of torture and one I felt sure I would have entered a plea to avoid, yet Corey endured it all. Throughout the day, crowds gathered, and he remained defiant: undeterred even by his execution. On and off Sherriff Corwen would stand on the ever-growing mound of rocks. He was as brutal as Corey; the only difference was Sherriff Corwen had God and the law on his side.

At night when he was alone with only me, at all times obscured from his vision, keeping my vigil; then it was a different story. Then he would sob, pleading for forgiveness, from my mother predominately, and occasionally God. He begged that they should forgive his foolishness. He was

433

an ignorant, greedy, and vicious brute of a man, but he was no witch.

On the morning of the nineteenth day of September, another two rocks were added to the pile and I watched Corey's tongue come out of his mouth. He looked ridiculous and grotesque, and some of the women present squealed in horror. Sherriff Corwen climbed on to the board and with his feet positioned on either side, straddling the rocks, he jabbed his cane hard into Corey's tongue in the hope of concealing it once again. It took a few goes and even though this man deserved no charity on my part, I still winced at the brutality of it all.

It was a strange experience. This man who had made my life a living hell. That bastard Giles Corey who had treated me worse than folks treat their dogs; I would've traded places with Mary Sibley's dog any day. Perhaps it was compassion, perhaps it was simply the knowledge that he was innocent of witchcraft, or perhaps it was just an emotional response to knowing I was finally rid of him. Either way, a tear rolled down my face as I listened to his final rasping words,

"More weight. More ... wei ...

JANET HORNE
(died 1727)

In 1727 Janet Horne became the last person to be tried and executed for witchcraft in the Both she and her daughter were arrested and jailed in Dornoch. Her crimes were turning her daughter into a pony and riding her in order to get Satan to her shod. At the time of her execution Janet Horne was showing signs of what would be recognised today as senile dementia. Her daughter suffered from deformed hands and feet which was possibly hereditary. The trial was presided over by Captain David Ross, sheriff-depute of Sutherland. He trial appears to have been rushed, possibly it only served as a formality as he quickly decided their guilt; sentencing both to be burned to death the following day. The daughter managed to escape but Janet was was stripped, covered in tar, and paraded through Dornoch in a barrel. On arriving at the fire, she is reputed to have smiled and commented on both the number of people present and the fire itself.

Maternal Kiss

THE DIVIL OF INSCH
Diane Narraway

The sunlight drifted through the cracked window casting shadows, which danced around the room. The small girl skipped gaily, laughing as she weaved her way in and out of the shadows; it was a typically happy scene. Then, the inevitable crash: a pottery vase shattered, alerting her mother to yet another disaster, and awakening her father, who was face down on an old coffer sleeping off the day's drinking.

Janet arrived in the drawing room just in time to reach her daughter before her husband properly came to.

"Oh, Annie. I despair of ye – ye are a gawky lass, to be sure."

"I'm sorry. I don't mean to be."

"I know, but we can scarce afford food and clothing."

"I tell ye Jannie, the lassie's a divil. Ye only gotta look at her to see that."

"Stop it, ye'll scare the lass." Janet placed her hands over Annie's ears.

"Nae a lassie. I'm tellin' ye, a divil."

"Well, it'd be yer doing if she is a divil; does the Lord nae visit the iniquity of the fathers on the children?"

"Hush woman, with yer scripture quoting; ye know nothing of the Lord's words."

"I know he's a darn sight more merciful than ye, Alisdair Duncan Campbell Horne." His name left a bitter taste on her tongue.

Alisdair Horne was his wife's biggest mistake: a drunk and a womaniser, who spent more time in taverns and brothels than anywhere else. Possibly due to his heavy drinking, he harboured a warped view of many things, including his daughter, who had been disformed at birth. Alisdair was of the belief that she was a changeling, or 'divil' as he put it and that somewhere in another realm was his perfect daughter. Of course, he blamed Janet for all of this and, in their more forceful arguments, even went as far as accusing her of using their child to bargain with Satan. Fortunately, because he only ever spouted off when drunk, the people he told were also drunk or just took it as the ramblings of a drunken idiot. The latter was certainly how his wife saw him.

She had been in service, had travelled extensively, and had become quite cultured for a maid. She, Janet, was what you would call a 'bonny lass': her eyes sparkled when she laughed, her red hair shone like fire in the sunlight, and she caught the eyes of men from labourers to lairds. Eventually, she caught the eye of Alisdair Horne, who in his heyday was equally attractive and could charm the birds from the trees. On the surface, they were both a 'good catch.' Alisdair had money and plenty of it, and Janet didn't want for anything. They were blissfully happy, at least to begin with.

They had only been married a few months when Alisdair began spending more and more time away from Janet, and more and more time in the company of whores and jezebels. Alcohol and women, particularly those who require payment for their company, are sure-fire ways of eating through the family fortune. And sure enough, within a couple of years, Janet was both pregnant and poor. Although she hoped that having a baby would rekindle their love and that Alisdair would see the error of his ways, she couldn't have been more wrong.

Annie was born with disformed hands and feet; Janet knew the fault lay with her husband passing her the pox but placing the blame was pointless: he would never accept responsibility. Alisdair had been away from home when Annie was born, and it was a good two days before he met his daughter. Immediately, he had attributed her disformities to her having been swapped for a changeling. Over the years, his conviction grew and, after a few ales, followed by a few more, his opinion of little Annie became more vocal. Janet grew to despise him. They were poor and Annie was clumsy, awkward, and prone to breaking things, as on this particular day.

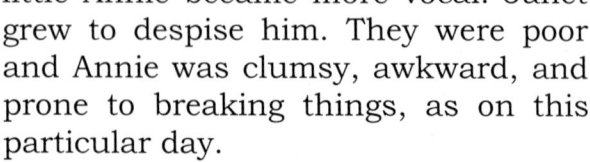

Janet ushered Annie into the kitchen, while Alisdair continued ranting about her being a divil before he stumbled off out to the ale house for a top-up.

Annie knew all too well her father's opinion of her, but as long as her mother was there she felt safe. Janet knew it was only a matter of time before Alisdair opened his mouth to the wrong person and so, right at that moment, she made the decision to leave him.

She grabbed what food she had, took Annie's hand, and set off on the long walk from Insch to Dornoch, where she hoped she still had family. The journey would take several days on foot, maybe a week with Annie struggling to keep up. Janet didn't care how long it took; she loved Annie and would not subject her to any more of her husband's twisted, drunken rantings. The days they spent on the road were pleasant days that passed by much quicker than she had anticipated. Both Janet and Annie learned much about each other, and the mother and daughter bond grew stronger with each step. Food had run out after a couple of days but even hunger and sore feet didn't daunt their spirits. Anything was better than life in Insch.

Eventually they reached Loth.

When Janet neared the gate of their family home, she could see her Aunt tending the garden; she looked old and frail. She opened the gate and the old lady turned to see her niece and child.

Janet looked exhausted; she had eaten very little in order for Annie to not go hungry. Her Aunt immediately stopped what she was doing and hurried towards them, flinging her arms round Janet before scooping Annie up in the biggest hug she had ever had.

"Come in child; ye look wiped out. And this must be Annie: ah she's a bonnie wee thing, such pretty eyes and those curls."

It warmed Janet's heart that someone else could see her daughter as beautiful and not as Alisdair would have everyone believe – a divil.

They stayed in Loth and life was good: Annie was happy, and Janet had almost erased her husband's drunken accusations about their daughter from her mind. In a happy environment, Annie grew and became much less gawky. She was smart too: a quick-witted lass by all accounts and when Aunt died, it was she who inherited the cottage and no small amount of land. Janet was not so fortunate and Alisdair's womanising and drinking had left her all-but penniless. She was also gripped by the later stages of the pox, her eyesight was fading, and she struggled to remember what day it was. Often she lashed out at her daughter, believing her a stranger. Annie coped well, considering her mother's erratic behaviour and was undaunted by the local tongue-waggers and finger-pointers, who saw her mother as a source of entertainment. Mostly Annie just shook her head, but occasionally the gossips felt the sharp edge of her tongue.

This all changed dramatically when a woman from Insch showed up. She had worked in the alehouse and immediately recognised Annie in the marketplace by her disformed hands.

"Why, tis the Divil of Insch." she declared, in a voice designed to attract as much attention as possible.

"Away with ye. What do ye know, tavern wench?" She stared long and hard at the woman, whose uneasiness could be felt by all present.

Annie turned with far more dignity than would most people, having just been accused of being a devil. This was only the start and she knew it.

Two days later, there was a loud knock at the door. Janet, who was unable to cope with loud noises, hid under the kitchen table shaking. Annie answered it, to an overweight man sporting a tatty powdered wig.

"Annie Horne? Is that ye?" His voice was stern and purposeful.

"Aye, ye know it is."

"I'm here to determine whether ye are a witch or nae." He announced, barging his way past her and closing the door himself. "Of course," he began pompously, "ye do realise that I have the power over whether ye live or die ..." His voice trailed off, as he caught sight of Janet shaking under the table.

"Well, what have we here lassie? Is she bewitched?"

"She is nay such thing;" snarled Annie "she is old, scared, and confused and ye are the one scaring her.

Whatever ye're here to do, just get on with it."

He, however, wasn't blind and could see full well how striking she was.

"Well, lassie, perhaps we could come to some arrangement." he muttered, eyeing her up and down.

It was obvious to Annie what this arrangement was and as hateful as he was, she knew it may be the only way to keep her mother safe. Truthfully, she had no interest in sex and her disformed hands and feet meant that, beyond sex, most men would have no interest in her.

"Well." he said. The tone of his voice indicated to her that he wasn't about to change his mind, so she beckoned him towards her bed chamber. Janet remained under the table, shaking until he left, and Annie managed to coax her out.

"It's OK, he's gone now." Annie said gently, offering her hand for Janet to take it.

Annie somewhat naively believed that was that, but the following morning he was back, with half a dozen other men waiting at the gate.

"We have received an accusation that yer mother is a witch."

"So, yesterday it was me and today it's my mother. Surely, ye have nay interest in fucking her. Or am I required to save her too?" She was more than aware of the possibility that she may be expected to have sex with all of them.

"Neither." he replied sheepishly. "I have orders to bring ye both in for trial."

Annie's heart sank and he could see the sorrow in her eyes. "What have either of us done to deserve such an accusation?"

"A man in Insch claims that ye are a changeling: that yer mother made a pact with the Divil and swapped her child for ye. And that she does transform ye into a pony and rides ye to the Divil, to get shoes for ye."

Annie didn't need to guess which man in Insch had made the accusation. She assumed the barmaid had returned and told him of their whereabouts. Her mother had no chance of reasonably answering anything; she could scarcely remember her own name. Frightened and confused, Janet Horne was led out of the cottage followed by her daughter. The only crime Janet had committed was to marry Alisdair Horne: a drunken womaniser who passed the pox onto his wife.

Riddled with the final stage of syphilis, terrified and confused, Janet Horne and her daughter were taken to the old tollbooth in Dornoch.

"I'm sorry." their captor whispered, in a compassionate voice as he closed the door.

Was this really the same man, who only a few days previous had demanded they come to 'an arrangement'?

Annie hugged her mother tightly, as they were swallowed by the darkness of the tiny room. She had spent the night praying and hoped above all else that God was listening to her. It appeared he was not.

At first light, they were collected for trial. Annie was more afraid for her mother than herself. Janet was afraid, confused, and had no idea what day of the week it was, let alone what she was being charged with or why.

A fair crowd had gathered for the trial; they jeered at her and her mother, as they stood quivering. Annie knew it wasn't going to be a trial in the true sense of the word: that it was nothing more than a kangaroo court based on hearsay, rumours, and superstition. It was presided over by Captain David Ross, Sheriff-Depute of Sutherland. Captain David Ross was known for his fear and dislike of witches and was no more tolerant than Annie's father. The trial was farcical, the charges absurd, and the outcome inevitable.

"Janet Horne, ye stand today accused of witchcraft and sorcery. That ye did wilfully exchange yer own daughter, Annie, for a divil to turn into a pony with the sole intent of riding to Satan himself. Whereupon he shod her and in haste you failed to return her, leaving her hands and feet permanently disformed and hoof like; an act which only serves to prove yer guilt. Ye also stand accused of bewitching pigs and poultry, specifically Aggie MacDougal's hens, which haven't laid an egg since last Hugmonay. How say ye?"

"I'm sure I've tried to lead a good life, but these people are strangers to me. My Annie has a twisted hand and folks are dreadful, whispering stories about us. Why do they hate us so?"

"Step forward and speak up woman; I can barely hear ye."

Janet stepped forward. It was cold, so it was hard for Annie to tell if she was shivering from the cold or fear. She began to speak, but Captain Ross was far from charitable and it was very clear that he had already decided that they were guilty.

"Recite the Lord's Prayer."

"Excuse me?"

"The Lord's Prayer."

At this point, Annie knew their fate was sealed. Her mother couldn't remember her own name half the time, so there was little hope she would remember the Lord's Prayer, and certainly not under duress.

"Our father ..." she began slowly, "who wert in heaven ..."

"Guilty as charged." This was proof enough for Captain Ross. One word she got wrong, just one.

"It's 'art in heaven,' as any true God-fearing Christian knows. Clearly ye are nay such thing." He shrieked, "... Art! Take them away; they are to be burned alive at first light. May the Lord have mercy on their souls; although I very much doubt he will."

Annie's heart sank. Her mother's fear was short-lived as they were led back to the tollbooth,

Annie knew by the morning her mother would've forgotten the whole trial; if indeed, one could even call it a trial.

It was around 3am when the same arresting officer with whom she'd had 'an arrangement' could be heard outside. She knew his voice only too well, from thunderous demanding to apologetic whisper. The tollbooth door opened quietly, and the lamplight cast shadows that flickered around the cell.

"Hurry, there isn't much time." He kept his voice hushed as he reached down to offer her his hand.

Her eyes flashed around the room: her mother lay curled up asleep and waking her would certainly have drawn attention. So, instead, she took his hand and allowed him to lead her off into the night.

At first light the guards appeared, along with Captain Ross. The man was thorough if nothing else; he was going to see his trial through to the end.

"The daughter's gone ... vanished."

"What do ye mean, vanished? People don't just vanish." Ross scowled hard at the young and, he believed, inexperienced if not idiotic guard.

"Look for yerself, Sir."

Sure enough, the only occupant of the cell was Janet. Ross's hatred was evident as he spat the words, "Bring the Witch and I hope her divil daughter is hiding in the crowd watching; I want her to witness every moment." His face screwed up pensively, as he considered the best course of action. What would be a fitting deterrent to other witches and what would break her daughter's heart should she be witness to the execution?

"Strip her ... and pitch her." The two officers began stripping the old woman, who was shrieking hysterically.

"When ye're done, parade her through the streets and take the longest route. I want to make sure everyone gets a look at what happens to those in league with the Divil. I especially want that daughter of hers to see her mother's fate."

And so, on a bitterly cold February morning, Janet Horne, whose only crime was marrying a sanctimonious, womanising drunk, was stripped of her clothing. She pleaded with them to stop and begged tearfully to know why they hated her so. The men ignored her questions, carrying out their duty in as cold and calculating a manner as their spirits would allow. All the while they were watched over by Captain David Ross, whose gaze flitted between the petrified prisoner and the crowd, hoping to catch a glimpse of her daughter. It was a pleasure he was denied: Annie was long gone, along with one of his highest-ranking guards. Neither would ever be seen again nor would the child, which was growing in her belly, at least not on this side of the Atlantic.

Janet made her way through the streets, paraded on a barrel. The sight of her: pitched and barrelled, and the sound of her wailing and sobbing as the hot pitch seared her flesh would be etched for ever on the minds of all those present. She was old, frail, and syphilis had taken its toll on her mind; her madness was evident to all as she neared the fire.

"So many folks. Have they all come to see me?"

"Aye that they have. They come to see ye burn, witch."

"How lovely they all look." There was little sign of sanity, but whether Ross knew of her illness or not was irrelevant; he was determined to paint her as black as he could. "See her defiance? Even now she refuses to repent." And as they lit the blaze beneath her he goaded her one more time, "What say ye now, witch?"

"Tis a bonnie blaze for sure."

"Let the Divil take her" Ross exclaimed triumphantly "and may he never be seen here again."

The Devil has never been seen in Scotland since.

BRIDGET CLEARY
(circa 1869 – 1895)

Most of the histories of witch burnings describe the savage punishments ordered by the established ruling classes, but such fervour ran deep through the bones of society, fuelled by ancient beliefs. Responsibility was not always passed to the justice system. Judgements could be brutally meted out at home, most frequently against women and children.

Bridget Cleary was good-looking, literate, independent, and different, dangerous qualities to have in a small rural community like that of Ballyvadlea, Tipperary. Helping matters little, she and her husband moved into a cottage recently built by the Poor Law Guardians on a *rath,* 'a fairy fortress.' Rumours abounded, fired by legends told by the *shanachie,* local storyteller, Cousin Jack Dunne.

Towards the end of an exceptionally hard winter, Bridget fell ill, probably with bronchitis, but her husband believed his wife exchanged for a sickly fairy, and the legends told him how to deal with it.

Bridget Cleary's death is regarded as the last witch burning in Ireland. No mourners attended her funeral as the locals remained suspicious the body was not human, so it was conducted by four policemen and took place after dark.

Her husband and killer, at a time when murderers were hung, served just fifteen years for manslaughter.

TIPPERARY WIFE
BURNING.

T'is Not My Wife, T'is Another's Life

IF OF THE DEVIL YOU ARE, BURN
Sem Vine

'Are you a witch or are you a faery?
Are you the wife of Michael Cleary?'

Granny said she was always going to be trouble; her, with her books and her airs and her fancy hats. So, when Mother was a little girl, she was never allowed to go near her. But Mother longed for something Bridget had made, for Bridget made such pretty things, and a thing of beauty warmed and lighted up those hard and dreary days. Mother said that sometimes, careful not to worry the chickens into a rackety fuss, she would wander close to Bridget's cottage, for Mother loved to listen to her singing as she sewed, her machine gently chugging, her full skirts softly swishing, brushing the earthen floor as her feet heel-toed rhythms on the treadle. It was as if she threaded music into her sewing, and by her nimble fingers all kinds of fabric grew into wonderful things; some that tied round the neck of a man or the waist of a woman, or that swaddled the tiny shape of a babe. But Mother said that Granny was glad her eyes were still good enough and she didn't need Bridget's help.

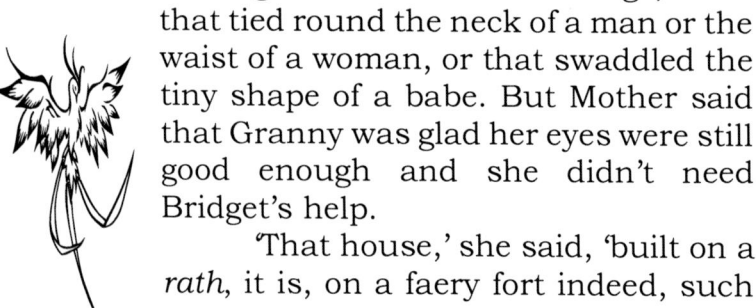

'That house,' she said, 'built on a *rath*, it is, on a faery fort indeed, such a hapless place for a home, let alone for one as cursed as she.'

Mother said she was only just twelve in '95, when that cruellest of winters was coming to an end. The spring was beginning to brighten the days at last, but then one March morning, the winter's chill returned in the villagers' whispers, saying that Bridget was missing.

'She took off in the night. I saw her,' her father swore, but the police came and took him away, and his sister and his sons, and they dragged Bridget's husband out of his house and away to Clonmel Gaol, him shouting all the while.

'It wasn't human, I tell you, it wasn't her, not my Bridget. My Bridgie was a beauty, a songbird, not that wailing thing, coughing blood and talking in tongues!'

And Granny nodded.

'Yes, yes, I heard the coughing too, I did. Days of it, I heard, I did. Even from my door I heard it. They always steal the ones they watch and leave their sickly things instead.'

Then a few days passed, and Bridget's wasted body was found in the boggy earth, shabbily buried and burned all black. Mother watched as the poor bony form, barely shrouded in a stained and tattered cloth, was wheeled through the village. The body seemed to tremble with the totter of the ramshackle cart. Onlookers shook their heads, their murmurs humming beneath the steady clop of hooves.

'Everyone knew she was bound to be taken. The *shanachie*[1] tells us these things so we know.'

These days, Mother said, they look at the tiny things, nigh invisible snippets, teeth, and all bits of scraps that mean you're you; but back then, it was a lock of hair, a ring, a shoe, a secret blemish. Those who'd known you through your life could simply say, 'Yes, I know you,' just as when you walked and breathed; but Bridget, see, while near all of her was burned, her face was whole beneath the cloth, one earring left glinting in her ear. Yet, even so, with all her face so clear to see, still her kin could not proclaim the body from the shallow grave belonged to Bridgie Cleary. Michael, who had laid the body there, told them all to ask the *shanachie* the truth; ask the *shanachie* they'd send her back, they will, and he must wait on Kylenagranagh Hill.

'They'll send her back, my Bridgie, all well and bright and singing, and fastened to a faery horse, and I must free her.'

★

'Take it, you witch!' hissed Michael on the night he challenged the changeling, pouring bitter herbs and beestings into her screaming mouth. Granny said it took four grown men to hold her down and make her drink the newborns' brew. Then, like the old ones say to do, they took the pisspot, made it full to slopping, and poured the piss all over her, and Michael, his lips peeled back and his teeth all bared, took up the poker, as instrument of iron and fire, and jabbed it at her again and again. Then, when that was done, they held her o'er the hearth, they did, to send the changeling back; and all the while she'd screamed like a wild thing, wailing words not one there could understand, her foetid blood sizzling and smoking on the hot bricks.

'Say your name!' demanded Michael of his wife.

'Say your name! Now! In the name of God!'

For a moment, Michael held his fervour, caught his breath, but not for long, for soon he was on it again. Granny said he locked everyone in and pocketed the key. He stripped Bridgie down to her calico shift and came at her with a burning log. When her shift began to catch, Michael grabbed the lamp and poured out all the oil into the flames, hurrying, for it must all be done by midnight.

'The filthy thing, I sent it up the chimney ...'

'Oh God! Bridgie is burned!' cried Cousin Hanna.

★

'That Michael Cleary,' Mother used to say, 'such a strong man, that he was.' She said she would often see him slide out of the pub opposite, slowed by the drink, with his face all shiny and his clothes all wrong. He'd drop his hat and stumble home to where his beautiful wife sang to the rhythm of her sewing. 'Come away from the window!' Granny would say. 'There's jobs to be done!'

Once or twice, Mother said, she would see a tall man come out of Bridget's doorway. Bridget, looking all pink and plump and smiling, would hand him some eggs. Mother would wonder if the man was so handsome because Bridget had woven her songs into his fine gentleman's clothes. Later though, when Mother knew the world better, she thought that maybe it was the man who wove the light into Bridget's smile and the beauty into her songs, and that Michael - if he hadn't gone mad – would've killed her anyway, if he'd known.

'Go to the faery place,' the *shanachie* told him.

'Go meet her there and cut the cords that bind her.'

But Granny said they'd never send Bridget back for what Michael had done to their own.

'That's why, when all was said and done, he upped and left for Canada,' said Mother. 'He just got tired of waiting, and not one of us heard of him again.'

---

[1] Anglicised form of Gaelic seanchaí or seanchaidhe, local storyteller and keeper of old lore

AMA HEMMAH
(1947-2010)

Ama was a Ghanaian woman burned alive for allegedly confessing to be a witch in Tema, Ghana. The suspects claimed the olive oil, which was used in an attempt to drive out the evil spirit was what caught fire. There was no evidence that she was any more than an old woman with dementia.

Let My Spirit Slip Away

'BURN BITCH BURN'
'Fly Free Upon the Winds'
Diane Narraway

They call me witch and they say
That the devil rules my soul,
But truth to tell it weren't no demon
Just the trials of being old.

My eyesight like my beauty
Has been lost to the passing years,
And the ramblings of an old woman
Ignite their superstitions and their fears.

I wander and I roam,
With no thought to where I be.
I cannot tell my house from yours
My vision fades, and I can barely see.

They say it was the work of demons,
That led me to the place
Where I was found, and accused
Of sorcery, from those so full of hate.

I had no idea why I was
Not safe within my home,
But I was only wandering
Lost, tired, and alone.

Witch they screamed; those five,
Who condemned me to my death.
Witch they screamed ever louder,
Witch! With venom on their breath.

Out demon, leave this woman.
Pastor Fletcher, a pious man,
Watched as the others held me down
And someone yelled "Go fetch the can!"

I felt the cold liquid, as it ran
down upon my face,
Mixing with my tears; I'd
know that smell any place.

"Oh... Please, don't do this to me,
Pastor, please tell them I no witch"
But the only words I heard were
"Burn the fucking bitch!"

I screamed and screamed.
The pain was so hard to bear,
Of my flesh charred and blistering,
And the stench of burning hair.

Suddenly the dark enveloped me
And I felt the flames subside.
I could feel the touch of a
woman:
An angel by my side.

I spent a long night,
As they tried and tried in vain,
But my spirit was tired
And my body lost to pain.

In my final moments I cry out
To my god, and all those damned,
To rid the world of all this suffering,
This pious scourge upon our land.

Mine is not the god of those who did this,
For he had left me there to die.
But my god. The god of truth whose power
is not tainted with broken promises and lies.

And so, I closed my eyes and
Let my spirit slip away.
And left they who caused all this
To survive another day.

I was safe in the knowledge that
My god would see me right,
And they would be tormented
In the still small hours of the night.

And while my spirit flies free
Upon the sacred winds of change,
The bitter taste of my tears forgotten,
Along with the miseries of age

I will soar high above the oceans
And fly free upon the winds,
Dancing with the sparks from Sabbat fires
As they fall upon the Earth.

As for those who tortured me
They can torture themselves
instead.
My screams burnt into their memories
And my face forever in their heads.

THE VVYTCH
Sam R Geraghty

These eyes have seen the terror
This day brings, upon the tyrant's scaffold
The four winds sing my name
For it was me upon the mountain,
I sat with you o'er a blazing fire
We spoke to the Old Ones, they beckoned me ...
On into their eternity

To dreams where with younger heart
Blessings, in those hallowed hours of youth
Of the dawn that brought my sight,
To this dusk that leads me into the noose
I sigh, my last breath of life!

But my eyes will see All, past the gate
Broken only is the body, say my name
VVytch ... and watch for my children
For their laughter will be my revenge.

GLOSSARY

Can't	Cannae	Won't	Wilnae
Couldn't	Coudnae	Wouldn't	Woudnae
Didn't	Didnae	You	Ye
Don't	Dinnae	Hogmanay	
Havn't	Havnae	Hugmonay	
No	Na/Nay	Deformed	Disformed
Not	Nae	Devil	Div
Now	Nu	Church	Kirk
Lord	Laird		
Wasn't	Wasnae		

Hattock – Scottish (rarely used in modern language) A little hat.

Hors and Hattock - Horse and Hattock: spoken by witches or faeries in order to travel magically to another place/realm.

Mickle – A large unknown amount/quantity

REFERENCES

THEORIS OF LEMNOS
peoplepill.com/people/theoris-of-lemnos/
en.wikipedia.org/wiki/Theoris_of_Lemnos
en.wikipedia.org/wiki/Demosthenes
Demosthenes the Orator Kindle Edition, Oxford 2009 ISBN 0199287198/ASIN B006BY2CUA

PETRONILLA DE MEATH
The Sorcery trial of Alice Kyteler, Pegasus Press 2004. Edited by L.S. davidson and J. O. Ward.
The First Execution for Witchcraft in Ireland, William Renwick Riddell. Pranava Books, Classic Reprints. India.
historyireland.com/medieval-history-pre-1500/the-sorcery-trial-of-alice-kyteler-by-bernadette-williams/
headstuff.org/culture/history/terrible-people-from-history/petronilla-de-meath-irish-witch/
historyhit.com/the-infamous-witch-case-of-alice-kyteler/
en.wikipedia.org/wiki/Richard_de_Ledrede
ancient-origins.net/history-important-events/alice-kytelerria.ie/news/dictionary-irish-biography/alice-kyteler-irelands-first-witch
en.wikipedia.org/wiki/Great_Famine_of_1315-1317

AGNES PORTER
woottonbridgeiow.org.uk/manors.php

archive.org/stream/isleofwightitshi00adam/isleofwightitshi00adam_djvu.txt
Wicked plants – Amy Stewart – Page 1 - Published by Timber Press inc 2019 ISBN 9781604691276

AGNES WATERHOUSE
Folklore Myths and Legends of Britain, Readers Digest 1973.
Rainbow Fact book of British History, Grisewood & Dempsey Ltd. 1984.
Antonio Fraser, "The lives of the Kings and Queens of England," Book Club Associates,
Karen Farrington, "History of Supernatural," 1997.
Diane Canwell & Jonathan Sutherland, "Witches of the World" Ermine Street Books 2007.
www.occult-world.com
Agnes Waterhouse Essex voices past
The Burning Times www.angelfire.com

GILLES GARNIER
en.wikipedia.org/wiki/Gilles_Garnier
executedtoday.com/tag/gilles-garnier
occult-world.com/garnier-gilles-1873/
serialkillers.briancombs.net/tag/gilles-garnier/
en.wikipedia.org/wiki/Gilles_de_Rais

AGNES COLLINS
legalhistorymiscellany.com/2019/06/30/elizabethan-witch-trials/amp/?_
archive.org/stream/isleofwightitshi00adam/isleofwightitshi00adam_djvu.txt

URSULA KEMP
en.wikipedia.org/wiki/Ursula_Kemp
ursulakemp.co.uk/history.htm
mysteriousbritain.co.uk/occult/ursula-kemp-and-the-st-osyths-witches/
museumofwitchcraftandmagic.co.uk/library/7076-ursula-kemp/
England's Witchcraft Trials – Willow Winshom – Published by Pen & Sword History 2018
ISBN 9781473870949

JOHN FAIN
Francis Hepburn thehistoryjar.com
Scots Discovery of Witchcraft 1651 kindle edition
Amazon Media EU S.à r.l. ASIN: B01CQ488MY

ANNA MUGGEN
peoplepill.com/people/anna-muggen/
en.wikipedia.org/wiki/Anna_Muggen
https://www.history.com/topics/middle-ages/hundred-years-war

RICHARD WILKYNS
Witchcraft in Exeter 1558 – 1600 Mark Stoyle 2017
Instruments of Darkness, Witchcraft in Modern England, James Sharpe

JOAN, MARGARET AND PHILLIPA FLOWER
bottesfordhistory.org.uk/content/category/topics/bottesford-witches&ved
en.m.wikipedia.org/wiki/WitchesofBelvoir&ved

J Barnes, The Wonderful Discovery of the Witchcrafts etc..(Terrumun Ltd. version) Op cit. p17
thespruceeats.com/history-and-types-of-british-tea-
en.m.wikipedia.org/wiki/Tea_in_the_United_Kingdom&ved
en.m.wikipedia.org/wiki/Francis_Manners,_6th_Earl_of_Rutland
bottesfordhistory.org.uk/content/category/topics/bottesford-witches
quod.lib.umich.edu/e/eebogroup/

GOWANE ANDERSOUN
Royal Privy Council 2nd S, v1 p. 469

ELIZABETH   CLARKE
en.m.wikipedia.org/wiki/Elizabeth   Clarke
en.m.wikipedia.org/wiki/Matthew Hopkins

ISOBEL GOWDIE
Emma Wilby "The visions of Isobel Gowdie: Magic, Shamanism and Witchcraft in seventeenth century Scotland," 2010 ISBN-10: 1845191803
ISBN-13: 978-1845191801
Robert Pitcairn "Criminal Trials of Scotland," 1829
Walter Scott "Letters on Demonology and Witchcraft," 1830
J.W Brody-Innes "The Devil's Mistress," 1974
Jane Pankhurst "Isobel," 1977

LISBETH NYPAN
Malleus Maleficarum Folio Society; Folio Soc ed. edition (1968) ASIN: B0000COBMZ
ansatte.uit.no/rune.hagen/nypan.

MADDALENA LAZZARI
Brenda Ralph Lewis "Dark History of the Popes" 2009 ISBN-10: 1906626243/ISBN-13: 978-1906626242/ASIN: 1906969000

TEMPERANCE LLOYD
The pdf book by frank gent - gent.org.uk/bidefordwitches/tbw.pdf
The town of Bideford (with grateful thanks for not calling the police on a vagrant)

TITUBA
en.wikipedia.org/wiki/Tituba
history.com/salem masachusettes
en.wikipedia.org/wiki/Samuel Parriss
en.wikipedia.org/wiki/Elizabeth Parriss
en.wikipedia.org/wiki/Betty Parriss
en.wikipedia.org/wiki/Abigal Williams
history.com/news/salem-witch-trials

GILES COREY
en.wikipedia.org/wiki/Giles_Corey
en.wikipedia.org/wiki/Martha_Corey
history.com/salem masachusettes

JANET HORNE
Rossell Hope Robbins The Encyclopaedia of Witchcraft and Demonology Springbooks. 1970

ISBN-10: 0600011836/ISBN-13: 978-0600011835

BRIDGET CLEARY
Bourke, A., (2006), The Burning of Bridget Cleary: A True Story, Pimlico
ireland-calling.com/bridget-cleary/
nationalarchives.ie/article/behind-scenes-bridget-cleary/
stairnaheireann.net/2016/03/15/1895-bridget-cleary-is-burned-to-death-by-her-husband-michael-who-believed-her-spirit-had-been-taken-by-bad-faeries-and-replaced-with-a-changeling-3/
historywithatwist.wordpress.com/2014/10/25/bridget-cleary-the-irish-changeling/
en.wikipedia.org/wiki/Irish_Home_Rule_movement
htmentalfloss.com/article/539793/bizarre-death-bridget-cleary-irish-fairy-wife

AMA HEMMAH
En.wikipedia.org/Ama Hemmah
bbc.co.uk/news/world-africa-11848536
modernghana.com/news/1020179/savagery-in-the-name-of-religious-belief.html

THE INQUISITION BY DIANE NARRAWAY
Was first featured in Songs of the Black Flame published by Black Moon Publishing.
blackmoonpublishing.com